THE WHITE GUNS

VE-Day, 1945—a time of rejoicing and disbelief for Britain and her allies, but for many of her victors, also a time of tension and suspicion. Nowhere is this more apparent than in the great harbour and naval base at Kiel, where Lieutenant Vere Marriott, in command of his own small motor gunboat, is stunned by the enormity of the task awaiting the occupying forces and the surrendered Germans, and torn by his conflicting emotions. And now, face to face with their old adversary, Marriott and his crew discover that there is more to victory than survival, and out of the devastation and mistrust there begins to emerge a fresh understanding, compassion where there had only been hatred. And also for Marriott, from the ashes of war arises an unlikely and unexpected love—without which victory, and sacrifice, would have no meaning.

THE
WHITE GUNS

Douglas Reeman

To Dick —

Happy Reading!

Douglas and Kim

3-11-87

CHIVERS PRESS
BATH

First published 1989
by
William Heinemann Ltd
This Large Print edition published by
Chivers Press
by arrangement with
William Heinemann Ltd
1989

ISBN 0 86220 329 5

British Library Cataloguing in Publication Data

Reeman, Douglas, *1924–*
The white guns.
I. Title
823′.914 [F]

ISBN 0–86220–329–5

To Kim,
the girl on the beach,
with my love

With this signature the German people
and the German armed forces are,
for better or worse,
delivered into the victors' hands.

Colonel-General Gustav Jodl
after signing the German surrender
to the Allies, May 1945.

CONTENTS

1 The Victors   1
2 And Then There Were Two   24
3 Twenty Crosses   44
4 Allies   66
5 Viewpoint   87
6 Reunion   116
7 Mayday   137
8 Yesterday's Enemy   163
9 Old Scars   183
10 Vodka Diplomacy   202
11 Out of Luck   220
12 The Last Watch   242
13 Without Fear or Favour   262
14 The Same Men?   286
15 Innocence   313
16 Until We Meet Again   335
17 Victims   358
18 A Promise Kept   381
19 White Guns   398

   Epilogue   417

THE WHITE GUNS

CHAPTER ONE

THE VICTORS

The confined waters of the Baltic Sea have moods and hazards as varied as the countries which enclose it, from Finland in the north to the gentler shores of Denmark and the turbulent currents of the Kattegat which divides it from Sweden.

This particular morning, with May just a few days old, was no exception; if anything, the air, chilling and heavy with damp, was hostile, as if it knew the reason for this day being different from any other.

The early sunlight was masked by low clouds, and when it touched the sea's face it was hard and metallic, so that the water looked like burnished pewter. When the sun was hidden, the same sea appeared darker, the colour of lead.

The small flotilla of vessels moving slowly south towards the approaches to Kiel Bay kept station close together, as if they too sensed the air of menace and uncertainty. Their engines, throttled down to hold the group in visual company at all times, rumbled across the water, and as an occasional glimpse of land loomed up to starboard the crews who stood to their action stations could hear the echoes thrown back from the shore.

It was a place very few had been before, and only those old enough to have recalled the days of peace might have remembered or recognised the names on the chart.

For this was May 1945, and after nearly six years

of war British ships were penetrating the Baltic, where none but a handful of reckless submariners had been able to grope their way to carry their particular skills to the enemy's coastal convoys.

This group of vessels was small but no less deadly. A pair of lithe motor gunboats, butting through the choppy water as if they resented being reined down from their spectacular thirty knots—*more with a following wind* as some claimed. A trio of motor launches, very similar in design with their low bridges and raked bows, but lacking the MGBs' formidable armament, followed by a long-funnelled salvage vessel. Dull grey like the clouds, all the hulls glistening in spray, guns manned as if expecting to be challenged.

The leading MGB, her number 801 painted on either bow, might appear to any landsman to be as smart as the day she had first tasted salt water in 1942. But the old scars were still visible despite the paint. Three years of war at close quarters. Seeking out the enemy, E-Boats and other such vessels, whose crews were just as dedicated and determined to win, or simply to survive. From Iceland to the Med, the English Channel and up to the North Sea, manned for the most part by hostilities-only officers and ratings, schoolboys and clerks, milk roundsmen and taxi drivers, they had proved in blood that they were more than able to adapt to the demands of war, despite the cost which had hit them harder than most.

Lieutenant Vere Marriott, the commanding officer of MGB 801, rested his elbows on the screen and levelled his powerful binoculars on a spur of land; as he had done countless times, so many that they were beyond measure. He was twenty-six years

2

old, and apart from getting the 'feel' of the navy in an elderly V & W class destroyer had spent all his time in Light Coastal Forces, in both MTBs and gunboats like this one. Covering the desert army in retreat along the North African coast, then turning to share the unbelievable change of fortune when the battered, bloodied veterans of the Eighth Army had stood firm at a place called El Alamein, a name which had previously been barely worth noting on any map or chart. After years of setbacks, both naval and military, their luck had changed. Rommel's crack Afrika Korps had been driven back. It never stopped until the German divisions were out of Africa and across to Sicily and Italy, harried all the way by craft like this one.

Marriott half-listened to the muffled growl of the four great Packard engines and watched some bobbing wreckage drift slowly abeam.

His had been a different command then. Once again he felt his stomach muscles contract as if anticipating a blow, his jaw tightening while he tried to push the memory from his mind.

This should have been a different day. Eleven months since the great Allied invasion of Normandy, and now they were here, following the German coastline, heading for Kiel. A place often mentioned in news bulletins, being bombed around the clock but still able to hit back, to build and offer sanctuary to the U-Boats which for the second time in a generation had almost brought Britain to starvation and defeat.

To most, Kiel was more legend than reality. Marriott recalled seeing a film before the war called *The Spy in Black*, with Conrad Veidt playing the Kaiser's U-Boat captain who had been chosen to

3

penetrate Scapa Flow and attack the Grand Fleet. It was just a coincidence, perhaps, that Günther Prien had done exactly that in this war in U-47, and had torpedoed the battleship *Royal Oak*, and laid her on the bottom with great loss of life.

He heard seaboots clattering up from the chartroom, which was hunched just forward of the square, open bridge.

Sub-Lieutenant Mike Fairfax RNVR, second-in-command of MGB 801 but still weeks away from his twenty-first birthday, watched him gravely before saying, 'It *feels* different.'

'Yes, Number One.' Marriott wanted to shake his hand, to laugh, even cry, but could find no proper emotion. All those faces, wiped away but not forgotten, the months and the years, the elation and the stark terror which tore at your guts like claws. *It was over*, they said. All but the actual signatures and the flag-waving.

Germany had collapsed. The impossible dream was still as hard to face, let alone accept, as the fact of their own survival.

Of course there was always Japan, the other theatre in the Pacific. Errol Flynn's war. But that was later. This was here and now.

He glanced over the screen at the forecastle, the power-operated six-pounder with leading Seaman Townsend testing the sights, the slender muzzle moving very slightly from bow to bow. Was that how *he* felt?

Like other MGBs of her class she carried a company of thirty officers and ratings. The boat had served them well and was paying for it. The hull had been holed and patched many times. Exploding bombs from the aircraft nobody had

4

spotted in time. Enemy tracer, cannon fire and white-hot splinters which could rip a man apart. The thick pusser's paint covered a multitude of sins. But her engines were good and she could still respond when roused. Stronger than anything faster. Faster than anything stronger. That combination had saved their bacon many times. For her size she was heavily armed. Along her one hundred and fifteen feet she mounted two six-pounders, the slender-barrelled Oerlikons and a selection of machine guns both heavy and light, as well as a few unlawful ones which they had 'come by' along the way.

Fairfax gauged his mood with practised care. He had joined the boat just before last Christmas after serving as third-hand in a smaller Vosper boat at Felixstowe. He could still recall his dismay when he had been told who his next skipper was to be.

Lieutenant Vere Marriott, holder of the DSC and Bar, had been one of the legends in Coastal Forces. But that had been earlier, before D-Day and the Normandy invasion. In these boats life was fast and furious. When they had nothing more interesting to write about, the newspapers would sometimes describe these young veterans as heroes. It usually brought derision from Fairfax's companions. In their kind of warfare there were only two sorts. The quick and the dead.

Marriott had been twenty-six. That had seemed incredibly old to Fairfax. His friends had suggested that Marriott might be *over the hill*. It had not helped.

But, in the months since then, Fairfax had come to feel something for his grave-eyed skipper which was closer to love than mere respect. The latter

5

seemed insignificant when he had seen what Marriott had done to weld a mixed collection of characters into a team, into one company. Many of the hands had come from other boats. Men who had seen their comrades drown or die in a dozen different ways. Those who had trod water and had watched their boats take that last dive. In their small, compact world each man relied on the other. He had to. There was nobody else when the flak started to fly.

Marriott had spared nobody, least of all his first lieutenant. The real test had been when they had encountered E-Boats off the Hook of Holland. They had been sent to cover an attack by MTBs on a small enemy convoy. With day and night air raids reducing Germany's railways and roads to a shambles, such convoys had become doubly important. It had been a quick, savage embrace, with two E-Boats and one MTB blasted apart, lighting up the night sky in their death agony before darkness closed in again, and friend and foe alike ran like assassins for their bases at full throttle.

Marriott's behaviour then had taught Fairfax much about his commander. He had handled the boat like a thoroughbred, not one which had almost come to the end of her useful life.

Marriott felt he was being watched and thought he knew what Fairfax was thinking. He liked Fairfax. He was bright, cheerful, and good at his job. In action he behaved like a veteran, but he succeeded in looking like a hurt schoolboy when Marriott had torn him off a strip. *Schoolboy*. He had been just that when he had joined up for the duration.

Marriott had sworn he would never allow himself

6

to get too close to anyone else again. Not after . . .
He slammed the door on his thoughts and said, 'I
wonder how Cuff is getting on back there?'

Lieutenant Leo Glazebrook, known as 'Cuff',
commanded another of the MGBs which had been
detached earlier to investigate a W/T report of small
craft moving along the coast.

Cuff was one of the originals of the flotilla.
Marriott had bumped into him several times during
his service. In the Channel, then out to the Med
where he had been sent to run guns to Tito's
partisans in Yugoslavia who were fully stretched
fighting their own war against the German and
Italian occupation forces.

Then Normandy. Cuff was always around.
Marriott bit his lip. So what was it, envy? Because
Cuff was ending the war in his own boat, one he
had commanded for over two years—a lifetime in
this regiment?

Marriott glanced at the men around him, taut
and tense, watching the sea, the sky, everything.

Why could he not accept this boat as his own? He
looked at the coxswain as he stood swaying slightly
behind the wheel. A one-badge petty officer named
Robert Evans, or so it said in his paybook. Another
mystery. A bloody good coxswain, always the vital
link between officers and ratings. He had dark hair
and a swarthy skin, a firm mouth, and eyes which
were very steady, unnerving sometimes when he
looked at a defaulter or some skate who had
overstayed his run ashore. Like black olives.
Originally Welsh, but one who had lived for much
of his life in the Channel Islands.

Evans had worked with the Special Boat
Squadron, the cloak-and-dagger brigade. He spoke

fluent French, perhaps because of his time in the Channel Islands, but there was something more to him than his papers explained. How did he feel now? Jersey, his home, had been the only part of Britain to be overrun and occupied by the Germans. If he had family there he said nothing of them. A withdrawn, remote man, but one who was respected by the youthful company and even the hard men who had been no strangers to the navy's detention quarters.

Marriott's thoughts returned to the missing MGB. Cuff was taking his time. It was to be hoped he was being careful despite the alleged victory. Marriott recalled their arrival off Copenhagen. When was that? Yesterday? The day before? He bit back a yawn. None of them had slept much since leaving England.

But that was how he had imagined it might be. The wildly excited, often tearful Danes, hugging the begrimed, grinning Tommies as they had marched up from the harbour. The announcement from Field-Marshal Montgomery's HQ that all German resistance in Holland, North-West Germany and Denmark was at an end. Even Heligoland and the Friesian Islands had surrendered.

The MGBs had paused only to take on more fuel from an army supply column and had been instantly swamped by elated townspeople from that enchanting city. Hugs and kisses, hoarded aquavit and brandy—Marriott had had his hand pumped by so many people he had been dazed by their gratitude.

How long would it last, he wondered? As in France, the so-called patriots would soon be revealed as collaborators by the dedicated few of the real Resistance whose strength had been sustained over the years by hate, by seeing their friends captured and executed.

'*Ship*, sir! Port bow!'

'*Stand to!*' Marriott raised his glasses and felt his heart pumping against his ribs. *Surely not now?* There had been talk of some German commanders refusing to give in, of those who had scuttled their vessels rather than surrender them to their old enemies.

It had even been reported that the island of Bornholm was being reinforced by troops fleeing the Russian advance, and that the German commander was preparing to defend the town from anyone who came near.

Fairfax lowered his glasses and gave a quick, tight grin.

'It's Captain (D), sir.'

A figure at the opposite corner of the bridge straightened his back.

Leading Signalman Silver, nicknamed *Long John*, needless to say, gave a grunt. 'Here they come, bags of swagger—showin' off as usual!'

The big destroyer tore down on the slow-moving group, a huge moustache foaming from her bow-wave, the spray a dirty yellow in the strange glare. Beyond her would be other destroyers and some cruisers, support craft, and landing ships packed with soldiers.

Marriott watched the impressive display, the glint of filtered sunlight on the destroyer's glass screen, and those further away as they swung in obedience to their leader.

A light stabbed across the water like a

diamond-bright eye.

'Signal from Captain (D), sir.' Silver's lips moved soundlessly as he read it. '*Take care. No one is completely on your side!*'

Marriott thought of all the brittle but witty signals he had seen and heard even in the face of death. What was wrong now? Nobody laughed. He stiffened as a loud boom echoed through the haze and spray and felt the explosion sigh against the hull as if it had touched a sandbar. They looked at each other and then Silver added, 'From Captain (D), sir.'

Marriott faced him. 'Well?'

Silver showed his teeth. '*Re my last signal. Delete "completely".*'

'That's all we need!' Fairfax spoke with feeling.

But a few moments later they saw the ungainly salvage vessel signalling from astern.

Cuff was coming to rejoin them. The explosion must have been his.

Marriott thrust his hand into his oilskin's pocket and closed it around his pipe. Even that felt damp.

Perhaps they had all just been holding on and nothing else? And had no more to give?

'Signal, sir.' Silver was studying him impassively. '*Take station on me.*'

'Very well. Bring her round to port, Swain.'

He turned to watch his men at their familiar stations, their white sweaters touched with grease from the guns, their eyes peering into the clouds and towards the hazy shoreline.

At Normandy it had been almost a frantic, last-ditch display. Best uniforms, cheers and madness even when the bombardment had engulfed the brave little ships. In the midst of it all, the

10

blazing tanks as they were marked down within minutes of rumbl)ng from the LSTs, the smoke and the roar of gunfire from the bombarding squadrons beyond the horizon; as men cursed and died, others had pressed forward; there was even that crazy soldier with the bagpipes. What would make a man act like that with death just yards away?

The men near him looked worn out, old before their time. Yet there were only six aboard who were over twenty-one. You would never have known. A grimy hand passed a signal flimsy up to the bridge from the W/T cabinet. Marriott read it carefully, then re-read it as his eyes blurred. He knew that the third-hand had joined them, as if he had guessed. Sub-Lieutenant John Lowes was eighteen years old, with this his first proper appointment. For him at least it had to be right. Marriott tried to picture the others he had known as if he could feel them too. Watching, waiting for him to make it worthwhile even though they could never share it. Now.

He said quietly, 'Pass the word. This is from the Admiralty. Official. All German armed forces have surrendered. The war is over.' He looked at the youthful Lowes. 'Put it in the log, Pilot. May the eighth 1945 is to be known as Victory in Europe Day.'

He stared blindly up at the gleaming ensign which curled above the bridge—ragged, holed, faded, but no less proud than those at Agincourt, Trafalgar even. But he saw only what he had lost.

Fairfax thrust out his hand, the coxswain too, while they studied each other like strangers.

Silver removed his cap and let the wet breeze ruffle his untidy hair. A Londoner from Dalston, he had been a tick-tack man at a greyhound stadium before the war. Perhaps not that much of a change, for him at last. But even he was at a loss, for once.

Silver said, 'I dunno what to say, sir.'

Marriott turned away. 'Be on your guard. They could be wrong about some of the more dedicated ones . . .' But he was thinking of England, how it would be back there. The long years. Bombed, sometimes starved, but always defiant. Without the ordinary civilians' determination, their faith, the warships and bombers would have counted for nothing.

He heard himself say, 'We shall enter harbour as directed but remain at action stations.' He let his words sink in. 'Tell the engineroom about the signal, Number One.' It was always the same in these boats. The engineroom crew were the last to know anything, unless they received a direct hit.

He heard the mounting roar of Cuff's engines and saw the boat planing past the MLs and the salvage vessel, his familiar yellow scarf whipping above the screen like a pennant. The other colour was provided by a line of swastikas below the bridge on red and white painted shields, each one a kill. As he drew abeam, Cuff switched on his loud-hailer. It was strange, but you hardly noticed his Yorkshire accent at any other time.

'Drinks on me when we get in!' He waved his gloved fists in the air. *'God damn it! It's bloody well over!'*

The MGB swung away to resume proper station on their quarter.

He at least was able to give way to his feelings. Some of his men were waving and cheering to one of the destroyers.

'I'm going to look at the chart, Number One.

12

Take over, right?' Marriott stepped down into the chartroom with its familiar musty smell. Dry rot, wet rot; no hull was safe when they worked them so hard in all weathers.

He switched on the chart light and stared at the uneven coastline of the peninsula, Denmark and down into Schleswig-Holstein. Kiel. *Germany*. He spoke the last name aloud as if to convince himself.

He heard the two subbies chatting near the voicepipes. Fairfax bewailing the fact the war had ended before he had got his second stripe, and Lowes because the war had passed him by altogether.

What would become of them all? *Of me?*

He searched his mind for the other faces, but they had gone now, their part played.

He thought suddenly of Cuff. As always, the survivor. The winner. And wondered why he had never really liked him.

*　　*　　*

Sub-Lieutenant Mike Fairfax flattened the creases on the ready-use chart and tried to prevent the instruments from rattling as the boat shuddered over some short crests. The atmosphere in the open bridge was as tense as he had known it in battle, and he knew he was only fiddling with the chart to hold his own nerves in check.

He heard Marriott say quietly, 'Dead slow. Keep clear of that wreckage, Swain.' He also heard Evans's noncommittal grunt. How well those two had worked together although, even in Fairfax's youthful opinion, Marriott and the swarthy petty officer were like chalk and cheese. Feet shifted on

13

the deck and in gun mountings, fingers played warily with sights and ammunition. It was electric and yet it felt dead. *Numb*.

Fairfax watched Marriott's even profile. Steady grey eyes, a sensitive mouth which had sometimes hardened as if to a command only when it had been required. Fairfax had come to recognise all the signs in his captain. The way his brown hair flapped from beneath the old cap with its tarnished badge, the tell-tale marks of grey in his sideburns. Wrong for a man of twenty-six, but Fairfax had seen it in others. Men like Marriott, young only in years, eyes lost in experiences he could only imagine.

Fairfax licked his lips and tasted grit on his teeth. It felt out of place at sea. He realised that what he had taken for sea-mist or perhaps inshore drizzle was in fact smoke; he could taste that too, so that his stomach rebelled at the stench of burning. A city, a port which had been crushed by war.

Silver called, 'Motor boat approachin' from starboard, sir!'

Fairfax raised his glasses and, from a corner of his eyes, saw the twin barrels of the paired Oerlikons train soundlessly on the small grey launch, then turn away disdainfully as if they and not the gunlayer had seen the huge White Ensign flapping from its stern.

He saw a bearded lieutenant-commander in battledress with a megaphone in one fist as he waved to signal his intentions to come alongside.

Marriott said in the same unemotional tone, 'Side-party, give him a hand. But we don't stop.'

The officer was hauled unceremoniously aboard and arrived on the bridge panting heavily.

The interwoven lace on his shoulder straps

14

proclaimed him to be an RNR officer, most likely a pre-war first-mate in some shipping line or other. He had a thick, raw voice and had probably been shouting at various vessels since dawn.

He shook hands with Marriott and glanced swiftly around the bridge, his eyes red-rimmed with fatigue.

'I'm acting harbour-master.' He waved his hand over the screen. 'There aren't just wrecks in the harbour, there are bloody *layers* of 'em, so we must make sure you don't join 'em, eh?'

Fairfax saw Marriott give a tired grin. 'I'll do my best.'

Sub-Lieutenant Lowes touched Fairfax's arm so that he jumped, without knowing why.

Lowes was pointing across the port bow towards a tall, gaunt tower which stood above the drifting smoke like an abandoned lighthouse. It must have been well over two hundred feet tall.

'What's *that*, for God's sake?'

Fairfax stooped over the compass and took a quick fix while he steadied the azimuth ring against the jerking engines. He consulted the chart, then replied, 'The German Naval Memorial at Laboe.' He did not notice the admiration in Lowes's expression. Nor did he realise how confidently his assessment had come out. Just months ago he had been nervous, unsure still at taking a watch at night alone with his doubts and misgivings. Marriott had given him this confidence. The realisation came to him only then, and he thought bitterly, *What good will that do me now that it's all over?*

A small escort destroyer, one of the hard-worked Hunt class, stood motionless inside the harbour approaches, surrounded by boiling froth from her

15

screws as they thrashed the water first ahead, then astern. A salvage tug was already nudging around her quarter, and the RNR officer said testily, 'She's hit one of the wrecks.' He looked ahead again. 'These destroyer types. Always making a big show. He'll be lucky if he gets off without punching a few holes in his belly!'

Fairfax took his eyes from the grim-looking memorial and watched the great harbour opening up ahead, then moving out to embrace the slow-moving MGBs on either beam.

I must remember every single thing on this day. Fairfax was not sure if he said it to himself or spoke aloud. But none of the others would have heard anyway. Each man was transfixed, only hands and eyes moving out of practice and hard necessity. On Cuff's boat, which was the nearest, Fairfax saw the others acting in the same stricken fashion when earlier they had been yelling and cheering.

There was smoke everywhere, and the water was thick with oil, so that when Cuff's boat pushed through it the sea showed itself like a blue thread before vanishing again as the filth closed in astern. Drifting ashes, patches of smoke which stung the throat like acid, bobbing flotsam, upturned floats and boats—a place of the dead.

The harbour-master cleared his throat and the starboard machine-gunner started with alarm.

'Use that pier yonder, Skipper. I can't let you inside the yard until we *know*.

Marriott turned and looked at his first lieutenant. It seemed like minutes, and Fairfax had the strange feeling that they had never been so close, nor would be again.

'Foc's'le party, Number One. Clear away the after

16

guns and use as few hands as possible.' Again the sad smile. 'You'll feel a bit naked up front.' He touched the wet screen. 'Don't worry. If anything gets nasty, we shoot first and argue afterwards.'

He saw Marriott look away as something huge and solid seemed to rise from the seabed in one last act of revenge.

The big German cruiser *Admiral Hipper* had been rarely out of the headlines from the very start of things. She had served in most campaigns from the invasion of Norway to the attack on Russia, and later to cover that same army in retreat.

A familiar sight in Kiel, and her life had ended here. Like a shattered leviathan she lay half-submerged, smoke still pouring from her towering bridge and slewed gun-turrets. The RAF had put her out of action a month ago, and her masters had seen fit to scuttle her by exploding depth-charges deep in her hull. That had been about a week ago and she was still burning, her oil joining all the other thousands of gallons in the harbour like her own life blood.

The RNR officer pointed at another massive wreck, only her side showing above the drifting procession of flotsam. But her name was still clearly visible on one bow: *New York*.

He said with something like respect, 'One of their old Hamburg-Amerika liners. Knew her well.' He stared at the shattered wreck and added bitterly, 'I hope they're all bloody satisfied!'

'Were you in a liner?' Marriott studied him gravely.

The man shook his head. 'No. I ran bananas.' He turned away to watch Fairfax and a handful of seamen hurry to the bows with ropes and fenders.

17

'At least it was a clean life.'

Marriott nodded, strangely moved by this man whose name he did not even know. The love and brotherhood of the sea was something else lost here.

'Slow astern.' He saw one seaman drop over the bows then reappear with the mooring rope. The first of their little band to set foot in Germany. The seaman must have realised it and was grinning up at his mates. That was Scouse Arkright, a real 'skate' who had been inside more naval D.Q.s than at sea until he had popped up in Coastal Forces. It had appealed to his independent spirit apparently.

The other MGBs were nudging their way to the out-thrust arm of the jetty. It was more like an empty ramp, Marriott thought, the rest had been blasted away in the bombing.

Cuff's boat was coming alongside in a cloud of high-octane vapour as her powerful screws thrashed astern before coming to rest.

These boats had been built originally to do service as both MGB and MTB. The bows of Cuff's command were scalloped like Marriott's 801 so that torpedo tubes could be fitted, but they never had been.

Marriott glanced now around the littered, broken harbour. Torpedoes were the last things they needed here.

The launch was panting fussily on the outboard side and the harbour-master thrust out his hand. 'Must be off. Long queue by now, I expect.'

Marriott thought of the bottle of brandy he had brought for this moment. The original one lay with the remains of his old command. In pieces like his men.

His eyes smarted and he wiped them with the

18

back of his hand.

The ex-merchant navy man prompted gruffly, 'Rough, was it?'

Marriott stared back at the tall memorial. It seemed to be mocking them. It had survived for the dead when all around had been laid low. He could see part of the town now; the light must be stronger, but there were only ruins, undulating piles like dunes in a desert. Where were the people? Dead or still trapped and buried there, gasping out their lives beneath their workplaces and homes, in the smouldering fires because there was nothing with which to fight or extinguish them?

Marriott replied vaguely, 'Thought you might join us for a tot.'

But, when he looked again, the launch was shoving off and heading back into the smoke.

Fairfax clattered back into the bridge, as if he only felt safe here. He touched his cap. 'All secure, sir.'

Marriott saw Ginger Jackson, a torpedoman who also acted as a messman for officers, emerge through the hatch which led down to the wardroom and W/T office. He had a huge grin, but then he usually did.

'I fetched it, sir.'

Marriott took the bottle from the towel in which he had wrapped it for safety. There were only enamel mugs available; all the rest had been smashed in the vibration when they had charged into Denmark expecting some last resistance.

Below the bridge the few who were entitled would be sharing their hoarded tots of rum with those still too young to draw it.

But here, on this small bridge, Marriott's world,

where it had all happened, this was their moment.

They all watched as the brandy slopped into the mugs.

The harbour, the stench of death and destruction, the scenes of horror yet to come, even the presence of the other boats nearby were all excluded. Marriott raised his mug and felt his grip tighten to prevent his fingers from shaking. Fairfax and the fawn-like Lowes. The black-eyed Evans, Long John Silver, and the others of this small team. Behind each man another seemed to stand like a shadow. Marriott felt that if he moved he would see them, that they would be as they had once been.

He said, 'I wanted to make a speech. To talk to you about victory and not what it cost us to get it.' He glanced up at the restless ensign as it jerked from the gaff. Like the RNR officer's banana ship, clean against the filth of battle.

'Instead, I'll just say *thank you*.' He studied their tired faces, their expressions of astonishment and disbelief. Perhaps the stilling of the great Packard engines made the realisation all the more poignant.

They downed their drinks and held out their mugs for a refill. Marriott felt the brandy stinging his throat, burning his stomach, and realised dully that he had not eaten since . . . He shook his head. He could not remember that either.

The Chief, Petty Officer Motor Mechanic Adair, popped through the hatch with a mug of something in his greasy fist.

'Cheers, everybody!' He gave his terrible grin before swallowing his neaters.

As a young mechanic he had been hurled against a piece of unyielding machinery in rough weather and had had all his front teeth knocked out. He never wore his dentures at sea in case he lost them or had them smashed in the roaring pit of his engineroom. At twenty-five, Adair was one of the *old men* of the flotilla.

Marriott shook his hand, saying nothing. Their eyes said it all.

Adair of all people would settle down better than any of them, he thought. He had set his sights on a small garage and tea-room, somewhere quiet in the West Country. Catch the day-trippers that way, he had said more than once.

Marriott had no doubt he would do just that.

'They're coming, sir!'

Marriott strode to the side and saw the men on the other MGBs returning to their weapons.

He watched as first the heads and shoulders, then the bodies of a great tide of shambling figures seemed to rise from the dockyard rubble and advance on the moored boats. No order or discipline, no formation, just a dull sense of purpose.

There were thousands of them. All in blue uniforms, some bandaged or limping, petty officers and seamen, like a silent army, their feet stirring up the dust and dead ashes as they moved closer.

The German navy, the invincible *Kriegsmarine*. It was beyond belief and imagination.

Despite being involved in so many close-actions Marriott was like most sailors; he had rarely seen the other side. Not as people, anyway. The flash of gunfire or an exploding mine, the eye-searing balls of tracer which would rise with such delicate precision before tearing down across the deck like hammers of hell; they were all commonplace enough. Then the corpses. Rolling as if asleep in stinking oil fuel, or torn apart like fresh meat in a butcher's shop. Even that was different.

As if to an unspoken signal, the tide of blue figures came to a halt, those at the rear moving up last until they were all standing shoulder to shoulder and yet, Marriott felt, completely isolated from each other.

One of the MGB gunlayers yelled, '*Ready*, sir!'

What was that? Madness, hate, the need for revenge after all that had happened to that man? A loved one killed, a home destroyed perhaps? It only needed a single spark to send every gun blazing into action. Marriott could feel the wildness in himself too.

Why not? The words seemed to scream out in his mind.

The flotilla's senior officer, 'Spruce' Macnair, was delayed at Copenhagen with engine trouble. Marriott felt the chill at his spine like ice. Cuff was the next senior for this moment of history. He glanced across at his wind-reddened face. Perhaps that more than anything decided him. For just those seconds he had seen himself in Cuff's expression. A lust to kill. To keep on firing until there was nothing.

Marriott switched on his loud-hailer. '*Secure guns!*'

He heard the click of cocking levers, the snap of magazine, and saw the way some of his own men looked at each other, almost sheepishly, as if they knew how close it had been.

Then he looked along the ranks of watching Germans.

After all this time. *So this is the enemy*.

Silent, apathetic, without hope.

22

Fairfax whispered, 'They don't have any officers, sir.'

Marriott glanced at his pale features. What had he expected, he wondered? Then he touched his arm. 'Orders will eventually come from on high, Number One. Until that happens these Germans are our responsibility.' He looked past Fairfax and saw Cuff watching him, his face expressionless above his line of painted kills.

It was obvious that the Admiralty had expected to get their bigger warships into Kiel for a proper show of force. If a small Hunt class destroyer could come unstuck, her larger consorts would be in a very bad way if they tried it.

'*Look*, sir!'

Marriott turned and saw a solitary figure moving from the centre of the silent crowd in the dockyard.

A petty officer by his appearance, and he was walking quite alone towards the jetty. It could have been rehearsed, but Marriott could tell from the way some of the others leaned forward to stare that it was not.

He said, 'I shall step ashore, Number One. Want to come?'

Silver gasped, 'Jesus, sir, you ain't even armed!'

Marriott shrugged. 'It would be rather pointless.' They all looked up, startled, as the outside machinery of war intruded and three Spitfires roared overhead, their wingtips almost touching.

The coxswain asked, 'Can I come too, sir?'

Marriott nodded. 'Yes. Let's meet the enemy.'

CHAPTER TWO

AND THEN THERE WERE TWO

Lieutenant Commander Ian 'Spruce' Macnair, DSO, DSC and two bars, the depleted flotilla's senior officer, waited for his assembled subordinates to settle down, to find a place to stand or sit in the tiny wardroom.

There was nobody in Light Coastal Forces who did not know Macnair, either personally or by his considerable reputation. He was probably most people's idea of the best type of RNVR officer, who had attended peacetime drills and served regular periods of training with the fleet. He was one of the very few who had been the backbone of the hostilities-only navy who had come through it unscathed. He seemed to have a kind of inner knowledge of the men he trained and led, and his *brood*, as he called them, owed him much, if not their very lives. In peacetime he had been a lawyer in Edinburgh, but his list of decorations proved he was able to forget this existence, discard it like a barrister's wig for the duration.

He was respected and also held in deep affection by all those who were closest to him. The right words when a comrade was killed or lost at sea, a quiet warning when someone over-eager stepped out of line at the expense of the rest of his *brood*. Even his nickname, Spruce, was part of the man. It was his own word for keeping up appearances no matter how bad things had been.

Marriott, whose boat had been chosen for the

meeting only because it was nearest to the sagging pier, said, 'All present, sir.'

He wondered about Macnair. Another one who had given all he had, held down his own fear or grief so that others would find comfort in his apparent strength. A lean, hawklike face, the hair patched with grey like frost, deeply lined around the eyes and jaw, he had just turned thirty, but looked old enough to be Fairfax's father. His boat had followed the rest to Kiel two hours after Marriott's strange meeting with the German petty officer.

Like their entrance to this stricken harbour, even now in a wardroom he knew as well as his own right hand, it had been unreal and dreamlike. He knew it was because he was worn out, tired and probably too famished to think properly. Hours on the bridge, watching for a last-minute hitch, sudden treachery or even ignorance that the war, which had been their lives, had ended.

He could see the unknown German now as he had halted in the flattened no-man's-land of crushed rubble. At the very last moment he had reached into his pocket, and had fumbled for something.

Marriott had felt his stomach twist, the brandy like fire. This one man was going to end the war in his own fashion. Nobody could help Marriott, the boats could not fire without cutting him down with Fairfax and Evans. Thoughts flashed through his mind. Silver protesting because he was going to meet the enemy unarmed, Cuff's bitter words on many previous occasions: 'The only good Kraut is a dead one!' He had even imagined Cuff's unspoken comment, what he would say after the German pulled a pistol from his jacket and ended it. 'I told

25

him not to be such a bloody hero!' But when the petty officer's hand reappeared it was holding not a gun but a crumpled white handkerchief which he held in front of him like a talisman. A small, pitiful flag of surrender.

Marriott tried to shake himself out of it and prepare to listen to what their senior officer had to say. But instead he heard the German's clear but halting English. 'Herr Leutnant, will you *help* us, *bitte*?' If he had shouted one last obscenity or threat Marriott might have been ready. The simple request had moved him more than he dared to admit.

Lieutenant Commander Macnair cleared his throat while he looked at their set expressions. He was probably thinking that the four gunboats were all that he had left from his original strength. Was he looking for the lost faces too?

'Well, gentlemen, this is a moment we've all been waiting for.'

Cuff murmured, 'But not expecting, sir!'

Someone chuckled, but it was a hollow sound.

Macnair continued, 'I am being replaced. You'd better get used to the idea of managing on your own.'

There was a babble of protest and he smiled, the effort wiping aside the years and the strain.

'We have won a victory here, but in the Pacific the fight goes on. I have to work up some new boats and their crews, prepare them for that war, a different ocean, a far cry from the Channel or the North Sea.' He hurried on, 'Because of the terrible state of the harbour and communications here, you'll all have your work cut out helping to put things in order. It will mean *changes*.' He looked at

26

their faces, feeling their resentment at something different from what they had known, about to take over and disrupt their lives even before the dust of victory had settled.

He gave a tired smile, one they had seen so often over the months. 'I don't like to insist, but you must try to spruce up a bit before your new commander comes to visit you.' He shook his head as Cuff made to speak. 'I know from long experience, Lieutenant Glazebrook, that I have left it a bit late to discuss with you the matter of *tact*. However, you must accept that our roles here have changed, so too have the methods which will be used to re-open this port, and join with the other services in co-operation with our allies to get things working again.'

Cuff muttered, 'I suppose we'll be giving the Krauts a pound or two out of the poor-box next!' He sounded angry.

Macnair looked past him at another lieutenant. 'James, your boat will be sailing with mine tomorrow morning. You'll get your orders presently.'

The others stared at the lieutenant. One or two slapped him on the shoulder, or pumped his hand.

'Jammy bastard, who do *you* know in Whitehall?'

But they were already missing him, another survivor, a call-sign on the R/T, a show of a towering bow-wave as his command had dashed in to cover their flanks in a pitched battle. Also, some of them were seeing their world shrinking even as they stood here. Coastal Forces were a bit like submariners, a navy within a navy, a family.

Macnair continued calmly, 'Cuff, you will take over as S.O. *but*, like most of the other

27

miscellaneous craft here, you will accept your instructions from the new commander.'

Tommy Updike, Cuff's Number One, also a Yorkshireman and not by coincidence, gave a loud groan. 'What's happened to the Glory Boys, sir? Miscellaneous now, are we?'

Macnair said, 'Get into your Number Fives.'

They stared at each other. Battledress, or working-dress as the navy chose to call it, was their stock-in-trade. You stood your watches in it, usually with grey flannel trousers rather than scratchy regulation ones, you slept in it, and too often you died in it.

Number Fives were for that other navy, Divisions, eating ashore, walking the quarterdeck of some sedate cruiser or destroyer.

Macnair added quietly, 'This is a different ball-game, my friends. The Germans have to see you as the victors, not find cause to believe that it was the mistakes of their leaders which lost them the war.' His tone sharpened. 'So jump about. Spruce up, no matter what you may think, and I shall bring the new commander aboard at the end of the afternoon watch.'

Marriott saw him to the side and watched a squad of khaki-clad soldiers marching along the dockside.

Was it just this morning he had stood with Fairfax and Evans to confront that silent mass of German sailors? It seemed that the whole area had been swamped by British soldiers just moments later, while tanks had rattled and swayed over the rubble, guns swivelling with silent menace, their crests with the all-seeing eye showing them to be of the Guards Armoured Division. It was comforting to know they were on hand if there was still a

28

suspicion of trouble.

They had had it ingrained into them before they had left England. Talk of *Werewolves*, as the youngsters of the Nazi Youth were called, going to ground to wait their chance to sabotage, to delay, and to kill. Even the Kiel Canal was said to be mined and booby-trapped, with the same lurking horrors here in the harbour.

He saw the squad stamp to a halt and come about with a slap and crack of rifles. Their uniforms were none too clean, their boots even worse, while their familiar helmets still carried the twigs and grass of camouflage. These were not the troops you often saw in the pubs and dance halls in Britain. These were the real army, who had marched all the way from Normandy, who had fought through every town and village, field and sewer, winkling out snipers and crack soldiers of the Waffen SS alike. Many must have fallen on the way, for many hundreds had first begun their long hike in El Alamein.

Young and fit, faces round and red in the weak sunshine, they were behaving as if they were on parade. Marriott had already noted the Tommy's ability to remain clean-shaven, no matter what. He had seen it at Tobruk and in Sicily, in the Messina Strait and at Anzio.

He heard the sergeant say loudly, 'I don't want no loungin' about, *see*? The Jerries'll be gawpin' at you lot, an' I don't need some snotty subaltern takin' the piss out of my lads because they don't know 'ow to behave, *see*?'

Macnair said softly, 'That was what I was trying to say down below.' He looked at Marriott keenly. 'You and the others have got quite a task ahead of

29

you. Some probably won't see the reason, others will only be thinking of getting back to Blighty. We won this war because we learned the hard way. We trained for it when, between the wars, the top brass became as stagnant as this bloody harbour.' He nodded to the two young seamen with belted pistols around their waists who guarded the outboard side. 'But they are totally untrained for peace—unready for it too. You'll have to watch them all the way.'

Marriott thought he knew Spruce Macnair well enough to ask, 'Are you really going home for the reason you gave, sir?'

The hawklike eyes settled on him, stripping him down as they had so often.

'You always were the quiet one, the thinker. I was so damn glad when—' he shrugged. 'Well, from all the odds, you should have bought it too.'

Bought it. So easily said in their world.

Then he replied, 'No, as a matter of fact, it isn't. I saw the PMO.' He briefly touched his chest. 'Not too good apparently.' The eyes flashed again. 'If you breathe a word to the others, I'll bloody well come back to haunt you!'

Marriott watched him leave, his hand still at the salute after Macnair had vanished aboard his own MGB.

He wished he had not asked, and yet he was glad Macnair felt he could share it. Another victim, just as much as one taken by cannon shell or bomb.

He had always thought Macnair to be indestructible. They all had. His heart felt suddenly heavy and he was reluctant to go below and join the others. His lips moved in a small smile. *Get spruced up*.

When he did go below they were already leaving

30

to hunt for their uniforms, grumbling, voicing their uncertainties, glancing at the land wehre the sentries were now very much in evidence with their rifles and automatic weapons.

Cuff said, 'They look as if they're put there to keep *us* from going ashore, rather than protect us, eh?' His head swivelled round, his eyes searching. 'You were a bit sharp off the mark this morning! Made me look a bit of a prat in front of my chaps, I'd have thought.'

Marriott replied, 'I'm sorry about that. I wasn't thinking. Just had a feeling that someone was going to start firing.'

Cuff grinned, his good humour apparently restored. 'Wouldn't have seen me shed any tears!' He gave a loud laugh and Marriott could smell the gin in spite of the brandy he had used to toast their victory. It was rumoured that Cuff drank half a bottle of Plymouth gin every morning either before or instead of breakfast.

Marriott studied him again. A year older than himself, but he had certainly abused his health. He had once been a rugby player and had the height and the weight of a front-row forward. But he had gone to fat, so that his blue working-dress looked too tight for him, and his neck bulged over his collar. He sweated too, as he was now despite the cool breeze.

He said, 'Starting already, what did I tell you? The top brass and all the little desk-heroes can't wait to get out here and throw their weight about. God, it makes me puke!'

Marriott tried to change the subject. 'What will you do?'

'God knows. Probably end up in the Pacific. The

31

bloody war might last for years out there. I'll likely get my half-stripe before much longer.'

'I knew you were up for it.'

''Bout time.' He glared at the soldiers on the dockside. 'I'll be glad to get shot of this dump. Go somewhere where there's a bit of *life!*' He walked to the guardrails and half-turned. 'Don't forget what I said about this morning, eh, old son? Do it again and I'll come down on you like a ton of shit!' Then he laughed, but it did not reach his eyes.

Marriott dropped down to the wardroom and made his way to his cabin. *Cabin*, it was more like a large cupboard, with the hateful red telephone just above the cot-like bunk.

He heard the messman, Ginger Jackson, announce cheerfully, 'Well, gents, 'ow about tinned bangers an' mash?' The two sub-lieutenants groaned and the irrepressible Ginger said severely, 'Now, gents, just because you've won a war don't mean you can get choosy! An' anyway it's all we got 'til the ol' grub ship gets 'ere!'

Marriott leaned back in the only chair and massaged his eyes with his fingers. Then he opened a drawer and studied a half-empty bottle of brandy. He shut it again. Perhaps not, with the new boss coming aboard. He thought of Spruce Macnair, of the German petty officer, the men he could hear chattering on their messdeck, the vague strains of music interrupted at irregular intervals by loud static from the W/T office. He opened another drawer and took out his folder in its waterproof bag. A few photographs, a last letter from his brother Stephen who had gone down in the *Repulse*. Was that all there was left of a man?

He made himself open his metal trunk and after a

32

moment's hesitation he shook out his best reefer with its wavy gold lace, the blue and white ribbon on the left breast. Then he stripped and stood shivering at the tiny basin and washed in cool water. He shaved with deliberate care, watching his eyes in the mirror, half-listening to the sounds around him. Hard to accept that there was no chance of a sudden alarm, the screaming clamour of bells or the nerve-jangling telephone in the night. Just the lap and gurgle of that filthy water alongside. They could have been on the Thames. Anywhere but Kiel.

The uniform seemed loose and he wondered if he should have the buttons moved. He shrugged his shoulders. And it felt damp. He recalled seeing Stephen on that one leave they had shared together, a rare thing in wartime.

He touched the gold lace on his sleeve. There had only been one stripe then, and he had been serving aboard an elderly destroyer working out of the Western Approaches.

His brother had brought a girl home to the house in Surrey where they had been born and had grown up together along with their sister Penny. It was as if they had all grown up too soon. He could remember his mother's disapproval because of the girl. She had said nothing directly, other than touching on the subject of her limited rations in the house, but it had been plain enough.

The girl's name was Mimi, or rather that was the one she had given herself. She had been set on becoming a professional opera singer and, although she had only played a few roles in theatres well outside London, she certainly acted like a star performer.

Marriott smiled to himself. *Exotic*, that was the only word for her. She wore striking make-up, and had her dark hair curled about her cheeks like a Spanish dancer. Her clothes, too, in fact everything about her, had been striking.

Stephen had confided to him that he was going to ask her to marry him. From other things he had said, it was pretty obvious that they were already very close and had probably spent a few days of his leave together.

Marriott could recall his own feelings of envy, the sense of being on the outside. He had had little experience of girls. Before the war he had been working like a slave studying to be a surveyor and draughtsman for a friend of his father's. A proper old tyrant he was too, making a fortune now out of repairing bomb-damaged buildings. A lifetime's work. There had been one girl, but they had grown up in the same road, even went to the same school for part of the time. The result was that they had behaved like brother and sister.

Then Stephen had gone back to his ship, the elderly battle-cruiser *Repulse* which was soon to be sunk by Japanese aircraft off the coast of Malaya with her powerful consort *Prince of Wales*. Both had been lost within half an hour, and the balance of naval power had shifted to the enemy. Singapore might not have fallen had those two great ships endured. But the admiral had not waited for air-cover. Marriott thought of Spruce Macnair's summing-up of the peacetime minds which had almost lost the war. Would they never learn?

On his next leave Marriott had expected to find his mother still in a state of shock.

But all she said was, 'I *knew* that girl was no good

for him!' As if in some way she had been at the root of it.

Marriott had found the London street where Mimi had lived. A rather scruffy area of houses turned into flats. There had been a lot of bombing for it was close to Clapham Junction with its big railway sidings and yards. An old watery-eyed man, who had called himself the caretaker, had explained apologetically that the girl had died.

Marriott had stared at the shabby building but it was unmarked. The old man had shaken his head wearily. 'No, she cut 'er wrists arter she 'eard about yer brother.'

Poor Mimi. He could still remember everything about her, even the strong perfume she used. It might not have worked out, but he hoped they had found happiness together, even for so short a while.

He glanced at his watch. The new boss was soon to descend on them. Marriott stood up, then pushed the package back into the drawer. What was left to go home for now? Perhaps Cuff was right to hope for the Pacific. He sighed and switched off the light.

What was the matter with him? *Nobody lives forever!*

★   ★   ★

Marriott waited below the bridge and watched the little procession clambering from one boat to the next.

Sub-Lieutenant Fairfax whispered, 'All ready, sir.'

Marriott nodded without taking his eyes off the small group as it vanished into the boat alongside.

He had not yet got a glimpse of the commander, but he had seen his cap. It was obviously new, bought for the occasion, the oak leaves around the peak shining in the May sunlight whenever it managed to probe through the drifting smoke. Most likely a regular officer. Getting off to the right start, as Cuff would have put it.

He saw Macnair emerge from a hatch and rest one hand on a stanchion. Short of breath, or was it just a casual gesture? Marriott felt his jaw tighten until it hurt. It was like sharing a terrible secret. Spruce, of all people, leaving his flotilla, being recalled. If he was that ill Marriott felt certain that Macnair would have preferred to remain with *his brood*, especially after all he had given to make this moment possible. He saw Cuff too, huge and towering above all of them; as acting S.O. he was part of the procession. Marriott wondered how he felt about being part of the Establishment, as he always called anyone who was a link in the chain of command.

Marriott said, 'Our turn now, Number One.'

Fairfax called, 'Ship's company, *'shun*!'

How different they all looked in their uniforms and gilt buttons. Even the hands were in fresh white jerseys. As fresh as they could be without proper facilities.

They saluted and Marriott stepped forward. He could feel the same resentment as he had sensed in the others. Because of Macnair, or because a stranger was taking over.

As Macnair made a brief introduction he took a few seconds to study the man beneath the gleaming cap.

Not very tall, with a dark, impassive stare and

36

tight, unsmiling mouth. He wore a raincoat which, of course, showed no rank. It seemed to make the oakleafed cap all the more prominent.

Marriott realised that the man's eyes were passing over him. A cursory glance, but missing very little. They were deep-set and in shadow in the afternoon sunlight. They flickered from Marriott's features to the ribbon on his chest and back again.

He did not offer his hand but said, 'Commander Meikle.' His voice was higher than Marriott had expected, crisp and with all expression honed from it. 'I shall, of course, get to know all of you in time.' He looked across the deck to the leaning wreck of the great liner *New York*. 'There will be a full meeting of all my officers tomorrow, eight o'clock. There is a lot to achieve here, and although several naval parties have already arrived, and others are expected in the transit camp in Cuxhaven, ours is the first real challenge.'

He looked at the sky. 'Clearer now.' He slipped out of his raincoat and tossed it casually to a leading writer who was at the tail-end of the procession, a large notebook grasped in one hand.

Marriott stared at the commander's reefer jacket. It bore three wavy stripes. The rank of commander RNVR was still a rarity, and, to top it, Meikle did not have a single decoration as some sort of reason for his advancement.

Behind Meikle's back Cuff stood like a fuming bear, his face the colour of raw meat. Obviously he had already suffered during the inspection or whatever it was supposed to be, and could barely keep his fists under control.

Meikle said sharply, 'I understand that you are the officer who spoke with the prisoners this

37

morning?'

Marriott saw a warning in Macnair's eyes and replied, 'I didn't know they were prisoners, sir.'

'They are *all* prisoners until they have been checked and vetted. I will not have my officers playing God. The Germans respect discipline, or they will under my command, I can assure you. It is forbidden to fraternise with the Germans at any level except in the line of duty. So don't be sentimental or careless, and keep tham at a distance at all times.' He sounded as if he was quoting from a rulebook.

Marriott retorted, 'I think I know how to behave, sir. I've been in this war from the beginning.'

Meikle said offhandedly to Macnair, 'Another one, eh?'

Then he added, 'All vessels here must be kept up to scratch.' He turned to Cuff and added, 'And get those swastikas painted out. This is the Royal Navy as far as the Germans are concerned, and everyone here is a representative of that service.' He nodded to Marriott. 'Tomorrow then.' He sought out his leading writer. 'Rust. The first sign of slackness is rust, so make certain it does not occur.'

Cuff said thickly, 'No fear of that, sir.'

He could barely contain his triumph. 'These boats are built of bloody wood!'

Meikle walked past him. 'I will see that officer before the meeting tomorrow, Macnair.' He seemed to remember. 'But, of course, you will be gone by then. Pity.' Again the searching glance. 'Regulation working-dress will suffice henceforth—'

More salutes, and Marriott watched the boats swaying as the small procession melted away towards the pier.

38

Cuff exploded, 'Bloody little bastard! I'll give him sodding swastikas and I know where I'll shove 'em!'

Marriott said, 'You really got off on the right foot.'

Cuff clapped him on the shoulder. 'You didn't do so bad either, chum. *I've been in this war from the beginning* indeed. I'll lay odds our desk-bound hero just loved that!'

Macnair came back and looked at them sadly. 'Things will settle down. There's too much to be done here for petty disagreements.'

Marriott asked, 'Where is he now, sir?'

'Inspecting the MLs. His temporary HQ is in one of the U-Boat pens. God, the place is in a terrible mess. I never dreamed it was like this.'

Cuff cut in angrily. 'Where does he fit in, sir? I mean, well, he's not one of us!'

Macnair eyed him thoughtfully. 'He was a lawyer, still is. I knew of him before the war. Lately he's been working with the Judge Advocate's Department. But don't push your luck, and instil that in your people. I recognise all the signs.' Again the tired smile. 'You forget, I was one myself!'

He was getting weary. 'I'll be off now. Don't make a fuss tomorrow. We'll be under way first thing.' They shook hands, making light of it as usual.

Then Macnair said, 'I'll miss you lot.'

They watched him go and Cuff muttered, '*Rust* indeed!'

Marriott leaned on the guardrails and stared at the swirling water with its awful stench. Dead ships, dead people, too, probably. He saw some German sailors marching along the top of some

39

rubble, in step, swinging their arms, two petty officers barking out orders until they reached a solitary tractor around which was a group of Royal Engineers. There was a great pile of picks and shovels, jacks and pit-props although nobody had seen them arrive.

The senior petty officer stamped to a halt and shouted, 'All present, *sir*!'

A young captain of the RE sounded relieved that somebody had chosen a PO who spoke English.

He said, 'Tell your men that we are going to begin here.' He picked up a shovel and jammed it between some bricks. Then he opened a large plan and added, 'You will start to clear the road to the gate over there!'

The Germans listened to the repeated orders and then stared at the endless heaps of rubble. Even they must have forgotten there was a road there.

Marriott said, 'God, it'll take years, and this is just the fringe of it.'

Cuff said savagely, 'So what? They bloody well started it!'

A British sergeant climbed into the tractor and revved the engine. The sound seemed to move the watching sailors into action and moments later the air was filled with the ring of shovels.

Marriott looked away. It was not much, and the young captain in the Royal Engineers would know it. But it was a start, like a feeble heartbeat.

They didn't look much like prisoners of war, he thought. Many would be waiting to get away from here, to find their families if they were still alive.

He glanced at Cuff but saw only coldness in his eyes, resentment.

Marriott climbed down into his own boat once

40

more and found Lowes busy writing a letter, probably to his mother. It nearly always was. His forehead was lined with concentration.

Marriott looked around the place which had been their refuge, their home. The worn cushions which were supposed to keep you afloat if the worst happened. A rack of pistols and two Lanchester sub-machine guns. A picture of the King which had been moved to cover yet another repair where a cannon shell from a German fighter had found its mark off the Belgian coast. Old magazines, and a photo of a smiling full-breasted nude whom Fairfax insisted was his aunt.

He could not picture the boat being sent to the Far East in the future or at any time. The pumps were running twice as much now, the hull was leaking badly, but he doubted if she would ever get another refit. He looked at himself in the stained mirror and grimaced. *Like me. Bloody well shagged out*.

Lowes looked up, a lock of fair hair falling across his wide, innocent stare.

'When can we get ashore, sir?'

'Good question.' He thought of the picks and shovels, the grim faces of the British sappers. 'I'm not sure we'll like what we find.'

Lowes touched his teeth with his pen. 'I'll bet Lieutenant Commander Macnair is going back to something *really* special. All those *gongs*—I mean, sir, they must give him something?'

Marriott tightened his mouth and saw the young subbie flinch. *He's going home to die, don't you understand?* But he heard himself say, 'I'd like you to join us tomorrow morning. See him off properly.'

41

He saw the cloud pass from the youth's face. God, Fairfax was once like him. He tried to shake off the mood and added, 'Open the bar. Let's drink to Spruce.'

He watched Lowes unlocking a cupboard which they called 'The Bar'.

We were all like him, a thousand years ago.

But it was not just Marriott and his two sub-lieutenants who were on deck at dawn. Silent figures lined the four hulls, two of which were spewing out octane smoke, and tugging restlessly at their lines.

Marriott clamped his teeth on an unlit pipe. *And then there were two.* It was a wonder they didn't order the lot of them back to the UK. He watched the pale sky, another fine day above the drifting smoke. It was eerie to watch it writhing endlessly above the strewn wrecks in the great harbour and through the gaunt buildings, shattered cranes and gantries.

There was a small cheer as the two boats thrashed astern to leave their consorts by the pier. Just like all those other dawns, when your heart seemed to fill your mouth so that you could barely breathe. Except that this time there was a small launch here to guide them out. It was so strange to see lights displayed again without a thought for blackout or darken-ship. He saw the pilot launch rocking in the swell, her red and green lights like bright, unmatched eyes reflecting from the oily water. Cuff must have decided to disregard Meikle's warning about behaviour and his boat's horn blared over the harbour in a drawn-out banshee wail. Marriott found that he had his cap in his hand, caught up by the sadness, the wild elation, too, of this moment.

'A cheer for Spruce, lads!' And they were all at it. Remembering, thinking of lost friends, knowing that things would never be the same again.

The only one who did not cheer was the coxswain, Petty Officer Robert Evans.

He had seen some shadowy figures moving along the dockside, groping their way to an early start on clearing away the destruction. He considered his feelings, as he had from the moment they had tied up here and when with the Skipper he had confronted that great mass of Germans.

He had felt his heart beating faster, his body go cold when he had seen their faces so close, had even smelt them. His fingers closed over the little leather case he carried in his pocket, the reward he had not been allowed to wear in case he was captured. The *Croix de Guerre*. Tomorrow he would have it added to his other ribbons, watch their faces when he went amongst them. He probed his reactions yet again. It was still as before. Hate was not strong enough, nor loathing either. It was like a dedication and a pledge. It would not bring his family to life but he would make them pay for what they had done.

Marriott said, 'See what you can do about breakfast, will you, Swain?'

Evans stared at the harbour but the two motor gunboats had already faded into the shadows.

'Aye, aye, sir.' Even the quaint British phrases had become second nature by this time.

Marriott regarded him closely. 'All right, Swain?'

'I was remembering, sir.' He replaced his cap and adjusted it with care as he always did. 'And thinking how it would have been if *we* had lost.'

Marriott fell in step beside him. 'If ever you want to talk to me about anything—' He did not need to

43

go on.

Evans regarded him for several seconds. 'I am not an officer, sir, but I hope you would allow me the same privilege.'

Marriott lowered himself into the hatchway and heard Ginger Jackson rattling cups in the wardroom.

He had been touched by what Evans had just said. There was a lot to him they might never discover. There was danger too, although he did not understand why.

Fairfax banged through the door. 'Another day, sir. What wouldn't I give for a pretty girl and a walk through some Hampshire grass!'

Ginger Jackson put their plates down with elaborate care. 'I found some sardines, gents.'

Lowes exclaimed, 'For *breakfast*?'

Marriott looked at the plate, with Ginger's familiar thumb-print on its rim like some exclusive hotel crest.

No, nothing would ever be the same again. Not for any one of them.

CHAPTER THREE

TWENTY CROSSES

Marriott stood by the break in the guardrails and looked towards the dockyard. He shivered in the early morning sunlight but knew it was not because of the air. So short a while, and yet this place had changed him in some way. Like being on a devastated island or in some man-made prison. He could not explain it. Even a pot of Ginger Jackson's best coffee and some powdered eggs had made no difference.

Alongside, Cuff's command creaked uneasily against the rope fenders, while just astern of them the three long Fairmile motor launches were astir with early activity. Decks being swabbed down, white sweaters moving in the smoky light as some of the hands prepared to receive fresh stores and supplies, although God alone knew how they would get here.

Marriott glanced at his watch and thought of Macnair. *Getting spruced up.* In another half-hour, colours would be hoisted. It did not matter if it was Dover or Rosyth, Alexandria or Port Said, routine went on. Perhaps it was why they had won. They had not been prepared for defeat. In the navy, routine and tradition were everything.

Marriott heard Fairfax coming along the wooden deck and smiled despite his uneasiness. He thought of Cuff's incredulous anger when the new commander had made his comment about rust.

Fairfax saluted. 'I'll hold the fort in your absence, sir.'

Even in the familiar working-dress again, he seemed different. Marriott was conscious of his own clean shirt, collar and tie beneath the rough serge battledress blouse instead of his favourite sweater, the polished shoes in place of the comfortable scuffed seaboots. He knew Fairfax was watching him as usual, waiting to begin the new day in the same fashion as any first lieutenant, no matter how small the ship.

Fairfax said, 'The Jerries must have been up and digging since dawn, sir.'

45

As he spoke, a German sailor, his uniform grey with clotted dust, appeared out of the fallen masonry above the pier, pushing a wheelbarrow full of broken bricks where just yesterday there had been a solid barrier of rubble. More likely they had had men working all night. Marriott realised that before getting up to see Macnair's departure he had slept like a log. He could not recall the last time he had been able to do that.

Fairfax added, 'I'll take on stores as soon as we get the buzz.' He hesitated, sensing Marriott's mood. 'Will you be long at the, er—HQ, sir?'

'Hope not. It'll probably be a lecture. A pep talk on how to behave.'

He saw the coxswain mustering a small party of men below the bridge, his face as expressionless as ever.

Marriott said, 'I'll be off then,'

As he stepped ashore he glanced at the hill of fallen bricks and girders as if expecting to see the silent army of Germans still waiting for orders, for some authority who would reveal what lay in store for them. Instead, a naval patrolman, extremely smart in white belt and gaiters, with a Thompson sub-machine gun slung over one shoulder, stepped out of a makeshift sentry-box and saluted. 'I'm to show you the way, sir.' He gestured to the other boats. 'Someone else will guide the rest of the commanding officers, sir.' He had a homely West Country accent, which made Marriott feel that neither of them belonged here.

As they fell into step together Marriott looked around him, knowing that he would never forget what he was witnessing. On every hand there was devastation of such magnitude that it seemed impossible it could ever change. The RAF's massive 'blockbusters' had changed the order of a naval dockyard into one giant scrap-heap. It was a nightmare of impossible proportions. Beside one dry dock, towering above them as they strode past, was a complete destroyer, lifted bodily by a single bomb and dropped on the land. Vehicles, caught by falling debris and collapsing dockside sheds, had been flattened. Marriott was used to the sights of war, but he found himself staring at an out-thrust arm in field-grey uniform which hung out of the window of one of the crushed lorries. The vehicle, like its occupants, had been wiped out, but the man's arm seemed strangely lifelike.

The sailor remarked, 'Hundred like that, sir.' He lowered his voice as if in respect for the dead. 'At the U-Boat pens where I'm taking you, the RAF caught two submarines while they were inside. One was ready to sail when the roof caved in. She's got her whole crew inside. Stinks a bit, I can tell you, sir.'

Marriott stared at the out-thrust arm. The skin was tanned, with a pale line where a wrist-watch had once been.

The sailor saw his glance and grinned. 'Someone got there before me, lucky bugger!'

The closer they drew to the huge slablike U-Boat pens the more unreal it became. Figures wandered amongst the wreckage like puzzled ants. Khaki battledress and the dark blue of the navy. Germans marched this way and that, usually with a British petty officer or army NCO in charge. The order *'Eyes right!'* as one party trooped past Marriott and his escort made it all the harder to accept. The Germans *saw* Marriott, and yet they did not seem to

47

realise what was happening. Empty, apathetic, like the living dead.

Ashes swirled over the U-Boat pens and Marriott heard the muffled stammer of pneumatic drills and the clash of shovels. The army had got power from somewhere, and he thought he could smell baking bread. It was almost as unbelievable as the total destruction.

'Here we are, sir.' The man pulled aside a sacking curtain and gestured into a long room with concrete walls. It had probably been a last briefing room for some of the U-Boats which had sheltered and refitted beneath the massive concrete, Marriott thought. He recalled with sudden clarity his own brief time in a destroyer-escort in the Western Approaches. The long, pitiful lines of rusty freighters and precious tankers. Preyed upon by U-Boats from the moment they left England, and from the instant they began their return voyage with the food and fuel of survival.

And always the hated signals from the far-off Admiralty. *There are now ten U-Boats in your vicinity. There are now fifteen U-Boats in your vicinity.*

Then the roar of torpedoes in the night, the blazing fires on the black Atlantic, a stricken ship falling slowly astern, to sink alone or be finished off by another U-Boat.

Close the gap. Don't stop. Don't turn back.

Marriott hesitated and then walked back from the entrance and stood for a long moment looking down into one of the docks. The U-Boat was afloat, untouched by the bombs, ready to leave to join one of those packs in the Atlantic perhaps, when the surrender had been ordered.

48

Even here in defeat she looked evil.

Marriott breathed out slowly. And it was the first one he had ever seen. Perhaps it was the fear which had offered all of them the hatred, the fire to hit back and finally to win, when the odds had seemed overwhelming.

Someone coughed discreetly behind him and he turned to see the same harassed leading writer peering at him anxiously.

'I—I wondered where you were, sir.'

Marriott sighed. 'Lead the way, or has the meeting started without me?'

'Commander Meikle will see you now, sir.' It was not really an answer.

Marriott followed the leading writer's scurrying figure into the cold shadows of the concrete room. He reminded him of the White Rabbit, the way he was muttering to himself and consulting his watch. Perhaps the new commander made his subordinates like that.

'Won't keep you a tick, sir.' Another peep at his watch and the door closed again.

Marriott stared around the room, the bare benches and much-used canvas-backed chairs. The U-Boat officers must have gathered here too.

The White Rabbit reappeared, a sheaf of signal flimsies clutched in one paw.

'This way, sir.'

The adjoining room was brightly lit by freshly rigged lights, the cables of which snaked through another door like part of a film set. In the dead centre of the room was a desk, completely covered with files, signal clips and a jar of freshly sharpened pencils. On one wall, illuminated by its own special lamp, was an enormous map of the area,

49

Schleswig-Holstein and the Danish border right down to Kiel and the bay of Lübeck. To the east of the sector was a thick red line marked with several Russian flags. Perhaps for the first time Marriott began to see the full extent of their responsibility and authority. It was huge, with the sprawling mass of Kiel but a tiny part of it.

God, if it's all like this . . .

He looked at the scattered cases and metal cabinets which littered the room, a nerve-centre, which even now was reaching out beyond the chaos to naval vessels and personnel and heaven knew who else.

Meikle entered from the other door wiping his hands on a small towel. Without his elegant cap he looked younger, but his thick curly hair in its neat regulation cut was iron-grey, brushed back from a high and intelligent forehead. He merely glanced at Marriott and then gestured to a chair, which apart from his own was the only one present.

Even Meikle's blue working-dress was impeccable, and the shirt cuffs which showed evenly at each wrist were crisp and starched.

'All settled in, Marriott?' Again the quick scrutiny which missed nothing. 'I gather Macnair had a rowdy sendoff this morning.'

Marriott thought of Cuff's blaring horn, their combined sense of pride and loss.

'Hope we didn't wake you, sir.'

Meikle was searching through a file and did not look up.

'Hardly. I was down in Plön for most of the night with the military commander there.'

Marriott stared. Meikle looked as if he had just showered after a good night's rest. Instead—

50

Meikle said, 'I wanted to speak to *all* my commanding officers separately. Something which, I gather, was rather unusual under your previous arrangements, hmm?' He did not pause for a reply. 'I have to know my people, even if I cannot always be with them. If I can't work with someone—well, that's something else.'

Marriott saw his lips tighten and could guess what the *something else* implied.

Meikle looked at him directly for the first time. His eyes, like the glance, were dark and deep.

'Your duties under my command will be as varied as the situation here demands.' He looked down at the papers again. 'I shall recap. Two of your flotilla remained in Denmark to be used at the discretion of the N.O.I.C. there. Two left this morning for the UK. That leaves your 801 and Lieutenant Glazebrook's plus the three MLs, some trawlers and the salvage vessel HMS *Sea Harvester*. She is under the command of one Lieutenant Commander Crawford, something of a diving expert.' He pursed his lips. 'He's going to earn his bread-and-butter in this harbour.'

Marriott blurted out, 'But the flotilla, sir? Surely it will be regrouped.'

Meikle shook his head. 'I think not. The Pacific War—well, that's hardly our concern, not yet anyway. Our work is here in Kiel and our adjoining responsibilities. The Naval-Officer-in-Charge is setting up his own HQ and a full operational and communications staff as well as a minesweeping command are sorting out their allotted stations.'

Marriott stared at the big wall-map, but all he could see was the dismantling of his flotilla. New faces had replaced those killed and wounded,

51

different boats from time to time had filled the gaps. But always the *same* flotilla. He could almost hear the voices of those lost faces singing their old morbid song after some particularly hairy raid or close-action.

What is left of our poor squadron? . . . Twenty crosses in a row!

To be no more. Because of some brasshat's order they had been wiped out, something which even the enemy had failed to achieve.

He searched Meikle's features for some indication of his feelings, but there was nothing.

Marriott said abruptly, 'So that's all they care!'

Meikle did not rise to the bitterness. 'I am not completely blind, Marriott, nor am I a fool. I saw the display of medals when I arrived when you were ordered to change into your Number Fives, knowing it would further illuminate that I have none.'

His tone was completely calm and Marriott could imagine him using it when summing up the evidence of guilt at a court martial, or in his pre-war legal days when Spruce had known him.

Meikle continued in the same unemotional way, 'Of course I am aware of your courage, just as I admire it in others. The policeman on his beat in the blitz, the nurse staying with her patients beside a landmine or unexploded bomb.' His lips moved in the hint of a smile. 'There has been all manner of gallantry in the past six years. Even the conscientious objector driving his ambulance under fire is not without it.' His tone hardened. 'Although I dare say there are no medals for *him*.'

Marriott felt beaten and drained. 'Is that all, sir?'

Meikle ignored the question. 'How long have you

52

known Lieutenant Glazebrook?'

Marriott regarded him coldly. 'I know him well enough. He is my senior officer and . . .'

'Lucky for you too.' He leaned forward to emphasise each point. 'When you were on passage here, Glazebrook detached his boat to investigate a shipping-movement report, yes?'

Marriott nodded, caught out by the change of tack. It was odd that it had happened just two days ago and he had all but forgotten it.

Meikle turned another page. 'They were fishing-boats under enemy control.'

'That was common enough, sir.'

'Why are you always springing to someone's defence or taking a general criticism as something personal? I was about to say that Glazebrook signalled them to stop and to obey his signals.' He closed the folder and kept his eyes on the grave-faced lieutenant opposite him as he added, 'He says in his report that they tried to avoid him, in fact to escape. So he closed with them and dropped two depth charges between them. I don't have to spell it out to you what must have happened to the fishing-boats with *wooden hulls* at close quarters—not someone of your *obvious* experience.'

Marriott saw Cuff's face as the mass of German sailors had advanced towards the gunboats, and recalled those other times when because of the war, and the daily presence of death, those you knew and cared about, Cuff's hardness had gone overlooked.

Meikle's voice was surprisingly gentle. 'I do not like the Germans, but we are here to administer and to govern until order is restored. We will never achieve anything but hate and disgust if we merely use our power to emulate their Nazi doctrines.'

'I didn't know, sir.'

Meikle looked at the outer door as the leading writer peered in at them.

'Very well, Lavender. I shall be free in two minutes.'

Marriott looked at his hands, almost expecting to see them shaking. *Lavender*. It would be. Just the right touch of unreality along with all the rest.

He heard Meikle say, 'We need to set an example here, and to get things done. Harbour clearance, the removal of corpses from the sea and the town, and we must have the ability to provide food and shelter for those who cannot hope to fend for themselves. No fraternisation, no sliding standards. I can imagine your experiences merely by reading about them. Let them be an asset, not a conceit.'

He pressed his fingertips together.

'I don't care what you or anyone else thinks of me. All I want is to get the job done. But if somebody should stand against me, he will go, that I can promise.'

It was almost over and Marriott stood up, groping for his cap.

'And *my* orders, sir?'

Meikle was reaching for a telephone in its leather case. 'I want you to be ready to put to sea at one hour's notice. There is something which I must decide.'

Marriott hesitated, angry that he had lost so completely to this self-contained man, and yet somehow grateful that he was still 801's captain.

Meikle looked at him and gave a dry smile. 'We *are* both on the same side, you know.'

Marriott walked out into the drifting ashes and smoky sunlight and found the patrolman waiting

54

for him.

'I can find my way back, thank you.'

The patrolman slung his sub-machine gun over one shoulder and grinned. 'Sorry, sir, orders say otherwise. *Nobody* moves alone in this place.'

They walked past the smashed vehicles and Marriott saw the outflung arm almost hidden now in rubble thrown up by passing tractors. How long had the dead soldier been there, he wondered? How much longer before his journey would finally end?

He found Fairfax and Lowes waiting at the guardrails with mixed expressions of anxiety and hope.

Marriott glanced along the deck, the activity which was part of his life. In his absence the ensign had been hoisted like the others on nearby warships and supply craft.

Did this old clapped-out gunboat mean that much to him, after all? How many hundreds of miles she must have thrashed with her four big screws; how many thousands of rounds of cannon shells and bullets. Three commanding officers. *And I shall be the last.*

He said, 'We are in business again, gentlemen.' He saw their grins. Was that all he had to do or say? 'One hour's notice.'

He saw to his surprise that Cuff's boat had been warped further along the pier.

Fairfax explained, 'Tommy Updike is preparing to take on stores, sir.' He faltered under Marriott's gaze. 'Cuff—that is Lieutenant Glazebrook—has gone to see the N.O.I.C. wherever he is, sir, to make a report in person.'

Marriott looked across the swirling waste of oil and filthy flotsam. He could picture the exploding

55

charges as if he had been there. And to think he had been worried for Cuff's safety. They had dropped plenty of charges in their time. Not to sink submarines but to blow the bottoms out of coasters and the like, or armed schooners which they had encountered in the Med. To use them against unarmed fishing-boats, knowing that hostilities had ceased, was little better than murder. He could almost hear Cuff saying the words he had used right here.

They started it.

He had met his match in Meikle, but as always would come out of it whiter than white. It was his way.

Lowes asked timidly, 'Is there a flap on, sir?'

Marriott smiled and felt some of the tension draining away. Lowes made a habit of using the slang and jargon of the war he had been too late to fight. *Is there a flap on?*

'It could be anything. Just be ready for it, Pilot.'

As the youth bustled away, Fairfax said, 'I'm glad we're still together, sir.'

Marriott eyed him thoughtfully. 'Thanks, Number One. I hope you can still say that in a week's time in this place!'

The coxswain turned as Fairfax laughed, then tried to concentrate on what Sub-Lieutenant Lowes was telling him about readiness for sea.

So they were leaving harbour again already. Evans stared at the shore where some German sailors were pausing to take soup and break from an army jeep.

There would be plenty of time, he thought. He had nothing else to think about now.

He straightened his cap and nodded. 'Right

56

away, sir.'

He had not heard much of what Lowes had been saying. But that rarely seemed to matter.

Alone by the bridge Lowes, unaware of Marriott's amusement or the coxswain's contempt, settled down to watch the slow-moving *Sea Harvester* as she steamed ponderously between two wrecks, puffing out smoke while she prepared to lay marker buoys for her divers.

It was all so exciting. He had seen no fighting. *Yet*. His eyes were far away. *But one day* . . .

Fairfax glanced along the sidedeck and chuckled. 'Dreaming again.'

Marriott thought suddenly of Stephen, how it might have been if they had shared this victory together.

'Dreams, Number One.' He touched his arm, then turned away as another face seeemd to overshadow Fairfax's. 'Leave him those at least.'

*　　*　　*

Marriott leaned on the rail beneath the bridge screen and watched the familiar activity on the forecastle, where Leading Seaman Townsend was supervising the mooring lines while Lowes, very dashing with a white silk scarf around his throat, tried to keep out of everyone's way. The gentle purr of generators and the rising vapour alongside told Marriott all he needed to know about the engineroom department. The Chief would make the hull move with his bare hands if need be.

Fairfax climbed to the bridge. 'All our people are aboard, sir. Ready to proceed.'

Marriott nodded. There was not much fear of

leaving without a full complement, he thought, not with all the sentries and armed shore patrols.

It was evening and the sky still bright. What was strange was that you hardly noticed the smoke any more. It was part of it, like the oil slicks and the smell of decay. It was warmer too. Not much, but Marriott could feel his shirt clinging to his skin. Or was it just nerves? Leaving harbour like all those other times, but with the knowledge that barring accidents they would be back alongside, perhaps this time tomorrow.

He saw a seaman walking along the dockyard wall with a large satchel slung over his shoulder, chatting to a patrolman.

Fairfax followed his glance. 'Postman, sir?'

Marriott shook his head. 'Too soon. Maybe in a day or so.'

Letters from home, newspapers to tell them about that other world where the end of the war in Europe would mean so much in so many different ways.

There might be leave soon. Marriott tried not to think about it. Everything would be so different now. With Stephen gone, and Penny probably still away, it would be an awkward affair.

He thought of Penny and smiled sadly. The baby of the family, so lively and vivacious and as changeable as the wind. Even at school she had been convinced she would be a writer or an actress, something artistic. She had got on well with poor Mimi, much to their mother's disapproval. It was probably no coincidence that Penny had joined up immediately after Stephen's death and Mimi's wretched end. She was now serving in the plotting room of a fighter station in Kent and was a corporal in the WAAF. The small airstrip had been constantly involved in the daily defence of London and later the support of the army across the Channel. Reading between the lines, Penny had had several wild crushes on some of the young fighter pilots she knew. Some had moved on, others had never returned from dog-fights and sorties over the Channel.

Something had happened to change her. She had written to him more than once of a man she claimed she would marry if he asked her. He was the Met Officer at the station, an older man, or a *wingless wonder* as she affectionately called him. There was a snag; he was a Canadian and would want her to go with him when the war was finally ended. What would their mother have to say about that?

Leading Signalman Silver called, 'Five minutes, sir!'

'Single up all lines!' Marriott caught Fairfax's sleeve. 'Hold it!' A jeep with RN painted on the side was pitching and bucking over the rubble like a boat in surf.

Marriott saw the flashing gold leaves around Meikle's cap, the rabbit-like Lavender sitting beside him with a briefcase clutched across his lap. while two armed seamen occupied the rear seats. So Meikle liked to drive himself. Another surprise.

'I'd better go to him.' Marriott felt both uneasy and vaguely annoyed. Did Meikle not trust him to take his boat out of harbour without his supervision?

Marriott clambered through the guardrails and jumped down on to the pier. By the time he had climbed up the crumbling slope Meikle had left the jeep and was studying the day's progress. The narrow track had widened, and even part of the buried gateway had revealed itself.

But he said, 'They'll have to work faster than this!' He returned Marriott's salute. 'You've read your orders?'

'Yes, sir.' It must have sounded like *of course*.

Meikle snapped, 'There may be problems. You are to find and rendezvous with the ship in question, board her, and if necessary take control. She is said to be carrying German servicemen who have already been listed as *war criminals*.' He saw Marriott's expression and added, 'What—didn't you know there were such creatures?'

'I don't see what difference that will make, sir!' Why did this man always manage to rile him so easily, to make him feel clumsy and foolish?

Meikle said abruptly, 'Intelligence have reported that the Russians already know about this ship. I want no incidents, no confrontations. Whatever we may think about their methods, and not without some justification I can assure you, the Russians are our allies, *right?* The ship is their headache.' They both turned as a squad of tired-looking soldiers crunched along another winding track of cleared rubble with a mixed assortment of Germans following in single file. The latter had their hands on their heads and had been stripped of their weapons and equipment.

A tough-looking sergeant held up his hand and halted the weary procession, then stamped his heels together and saluted.

'Prisoners, sir.' He spoke like a man who was beyond surprise or disappointment. ''Idin' in a pump 'ouse. I'm takin' 'em for interrogation.'

Meikle looked thoughtfully at the 'prisoners'.

60

Most of them were old enough to have served in the Kaiser's war, and their uniforms were ill-fitting and threadbare. The remainder were just boys of around fourteen. One of them was sobbing and holding his cheek.

The sergeant glared at him. ''Itler Youth, that one, sir. Spat at Roberts, my lance-jack over there, 'e did. Little bastard!'

Meikle said coolly, '*Volksturm*, Sergeant. Their equivalent of the Home Guard. Any weapons?'

'Nah, sir, ditched 'em probably while they waited a chance to sabotage somethin', I shouldn't wonder.'

Marriott watched the soldiers, especially the one called Roberts. He had the feeling that but for the sergeant the lance-corporal might have shot the lot of them.

As if reading his thoughts the sergeant lowered his voice and said, 'Roberts lost all 'is family in the blitz. Not the chap to spit on under the circumstances!'

Surprisingly the soldiers nearby broke into broad grins. But, for men who had been killing the enemy because they were ordered to, and had seen their friends die or be sent home to Blighty as broken things, it was a taut margin. Like the MGBs' guncrews, here, where the Germans had surrendered under a soiled white handkerchief.

Meikle nodded. 'You did right, Sergeant. I shall say as much to your CO. Now take them off to the MPs.' He met the sergeant's gaze. '*All* of them.'

As they shambled away Meikle said, 'Something troubling you again?'

Marriott said, 'I don't think so, sir.' But it was a lie. His own father, desperate to do something for

61

the war effort, had joined the Home Guard. He was probably the same age as the veterans he had just seen. He thought of Evans's comment. Suppose they had lost the war? What chance would men like his father have stood against Tiger tanks and dive-bombers?

Meikle saw Lavender peering at his watch and said dryly, 'With him around I don't need an alarm clock.' The mood changed just as quickly. 'Be off with you. The pilot boat will see you clear.' He sniffed the breeze. '*Sea Harvester* will begin work tomorrow.'

They both looked at the listing wrecks, their sides already in shadow. It required no imagination to picture what the divers would find in the bombed and shattered hulks. But nothing could move until they were cleared.

Meikle stood back and added softly, 'Remember what I said. No confrontations. Things are touchy enough already and the dust hasn't settled yet!' He turned and climbed into his jeep, then without looking back at the gunboat he drove swiftly into the dockyard.

Marriott clambered on board again and strode to the bridge. He was suddenly eager to leave, to find the freedom of open water again, away from all the planning and the endless devastation.

'Start up, Number One!' He felt the bridge shake wildly as Adair brought his beloved engines to life.

Marriott climbed on to the gratings and peered astern. 'Let go aft!' He saw Evans's hands moving the wheel very slightly. Ready for anything. 'Slow astern, starboard! Let go forrard!'

He watched the stern swinging very slightly away from the sagging pier as the breeze thrust the boxlike hull clear. 'Slow astern, port outer!' He saw the backwash from the screws churning the scum and scatterings of charred woodwork against the piles. *A dead place.*

He saw the red and green eyes of the pilot boat rocking on the slight swell, then raised his glasses to look for the nearest wrecks. 'Slow ahead together! Take her round, Swain!' He had seen the new ribbon on Evans's jacket and wondered why it had been omitted from the coxswain's personal documents. He would ask him. Maybe.

Fragments of something bumped against the hull and the seamen on the bridge glanced at one another and grimaced.

Soon the tall sentinel-like memorial of Laboe loomed abeam and Marriott felt the deck lift under his feet as if eager to be free, like himself.

'Half ahead. Course to steer, Number One?'

A lamp stabbed across the unbroken water from the pilot boat and Long John Silver triggered his Aldis in reply.

Aloud he said, 'An' good luck to you, mate!'

Fairfax called, 'Steer North-fifty-East, sir!'

Marriott glanced at the sky and smiled. *Sharp as a tack.* He had learned a lot, and quickly. He touched the screen bathed in bright green by the starboard light. The first time he had seen it switched on since he had taken command. It was a wonder it worked.

Marriott said, 'Take the con, Number One, and call me if—'

Fairfax's teeth gleamed in the fading light. 'I know, sir. *If . . .*'

Marriott went below to his cabin and heard Ginger Jackson humming contentedly as he unpacked some of the new supplies.

It was funny that in war the simple things were all that counted.

In his tiny cabin Marriott changed into his seagoing clothing and scarred old boots. He could feel Meikle's disapproval even from here. He switched on the little reading lamp and opened his curtly worded orders.

A rendezvous with a strange vessel. Just the thing for Lowes's next letter to his mother.

Then he frowned and opened his personal chart, his eyes lingering on the lines and bearings of the Russian sectors. The carve-up, as Cuff had called it. It was odd that Meikle had not mentioned the meeting with the N.O.I.C. Perhaps Cuff would be transferred to another command? He heard Fairfax moving on the bridge overhead, the clatter of tin mugs as tea was passed around to the watchkeepers.

It was all they knew. The amateurs who had become the professionals. The veterans. The survivors.

He thought of how 801 would appear from the land as she slipped across the bay, a low shadow apart from her navigation lights. What did they really think—the *enemy*?

He lay down on his bunk and closed his eyes. The engine's regular beat, the sluice of the sea against the long mahogany hull, were like parts of his own being.

He stared up at the deckhead and then closed his eyes.

The very next instant, or so it seemed, he was sitting bolt upright, his whole body screaming in protest.

He snatched the handset and said, '*Yes?*' He

could feel his chest heaving, wet with sweat, the handset slipping in his fingers.

Fairfax's voice sounded miles away. 'Sorry, sir.' The usual hesitation. 'Are you all right, sir?'

Marriott made himself unwind, piece by piece. So it had not gone away. The shrill of the telephone still brought the memories. The fear.

'Yes.' He peered at his watch. It was unbelievable. He had slept for four hours.

He heard himself ask, 'It's not time to alter course, is it?' He shook himself. What was the matter with him?

'No, sir. The Chief is worried about one of his pumps. Wants to slow down. Better still, to stop altogether. He says he can clear it in no time.'

Marriott nodded although Fairfax could not see him. He felt his breathing, like his heartbeat, returning to normal. The intakes had probably sucked up some extra filth from the harbour. Better now than later. He made up his mind.

'Is it all clear?'

'Yes. No shipping. Sea's pretty calm.'

'Right. I'll come up.' He replaced the handset. 'Getting past it.' He spoke aloud without realising it. Then he swung his legs to the deck and rubbed his eyes.

He was the captain again.

CHAPTER FOUR

ALLIES

With her engines stopped, MGB801 drifted broadside-on to the sea. The motion was sickening so that even Marriott felt his stomach heave in the familiar, musty confines of the chartroom. He jammed his elbows on the chart table and studied the pencilled lines and bearings, the neatly worded notes beside the small light. Lowes as the third-hand looked after the charts and attended to the log. It earned him the honoured nickname of Pilot, but in fact his work was little more than a navigator's yeoman in any larger vessel. He heard Fairfax breathing at his elbow, his eyes doubtless watching every move as he checked their approximate position, the brass dividers glinting in the small glow.

Marriott said eventually, 'I estimate that we're about here. Some ten miles north of Rostock. We could get a good fix if it was daylight, good *enough* anyway.' He swore silently as something metallic crashed down in the engineroom. 'God, he's taking his bloody time!' He peered at his watch, knowing he was getting rattled, worse, that Fairfax would know it.

Fairfax asked, 'Will it make much difference, sir?'

It sounded as if he was blaming himself. *Just as Meikle accused me of doing.*

He replied, 'As soon as we can get under way again I shall call for revs for twenty knots. I know all the warnings about fuel consumption, but I want to sight Bornholm by dawn. The ship should be easy enough to find. According to Operations she can only make seven knots.'

Fairfax watched him, seeing the emotions, the doubts crossing his face.

'What will we do, sir?'

Marriott sighed. 'We have to turn them back. Germans they may be, but they're from the Russian sector.'

Fairfax said, 'Trying to get away. Sweden perhaps?'

'Doubt that. After being so pally with the Nazis during the war I don't expect the Swedes will want to antagonise Uncle Joe more than they have already.' He touched his forehead. It was damp and cold. A sure sign. It was all he needed, to throw up in front of the others. They climbed up to the open bridge and Marriott stared at the mass of tiny stars which seemed to pitch from side to side in the motion.

He said, 'Ask the Chief—' He added, 'No, don't. He'll be doing all he can.' He took several deep breaths. How clean it tasted after Kiel. That was better. He groped for his pipe then stiffened as Silver called, '*Engines*, sir! Fast-movin'!'

Marriott grasped the rail and turned his head this way and that. He could feel the hair rising on his neck. Would it never go away? All those times in the North Sea and Channel when they had drifted, engines stopped like now, waiting and listening. Even when you expected it, there was always a sense of shock. The *thrum-thrum-thrum* of the E-Boat's powerful Daimler Benz engines. Usually returning after a successful attack on coastal shipping, or on their way to seek out fresh targets. To hear them first was to hold the winning hand. Your own engines cut out every sound.

Like the time this boat had been raked by a German fighter on their way back to base. Too many aboard thinking of getting home in one piece. Or getting back at all, and perhaps a lookout peering for a first sight of England instead of watching astern. It had cost the boat two lives.

'Got it!' He gestured over the swaying glass screen. 'South-East of us, I'd say.'

He swung away, his mind empty of everything but the facts. Like those other times. *Observation—Conclusion—Method—Attack!* Except that this time there would be no battle. He felt his mouth harden in a tight grin. Or no confrontation, as Meikle would have it.

He said sharply, 'Darken ship!' He hesitated, his thumb on the invisible red button. Too jumpy? Over-reacting? *To hell with what they think.* He jabbed it down hard and heard the alarm bells yammering through the hull.

Silver chuckled. 'That'll stir the idle buggers!'

Fairfax lifted his face from a voicepipe. 'Chief, sir! Ready to proceed!' He added in a surprised tone, 'Didn't mention the alarm, sir!'

Marriott moved to the front of the bridge and heard the thud of feet on ladders.

But for Adair's concern for his charges they might not have stopped, and the unknown vessel would have remained a mystery.

He snapped, *'Start up!'*

★   ★   ★

Sub-Lieutenant John Lowes sat wedged into a wardroom bench seat, unable even to think of sleep in the awful, swooping motion. He had even heard some of the old hands spewing up in the heads. One smell of that and he was done for.

In the navy, *the Andrew*, another titbit of slang, there was no sympathy for the ones who suffered from seasickness. At best, the old sweats remarked that even Nelson had been seasick but it never stopped *him* from winning battles! The less charitable enjoyed describing possible 'cures'. Like swallowing a lump of pork fat tied to a piece of string and pulling it straight up again.

Lowes watched as Ginger Jackson wandered into the tiny wardroom, his eyes everywhere as he searched for nooks and crannies where he could store his fresh supplies. Cans of corned beef and those awful square-shaped sausages. Drums of powdered egg and soup. Tinned herrings in tomato sauce, the sailors' favourite.

Lowes groaned and swallowed violently. He must stop thinking about it. Ginger paused and regarded him cheerfully. He was never seasick. But he liked Lowes. He reminded him a bit of his kid brother. Apart from his posh accent, of course. Ginger came from Kentish Town and had had to fight his brother's battles many times. Trouble was, he looked a bit effeminate. Rather like the subbie. His brother was a sickberth attendant in the battleship *Rodney* now. He grinned. They'd be fighting *for* him!

'Soon be movin' again, sir.' Ginger leaned against the door and sighed. 'Then back to Kiel, the poor man's Brighton!'

Lowes grimaced. 'I want to get ashore and see
69

things.' He flushed. 'You know, get some souvenirs before they all get picked over.'

Ginger regarded him thoughtfully. As messman he was the only man in the boat who had stepped into the dockyard, apart from the Skipper, that was. Funny when you thought about it. But Jimmy the One had sent him to find the supply truck which was delivering stores for the naval vessels in the harbour. He had met a jolly little corporal, one of the army cooks there. He had learned quite a lot from him. They would do some business together if he was not mistaken.

Ginger groped into his overalls and pulled out a folded handkerchief. He laid it on the table and opened it, but kept his eyes on the young officer. He was taking a chance. But Lowes was like his brother in another way. A bit thick.

Lowes peered unblinking at the little glittering collection of medals. At least two Iron Crosses and some others with different coloured ribbons. A watch too, marked in precise seconds, the sort a German gunnery officer might use.

He gasped, 'H-How much did you have to pay for these?' His seasickness had gone completely.

Ginger did not reply directly. 'You don't smoke, do you, Mister Lowes? So what d'you do with yer ticklers, yer duty-frees?'

Lowes stared at him, his eyes blank with surprise. 'I save them for my mother. They're hard to get at home.'

''Arder still 'ere, sir, in fact bloody impossible. The Jerries 'ave no fags nor tobacco, coffee neither, it's their *currency* now. Money's useless.' He decided not to mention all the other things which could be obtained on the new black market. It was a

70

lucky thing he had found the little army cook.

'But—but—' Lowes was further confused. 'I thought it was against the law? No fraternisation, that sort of thing?'

Ginger folded the handkerchief. 'Well, of course, sir, if you're not interested—'

Lowes licked his lips. When he went home he would go and see Monica. What would *she* think when he produced an Iron Cross? *Back from the war.* The words seemed to shine like the title of a big film.

He said hesitatingly, 'Well, we *are* the ones who are taking all the risks.'

Ginger nodded gravely. ''Course we are, sir. Fair rations for all, I says.'

Lowes was hooked. Ginger had not made a mistake. As an officer, no matter how junior, he had access to other useful stores.

Ginger stared around the wardroom. *They don't give a toss for us now that we've won the bloody war for them. It'll be good old Jack, then off to have a bash at the Nips next.*

He added, 'Just between us, o' course, Mister Lowes.'

But Lowes was miles away. With his friends in the fashionable hotel which was for *officers only*. An Iron Cross. For a start anyway. When the alarm bells shrilled through the boat Lowes was unable to move. It was like seeing a mirror shiver to fragments even as you were looking at it.

Ginger grabbed his arm and shouted, 'Jump about, sir! They ain't bleedin' weddin' bells!'

The coxswain strode past, his face like stone as he brushed some crumbs from his jacket. So he had been unable to sleep too? But then he never seemed

71

to.

Lowes snatched up his cap and ran for the ladder even as hatches slammed shut and lights vanished as if they had been switched off by a single hand.

The engines suddenly roared into full throttle and caught the breathless Lowes off balance. But for Silver's quick hand he would have pitched headlong into the bridge.

Marriott said from the darkness, 'Sorry to get you out of your pit, Sub, but it was the quickest way to do it.'

Lowes stared round at the dim, crouching figures. The wind was whipping at the halliards as the speed mounted, and he could see the bow-wave spreading back from the stem as if lifted from the sea and made a pale arrowhead on the black water.

As always he was the last at his action station even though he had been up and dressed. How did they do it, he wondered?

He heard one of the machine gunners wrestling with his gleaming belts of ammunition but whispering a filthy joke to his mate at the same time. Lowes did not know how to react. There was no fresh outbreak of war, after all. He looked at the others. The Skipper standing beside the coxswain, hatless, his hair blowing in the wind across the screen. Fairfax must be down at the chart table, while Long John Silver was calmly untangling some of his signal halliards.

No war. But they were still needed. His heart swelled. And he was part of it. One of them. *Accepted*.

He began to dream while he clung to a rail as the hull slammed across the water, throwing up the spray like huge wings.

72

All he had to do was to explain to his mother why there would be fewer duty-free cigarettes from now on . . .

*　　*　　*

'Dawn'll be up any moment, sir.'

Marriott did not answer, his ear pitched to the steady beat of engines, slowed now as they approached their estimated position on the chart. They had stopped engines several times to listen, but had heard nothing but sea noises, as if they were alone in the Baltic. An intruder.

He wiped his powerful night-glasses with a twist of tissue and tested them on the horizon, where dawn would first show itself. The air was cold and he felt chilled to the bone. Or was it just his edginess?

'Select three extra lookouts, Number One, and issue them with binoculars. Take them from aft.' He thought briefly of Cuff's angry face. 'We'll not be needing depth charges, I think.'

He waited for Fairfax to pass his orders then said, 'She's an old ship we're looking for, a coaster, about two and a half thousand tons.' He pictured the sparsely worded orders which Meikle had given to him, with Operations' additional intelligence clipped to them. He added, 'She's named *Ronsis*, although she's not listed on my brief. Latvian, until the Germans marched in and took over. They've been using her for local supplies.' Why was he telling Fairfax all this? He took a quick glance at him as he trained his glasses abeam and adjusted the focus. *Is it that I don't want him to go, and if so, why not? Perhaps because I think he can't handle it.*

Fairfax said hesitatingly, 'The *Ronsis*, sir. I suppose we can't just let her through?'

Here we go. He replied curtly, 'No chance.'

Fairfax thought about it. 'I—I mean, *refugees*, sir. What do they matter?'

Marriott dropped his voice. 'Just forget it. Wait until we've had a look, right?' He felt a barrier drop between them. He was angry and knew it was because Fairfax had voiced his own thoughts for him.

Surely it didn't matter who finally vetted the refugees and weeded out Meikle's 'war criminals' and the Nazi leaders trying to escape Russian justice? More like revenge after the devastation of the German armies' thrust eastwards to the gates of Stalingrad itself. Millions, not thousands, had died in the savage battles, many of which had been fought in waist-deep mud or worse, in temperatures so low that guns jammed and men froze to death in their fox-holes and trenches. No mercy, no quarter given by either side. No wonder they wanted to get home even if their town or village was occupied by the Allies. Anything might seem safer than under the Russian heel.

Silver muttered, ''Ere it comes!' He thumped his palms together so that Lowes jumped with alarm.

Marriott raised his glasses and watched the first hint of daylight touch the sea, to create a margin between sky and water.

Suppose there was no ship? Marriott moved the glasses very slowly, his legs straddled against the slow roll. He knew he was hoping the sea would be empty.

Refugees. His mind lingered on the word. Right from the start of the war he had seen them, mostly

74

on the cinema newsreels, all sorts of nationalities, and yet sharing the same despair and fear. Pinched faces peering at the sky, dreading the banshee scream of Stuka dive-bombers or the rattle of machine-gun fire as crowded roads were torn into bloody havoc. To create fear and to demoralise as well as to delay a defending army. French, Norwegian, Greek, Polish—the list seemed endless. Even the road always looked the same. Pathetic farm wagons loaded with small possessions, the old and the sick, and of course the children.

Now the Germans were learning the same brutal lesson. So why should he care?

More sunlight now, pale and watery, spilling over the sea's edge to make it shimmer, to discover some colour for the first time. *A fine day*.

He heard Lowes remark, 'We *should* have radar. We'd soon find it then.'

Nobody answered. All the hands on the crowded bridge had said or thought the same thing many times. When it had really mattered.

Marriott bit his lip. They had always been at the wrong end of the queue. Like the minesweepers, they had been expected to *feel* their way.

He stiffened as his glasses settled on something black and solid. Silver had seen it too. It was the island of Bornholm where the Germans had threatened to hold out to the last man. But they had not. How close it looked.

Marriott said, 'Go round the boat, Pilot. Check each action station.' He added as if speaking to all of them, 'This is not a drill.'

Lowes bustled away, pleased to be doing something so important.

Marriott said, 'He's right, of course.' His words
75

reformed the link between them and Fairfax moved closer. 'If there is anyone else hanging around it would be nice to know.'

'*Ship, sir!* Bearing Green four-five!'

They all craned forward, every pair of binoculars training on the bearing.

Marriott said between his teeth, 'Good work, Rae.' The starboard machine-gunner had eyes like a cat. He was a veteran, one of 801's original company, and had used his eyesight to full advantage many times. Even now he was swinging his twin three-oh-three machine-guns towards the far-off blur which had suddenly become framed against the strengthening sunlight.

Marriott held his breath and tried again. It must be the *Ronsis*. He could just distinguish the old-fashioned straight stem and solitary funnel. He could even see the thick trail of smoke which seemed to be resting on the water. There was only the tiniest hint of white at her bows. She might even be stopped.

'Switch on navigation lights!' Marriott had ordered them to be kept shut off when they had first stopped at Adair's request. After hearing the high-speed engines he had decided to leave the boat in darkness. Now, even in the growing daylight, the navigation lamps seemed unnaturally bright.

Fairfax said, 'She's not showing any lights, sir.'

Would you? Aloud he said, 'Prepare the dinghy for lowering.' He added sharply, 'Not you, Number One. Let Leading Seaman Craven handle it.'

Fairfax hurried to the rear of the bridge, his voice hushed as if he thought the distant ship might hear him. She was a good three miles away. There was no chance she could slip past them, or escape in darkness.

'Increase to half-speed.' Marriott studied the solid silhouette. No response, or sign of life. Maybe . . . He dismissed the idea and rapped, 'Signal her to heave-to. Tell her who we are.'

The lamp clattered busily and as Fairfax came back Silver called, 'There, now! Like a bleedin' Christmas tree!'

The other vessel had switched on her masthead and navigation lights, while from somewhere beneath her bridge a whole line of scuttles lit up like lanterns.

Then, very slowly, a lamp stammered across the gap between them.

Silver did not bother to use his glasses. 'She's the *Ronsis*, right enough, sir.' He watched the light again. '*I await your company*.'

The seaman named Rae played with the cocking levers on his guns. 'What a pity!'

Marriott glanced at him. A young, homely face you might not even notice in a barracks or a big warship. But Marriott had come to know him well, especially as his action station was here on the bridge. It was an unexpected side to his nature. He had been hoping for a chance to use his guns. Just once more. The wildness was lingering there. *It's still in all of us*.

He touched Fairfax's arm. 'When we're close enough I want you to board her.' He tried to make light of it. 'At least we know from the quaint wording of his signal, someone speaks good English, eh?' But relief would not come.

Fairfax nodded, his face no longer in shadow as the weak sunlight explored the bridge fittings and gave personality to the watching figures in their

77

duffel coats and sweaters.

'Right, sir.'

Marriott continued, 'Just find out what you can, but tell the master he must turn back.' He watched the uncertainty and the doubt on Fairfax's face and added, 'There's *nothing* we can do about it.' He turned away, impatient, weary of it. 'I'll go across myself if you can't manage it!' It was unfair, but Fairfax had to understand.

Fairfax retorted, 'I won't let you down, sir.' But he sounded surprised. Hurt.

'Dinghy's ready for lowering, sir!' Any interruption was welcome.

Marriott said, 'Take Craven as your leading-hand, and make sure your party carry Lanchesters.' He added meaningly, 'Get a sidearm for yourself.' He called after him, 'And send Lowes up here, he's not a bloody passenger!'

Evans glanced up from the compass and looked at him but said nothing.

Marriott dropped his voice to exclude all the others. 'I know, Swain, but it's getting to me.'

Evans showed his teeth in a rare smile. 'I expect your first captain shouted at you often enough, sir?' He eased the wheel over again, taking in the slow drift of the other vessel with a practised eye. 'It does no harm.' He gave a shrug. 'It can also save lives.'

Marriott thought of his first captain in the old V & W destroyer. He had barely had the time to get to know him. But his first words when he had joined ship had returned to his thoughts.

The captain, a two-and-a-half ringer, had observed, 'I've just the two pieces of advice for your stay in my command. Do what you're told, and

78

keep out of my way.'

He had been a small, rugged Scot. Looking back he must have felt that his world was coming to an end as his regular officers were rapidly pared away to be replaced by the *bluidy amateurs*, as he sometimes called the RNVR.

How that had changed, Marriott thought. Now they were all professionals. Or dead.

'Slow ahead.'

The sea noises intruded again as spray dappled the bridge screens and made the six-pounder on the foredeck shine like silver.

Small in shipping terms perhaps, but the old *Ronsis* loomed over them like a rusty cliff. Most of her camouflage paint had been worn or scraped away and her tall side was a mass of dents.

Faces made pale blurs along the bulwark, and a man in a uniform cap had appeared on the bridge wing to peer down at the lithe Fairmile gunboat which dipped and rolled some twenty yards under the coaster's lee.

Fairfax stood by the bridge gate and faltered, one foot in the air. Marriott said, 'Take care, Number One.' Their eyes met. 'I need you around.'

Fairfax nodded and hurried aft, the big webbing holster flapping against his side.

Marriott waited, his eyes on the coaster until the little dinghy appeared around the stern. Thank goodness the sea was light. These little dinghies were not much use in foul weather.

Evans waited for the starboard outer engine to go astern for just enough revolutions to hold the hull parallel with the *Ronsis*.

'They're lowering a ladder.' He grunted. 'They dare not make trouble, sir.'

Marriott watched the dinghy grapple to the foot of the narrow ladder, then Fairfax's slim figure swarming up it with Craven close behind him. Leading Seaman Craven was another hard case. From Birmingham, and yet he had taken well to the navy. Once he had been heard to state that anything was *a sight better than Brum*!

A voice came from aft. '*Ship, sir!* Starboard quarter!'

The sea was shining more brightly now and in the reflected glare of the first sunlight it was hardly surprising that the newcomer had arrived unnoticed. Marriott found her in his glasses, conscious that he had his back to the old coaster, cutting himself off from Fairfax and what he was doing.

Lowes exclaimed. 'It's a *small* ship, sir.'

Marriott said sharply, 'Watch the *Ronsis*, Pilot!' He steadied his glasses again. It was just not Lowes's day. 'What d'you make of her, Bunts?'

Silver did not hesitate. 'Torpedo boat, I'd say, sir. I seen one like 'er at Murmansk when I was on the Arctic convoys.' He grimaced. 'Buntin'-tosser in a bloody corvette I was then.' He leaned against the side. 'This one 'as stopped, sir.'

'Call him up. Make our number. My guess is he's the one we heard in the night.'

The Aldis stabbed across the water but there was no reply. The other vessel, so low in the water it was impossible to identify either her shape or markings, stayed where she was. Like a crouching animal.

'Call him up again.'

Lowes shouted, 'It's Number One, sir!'

Marriott turned round and stared up at the

80

rust-streaked bridge. Fairfax had got a megaphone from somewhere and although it distorted his voice his anxiety was obvious.

'They were turned away by the Swedish navy, sir! They've been hiding from Russian patrols.' He gestured violently towards the far-off, black silhouette. 'There's one here already, sir!'

Marriott switched on the loud-hailer. 'Tell the master *he must turn back* and place himself under the control of the Russian commander.'

Fairfax stayed where he was, his voice pleading. 'There are wounded soldiers below, some in a bad way.' Craven's head appeared beside him and then Fairfax shouted, 'Women too! Nurses and civilians.' When Marriott said nothing he added desperately, 'We can't just leave them, sir!'

Marriott wiped his forehead with the back of his wrist. *What the hell does he expect me to do? I'm not God.* He looked at Evans's grim features. 'What's the Russian doing now?'

Evans gave an indifferent shrug. 'Still there. Waiting.'

Marriott stared at the handset and then spoke into it again. 'I'm going to make a signal. See what else you can find out!' He snapped down the switch and took the pad Silver was holding out. He had guessed what might happen.

Marriott waited for the strain to leave his eyes clear enough to write properly.

Then he tore off the flimsy and said, 'Give this to Sparks. Immediate.'

Even as he said it he knew it was hopeless. Was it for Fairfax? *Or for me?* It did not take long. Marriott watched the coaster and imagined all the people inside her ancient hull. Some too badly

81

wounded to care. Others who just wanted to get home. Civilians who were running away. Nurses too.

Silver came to the bridge and regarded him impassively.

Marriott asked, 'What did it say?'

Silver did not have to read the reply.

'*From N.O.I.C. repeated Admiralty. Permission denied. Ensure that Ronsis awaits escort. Do not, repeat not, interfere.*' Silver looked at the distant silhouette. 'That's the lot, sir.'

Marriott returned to the loud-hailer. 'No good, Number One. Tell the master to await escort and not to do anything foolish.'

Fairfax called bitterly, 'Like what, for God's sake?' Then in a more controlled tone he said, 'I'll tell them.'

A moment later his head and shoulders reappeared on the bridge wing and he called, 'Understood, sir.'

Marriott's voice boomed across the water, metallic in the loud-hailer. 'Return on board. Fast as you like.' He hesitated. He could feel Fairfax's anguish and wanted to understand it if not share it. '*It's over*, Number One.'

It seemed to take an age for the boarding party to clamber down into the bobbing dinghy at the foot of the ladder.

Eventually Fairfax reported to the bridge and saluted, the formality strangely alien here. 'They were making for Denmark, sir.'

'Tell me about it later, Number One.'

They both turned as the sound of engineroom telegraphs echoed across the choppy water, and moments later the *Ronsis*'s single screw started to

82

churn the sea into a mounting surge of froth. Her length appeared to shorten as she began to turn heavily, the gap between her and the slow-moving gunboat widening, breaking all contact.

Fairfax muttered, 'The ship *stank*, sir. They'd no proper medicine or dressings. I never thought—'

Marriott kept his distance, hating what he had to say and do.

'Just take it off your back. As I said, *it's over.*'

Someone shouted, 'Look at that! She's altered course again! She's makin' for the Swedish mainland!'

Marriott stared incredulously, but knew the ship's master must have been making this decision even as he had listened to their exchange across the water between them.

The Russian vessel had begun to move. Silver said, '*She's* got radar, right enough, sir!'

Rae grinned. 'The Ruski may be fast, but he'll never catch the old cow!'

Marriott could almost read the ship's captain's mind. Run his old ship aground, then the Swedes would have to take his passengers into their protection. It was a wild and unlikely scheme, but when you saw no alternative—

The lookout's voice was raised almost in a scream.

'*Torpedo's runnin' to starboard, sir!*'

Marriott flung himself across the bridge, all else forgotten as he stared at the thin white line which was cutting across the leaden water as precisely as a razor.

'Full ahead! Hard astarboard!'

Someone was shouting, 'Second torpedo running, sir!'

Twin parallel lines fired at extreme range, the torpedoes streaked past the motor gunboat even as her bows lifted to the great surge of her four screws and cleaved the sea apart.

Fairfax yelled, 'Call her up, man! For God's sake do something!'

Silver let his binoculars fall to his chest as if he could not bear to watch. He had seen so many vessels fall apart, theirs, ours, neutrals, even hospital ships. Nobody had been immune to the sea mine, the impartial killer, or the torpedo in the night. Death could take its choice. Like the youngster in his bomber, pressing the switch over Berlin or Coventry. What did it matter to him? His plane and crew were his first responsibility; they all knew that if one percent of their bombs ever found their proper target they had been lucky.

'Midships! Steady! Hold her, Swain!' Marriott wrapped one arm around a stanchion and felt it tearing at his muscles as the hull lurched upright from its fast turn. He saw the livid red flashes, just seconds apart, then the crash of the explosion rolled across the water and lifted the gunboat as if she was on a wave crest.

Evans was crouching over the wheel, his eyes slitted against spurting droplets of spray; he did not even flinch as the hammer blow boomed around the boat and over the sea, as if it would never stop.

Marriott raised his glasses and glanced briefly at the *Ronsis*, already gushing smoke and flames, her outmoded poop twisted as if the two torpedoes had broken her back. Then he swung round to seek out the other vessel but saw only the frothing backwash of her wake as she turned and headed towards the invisible mainland.

'Slow ahead.' Marriott glanced at the compass. 'Steer Nor'-East.'

He looked at Lowes. His face was white and he was shaking. Shock, the suddenness of disaster. The fact that such things were impossible according to the rules of war, and there *was* no war any more.

Marriott said, 'Fall out action stations. Stand by to take on survivors.'

He shook Lowes's arm. It felt limp, as if he had died in the explosion. 'Snap out of it, Sub!' Then he beckoned to Able Seaman Rae. 'Relieve the cox'n.' He saw Evans's quick nod as he stepped down from his grating. *Taking charge*, as he had done so often.

Marriott looked at Fairfax. 'Well?'

Fairfax replied, 'You were right, sir. It's over now. For *them* anyway.' His voice was bitter, hostile.

Marriott regarded him gravely. 'What did you want me to do, start another war? The Russians are our *allies*. They suffered because of the Germans. The *Ronsis*'s master must have known what might happen.' He waited, feeling the helplessness running through him, dragging him down. 'We had our orders. Furthermore, I suspect the Russians knew them better than I did.'

Another explosion, deep and throaty, shook the hull, and Mariott watched the old ship as she seemed to topple on her side, her tall funnel falling with the foremast and cargo derrick, machinery smashing through the hull which had been too old for war, probably for the first one as well. She was in halves, bow and stern pointing towards the mocking sunshine like ill-matched memorials.

Silver said tersely, 'She's goin'.'

The bow section went first, throwing up bubbles

85

and steam, then the high poop rolled over and Marriott caught his breath as he saw a liferaft with several tiny figures clinging to it, smashed underneath and carried to the bottom.

'*Signal to N.O.I.C. repeated Admiralty.*' Marriott saw some of his men lining the guardrails with scrambling nets and heaving lines; two even carried boathooks. There could not be many left alive. She had gone under in about five minutes.

Silver questioned softly, '*Sir?*'

'*Reporting Ronsis torpedoed and destroyed by unidentified warship.*' He turned away angrily. They could work that out for themselves at Kiel. He tried to calm his voice. '*Am picking up survivors. Request assistance. Will return to base as ordered.*'

A voice called, 'There's one, Jim! Get ready with the nets!'

Another gasped, 'Christ, look at *that*!'

As Marriott called for another reduction of revolutions he heard a woman screaming. It made him shudder, and when he looked at Fairfax he saw that he was reliving it, remembering that he had seen and probably spoken to some of them.

In the bows the coxswain stood with one arm outstretched, pointing to something or somebody in the water as the raked stem ploughed through the litter of flotsam, coal dust, and corpses.

It was a trick of the light, but Marriott could almost believe that Evans was smiling.

CHAPTER FIVE

VIEWPOINT

The blue-painted jeep with RN on the sides rolled across protesting sheets of steel which the sappers had laid to cover the edges of smaller bomb craters. Marriott gripped his seat and watched the hundreds of figures at work with picks and shovels, while bulldozers and tractors stirred up even more dust in the hazy sunshine.

It felt an age since they had put to sea to make a rendezvous with the coaster *Ronsis*, and yet nothing had changed, or had it? When Commander Meikle had driven to the end of the pier to collect him Marriott had noticed an army three-ton Bedford easing along a narrow track through the piled-up rubble and twisted girders. Just days since the young RE captain had driven a shovel into it to mark the end of the buried roadway. How they must have laboured, he thought, all day, all night, until it had become wide enough for the German sailor with his wheelbarrow. And now a three-tonner was able to get through. Easy for the army driver after what he must have seen in all the eleven months since Normandy, D-Day.

Meikle wrestled with the wheel and swung off the track to avoid a parked army tank, one with the Guards Armoured Division's crest painted on it.

He said, 'No consideration at all.' He could have been driving down the Strand or round Hyde Park Corner, Marriott thought.

They halted at some barbed-wire gates for a

cursory check, then with smart salutes from some red-capped military police Meikle accelerated out of the scarred gateway and on to the main road.

Marriott realised dully that it was the first time he had been outside the dockyard.

There was little difference here. Shattered houses, broken electric cables dangling from posts, craters, and still more craters, some so huge they had swallowed whole streets.

Like London, he thought grimly, where Wren churches and tiny back-to-back houses in the East End had seen it through on equal terms. Raids night and day, and then the 'flying bombs' which were launched from the Low Countries and flew until their rocket fuel ran out. Then they fell with deadly effect. But at least you could hear them, until the engine cut out. The huge V2 rockets struck from thousands of feet with the speed of light. Those who escaped death or injury often heard the explosions long after the rockets had found their target. Could they have stood it if the army had not overrun the rocket bases in time? He watched the passing scene, horse-drawn carts, busy army scout cars and lorries, and everywhere the khaki uniforms of the occupying power.

He tried not to think any more about the *Ronsis*. The opinion in the gunboat was divided. Some said it was all you could expect from the Reds. Others claimed stoutly that, but for Joe Stalin, Germany would have won the war.

Beyond the needs of duty and watch-keeping Fairfax had said next to nothing. It was like a cloud hanging over him, the reality of victory, the clinking of chipped mugs filled with hoarded brandy already forgotten.

Meikle had been waiting for them to tie up on their return to Kiel. He had waited, watching the army medics with their stretchers lifting some of the survivors on to the pier and to the waiting military ambulances. The sailors too, some from the moored MLs, had helped to carry or guide the dazed and bewildered people to safety. They had picked up twenty-three, but three of those had died within hours of rescue. Burns, broken limbs, shock, they had all taken their toll.

There were two women amongst the survivors. One a nurse in army uniform, the other a young civilian who had almost lost her reason. A German soldier who spoke some English had explained that she was trying to escape from the advancing Russian troops with her child. After the torpedoes had burst into the ship's side she had not seen the child again.

None of them really understood what had happened, and only those who had been on deck had realised what the *Ronsis*'s master had been trying to do. He had vanished when the bridge had been turned into one huge fireball.

That had been yesterday. Meikle had accepted his written report and had handed it to his leading writer who even now was crouching in the rear of the jeep. He had said little but, 'They'll want you at HQ tomorrow. There are bound to be repercussions. Working together won't be easy—I don't envy the negotiators when it comes to sharing out the victors' spoils.'

He had not been making a callous joke. It was just one of the known facts, as far as he was concerned. When he had returned to his jeep he had called back, 'There may be some senior officers present.'

Marriott wanted to reply, *What did they do to help? I asked for assistance, but none came, so what was I supposed to do about it?*

Now he was here in Meikle's jeep, the air rushing past the open sides, the floor bucking as the wheels skidded over badly filled holes and scattered bricks.

It had been a rough night. Marriott had stayed in his cabin, smoking his pipe and thinking about it. What could he have done? What *should* he have done?

Meikle said, 'That's the main railway terminus over there. Roof's caved in, of course, but we'll soon get some rolling stock on the move. We'll damn well need it before long.'

Damn from Meikle sounded like an obscenity. He never seemed to lose his temper. Cold, confident, and without feelings.

Marriott saw some women in rough working clothes sweeping rubble from a pavement. One was quite pretty despite her clothing and a kerchief over her hair to keep the dust and smoke away.

She glanced up briefly and their eyes met. Not afraid, but cautious, as if she expected them to call her to the jeep for some reason.

Meikle commented casually, 'Venereal disease is pretty rife here. That must be rammed into our people. The PMO will probably get some films and lectures going.'

'I thought there was a non-fraternisation order in force, sir?'

Meikle took his eyes off the road and studied him calmly. 'I've heard that sailors don't take much notice of orders of that sort, eh?'

Then he called, 'What time do we have,

Lavender?'

The White Rabbit replied instantly, 'Half an hour, sir.'

'Plenty.' Meikle swung off the road and braked hard. They waited for the dust to settle on the shimmering bonnet, and the warmth of the sun reminded Marriott that he had barely slept. Figures moved past, as if the jeep was not there, as if there was no purpose in anything.

Meikle said, 'Don't be taken in by hard-luck stories, Marriott. I've seen the reports already. They'll try to suggest ill will between us and our allies, expecially the Russians.'

'After what I saw, I think they may be right, sir.'

Meikle sighed, then snapped his fingers. 'Briefcase, Lavender!'

He laid it on his lap and dragged out a crisp new file. It seemed to be full of photographs.

Meikle said, 'Take a look.'

Marriott turned over each picture and felt his mind shy away, stunned and aghast at what they showed in every horrific detail.

Long trenches, only partly filled by bulldozers, showed the piles of skeleton-like corpses. Many were naked, men or women it was difficult to say. Some had their hands tied and had obviously been shot through the nape of the neck at point-blank range. Pictures showed corpses in heaps, staring and obscene. Almost worse were those who still stood on their sticklike limbs and stared at the cameras. They should have been dead, if only to save them from this final humiliation.

Meikle asked quietly, 'You knew about the concentration camps?'

Marriott went through the photographs again,

scarcely able to believe what he was seeing.

'Not like this.'

'In Poland. But there are many more. Machinery of mass-extermination. Hitler's much-vaunted final solution.' His voice was cool, matter-of-fact.

Marriott thought of the wounded German soldiers, the sailor with the little flag of truce, the injured nurse whose eyes told him some of the horrors she must have witnessed. Even the girl back there with the broom.

'Surely they're not all like that?'

Meikle tossed the briefcase back to his writer. 'We shall see.' He revved the engine and peered at the road. 'They're all guilty to me until I know differently.' Then he turned and studied Marriott's strained features. 'Getting your last command blown from under you wasn't part of some *jolly game*, you of all people must see that? You fought to survive, most of all to *win*! Just remember that the next time you want to pin your heart on your Number Fives!' He steered easily on to the road. 'If it had been me I'd want to make them pay for it!'

They drove the rest of the way without speaking.

*   *   *

The temporary headquarters for Naval Operations had once been a school. Later it had been used as a hospital for dealing with the mounting pressure of air raids, and as Marriott walked beside the commander he was aware of the start contrasts on every hand. The peeling remains of children's paintings and drawings, from last Christmas he thought, Santa Claus on his sleigh, reindeer and trees covered with snow. In one empty room where

92

desks had once stood, there were piles of rough palliasses, deeply stained with dried blood, awaiting disposal in one of the many fires which the army had built to rid the place of filth and the danger of disease. Parts of the roof had gone and, once, he looked up to see the sky, very pure and clear overhead.

A few German sailors were busily removing rubbish and unloading steel cabinets from some army trucks; they stamped to attention as the two naval officers passed, their eyes staring and empty. *How do they see us?* Marriott wondered. Then he thought of Meikle's photographs, the horror of that place, the appalling suffering which must have made death more than welcome when it came to release them.

He recalled what he had told Fairfax, and the young sub-lieutenant's face when he had spoken so harshly. Perhaps he had been wrong. Maybe it was better to keep your enemy in a periscope or gunsight, or through a bomb-aimer's crosswires.

Here, it was like seeing yourself in defeat.

Meikle snapped, 'Wait here.' He strode over to speak with a petty officer who was sitting rather self-consciously at a desk, isolated in the corridor, a sub-machine gun dangling from the back of his schoolroom chair.

Meikle came back and said, 'The Operations Officer has a visitor, but he wants us to enter all the same.' He sounded quietly irritated. 'Just remember what I told you.' He ran his eyes over Marriott's attempt at formality. But his reefer jacket needed a press, and he had made this particular collar last from the other meeting. 'Hmmm.' The room looked over what had once been a pleasant garden, a study or library, Marriott decided.

Maps and telephones were everywhere, and two RNVR officers and several telegraphists and signalmen were kept busy answering them, making and passing notes while a fat Yeoman of Signals waddled amongst them like an impressive guard-dog.

At one end of the long room were a desk and some chairs, rescued from nearby houses, one still scorched from a near-miss.

The Operations Officer was tall and angular, a regular, with the three rings of a commander on his sleeves. He looked very tired, but had a warm smile as he gestured to the chairs.

'I'm Rodney Boucher, Marriott. The *Bloke* here for the moment until better things are fixed up. Sorry to drag you up here—'

But Marriott was looking at the other officer who was sitting half-concealed by the back of a tall swivel-chair.

The Operations Officer hesitated. He had a studious, almost gentle manner which one would hardly expect from an officer who was trying to build some semblance of order in a shattered dockyard and the movement of naval vessels there.

'This is Commodore Paget-Orme.'

The seated figure swivelled round and regarded Marriott for several seconds. He was the sort of senior officer who would make anyone feel crumpled and uncomfortable. His reefer was dark and shining, the very best doeskin, and the single thick stripe around his sleeve was like the gold on Meikle's cap. New. *Bought for the occasion.*

He was clean too. Unhealthily so. Very pink and

94

scrubbed with neat, square hands which rested in his lap like watchful crabs.

The commodore said, 'I am here to hurry things along. I am responsible to the admiral.' He smiled gently, showing small even teeth. 'Nobody else.' It amused him, and his stomach, which even the perfectly cut reefer could not disguise, shook with silent mirth. 'A sort of God-figure!'

Marriott glanced quickly at the others. Commander Boucher's expression was one of patient resignation, Meikle's not far from dislike.

'Now, er, Lieutenant Marriott.' Commodore Paget-Orme readjusted one elbow on his chair and studied him critically. 'DSC and bar—one of the Glory Boys, they tell me?' He did not expect a reply. 'This affair with the vessel, er—'

The Operations Officer prompted, '*Ronsis*, sir.'

'*Quite.*' The smile was fading. 'Well, I understand that you were ordered to turn the *Ronsis* back from her attempted escape?'

Marriott pressed his knuckles against his side to contain his resentment. Perhaps this had been the headmaster's study? It was how it felt now.

'I ordered her to stop, sir.' He had made signals to this effect, written it in the log and again in his report. It was like talking to an unstoppable wave. 'Then I sent a boarding party who discovered there were wounded soldiers and some women aboard. How many, we can't yet find out.' He expected an interruption but the plump commodore was staring at him intently. The two pink crabs had scuttled up his chest to link together beneath his chin as if for support.

Marriott continued wearily, 'I made a signal to—'

The commodore nodded impatiently. 'I *know*
95

about that.' His eyes, which were very pale blue, swivelled towards Meikle. 'What was the response?'

Meikle said, 'The N.O.I.C. repeated that the original order was to be executed. That the ship was to await a Russian escort.' He looked at Marriott, his voice, like his face, empty of expression. 'The Russian senior naval officer was informed to this effect.' He gave a brief shrug. 'Our responsibility was then ended.'

The commodore ran his tongue over his lower lip.

'So the German-controlled ship then attempted to escape.' His eyebrows were raised slightly. 'An old freighter or whatever, against a fast patrol boat. Rather ridiculous, I'd have thought?'

Meikle said, 'We shall never know what the ship's master was trying to do. Maybe he wished Lieutenant Marriott to challenge the Russian's authority so that he could slip away, ground his ship maybe, throw himself and his passengers on the mercy of the Swedes or even us.'

The commodore gave a childlike smile. 'One hell of a lot of *maybes*.'

The Operations Officer said abruptly, 'I have a dispatch from the Russian admiral, sir. His explanation is that his patrol boat fired only when her commander believed that the *Ronsis* had outmanoeuvred or outwitted MGB 801's commanding officer.'

Marriott heard himself exclaim, 'It's a lie, sir! They murdered those people in cold blood! I could have taken her under my charge and put a full boarding party aboard if—'

The commodore nodded. 'Ah yes, Lieutenant Marriott. *If.* That one word which makes all the difference. But you did *not* and I am glad for you.' He was suddenly cold-eyed, all humour gone. 'You would have created a serious rift between us and the Russian command at a time when we are barely able to cope with matters here! And all you would have got would have been a court martial for disobeying orders! Let me assure you of *that*!'

The Operations Officer waited until the commodore had regained his self-control and said, 'If we dispute the Russians' explanation they will alter it. They always do. They will say that you were deliberately allowing the *Ronsis* to escape, to Sweden perhaps?' He looked at Marriott and added gently, 'Try to forget it. It was an aftermath of war.'

Marriott tried again. 'If you speak with the survivors, sir, it might give you a better bargaining point?'

The commodore examined one finger and frowned. 'They have gone. I ordered them back to the Russian sector this morning.'

Marriott pictured the stricken woman who had lost her child, the face of the army nurse, the wounded soldiers and a couple of Latvian seaman.

Paget-Orme looked at Marriott and asked, 'Why should you bother yourself? The Germans would have done the same if Russians had been trying to escape.' He became tired of it. 'Anyway, Marriott, I shall need your boat in a couple of days. I intend to carry out an inspection of local facilities, docking and salvage and the like.' It sounded vague. 'Do the Germans good to see a *veteran* in their midst!'

Marriott replied, 'I should have left them all to die.'

Meikle said harshly, 'Doubtless you've had to do

97

that often enough in the past!'

The words were still ringing in his mind when a car carried him back to the dockyard.

*   *   *

The motor gunboat's main messdeck was crowded to capacity, the air so thick with pipe and cigarette smoke you could cut it with a knife. Every scuttle and vent was wide open, and the stench of the harbour added its power to the humid atmosphere.

Many of the seamen sat around a mess table, peering over one another's shoulders to devour the two newspapers which had finally arrived from England. In the confined space beneath the low deckhead others pressed or 'dhobied' their clothes, or swapped yarns while they shared the handful of mail which had also been delivered by the same ship which had brought newspapers and parcels from home.

Leading Seaman Craven was saying, 'Christ, look at the crowds outside Buckingham Palace! I'll bet there was bloody fun-and-games that night!'

The others peered at the front page, the palace seemingly hemmed in by a solid mass of faces, flags waving, some figures squatting on the roofs of taxis, the delight and astonishment of victory so evident that, like Craven, most of the others were missing it. Wishing they had been there to share the rejoicing.

Another said bleakly, 'Look at these other pictures, Hookey.'

Craven stared hard-eyed at the stark review of a liberated concentration camp. The walking dead, the unspeakable horror of it.

98

Craven said, '*Bloody bastards!*'

Ginger Jackson peered in from the main doorway, dressed as usual in overalls scrubbed and laundered so often they were more white than blue.

'It's all part of it.'

Craven glanced up at him and grinned. 'An' what about your lot? You must have shipped enough gin to float the bloody *Hipper!*'

Leading Signalman Silver tied the last knot in some wool as he repaired another sock and said, 'Commodore's comin' aboard tomorrow, that right, Ginger?'

Ginger did a few mincing steps and lisped, 'An' he's bringin' 'is own *chief steward* with 'im!'

The sailor who was trying to press his shoregoing bell-bottoms into the seven desired creases on the gunboat's only ironing-board yelled, 'Watch out, Ginger, these are me best nookey trousers!'

Craven sighed. 'I dunno what you're expectin' when we *do* get a run ashore. From what it says in the little book, you're more likely to catch a dose of clap than anythin' else.'

A young ordinary seaman named Langford asked, 'What exactly *is* a commodore, er, Hookey?'

Craven stared at him. 'Speak, can you? I was beginnin' to wonder!'

Langford was just eighteen and had joined the company a few days before they had sailed from England to Denmark. It had been a short war for him. It was always hard for a newcomer to settle in and be accepted. Especially one so completely green. And besides, most of them still remembered the man whose place he had taken. Or was trying to take. He had been lost overboard in the Channel. The night had been pitch-dark. They had not even heard him cry out.

Sailors were a superstitious lot. A few had persisted that they had heard the luckless seaman since. Calling out from the darkness.

Craven considered it. 'A commodore is neither one thing nor t'other. If it was peacetime, I mean *real* peacetime, he'd be a captain who was 'opin' to make flag rank. 'E *could* fall back to bein' a four-striper, *or* he could rise to flag rank and be a big-'eaded admiral, see?'

Silver gave a dry chuckle. ''E *could* be dropped altogether, o' course, kicked out of the Andrew.'

Ginger Jackson pushed himself on to the bench seat and rested on his elbows.

To Craven he said quietly, 'I mentioned you-know-what to Mister Lowes.'

Craven and Able Seaman Rae, who had been reading the *Daily Mail* very slowly, his lips silently forming every word, both sat bolt upright.

Craven exclaimed, 'You done *what*, you stupid bugger?'

Rae muttered, 'Christ, I want my demob when this lot's over, not the sodding glasshouse!'

Ginger smiled gently. 'Oh, 'e's all right. Good as gold. Once we get started he'll get properly 'ooked.' He bowed his head and persisted, 'Look, mates, we need all we can get. It'll be a piece of cake, you see.'

Craven was unconvinced. 'All the same, Ginger, you're takin' a bloody chance. Snow White may be a bit wet, but 'e's still an officer, for Chrissake!'

Leading Signalman Silver chuckled quietly and studied the completed repair. A right bunch they were, he thought. They had not even begun their scheme to get rich at the Jerries' expense, and already they were in dispute. He folded up his
100

'housewife' and wondered what the Skipper was doing. He had seen him on his return, and their eyes had met as he had climbed to the bridge where Silver had been tidying up the flags and signal lamps. Whatever had happened at HQ, the Skip was taking it badly. Carrying it all, as he had carried *them* since he had assumed command. Silver had served with a few in his time, but Marriott was the best. He leaned back and tried to think about his life at the dogtracks as a tick-tack man, a skill handed down by his father. Would he ever be able to go back to it after this? Fights at the dogtrack bars or in the local at the end of the street. The coppers shoving everyone around with their usual good-humoured toughness. Until things got too rough, then it was the hurry-up van and a ride to the local nick with a few more thumps on the way for good measure.

He let his gaze move around the crowded messdeck. Their refuge, their home. Where they had swapped news from families and girl-friends, shared the bald notices about a bombed house, relatives wiped out while *we thought we were taking all the risks*.

Familiar faces, men he knew like his own people in London. Scouse Arkright, the best of mates in a battle, but a fighting maniac after a few jars ashore. He was bending over his banjo, his mind empty of all else as he adjusted the strings. It would be 'Maggie May' before pipe-down. *Again*.

And Leading Seaman Townsend who did a bit of everything. Apart from the coxswain they carried no deck petty officers. Townsend was not only the senior gunlayer but also acted as chief boatswain's mate, boss of the messdeck, and a ready ear if someone had dropped a clanger and needed advice.

Like most of the others Townsend would be leaving soon, he thought. To pick up his PO's rate and join some general service ship to be packed off to the Pacific.

The radio squawked and fragments of Vera Lynn's voice echoed above the buzz of conversation.

Someone shouted, 'Turn that row off! I just want a bit of crumpet, I don't need to hear a bloody song about it!'

Silver grinned. How could they settle down to civvy street when it was all finally over?

He realised that Rae was staring at him, his eyes wide and unblinking.

Silver asked, 'Wot is it?'

Instead of answering, Rae put one finger to his lips, then shook his head to indicate he did not want anyone else to hear.

Then he leaned over the table, his mouth to Silver's ear.

'There's something moving against the hull, Bunts.'

Silver glanced at the others but they were still chatting, reading, or doing repairs to their clothing.

Had it been anyone else . . . Silver nodded very slowly. They had all owed their lives to Rae's quick senses more than once.

He felt a chill run down his back in spite of the hot air. *There it was again*. Not driftwood this time. He tried to think clearly. They had all been lectured on the 'Werewolves', the Nazi youth who would hit back after the occupation forces had dropped their vigilance. Suppose that was one of them? Jesus Christ, the sound was right against one of the main

102

fuel tanks. A *limpet-mine*—

Rae said, 'You go. I can't get out without drawing attention—'

Silver nodded then threw one leg over the bench and made for the door.

He clambered up the ladder, his mind groping for an explanation. If he had shouted an alarm they would either have taken it for a joke, or could have cleared the lower deck with such a scramble that whatever it was alongside might blast them to oblivion.

It was an unwarlike scene on the upper deck.

Green, an AB who was standing in as gangway sentry, was leaning against the guardrails, his hand cupped to conceal a lighted cigarette. He saw Silver and blinked anxiously. 'Weren't doin' nothin' wrong!'

Silver snapped, 'Where's the O.O.D.?' He had almost called him *Snow White* like the others.

The sentry gaped at him. 'Back there aboard one of the MLs. There's a party for one of the officers, a birthday I think—'

Silver glared at him. 'I don't give a toss what he's doin'! 'Ere, give me the piece!'

The sentry unwound the lanyard from beneath his blue collar, then dragged the Smith and Wesson revolver from its holster.

'*Fetch* 'im then. Double quick!'

'But, but—' Green's eyes were popping with anxiety, and he probably thought Silver had finally cracked.

'Just tell 'im we may have a frogman alongside the 'ull!' He watched the man scurry along the pier as if the fiends of Chatham were after him.

Silver swallowed hard. *Just what we need*. And

103

neither the officers nor the coxswain on board.

He heard Craven's heavy tread and felt something like relief.

'Christ, Bill, I'm glad you came. I'm a buntin' tosser, not a bloody gunner!'

Craven took the revolver and flicked it open to check that it was loaded. Rae had obtained a Lanchester sub-machine gun and was watching the side of the deck as if he expected to see a mob of frogmen come swarming over the hull.

Craven said, 'It's between us an' the pier.' He sucked his teeth. 'Get ready to clear the boat. God, I thought we was past all this shit!'

For a big man he moved easily and fast and Silver saw him climbing beneath the shattered pier, groping his way single-handed amongst the rusty supports, the revolver shining in the shafts of sunlight through the gaps in the footway.

Craven was aware that he was more angry that afraid. Like those moments when he had been with Jimmy the One aboard the clapped-out *Ronsis*. Fairfax was a good enough officer, unlike some, but Craven had been astonished at the way he had reacted over the German passengers. What the hell did they matter after what they had done? He licked his lips and steadied his feet on an oil-covered spar. God, the whole place stank. Maybe it was just a bit more wreckage drifting past, but it was better to be careful than bloody well croaked.

He stiffened as he saw something moving slowly down the gunboat's smooth side. The water was so thick with oil and effluent it looked like a human head bobbing on the surface. One arm moved out of the water, a hand groped for some kind of hold, but the rest of the swimmer's body was completely

104

hidden in the dark, filthy harbour.

''Ere's one of the bastards!'

Craven heard the slither of feet, then Rae appeared beside him, dragging at the cocking lever of his sub-machine gun.

The swimmer was startled by the shouts and lost his hold, to vanish completely for a few seconds below the surface.

In that short time Craven had a dozen thoughts all at once. He had heard Sub-Lieutenant Lowes's footsteps running along the pier, a sudden din of voices from the moored gunboat. At any second the mine or whatever it was would explode against the hull, right by a fuel tank, and the whole pier would brew up and likely take the MLs with it. Like the time in Ostend when an MTB had blown up in the basin and had set all the others ablaze. But uppermost was the thought, *He can't stay down forever. I'll take one of the bastards with me!*

The head broke water right below his feet and he tightened his grip on the trigger and felt the hammer take the first strain.

Rae exclaimed thickly, *'Christ, it's a bloody kid!'*

Others were here now, and one seaman dropped on his knees and snatched the boy's hand as he slipped, gasping, into the oil again.

They pulled him up, none too gently, on to the pier. He was, at a guess, about ten years old, covered in oil and quite naked. Droplets of blood ran through the oil to show where he had bumped against the pier or the side of the gunboat.

He stood in a puddle of filth and stared at their strained, intent faces. Then he tried to smile, his teeth white through his coating of dirt.

'Haben Sie Kaugummi?'

Silver groaned. "E wants bloody chewing-gum!' Some of the others laughed, but Craven snarled, *'You fuckin' Kraut!'* As he turned away he stared at the revolver in his fist; it was shaking so violently it was a wonder it did not go off. Another second. Just that, no more, and he would have blown the boy's head off. He tried to stop his hand from quivering, knowing that some of the others were watching him.

He heard himself mutter, 'He's about the same age as my kid brother.'

Sub-Lieutenant Lowes pushed through them. 'What's going on?'

Silver gestured to the naked boy. 'The *enemy*, sir!' He wanted to laugh, to scream, anything. It had been a near thing.

Lowes peered severely at the boy. 'Inside the dockyard perimeter—that's a serious offence, Silver!'

'Then you'd better tell him, sir.'

Lowes hesitated. 'What d'*you* suggest?'

Silver reached out and grabbed the boy's wrist, swinging him round.

'Look at 'is ribs! Would you like a nipper of yours to wander amongst all this shit beggin' for food? *Chewin' gum*, as 'e put it!'

Ginger Jackson suggested, 'Probably got through the wire up at the wall. Left 'is clothes and decided to swim 'ere.' He grinned. 'He could have had his arse shot off!'

Rae uncocked the Lanchester and the German boy started with sudden fright.

He said calmly, '*I'd* have shot the little sod anyway.'

Silver sensed the sudden tension. 'Fetch a towel

106

and get some grub from the galley, Ginger. Best get rid of 'im before '*e* becomes another *incident*.'

Lowes rubbed his chin, worried and unsure, with the feeling he had handled it rather badly.

Craven was repeating, 'I could have *killed* him!'

Rae watched the other leading the naked boy to the gunboat's side. *Soft lot of buggers*. 'I thought you hated the bastards?'

Craven handed the revolver to the resentful Green. 'This was different.'

Silver sighed. Their first contact, and somehow he felt the unknown boy had won.

★   ★   ★

Lieutenant Vere Marriott lightly touched the peak of his cap in response to Fairfax's salute and said, 'A smart turnout.' He had just completed his rounds of the boat and for the thousandth time had been amazed at the way a sailor could live, sleep and work in such confined quarters.

In time of war there was usually more room. Only one watch stood at their stations on deck and in the engineroom while the remainder tried to pretend that being off-watch was being normal. In harbour Marriott, like most commanding officers, would send as many hands ashore as possible. To find relief on firm ground or to drown their sorrows as the mood took them. But now, with no shore facilities available, except for the occasional supply boats or the NAAFI manager's battered van which stood amidst the wreckage and desolation to dole out chocolate and shoe polish, magazines and elderly pork pies, they had had to look inboard at their own resources.

107

They had seemed cheerful enough as the coxswain had called the messdeck to attention and he had moved amongst the men he thought he knew so well. The same sharp comments from the coxswain about the cruder pin-ups, the same chuckles from those uninvolved.

Fairfax had done a good job, he thought. Even poor Lowes, who had come to him in dismay to reveal what had happened with the German boy's unexpected arrival in their midst, had worked hard.

He had blurted out, 'I thought the cox'n was angry, sir, but it was all *my* fault. I don't want anyone else on your report because of me!'

There was not a dishonest bone in Lowes's body, Marriott thought. With a face like his it would be quite impossible to lie anyway. He knew little about him, other than that he had been brought up by an indulgent mother who was not short of a shilling or two, his father having gone off with a showgirl when he had been just a child.

He had tried to reassure him. 'I'd have done the same myself.' Nonetheless it was worth looking into. If security was that slack at this stage, other visitors might be after something more than chewing-gum. Ginger Jackson had hinted that thay had packed the lad off with a bag of goodies. That too was typical. He had seen German survivors wrapped in oil-soaked blankets, shivering on the deck of the ship which had rescued them. Moments earlier they had been deadly enemies. Then it all changed, or seemed to. Cigarettes, mugs of scalding tea, and occasionally a tot of rum. How could men readjust so quickly from murder to small acts of kindness? The brotherhood of the sea? It had to be more than that. Perhaps it was like a fever which took some longer than others to fight away from?

Fairfax said quietly, 'I've not had the chance to speak with you about—'

They faced each other and Marriott said, 'Try to forget it. It's a different world here.' He saw the chief steward who had been sent to supervise the food and drink which filled the small wardroom, throwing some crusts over the side and looking up for gulls to eat them. Chief steward—he was more like a butler than that. During his rounds Marriott had remarked on the spread of food, the ranks of freshly polished glasses.

The butler had replied haughtily, 'We do our best, sir.'

He didn't know much about Kiel anyway. The gulls, like everyone else, stayed away from the harbour and its stench of death.

Fairfax followed him to the bridge, strangely tidy and deserted although they could hear the gentle murmur of one of the Chief's generators. Making certain that, when the great man came aboard, the engines at least would not let them down.

Fairfax said awkwardly, 'I read somewhere in orders that sub-lieutenants attached to naval parties in Germany can apply to be upgraded, sir.'

'I'm sure you're right.' Marriott, in all his six years of war, had never been able to become interested in the endless stream of AFOs, KRs and Admiralty Instructions which sometimes seemed more vital than the fight itself.

'Only—'

Marriott smiled. The edges had been knocked off the young Fairfax and he had come through better than expected. But at times like these his open face gave it all away.

Marriott said, 'You'd like to put up your second ring, right? Acting-temporary-lieutenant as suits their lordships? Forget it.' He saw the hope die and return just as immediately as he added, 'I've already made a request on your behalf.' He watched a staff car rocking and labouring over the rubble as it headed pointedly towards the pier. 'You deserve it anyway.' His face was expressionless as he saw the gold-leafed caps emerging from the car. 'Unlike some.'

He ran his eye once more over his command. 'Man the side, Number One.' The formality helped at times like these. Fairfax was about to share something with him. Not here, not yet. A voice seemed to whisper, *not ever, is that what you want?*

He said, 'Keep the upper deck cleared until the commodore is settled aboard.' He heard the discreet clink of glasses. 'That shouldn't take too long.'

The calls trilled, and Commodore Lionel Paget-Orme, a fine black walking stick in one hand, stepped across the small brow and returned their salutes.

Meikle, the bearded RNR harbourmaster, two army officers and the indispensable Leading Writer Lavender completed the party.

Paget-Orme nodded and gave a tight-mouthed smile of approval. 'Fine little craft, eh, Meikle? The eyes of the fleet, what?'

Marriott glanced quickly at a point above Meikle's shoulder. The commodore's description reminded him of the *Boy's Own Paper* or the *Hotspur*, which had once been his favourite at school.

They climbed on to the bridge and Paget-Orme clambered carefully into the tall chair which

110

Marriott or the O.O.W. used at sea. He noticed that the coxswain and Long John Silver, Able Seaman Rae and one other figure somehow managed to find and keep their places for leaving harbour. Paget-Orme put on some dark glasses and handed his black stick to Rae, who after a moment's hesitation slid it behind the voicepipes where it would not be trodden on.

'Start up, Pilot.' The bridge quivered to an immediate burst of power and acrid vapour rose on either side and made the commodore dab his mouth with his handkerchief.

'Single up! Back spring and sternrope!' He saw Fairfax wave an acknowledgement from the forecastle; the immediate intake of mooring wires, rope and fenders, a tangled mass to any landsman, but within minutes it had been secured and vanquished by the forecastle hands. Occasionally as Marriott moved through the throng on the small bridge he glanced at the plump commodore. He was enjoying every moment. As if he had never been to sea before in his life. He smiled to himself. Certainly not as a commodore anyway.

He cupped his hands. 'Slack off forrard!' To the seaman at the voicepipes he called, 'Slow ahead starboard outer.' He caught the man as he lowered his head. '*Dead* slow.'

The gunboat edged forward against the rope fenders beneath her great flared bow while the stern rope was paid out to allow for the hull to angle away from the pier. With luck they would receive a better berth when they returned.

'Stop engine—let go forrard—let go aft!' He collided with an apologetic major of the Royal Engineers and saw the bearded harbourmaster grin

111

at him in sympathy.

The motor gunboat slewed round and waited, rocking gently in a welter of froth from her vents, although the bubbles were like black glass. It was a wonder that Lowes's youthful intruder had not died of poisoning long before he reached the pier, he thought.

'Slow ahead together. Port fifteen.' The RNR officer stood beside him, his hands thrust into his reefer pockets. Everyone was dressed up today, Marriott thought.

'Follow the buoys, Cox'n.'

Marriott stared at the curving lines of green marker buoys, not full-sized but easy to see in the pale sunlight. To the harbourmaster he said softly, 'You've been busy.'

The man nodded, reached for his pipe, then glanced at the commodore's rounded shoulders and changed his mind.

'There's the *Sea Harvester*.' His eyes were troubled as the tall salvage ship loomed up on the starboard bow. She was surrounded by small craft and diving pontoons, while derricks swung out from her superstructure so that she seemed to be all arms and legs like a mechanical spider. He dropped his voice. 'Her people have got over two hundred corpses up already.'

His voice was not low enough. Meikle rapped, 'There'll be more too. We're only scraping at the job at the moment.'

The harbourmaster nodded with approval as the coxswain's hands moved gently on the wheel so that a puffing dredger passed well clear on an opposite course.

Then he pointed across the glass screen to two

112

lolling wrecks, their battered superstructures locked in a clawing embrace. 'We're moving those first. Eventually we'll shift all the unusable wrecks to the shallows up yonder, sir.' The last remark was addressed to the commodore.

Paget-Orme straightened his back and yawned. 'There will be more help arriving each day. Some serviceable vessels for accommodation and headquarters work too.' He showed his small teeth. 'A floating cinema no less!' He shook with laughter. 'We don't want poor Jack to lose all the comforts of home, do we?'

Marriott happened to turn and saw Rae making a gesture at the commodore's back. It was hardly surprising.

Past the half-submerged hull of the *New York* once again, the smoking goliath of the heavy cruiser *Hipper*, wrecks, pieces of wrecks, and God only knew what else underneath.

Meikle said, 'Some of the docks which contain vessels beyond repair are to be filled in, sir. It will get rid of a lot of rubble from the sheds and workshops.'

The harbourmaster said sharply, 'Starboard a bit, Swain.'

But Evans only nodded. He had already seen the warning flags. Somewhere beyond them men were working on the sea-bed in thick, clinging blackness.

'Minimum revs.' Marriott stood on a grating and watched two of the divers in their traditional red stocking-caps, sitting on one of the moored pontoons, their helmets beside them while their working party plied them with mugs of tea.

'I wouldn't have their job if—'

There was a dull explosion and the surface boiled

113

momentarily before falling flat again. Neither of the resting divers even turned to look.

Lowes gasped, 'Oh my God.' He turned away, his eyes shocked as the sea yielded up some more fragments. It must have been one of the very last air attacks, Marriott thought. He gripped the rail and then forced himself to relax his grip while he watched the pathetic remains swirl slowly in the disturbance. Corpses, unreal gaping faces, almost transparent in the sunlight. Two motor boats were already moving towards the gruesome remains and Marriott saw some Germans in overalls and wearing protective masks standing in the bows with nets and scoops. Marriott made himself watch, knowing that, with strangers around, his men would look to him. God, he thought, how much worse for those divers working down there, cutting and blasting, feeling their way, praying they would not lose touch with their companions. To be amongst death at such close quarters—

He heard Paget-Orme say loudly, 'Get a grip on yourself, Sub! There'll be far worse than this, y'know!'

Lowes did not answer; he was retching helplessly into a handkerchief.

Marriott looked at the commodore. *It was bravado. A lie.*

As if to confirm his thoughts Paget-Orme said brightly, 'Time for a gin, what? Take a break!'

The bridge was suddenly empty again. Except for the white-faced Lowes and the grim harbourmaster.

Marriott pulled out his pouch. 'Here, light up and I'll join you.'

The RNR officer smiled, 'No gin, then?'

'No. Not yet anyway.' He leaned over the chart.

114

If I start now I'll never be able to stop.

I should have been ready. Next time he might not be able to contain it. But for those few moments he had been back to Normandy, his mind and body cringing to the roar of gunfire and the insane clatter of automatic weapons.

And then the explosion. His life gone, as if he was abandoned with the bloody pieces with their obscene mutilations. *His own men.*

The harbourmaster blew a stream of smoke and wagged the pipestem in the air.

'Good stuff.' Then he added quietly, cutting out Evans and Silver, 'Have you thought about seeing someone about it?'

Marriott clenched his fists. 'You think I'm over the hill?'

The man shook his head. 'I think you owe it to yourself, that's all.' He cocked his head to listen as laughter floated up from the wardroom hatch. 'They're not worried. Why should you?'

'Because I *care*!' He wanted to remain silent. He still did not even know this man's name, and yet—he blurted out, 'And because there is nobody to share it with.'

Voices came up the ladder and the harbourmaster exclaimed, 'Oh, shit!'

Paget-Orme climbed into the chair once more and dabbed his mouth.

'Excellent, excellent.'

Marriott noticed that he did not look over the side at the water. He moved to the opposite side of the bridge. When he got some home leave would nothing change?

'A *word*, Marriott.'

He turned and saw Meikle watching him; he was

115

without his fine cap but curiously it made him less approachable.

'Something I wanted to ask you.' He studied Marriott's expression, as if to give him time.

Marriott could feel the anger running through him like fire. Just say one word more about *what it was like* and *leaving people to die. Do that, and the next time we meet will be at my court martial.*

'*Sir?*' The edge in his voice made the commodore stiffen, but he did not appear to be listening.

'Could you use a few days at home? Nothing much of course, I shall want you for—'

Marriott nodded, dazed and off balance. 'I'd like that, sir.'

The eyes were unblinking. 'Good. I need some documents taken across to Dover. You could use some spares for the boat, I expect?'

Marriott stared at the passing shoreline as Meikle joined the others in another discussion about wrecks and restoration.

The harbourmaster tapped put his pipe carefully in one callused palm. He had heard some of it and guessed the rest.

Afterwards he thought it had been rather like seeing someone come back to life.

CHAPTER SIX

REUNION

Spring in England. Marriot paused in the sunlight and watched the train pulling out of the station, letting it all wash over him, calm him like gentle

116

waves on a perfect beach. How green everything was, the trees almost meeting across the familiar road along which he had walked countless times from his home to the same station. On his way to school, to his first job, to his grandfather's funeral, that fine old soldier from Victoria's army with the straight back and twinkling eye. Then to his first ship.

Marriott put down the small case and slowly refilled his pipe while he listened to the birds. It was a place he had thought about so often in the long years. His had not been an adventurous upbringing when compared to some he had met in the navy. An ordinary, safe, middle-class existence; places and events, like Oxshott Woods, the racecourse at Esher, and the local village cricket team at Thames Ditton sometimes more important than the outside world.

It was fifteen minutes' walk from home to this spot, if you took it easily. Many were the times he had had to run all the way, his breakfast half-eaten, his school homework incomplete until he could meet his classmates in the cycle shed to compare their efforts and help one another to outwit the masters.

He picked up his case and walked beneath the trees. At the little green where Penny had learned to ride her pony and had taken her first fall from it, the long humps of the air-raid shelters were already overgrown with long grass and dead daffodils. He had often thought of people running for such shelters when the sirens had wailed night after night. Now they were just as suddenly meaningless and without menace.

The road was strangely deserted; even the local

pub looked asleep in the afternoon sunshine as he walked past. More memories. He had been there with Stephen before . . . He shut his mind tightly and thought instead of Dover when he had arrived the previous day.

An armed escort had collected Meikle's top-secret steel containers, and he had been surprised at the amount of shipping which filled the harbour and the roadstead. He had seen it too many times almost deserted, a daily target of the German cross-Channel guns. A battered, defiant place which had symbolised Britain almost as much as the White Cliffs.

He had left Fairfax in charge and had given him his telephone number. Surely nothing could go wrong in the two days leave left to him? There was local leave for some of the company, but none for those who lived in faraway places like Scotland and the North. *But just to be here.* He stopped again and eased his shoulders in the warm air. It was strange not to feel the pull of the gas-mask haversack on his shoulder. He kept thinking he had left it somewhere by mistake. So many things to get used to. He had phoned the house from Dover. His father had answered and he had the feeling he had been deeply moved by his unexpected arrival. He had not explained that it was for two days only.

His father was not a strong man and suffered more and more from arthritis, something he had deliberately suppressed in order to remain in the Home Guard. That could have done little to help, Marriott thought. By day getting to London where he worked in the offices of the Southern Railway, no matter what had happened in the overnight raids on the capital. Then, at night, patrolling with his platoon, or guarding the local reservoirs, manning roadblocks in case of a parachute attack. Like the rest of his companions he was a veteran of the Great War.

Marriott often thought it was a wonder that he had wanted so desperately to get into the Home Guard after what he must have seen and done on the Somme. He had never discussed it very much. But after Stephen had been killed at sea, he had opened up a few times. As if their common loss made them equals in some way.

A postman cycled past and waved to him. 'Nice to have you back!'

Marriott smiled at him and watched him cycle around the back of the Harrow. Outwardly closed, it always found a pint for Ted the postman. God, he must have carried a few heartbreaks in his bag. People he knew or had heard about. Dead, missing, captured, crippled.

That part at least was over. There was still Japan, but surely the Axis collapse would make even them have second thoughts?

Marriott felt something like apprehension as he reached the end of the road. Even this 'safe' place had not missed the war. A high gap had been gnawed out of the road and the one adjoining it when a buzz-bomb had fallen from the sky. Other houses had been damaged by near-misses or had lost their rooftops to incendiary raids.

All the same, it looked better than expected. As he quickened his pace he saw familiar pictures of Churchill and his V-sign in some of the windows, others of the King and Queen. A few sported flags, a gentle acknowledgement of victory.

A cat sitting on a windowsill stared, his eyes like

119

grapes in the sunlight, to watch him pass. At another house with the Air Raid Warden's badge and a couple of stirrup-pumps propped outside, an old dog dozed, unimpressed by the change.

Even the windows looked different, he thought, stripped of their dusty blackout curtains and screens, the glass shining where before it had been criss-crossed with sticky tape. It was supposed to prevent the glass from changing into flying knives when the blast blew them out.

He stopped and looked at his house. Tidy but shabby like all the others. The creeper already budding, the path neatly weeded, as he had known it would be.

The door opened before he could reach it and then he was holding his mother in his arms.

She said, 'This is a real surprise, Vere.' She slipped from his arms and closed the door behind him.

Looking back, Marriott had long realised that his mother had never been able to show much warmth, or perhaps had not wanted to. Afraid of her own feelings? *Perhaps that's where I got it from?*

He heard voices and then he was in the living room. The last time he had been here there had still been the steel shelter in the centre of the room, like a giant table with bedding underneath, and wire mesh around to preserve the inmates if the house collapsed on top of it. But the proper table was back. The window was open and he caught the smell of the garden. Half of it was planted for vegetables. Digging for Victory. But the smell was exactly as he had always remembered.

His father wrung his hand, his eyes shining with pleasure.

But Marriott was staring at the complete stranger who had just risen from the old armchair beside the wireless.

His mother said, 'This is Chris.'

Marriott waited. The man was about his own age, round-faced with heavy-rimmed spectacles. Despite the warmth from the sunshine and the garden he wore a heavy green pullover and a tie.

His mother explained, 'Chris is with the Ministry.' Then with something like defiance she added, 'He's got Stephen's old room.'

Marriott took the outstretched hand. The ministry of what? Not that it mattered. He was here, in this house. *Their home.*

The stranger said, 'It's a pleasure to meet you at last. I can't tell you how often I've envied you your exploits.'

His father said, 'We had the room, you see, Vere.' It sounded like pleading. 'With Penny still away and . . .'

His mother was watching all of them. 'I'll make some tea.'

The stranger beamed. 'I'll give you a hand, Mrs Marriott!'

They stood for what seemed a long while without speaking.

Then Marriott said, 'I've brought some duty-frees, Dad.'

His father sat down and eased his bad leg. 'Don't take it so hard. He's a decent chap. Helps your mother when he's not at his office.'

Marriott felt his eyes prick and turned away. 'I've only got two days. I—I think I'd like to wash before we have tea.' He almost added, *if my old room is still mine?* But his father's quiet anxiety was enough.

He said, 'It's good to be home, Dad.'

*   *   *

'You've hardly touched your tea!'

Marriott looked at the tinned peaches on his plate. She must have been saving them specially. *Like the brandy in Kiel.*

His father said, 'Easy now, I expect he's pretty tired. How is it over there?'

Marriott shrugged. Suddenly he needed a drink. Really needed it.

'We're getting on with the job. It's an enormous one.'

He had peered into his brother's room and had felt his mind in a vice. Only the wallpaper was the same. The books, the funny table he had brought back from his first-ever RNVR training, the one which had made Marriott sick with envy, everything had gone.

The times they had sat here. Sharing secrets, growing up, fighting off Penny's constant begging for loans to increase her pocket money.

I should have stayed with the boat.

Chris, whose other name was Pooley, said suddenly, 'Is Hitler *really* dead, that's what I'd like to know. A lot will depend on the truth. There'll be a general election pretty soon.' He looked around the table and nodded to emphasise its importance. 'The people will want to know!'

'What people?' Marriott watched him calmly. Even the name Pooley suited him.

'Well, the ones who have to decide.'

His mother leaned over with her teapot. 'Chris is with the Ministry of Education, you know.' She

122

smiled at him, sharing it. 'A job like that will mean everything. I can't remember the last time. All those poor men on the streets, no work, nothing.'

Marriott locked his hands together beneath the spotless cloth.

'I work with people too. I dare say they will get the chance to speak out when the time comes. In case you've not noticed it, there's still a war going on in the Far East!'

His father exclaimed, 'You're not getting posted there, surely? Not after all you've been through?'

Marriott eyed him sadly. His father was doing it again. Mending the holes. Protecting his wife from trouble. From reality.

Marriott replied, 'Not yet anyway.'

Chris persisted, 'The war must be seen from two aspects—'

Marriott said flatly, 'One was enough for me.' He was being unfair, rude too, but he could not help it.

Mercifully the telephone rang and Marriott said, 'I'll take it, if I may?' It was probably Fairfax. Marriott was sickened to discover that he hoped it was. A recall. Like all those other times. But it was a girl's voice, almost breaking with excitement and pleasure.

'Vere? It's *me*, you idiot, Penny! You're home!'

Marriott gripped the telephone until the pain in his hand helped to steady him. 'How did you know?' He could feel the others watching and listening.

She said in her breathless fashion, 'Heard it from a pal in he Wrens at Dover. Said you were—' She sniffed and tried again, 'Said you were there! Oh, dear, lovely Vere. I shall be with you in an hour. I need to see you, to talk—' The line went dead.

And I need you.

He faced the room, his voice controlled again. 'That was Penny. She's coming.'

His mother moved two plates and looked at the clock.

'Never tells you anything. I just don't know about that girl!'

She bustled out of the room and, after some hesitation, Marriott's father followed. He hung back by the door, looking somewhere between them.

'Your mother will be planning where everyone's going to sleep, what she's going to give you to eat, I expect!' His gaze lingered on his son. It said, *don't spoil things. Not now.*

But he smiled and added, 'A family again. Like old times.'

Marriott loosened his jacket and took out his pipe. 'Care for a fill?'

'I—I don't smoke, actually.'

Marriott watched the smoke being drawn through the open window and thought of the mist over Kiel. The watching faces, the out-thrust arm of an unknown soldier who had had his watch looted.

'Do you like your work?'

Chris smiled vaguely. 'I shall try for something better, more rewarding perhaps.' Then he blurted out, 'I was excused from the services.'

Marriott shrugged. 'It's none of my business.'

It made no difference. 'Anyway, my conscience did not allow me to take up arms.'

Marriott stood up. It was not working. *My conscience would not allow me to stay.*

Instead he said curtly, 'We managed. *Just.*' Then

124

he walked out of the room.

*　　　*　　　*

Sub-Lieutenant Michael Fairfax sat comfortably in one corner of the gunboat's tiny wardroom, completely relaxed, a drink within easy reach while he enjoyed the peace of the evening. He might easily have been the only soul aboard for, apart from the lap of water alongside, there was no sound. The boat too was enjoying a well-deserved rest, he thought.

It was so strange to be alone, able to think, to plan. All the hands were either on local leave, or enjoying a run ashore in Dover. The duty watch consisted of Leading Seaman Craven, a stoker and one AB named Farmer who had had his leave stopped anyway for getting into a brawl in a local pub. Twice a survivor from other boats, Farmer had got into an argument with some squaddies from a stores depot, doubtless on which service had played the greatest part in winning the war. It was usually that. After what he had gone through, it was hardly surprising he should blow his top. But Fairfax was *in charge* in the Skipper's absence and had awarded the punishment without misgivings.

He glanced at the clock. Soon time for Rounds with Craven. He reached for the large pink Plymouth gin and sighed. But until then . . .

He could have taken leave himself and shared the duties with Lowes. But he was happy to be left in sole, if temporary, charge. He had queued to use one of the telephones in the harbour and had succeeded in speaking with his mother. His father was, needless to say, at his hospital. He was a good

125

surgeon and much respected for his work on skin-grafts and trying to mend the appalling effects of burns. Most of his pateints were young pilots, as well as civilians caught in some of the many hit-and-run air attacks.

Fairfax's brother was a surgeon too, and he guessed that his family had been more than disappointed when he had chosen to enter the navy, albeit for the duration only, provided he remained alive.

Whatever they said to his face he could always feel that it was there. Like the time his father had commented, 'The navy's all very well, Mike, but it'll be time lost for you as far as qualifying is concerned.' It had not occurred to anyone that he did not want to become a doctor. He laughed aloud and checked himself. He was unused to drinking, especially alone.

He wondered how Marriott was getting on. If the brief escape from duty would do him any good. Since the incident with the torpedoed coaster he had been more withdrawn than before, and Fairfax had put off asking him about what was uppermost in his thoughts. The fact that Marriott had put him up for promotion under the new scheme showed that the bond was still there. He might ask him when he returned. Tomorrow.

After the war was over in the Pacific theatre the services would be cut to the bone. That was the snag. Fairfax had got round to his decision slowly and carefully, each step seemingly linked with an event or a memory during his own active service. Now he was certain. He wanted to remain in the navy. He had heard that it was more than just difficult. If you were a 'temporary gentleman' with navy stripes it was extremely unlikely you could transfer to the Royal Navy. But was the gap still that wide? With a reference from Marriott and perhaps a senior officer, he might just stand the chance, at least of an interview with somebody in a position to decide.

Feet grated in the doorway and Leading Seaman Craven nodded to him.

'Rounds, sir?'

'Like a gin?'

Craven grinned. 'A beer'll do me, sir, ta.'

'All quiet?' He watched Craven's huge hands deftly opening a bottle from 'the bar'.

The leading hand grunted. 'There'll be a few drunks when the libertymen come back.' He swallowed deeply, his eyes squinting against the deckhead lights. 'We doin' this run back an' forth a lot, d'you reckon, sir?'

'It seems we'll have to do a bit of everything. Better than staying in that damned harbour anyway.'

Craven rubbed his chin and revealed a heavy truncheon which was hanging from his wrist. Doubtless to pacify any unruly libertyman. He was thinking of the boy in the water, the last pressure on the trigger. It still made him sweat, although there was no sane reason for it.

Fairfax stood up and reached for his cap. 'Here comes the first one. Time for Rounds, I think.'

They left the wardroom and Fairfax collided with a figure at the foot of the ladder. It was not one of the libertymen, it was Lowes.

'God, what are you doing back so early? You're not due until tomorrow, or had you forgotten?'

Craven hung back, sensing that something was

127

badly wrong. He was too discreet to listen openly, but not so stupid as to ignore it.

Lowes gasped, 'Thought I—I'd come back and give a hand.' In the evening light he looked desperate. Trapped.

Fairfax took his arm. 'What's happened? Come on, John, perhaps I can help!'

Lowes shook his hand off. 'I'm *all right*, I tell you!' He lurched into the wardroom and closed the door.

Fairfax said, 'Suit yourself!' But he was worried all the same. It was like seeing an entirely different person.

Craven climbed up the ladder behind him, his mind busy with Lowes's odd behaviour. Ever since Ginger had told him about sharing their scheme, even partly, with Lowes, he had been bothered. If the subbie was about to go round the bend they might all end up in the rattle.

Alone in the wardroom Lowes sat and stared at the frayed carpet between his shoes, his cap moving round and round in his fingers. His heart throbbed so violently that his whole body ached as if he had been beaten all over.

He had blundered into a pub near the railway station without really knowing what he was doing.

The barman had stared at him suspiciously although Lowes was too upset to notice it. He had asked for a large gin and only when he had attempted to swallow it had he realised that the whole bar was packed with naval ratings, some with their girl-friends, others clinging to the local talent, painted whores who as Leading Seaman Townsend would have put it *were probably poxed up to the eyebrows*. There was complete silence in the room and all of them had stared at Lowes as if he had just dropped from Mars.

Still gasping on the raw gin Lowes had found a small alley and vomited against a wall.

The realisation of what he had done curiously helped to steady him. He peered down at his best reefer jacket and trousers but nothing had splashed on them.

He saw the gin bottle and seized it like a drowning man. He did not even bother to fetch a fresh glass but used the one left by Fairfax. This time he swallowed the neat gin slowly and despairingly, his eyes misting over with its fire as well as the stark memory.

As a boy he had always lived in his mother's shadow, on what he had seen as the 'grand scale'. His home was half of a converted mansion on the outskirts of Guildford, and when he had been collected from school or had walked dreamily up the winding drive he had imagined that the whole of the fine house was his, filled with people, pretty girls, and, of course, dogs. Lowes loved dogs.

The other half of the mansion had been taken over by the military soon after Dunkirk and was eventually used as a small convalescent home for army officers who had been so badly wounded that even though they had recovered their health they would never see active service again. Lowes had often watched them. Sitting in the sun in their blue dressing-gowns, hobbling about the garden, or being pushed by orderlies along that same winding drive.

When he had gained his coveted midshipman's uniform Lowes had made a point of marching past the little groups of quiet veterans. He had known it was cheap, but he had enjoyed their curious glances all the same.

He took another swallow and wondered how Cuff Glazebrook managed to drink so much of it before breakfast and still appear quite normal. He made to put down the glass, knowing he should stop. He watched his hand refilling it as if it had a mind of its own.

Lowes had always had his own key. *In case my little boy gets locked out.* It had been a warm afternoon and there was a khaki staff car parked near the front door. That was not unusual as there was quite often an overflow from the other half of the building, ambulances and the like. The house had been empty, and yet he knew it was not. His mother would spend quite a lot of her day taking care of herself, her hair, and her extremely large wardrobe. He had been thinking about his cigarette supply. His mother smoked a lot, more than she should, but he could never refuse her anything. She had had him when she was twenty-one, and was not yet forty. She was admired for her elegant, even aristocratic good looks, although he saw her as his adoring mother and nothing more. Always there to chase his fears and cares away, to stand up for him even at his various schools. He had once wondered why she had not objected to him volunteering for Light Coastal Forces instead of joining a cruiser, or better still some shore appointment.

He had climbed the familiar stairs, one palm sliding up the banister rail, until he reached the landing. She had even kept his old rocking-horse and it stood permanently on the landing, like a family heirloom.

Lowes exclaimed brokenly, *'Oh my Christ!'* He

stared round, shocked by his own anguish. But the boat was still, and only someone's footsteps reached the wardroom from right forward. Probably Fairfax checking the moorings. The rest had been a complete nightmare and it had not gone away. If anything it was worse, even more unreal in retrospect.

The bedroom door had been flung open and a tall figure had burst out of the room like a madman.

He had been tall and powerfully built and completely naked.

He had yelled, 'Who the fucking hell are you?'

All sorts of horrors had flashed through Lowes's cringing mind. His mother had been attacked, even murdered, and this intruder . . . Even that belief had disintegrated as his mother had appeared in the door. Her hair had been dishevelled, when usually there was never a strand out of place, and she was trying to cover her nakedness with a filmy negligée, one which Lowes had never before laid eyes on.

She had screamed. 'Don't hit him, Ralph! He's—he's my son!'

The man had swung away, breathing heavily, 'Why didn't he say he was coming?' As he pushed back into the bedroom Lowes had seen an army uniform strewn on the white carpet, as if he had leapt straight out of it while his mother had lain watching and waiting for him.

She had thrust out her arms. 'Don't look like that, Johnnie! You were going to be told! I love him, you see—'

The man, Ralph, had called harshly, 'Don't just stand there, tell him to piss off while we get dressed. Then we can talk about it. God, he's not a bloody infant any more!'

131

She had still held out her arms imploringly. *'Please*, Johnnie!'

Lowes had never seen his mother like it before. He had never seen any woman without clothes for that matter, except when he had seen Mrs Thomas's daughter through a hedge taking off her wet swimming costume.

It had been so terrible, so impossible to believe or grasp, that Lowes, after he had run down the stairs and along the drive, had not uttered a single word.

He stared dazedly at the table and the bottle, which was almost empty. All those letters he had written to her. The thoughts and hopes they had shared. And now she was letting that stranger, Ralph, use her like, like . . . he could not think of a suitable insult.

What would he do? There *was* nothing he could do. He had always depended on her. She had always been there. Suddenly there was a void. He shivered and thought he was going to throw up again. That brute, naked, like a savage. *In our home*.

Lowes reached for the botle and fell forward, his head hitting the table as oblivion temporarily offered him sanctuary.

He was still lying there when Fairfax returned.

He closed the door and rolled Lowes on to the bench seat and loosened his tie and jacket.

'Poor little bastard.' He wondered what must have happened. He would try and put him together again before the Skipper got back.

He realised what he had spoken aloud. Just two years difference in age, but a million in experience, he thought.

As he slipped Lowes's best jacket from his

132

shoulders his wallet fell from the inside pocket.

As he stooped to pick it up a photograph fell out. It was of Lowes's mother; he had shown it to him several times. With pride as much as love.

Almost guiltily Fairfax replaced the photograph inside the wallet. Or rather the two pieces of it. Lowes must have torn it in half.

So that was it.

Fairfax went into the tiny pantry and shook the coffee pot.

If I had not insisted he took some leave instead of me, he might never have found out whatever it was.

Welcome home.

★   ★   ★

The bar was only half-filled when Marriott walked down to the Harrow to buy something for the evening meal.

Penny would be arriving at any minute and it seemed that there was nothing but two inches of sherry left over from Christmas to celebrate this reunion.

He felt his jaw tighten. Perhaps dear Chris didn't drink, either? He looked around the snug bar as all the lights went on, while outside the inn-sign was also illuminated by a miniature searchlight. It was what he had noticed most at Dover. All the houses with their windows glittering like tiers of eyes. But no street lighting. The authorities had reminded everyone that, because of the war, there was still a fuel shortage. As if they needed any reminding, he thought.

The landlord watched him thoughtfully. Marriott was a far cry from the cheerful and optimistic young

133

subbie who had paused for a last drink on his way to Felixstowe to join his new flotilla.

He said, 'No Scotch of course, won't see any of that for years, I expect. Got a couple of bottles of red wine you might like.'

Marriott took out his pipe and filled it with care. 'Thanks. I'll have a gin—'

'Got plenty of brandy.' The man reached under the bar. 'Horse's Neck, that's what—'

Their eyes avoided each other. *What Stephen had had on that last reunion.*

'It'll do me.'

As the landlord went to search for the wine Marriott looked around the comfortable room with its smoke-stained chimney breast and horse-brasses. Lines of regimental badges and shoulder flashes too. All along one wall. Each had a story to tell, he thought as he sipped his drink.

Welsh Guards; they had had a training battalion at Sandown Park racecourse for the whole war. Men had come and gone, many had been lost in North Africa and Italy. Canadian badges in plenty. How much at home they had been here, when so far from their own country. The same war. The local anti-aircraft battery, balloon barrage, military police, all had left something.

Like it said on the memorial at Dover. *To remind us to remember you.* There would be a hell of a lot more names on it soon.

Now all the servicemen who had trained or been billeted around this district had departed, seemingly overnight. The sandbagged barriers and camouflaged nets which had hidden the big guns, part of the ring of batteries which had defended the sky over London, were abandoned. The fat barrage

134

balloons, which had dotted the skies like basking whales, were just a memory now, like the long, chilling nights in the shelters.

He looked at his glass. It was empty. *I'm getting morbid.*

The landlord returned and placed the bottles on the bar. 'Here we go.' Then he looked at the door as if he expected to see the blackout curtain billow inwards to engulf another customer. But he grinned. 'Here she is, bless her!'

Penny ran across the room, oblivious of the few who were sitting around with their drinks, her eyes filling her face as she wrapped her arms round his neck and kissed him hard on the mouth.

Then she clung there, searching his face, feature by feature.

She exclaimed, 'I was early. Thought I'd walk back with you! You look just great!'

She had altered in some way, he thought. The same rebellious hair which fought to escape her blue WAAF's cap, the same wide provocative eyes. He could feel her body against his own. That was the difference. She had become a woman.

With her arm through his they walked past the green. She glanced at it, remembering her pony probably.

She said, 'I wanted to see you and talk with you.' He felt her shiver, then grip his arm more tightly. 'Everything's different, isn't it?'

'You feel it too.'

She nodded without looking at him. 'It's not just the creepy lodger.' She gave her wicked chuckle. That at least was unchanged. 'That's awful of me, but he is!'

'I agree.'

135

She said suddenly, 'I wish you could meet my Jack.'

'Is he *the one*?'

She said in a quieter tone, 'Don't laugh at me. I've had a few affairs, nothing real. But when you serve alongside young men who you know are going to have their names sponged off the pilots' rota sooner or later, you can't help getting involved.'

'Tell me about Jack.' It was obviously very important.

'That's just it. I love him, I really do. I wish you had someone who—'

'Don't change the subject. If he loves you, where's the problem? They're bound to miss you when it happens but—'

She interrupted quickly, 'He asked me to marry him. I've got his ring in my pocket. Didn't have the nerve to bowl into the old home and display it like a battle trophy! I don't want anything to spoil it. It was important that you should know first.'

She put her head against his shoulder. 'What will you do when I've gone?'

So that was it. 'When?'

'He's been ordered back to Canada. If I marry him I can go with him.' She looked at him, her eyes shining faintly in the dying light. 'Three months at the most.'

'D'you *want* to go?'

She nodded. 'I shall be turfed out of the WAAF but I've done what I joined to do. Yes, I want to be with him. I don't care where it is. But I shall miss you most of all.'

He gripped her tightly so that the bottles clinked between them.

'Don't. *Please*.' He made another effort. 'I'm so

136

glad for you.'

She studied his profile. 'Together then?' It was what the three of them had always said.

He smiled, suddenly glad for her. '*Together.*'

CHAPTER SEVEN

MAYDAY

Sub-Lieutenant Fairfax stepped into the wardroom and waited for Marriott to glance up from the makeshift desk. They had just completed the usual muster of requestmen. He was relieved that there were no defaulters. Not this time. Mainly, he suspected, because of a lack of opportunity.

'That's the lot, sir.'

Marriott leaned back in the chair and unbuttoned his jacket.

In Kiel again, the brief leave already slotted like an interlude into his memory. Except for Penny. Lots of things might happen. She might decide to break it off with her Jack, or his transfer back to Canada could easily be changed. Only the unlikely was certain in the services.

Beyond the confines of the hull he could hear the rattle of drills, and felt the occasional thump as an underwater explosion sighed against the keel. In the short time he had been away many more vessels had made their appearance here. Salvage craft and tugs, trawlers, dredgers and, standing aloofly in the background like elegant spectators, a pair of graceful destroyers. There were some merchant ships too, already being converted into offices and

137

accommodation for the swelling numbers of naval personnel.

The stench was still very evident, and when they pumped out the heads the water which refilled the basins was as black as coal.

Marriott said, 'You did right not to make a big issue over Able Seaman Farmer's drunken spree at Dover. He's dipped his good conduct badge enough times already.'

Fairfax watched him, thinking of the men he had come to know so well who had just been up before the Skipper, like strangers in their best shore-going kit, their *tiddley suits*, resplendent in gold badges. It made a welcome change from overalls or oil-stained sweaters. Leading Seaman Arthur Townsend, the boat's 'core' in many ways, had been made up to acting-petty officer, while the keen-eyed machine-gunner Rae had been promoted to leading seaman. Both well deserved.

Fairfax said, 'I'm glad about Townsend.'

'Yes, get him to put up his rank today. It'll look right even if he can't change uniforms yet and get measured for his fore-and-aft rig. When he goes on his final course, we shall lose him, I'm afraid.'

Marriott looked up and added, 'Same applies to you.' He pushed an envelope across the table. 'Came aboard with the mail. Well done, *Acting-Temporary-Lieutenant*!'

Fairfax could not hide his pleasure. 'I'd like to buy you a drink, sir!'

Marriott closed his book. It was always a good feeling when there was no trouble at the table.

'There's one more thing. Fetch the cox'n, will you?'

Evans entered and stood very stiffly in the centre

138

of the wardroom.

'I've had a request, Swain.' He watched Evans's impassive features. *Would you ever got to know him*, he wondered. 'From Commander Meikle.'

'Sir?'

'He has asked me to sound you out about transferring to his staff.'

'I see, sir.'

Marriott had expected surprise, even resentment, but there was nothing.

'The fact is, Swain, that all our resources are stretched to the limit. The Military Government is organising every town and garrison, but they need more interpreters than they can find. Schleswig-Holstein was the last major part of Germany to surrender, so we are at the end of the queue.' He smiled wryly. 'But we know that's nothing unusual.'

Evans's fingers were pressing hard against the seams of his trousers.

'I do not understand, sir.'

Marriott looked at an open scuttle as the topmast of a small vessel glided past like a lance.

'You have an excellent service record, with two decorations for bravery. You were with Special Services and the SBS and you are used to co-operating with the army when need be. You speak German, and of course French—you would be a real asset to the commander. However, you are not obliged to go, I have made that clear.'

Evans looked past him, his face controlled like a mask.

Marriott added slowly, 'Obviously I should miss you. But in this situation you must always remember the first lieutenant's prayer. Look after

139

Number One!'

He saw Fairfax grin but Evans remained as impassive as before.

Evans said slowly, 'I will accept the commander's request, sir.'

'Very well. You can instruct our new acting-petty officer in your other duties.' What had he expected? Evans, no matter what his paybook proclaimed, was no more Welsh than he was. One of de Gaulle's Free French who, because of his life in the Channel Islands, had chosen to fight alongside the others who had escaped from their country to join in the war in their own fashion. And yet Marriott felt disappointment.

Evans said haltingly, 'I will say this now, sir. I have not met a better Englishman, nor have I served under a better captain.' He thrust out his hand. 'I belong here, sir. The boat will probably return to England, or be refitted for the Far East.' He nodded slowly, as if he had just felt the true conviction of his words. 'I will be of more use ashore.'

They watched him leave and Fairfax exclaimed, 'That's a turnup for the book, sir!'

He watched as Marriott put his signature at the foot of Meikle's formal request and wondered. Was it just a coincidence that Marriott had advanced Townsend's promotion? Or had he known in his heart that Evans was going to accept?

Marriott felt for his pipe. 'I'll miss the old bugger, all the same.'

Thuds echoed through the bulkhead and Fairfax said, 'I've got the hands hunting for leaks, sir. Not the hull this time but the deck. The mess was like a rain forest when we came through the Kattegat!'

There was a tap at the door and the gangway sentry called in, 'Visitor, sir.'

Marriott was still thinking about the coxswain. *Danger.* The word seemed to persist.

He made to leave. 'I'll see you later, Number One.'

But the sentry added, 'A visitor for *you*, sir.'

Marriott faced the door. It was nobody senior or the sentry would have alerted everybody in time to offer the welcome mat. Then who—

A slim and very tanned lieutenant stepped over the coaming, ducking his head as he did so. He glanced slowly around the wardroom and gave a gentle yawn.

Fairfax watched, fascinated, as Marriott strode across the worn carpet and threw his arms around the tall lieutenant.

'Beri-Beri! Of all people! Just what the *hell* are you doing here?'

Lieutenant John Kidd, known affectionately by his nickname because of the many injections and vaccinations he had endured, mostly it seemed without success, in his various outlandish appointments, smiled at the greeting.

'Got tired of Burma, thought I'd come and lend a hand, so to speak.'

'Have a drink?'

Beri-Beri tossed his cap into a corner. His hair was so bleached by the sun it looked like silver in the reflected glare from the scuttle.

'Thought you'd never ask.' He yawned again.

Marriott groped amongst the bottles. It was a tonic to see him. He had not changed much, still yawning. He had seen him fall asleep in a noisy mess or in the middle of a senior officer's speech.

141

He knew he had been ill several times. Burma was the last place they should have sent him.

He asked over his shoulder, 'Have you got a command still? ML the last one, wasn't it?'

'No command.' He took the glass and held it to the light. 'I'm an explosives-wallah now.' He chuckled. 'They tell me.'

Fairfax knew he was sharing something special. He had seen the strain drop away from Marriott, the genuine pleasure these two men shared in finding each other.

Kidd was a strange one, he thought. He had already noted the DSC and bar, plus a decoration he did not recognise. Another veteran, and about Marriott's age, he decided.

Kidd looked at him suddenly, his pale lashes flicking open like a cat when it is suddenly awakened. There was no sleepiness there now. Blue eyes which seemed to look right through you.

He remarked, 'We go back a long way. Never thought we'd get this far.'

Again, Fairfax saw the exchange of glances. Each one remembering, accepting the truth of that last comment so casually uttered.

Marriott said, 'I know.' He looked at him directly. 'A lot of good blokes, eh?'

Beri-Beri held out his glass, one of the boxful which Ginger Jackson had 'come by' from somebody in the dockyard.

'When I get out of this regiment I'm going to find a place of my own. No sea, no more bloody ships, none of the bullshit either.'

Marriott asked quietly, 'What will you do?' Someone had once told him that people who had suffered like Beri-Beri rarely saw out a full span of

142

life.

'*Do?*' His face creased in a grin. 'I'm going to *fish*, and that's the closest I ever want to get to the water again!'

He tapped his head. 'You're sailing this afternoon, right?'

Marriott nodded. 'I'm taking a passenger round to Neustadt.'

Beri-Beri gave a lazy smile. 'S'right, chum. *Me*. I'm supposed to check with the army about some demolition there. Your Commander Meikle wanted to send me by road, but I pointed out the stability or otherwise of some of these explosives is somewhat in doubt. Especially on the knocked-out roads I've seen!'

Marriott nodded. 'Welcome aboard then!'

'I'll go and fetch my gear.' He looked at the shabby wardroom. 'Not much different from my old command.'

Marriott called after him, 'What happened to her?'

He considered it. 'Ran out of luck. You know how it is.'

They heard him clamber to the deck and pause to speak with Lowes who was O.O.D.

Marriott folded his papers and thought about Kidd. Like Cuff, he was one of the originals. The old gang at Felixstowe, and then down to the Med. In the navy you often lost touch with those who had seemed like brothers. You had to forget too. Especially those who would never come back.

To give himself time to recover from the unexpected and moving reunion he asked, 'What's the matter with Pilot?'

Fairfax had still been thinking and conjecturing

143

on the meeting of these two. What had gone before. The warmth he had felt between them, that he could not share.

He replied, 'Oh, he's all right, sir.'

'You mean you're not going to tell me, is that it?'

Fairfax faced him warily. Even now he could not distinguish if Marriott was joking or in earnest.

'It's not that, sir—' He shrugged. 'He was upset about something when he came back from leave. He only took one day.'

Marriott heard the pipe. *Up Spirits!* Soon there would be the heady smell of rum. As much part of their routine as the answering cry to the pipe from some wag, 'And stand fast the Holy Ghost!' It never failed.

He remembered his own thoughts. *I should have stayed with the boat.*

'I know we're not getting shot at every day, Number One, but we still have to depend on each other. Especially now that we're so short-handed.'

Fairfax shifted under his grey eyes. 'He was always writing to his mother.' He hated it. Like a betrayal. 'You remember, sir?'

Marriott nodded. Short-handed was right. Only back in Kiel for a day and they were off again. But with Beri-Beri aboard it might be different. Someone to confide in, to share their feelings.

'Yes, I remember.' He had seen Lowes dragging about his duties. He had expected Fairfax, as his first lieutenant, to snap him out of it, and not leave Evans and the leading rates to carry him. The fact that he had not—

Fairfax said, 'Well, sir, when we came alongside yesterday, the mail was brought aboard. There were two letters or more for him. I think I recognised her

144

handwriting. She wrote to him all the time.'

Marriott thought suddenly of the evening meal with his parents and the ingratiating Chris. His mother's expression when Penny had told them about her Canadian, and produced her ring.

She had exclaimed, 'You're not, *not*—'

Penny had faced her, hurt and ashamed. 'No, I'm not pregnant, if you must bring it up in front of strangers!'

It had been awful. Afterwards he had heard Penny sobbing quietly in her old room.

Fairfax took his silence for impatience and said, 'He didn't even open them. I found them torn up in the gash-bucket.'

'I'm glad you told me.' It must be bad. What Commodore Paget-Orme would write off as an aftermath of war.

He stood up, needing to be alone before they got under way.

'Make Beri-Beri comfortable when he gets back, Number One. I'm going across the dock to visit Cuff.'

Fairfax followed him to the door and up to the deck where several of the hands were crawling about on their knees searching for open seams. It was warm and sunny, the misty blue sky making a blunt contrast with the shattered buildings and partly destroyed hulks. Men working everywhere, dust and smoke, parties of tired-looking Germans marching or shovelling, or patiently queuing at the army food-trucks for sandwiches and great mugs of sweet tea.

It would be good to get out of this place. Marriott turned as Fairfax walked to the break in the gangway.

'I forgot. You wanted to ask me something?'

Fairfax flushed and was surprised that he still could.

'It can keep, sir.'

'You want to stay in the Andrew when this lot's finally over, right?' He saw it go home like a bullet. 'All for it, are you?'

Fairfax shifted his feet 'Something like that. I—I wanted to ask you what you thought about it, my chances, if there are any.'

'What *I* think about it?' He touched his sleeve. 'I'm the last one you ought to ask. Think about it anyway, then we can talk.'

Fairfax saluted as he strode over the brow to the rubble-strewn jetty.

To himself he said, 'You are the only one I would ask. Don't you, *can't* you understand you're the sole person I want to talk to?'

Ginger Jackson interrupted his thoughts.

'Congratulations, Mister Fairfax. Not before time neither.'

Fairfax noticed he was carrying Townsend's best jumpers over one arm.

He replied, 'News travels fast, Ginger. Where are you off to?'

Ginger did not reply directly. 'If you'd like to let me 'ave one of yer uniforms I can get yer new ring stitched on, sir. Real nice job. I'm gettin' Arthur Townsend's PO badges done.'

'How can you know a tailor, Ginger? You've not even been ashore yet!'

Ginger tapped his nose and winked. 'Little Jerry bloke right 'ere in the dockyard. No bother, sir.'

Fairfax smiled doubtfully. 'Right then.'

'I got the O.O.D.'s permission to step ashore,

146

but I'll go an' get yer best reefer afore I leave.'

He strolled away whistling to himself.

Fairfax smiled. Not a care in the world. He saw Lowes standing near the working party, his face paler than ever.

I'll bet Ginger even knows what's up with him!

He called, 'Have you checked the chart, Pilot?'

'Chart?' Lowes stared at him dazedly. 'Which one?'

Fairfax pulled him out of earshot of the others.

'We're sailing this afternoon at 1600, for God's sake! What the *hell's* got into you?' He relented slightly as he saw Lowes's lip tremble. *At any second he's going to burst into tears in front of the hands.* He recalled the Skipper's words. *We still have to depend on each other.* 'Just snap out of it, will you, John? Look around you at all this bloody mess! Then tell me *you've* got troubles!'

Lowes stiffened and retorted resentfully, 'It's all right for you—'

Fairfax said quietly, 'I didn't hear that. Now fetch the right chart for the Bay of Lübeck and I'll lend you a hand, okay?'

Lowes nodded slowly, the fight going out of him as quickly as it had risen.

'Yes, of course, Number One. I shan't let you down. And I was glad to hear about your promotion.'

Fairfax smiled. 'Chin up then. You look like a wet Sunday in Cardiff!'

Ginger reappeared with the reefer folded over Townsend's jumpers.

Townsend asked, 'Wot's up with Snow White, Ginger?'

Ginger frowned; he was planning what he would

147

offer the German worker who was going to sew on the badges and Number One's extra ring.

''*Im?* Found someone 'avin' it off with 'is old lady, you mark my words!'

Townsend sighed. 'Wish someone would take mine off my hands!'

They both laughed so that Petty Officer Evans who was standing on the empty bridge turned to look down at them.

He had seen some of the terrible photographs in the newspapers. All those pitiful, broken faces.

He felt himself sway as if the boat had rolled against the piles, but she was unmoving.

Any one of them could have been his young sister.

At 1600 exactly MGB 801 cast off her lines and headed down the harbour. Fairfax stood with the line of forecastle hands, listening to the shrill calls as they ploughed past a destroyer with the thick black band of Captain (D) on her wide funnel.

All of this must count, he thought, carry weight when he was accepted for an interview.

'Fall out the hands!'

Fairfax turned and touched his cap to the bridge. It would be strange to look up and not see Evans, he thought. After this trip anyway. He saw two faces where Marriott usually stood; the other one was Kidd. Fairfax smiled. Beri-Beri. Perhaps he might tell him more about the Skipper.

He watched them laugh together.

He had never seen Marriott so much at ease. What must have happened to make him the way he was?

Fairfax watched the seamen stowing the lines and fenders, chatting together, like Ginger, outwardly unimpressed by everything.

He could almost hear his father dismissing his feelings as nothing more than *hero-worship*. One of his many clinical conclusions.

Fairfax shook his head and remembered the nights off the Hook of Holland and amongst the Belgian sandbars.

For once, his father was near the truth.

*   *   *

Marriott and Kidd leaned side-by-side on the chart-table while the hull swayed and shuddered around them.

Marriott traced their pencilled course and the various fixes already marked on it with his brass dividers and said, 'We should be up to Fehmarn Island and into the Belt during the First Watch.' He looked up at the chartroom's deckhead as something clattered across it and brought an angry bellow from the helmsman. 'It's this reduced speed, I'm afraid, Beri-Beri.' He smiled as the hull rolled again. 'But I want to stand well clear when we turn into Mecklenburger Bay and then reach Neustadt around dawn. The minesweeping boys are out in force. I don't want to run foul of them in the night!'

'How was Cuff, by the way?'

Marriott considered it. He had found Cuff Glazebrook slumped in his wardroom, an almost empty gin bottle his only company. He had made something of a show about his confrontation with the N.O.I.C., but it had lacked the old bluster one had come to expect of him.

'Kept on and on about those bloody depth charges! I still say I did the right thing. The

149

bastards had no intention of stopping. Anyway,' he had slopped the remaining gin into his glass, 'I don't change that easy. I won't start licking the arses of those I've been ordered to kill just days earlier!'

'But he's taking no action in the matter?'

'How could he?'

He had leaned forward as if to hold him in focus.

'The bloody war's moving so fast we'll *never* get to the Far East at this rate. Rangoon's been retaken from the Nips, and our Pacific Fleet battleships were in some big action last week according to the newspapers. I tell you, old son, the carve-up will leave us high-and-dry. Even the Yank Ninth Army have had to pull back across the Elbe because they might offend the bloody Russians if they hold on to what they captured!' He had tried to cheer up and had said, 'Heard about old Beri-Beri. We'll see some fun now. He'll shake up these po-faced gits who are trying to run things here.'

Marriott had felt almost sorry for him. 'What will you do when peace arrives, Cuff?'

'Not be like my father, *that's* for sure! His idea of enjoyment is a weekend at Blackpool and a plate of whelks with his cronies!'

Anyone who did not know would imagine that Cuff's father was some kind of a layabout. Marriott had known for a long time that the truth was a direct opposite. Cuff's old man was a millionaire and dealt in commercial vehicles. The war had made him rich, and there were few army units which did not use either some of his vehicles or at least their components. He had started life on the shop-floor of a factory which had been on the decline until the war had broken out. Where Cuff's father had found the money to buy the place and finance several others was a mystery and would probably remain so.

But Cuff did not see it quite like that. 'If the silly old sod thinks *I'm* going to learn the business right from the bottom as he did, he can think again. Jesus, after what I've been through—' His red-rimmed eyes had flashed in the dusty sunlight. 'I intend to begin at the top, with his bloody help or otherwise!'

Marriott looked at his friend. 'You know Cuff. All blood and guts. I don't see peacetime suiting him at all!'

They were laughing as Fairfax ducked down into the chart-house.

'We've just sighted some of the sweepers, sir. Three miles. Just exchanged recognition signals.'

Marriott peered at the chart again. 'Alter course. Steer Nor'-East until we're well clear. Then call me, and I'll order an increase of revs to compensate for it.'

Fairfax's eyes moved quickly between them. 'Ginger is making some fresh coffee, sir.'

'Right. We'll be there when you've altered course.'

Kidd yawned. 'Nice enough chap.'

'Between us, he wants to sign on as a regular.'

Beri-Beri's eyes crinkled. 'Serve him right!'

They were both on the bridge again as the gunboat altered course into the Fehmarn Belt and ploughed heavily through an offshore swell, the early blink of an island lighthouse barely reflecting on the dull-coloured water.

The watches changed and the two lieutenants settled down to watch the dusk making shadows on

151

the land while garlands of gulls dipped and pitched in the bow-wave, rosy pink in the fading light.

Marriott said, 'Good lookout tonight. There are several Swedish ships reported in the area.'

Evans waited by the signal locker. 'Darken ship, sir?'

'Yes. I don't want any more *strangers* slipping past us because they've seen us first!'

One of the lookouts laughed. The *Ronsis* was just another memory.

'Coming below, Beri-Beri?'

Fairfax, who had the watch, coughed discreetly. 'I think he's dropped off, sir.'

Marriott saw Kidd's fair hair flapping untidily in the breeze over the screen and smiled. He had fallen asleep in the bridge chair, one arm swinging in time with the boat's uneven motion.

He said, 'Leave him. He's earned a rest.'

Marriott lowered himself to the wardroom and saw Lowes lying on a bench, covered with a blanket and breathing heavily.

Marriott pushed past to his small cabin and wondered what he ought to do about him. Lowes was only pretending to sleep, and he had eaten hardly anything since they had slipped their moorings in Kiel.

He sat down in his cabin and watched his oilskin swaying from its hook behind the door. It was good to have Beri-Beri here, to know he was going to be around. For a while anyway. In the navy *a while* was valuable. He did not feel like resting but decided he would write a letter to Penny. It could go off as soon as they returned to harbour. She would at least know that he cared and was thinking of her. He rested his head/on one hand as he stared

152

at the writing paper and wished he had not watched the swaying oilskin. Seasickness could hit anyone, even the old Jacks—

He swung round, startled as the handset jangled above his bunk.

'Sorry to call you, sir.' It was Fairfax. Apologising again. 'Sparks has picked up a signal.' He swallowed hard. '*Mayday*, sir.'

'I'm coming up. Call the cox'n!'

'He's already here, sir—' But Marriott was already bounding up the ladder. He found Kidd wide-awake and Fairfax ducked beneath the protective hood on the ready-use chart-table.

'Got a fix yet?'

'No.' Beri-Beri shrugged. 'But I've got a nasty feeling.'

Fairfax withdrew his head and shoulders. 'W/T can't get more than a garble, sir. But she's one of ours, *that* Sparks does know.'

Long John Silver slid past them to his place at the rear of the bridge. Still a team. No matter what.

Marriott looked at his friend. 'Well, what about your feeling?'

'I think she's the ML that sailed ahead of you.' He added softly, 'The one I should have taken passage in.'

Marriott moved restlessly about the bridge. Beri-Beri did not have to elaborate. The ML had been taking the bulk of the explosives for the job in Neustadt. 801 only carried detonators and some steel jacks from the engineering department.

Rae stood by the voicepipes, wide-awake as ever when he was on watch. He was still astonished at getting his hook from the Skipper. It would show his family he'd not been completely unrewarded.

153

He lowered his face to a voicepipe and snapped, 'Bridge!'

Then he stood up and said, 'It's a fire, sir. Somebody's replied to the Mayday, Sparks thinks it's a supply ship somewhere astern of us.'

'Is the Chief up and about?'

Rae nodded in the darkness. 'He is, sir.' It sounded like *of course*.

Beri-Beri watched his indecision as he moved about the bridge.

'Might not be a *serious* fire.' That was Fairfax.

Marriott snapped, 'It's a Mayday, not an invitation to a party!' He relented immediately. 'See if you can find her call-sign.' He felt Silver move past him. 'We could try to call her up on R/T.'

Marriott was thinking aloud as voices echoed tinnily up and down the pipes, and an occasional stammer of morse escaped above the sea noises around them.

Down in the chartroom again, Marriott stared at the calculations and bearings until his mind ached.

Fairfax said, 'I think she's around the next headland, sir.' He rested his forefinger on the coastline. 'There's another lighthouse beyond there. Also it might explain why our radio reception is so bad.'

Marriott stared at him in the reflected chart-light. 'Good thinking. With luck the lighthouse keepers might summon assistance.'

He made up his mind. 'Pass the word, Number One. Full revs in three minutes!' Fairfax nodded, still feeling Marriott's praise when seconds earlier he had felt the lash of his contempt. Then he bolted for the ladder.

Beri-Beri was watching him, his eyes hidden as

154

his body leaned this way and that as if to follow his shadow on the bulkhead.

'If you close the land now you'll be right amongst the sweeping area, but you realise that, don't you? I know we're safe enough with our depth, but there may be a few drifters around.' He reached out and took his arm. 'But that *is* what you intend, isn't it?'

Marriott returned to the chart, the coastline and pencilled markings blurred as he tried to control his racing thoughts.

It was over. Done with. And anyway you couldn't leave them to brew up without trying something. *Not one of your own.*

He said between his teeth, 'When we do find the bastard I'll lay odds he's put the fire out and is on his way to Neustadt!'

Beri-Beri watched him, feeling his sudden anxiety. Torment was a truer word.

Silver swayed down the ladder with his recognition book, more dog-eared and stained than ever.

He said bluntly, 'She's Lieutenant Duncan's ML, sir. Call-sign *Vagrant*.'

'Yes, I see.' Marriott tried to clear his mind. He could see the ML's skipper quite clearly in his thoughts. A round-faced, cheerful Devonian from the River Exe. He had been in Coastal Forces for all of his service, and two years in command of this ML.

Now he was out there somewhere. *Fire.* Feared, dreaded more than anything else by sailors.

Fairfax called down. 'Ready, sir! Course to steer is South-Sixty-East!'

'Very well. Half speed. Bring her round, Number One. I shall be in the W/T office.'

155

Down in the hutchlike compartment with its shining bank of instruments and flickering dials, Telegraphist White peered over his shoulder with surprise.

'Nothin' more, sir!'

'Try R/T.' How dry his throat had become, and his back felt like ice.

He watched the telegraphist switch on, his eyes on Knocker White's fingers moving the dial, seeking the other vessel. Why did they call Whites *Knocker*?

'Hello *Vagrant*, this is *Otter*, do you read me—'

He felt the hull begin to jerk as the screws beat the sea into a mounting bank of foam. But the motion was easier. MGB 801 was at home in these conditions.

'Dead, sir.'

'Keep trying.' Marriott clambered back to the bridge, aware that every sheltered place was crammed with silent, watching figures.

'Full speed, Number One.' He groped his way to the chair where Beri-Beri was clinging to a handrail, his hair rippling, standing on end as the hull bounded forward, suddenly unrestricted as if cut free from a leash.

'Lighthouse, fine on the starboard bow, sir!'

They all saw the edge of the long beam waver then fade as the far-off lantern completed another turn. Regular, constant, reliable. No wonder old sea pilots called them their Silent Sentinels.

Rae said, 'No more signals, sir.'

Marriott gripped the back of the chair hard. In his mind's eye he could see the hidden mines, the ones which those sweepers were supposed to clear at first light, before he had even arrived here.

156

He raised his glasses and saw the tremendous arrowhead of white-banked water surging back from the bows. It was impossible to hold them steady. *Where the hell was she?*

Silver had relieved Rae at the voicepipes so that the bridge could have the benefit of his cat's eyes.

He yelled, 'Signal from HQ, sir! Plain language!'

Marriott knew what it would say. He replied, 'Repeat it!'

'Fire reported in area south of Staber Huk. No further details. Attention is drawn to—'

Marriott snapped, 'That's enough! We should see something soon!'

He heard someone retching and knew it was Lowes. Another rude awakening for him.

The hard glare of the lighthouse swept over the black water. It was a dangerous place for ships which had too much draft and too little power in their engines.

'Dead ahead, sir! Fire on the water!'

Marriott watched in silence, feeling Fairfax and Beri-Beri pressing against him on either side while they trained their night glasses on the flickering glow of yellow and orange flames. It was like being carried against his will. As in a dream when you can't run away or hide.

Fairfax shouted, 'Fire-parties to your stations! Stand by rafts and heaving lines!'

Marriott tried again to moisten his lips. 'Remain on this course. We must hold up to windward.' But it was like hearing someone else giving the orders. A robot.

Men blundered about in the darkness, sometimes blinded by the sweeping impartial glare from the lighthouse.

157

Marriott said, 'Half speed all engines.' The keepers must have telephoned about the fire. Germans seeing their old enemy in danger, but the code of the sea too strong to challenge.

The bows seemed to slide down and hurl the spray as high as the masthead. Men with torches were groping along the slippery foredeck, others called out for assistance, or cursed horribly as they fell over some immovable object.

'All ready, sir!' Fairfax was back on the bridge again, breathing fast, eyes shining in the glow.

Marriott raised his heavy binoculars very slowly and then stared at the fire on the water.

The outline of the ML's hull was sharper now, like a black line beneath a flicker of fire and steam, the latter probably from hoses and extinguishers.

Beri-Beri whispered, 'They've not got it under control. My guess is it was the engineroom. We might be able to grapple before she loses all her power!'

Marriott barely heard. He had seen a few tiny figures momentarily in silhouette against the flames. How small and vulnerable they looked.

'Call them up. Let them know we're coming.' He doubted if anyone had the time to man the W/T office, and he saw Silver's Aldis lamp clattering away, telling them in his own fashion that they were no longer alone.

He gripped his glasses more tightly to prevent them slipping from his grasp. He could not drag his eyes from the dancing, evil-looking flames. Men were hurt, perhaps dying, praying for rescue. And all Marriott could see was his own boat. Burning and burning, so that those same pitiful screams seemed to be right here beside him.

'*Stand by forrard!*'

Marriott felt his eyes stinging but still could not look away. Below the bridge he heard someone shouting above the engines' roar, to encourage those who would not hear. He wanted to find the man and shake him, tell him there was no hope. He recalled Beri-Beri's own words.

She ran out of luck.

'*Dead slow!*' Marriott tried to clear his throat and tasted the stench of burning for the first time.

Beri-Beri said, 'I'd not get too close.'

Marriott nodded. So he knew too. *The old instinct.* He heard Lowes sobbing quietly at the rear of the bridge and thought he was too frightened to care what the others thought.

But for once Lowes was not thinking of himself. He had heard the name of the stricken ML's commanding officer called from the W/T office, Lieutenant Duncan. It had been his birthday Lowes had been invited to share when the German boy had been dragged from the harbour.

Marriott said, 'Port fifteen.' He watched the flickering flame reflecting from the gently moving water, as if it came from the sea-bed itself.

Beri-Beri said, 'Why doesn't he abandon? He must have seen us!'

Marriott felt his hand shake as he pressed down the switch of the loud-hailer.

'D'you hear there? Abandon ship, I shall pick you up—'

He got no further. The flame seemed to flare straight up and then expand until the whole hull was engulfed. Then came the explosion, strangely muffled and yet so powerful that the complete deck and most of the bridge was hurled into the air in

159

flaming pieces, some of which hissed down right alongside.

Fairfax gripped a rail for support and stared aghast as the fragments continued to fall. He heard something solid drop on the foredeck, the instant response from someone's extinguisher.

He cringed in the fierce glare which made the men around him look like lifeless studies in bronze. For a few moments he saw Lieutenant Kidd with his arm around the Skipper's shoulders, and for a second more imagined that Marriott had been hit by a falling piece of timber or worse.

As he made to run towards him the light suddenly doused, leaving him almost blind in the impenetrable darkness. Only the lighthouse beam remained, licking out and over the swell, painting the bobbing pieces like silver.

Fairfax gasped, 'Are you all right, sir?'

Marriott turned very slowly, knowing that but for Beri-Beri's arm he would have fallen.

He said, 'Get up forrard, Number One. You know what to do.' He tried again. 'I'm relying on you.'

Beri-Beri snapped. 'And take that officer with you! Keep him bloody quiet!'

But when Fairfax reached Lowes he found Leading Seaman Craven speaking with him, his voice unusually quiet.

He was saying, 'In war, any bloke can get the chop. I've seen a-bloody 'nough of 'em go like that!' He bobbed his head towards the figures in the forepart of the bridge. 'Our Skipper 'as died just once too often, see?'

Lowes wiped his face with the back of his hand. 'Yes. Yes, I see—'

Behind his back Craven sighed. *Never in a thousand bloody years!*

The hull moved slowly across the water, torches and the bridge searchlight reaching out on either beam, finding and rejecting.

Beri-Beri murmured, 'I should have been aboard her by rights.'

Marriott came out of his thoughts as Fairfax called aft, 'No survivors, sir!'

Marriott shouted, '*Keep looking!*' To the bridge at large he added, 'There must be someone. There *has* to be.'

Beri-Beri watched his anguish and wished there was something he could do. He had been there when Marriott's boat had blown up. As close as they had been to the ML. He knew how Marriott had tried to overcome it, had given himself to his new command more than ever before. But after this . . .

Evans asked doubtfully, 'Shall I take her round again, sir?'

'Yes.' He swallowed hard, feeling the fear like something wild and alive. 'You never know. Think how it would feel to find hope and then see it sail away, leaving you to rot?'

When first light found them they were still circling the place where the ML had been blasted apart. The light revealed what the darkness had mercifully hidden. Bodies and pieces of men, familiar uniforms and badges, burned and bloodied in that last explosion.

Silver watched Marriott staring down into the water as they passed a floating corpse, afraid to interrupt his suffering.

'Minesweepers astern, sir!' He looked at

161

Beri-Beri questioningly. Marriott had not heard a word.

Beri-Beri said, 'Signal the senior officer. *There are no survivors.*' He had seen the long metal tanks which the minesweepers and salvage vessels had been issued with, for macabre relics like these. 'He can carry on from here.'

He looked at his friend. 'They had no chance. Neither did we.'

Marriott turned as Silver's Aldis clattered the signal towards the leading trawler.

'Would you tell Number One to secure his fire-party.' He moved to the bridge chair and rested his arms on its high back.

He knew that Beri-Beri was examining the chart and in minutes would put the gunboat back on course for Neustadt.

At any other time he would have objected, resisted anyone's attempt to help.

But he could barely move, any more than he could free his mind from that last searing explosion.

He felt the deck begin to shake, the sudden increase of power and the thrash of foam from the outer screws making the silent figures come to life again.

Evans was stepping down from the wheel, his place taken by Townsend, in more ways than one.

Beri-Beri joined him by the chair but did not look at him.

'You know what I think, Vere? I believe that *we* are the survivors.'

Marriott pulled out his pipe and jammed it between his teeth to prevent them from chattering.

He felt more like tears than he had believed possible. But it could not be like that. Meikle had proclaimed that it was not a game. He was wrong. How else could they have endured it, with survival just a joke?

He said, 'Quite right, Beri-Beri. If you can't take a joke, then you shouldn't have joined!'

Neither of them dared to laugh. Each in his own way knew he would be unable to stop.

CHAPTER EIGHT

YESTERDAY'S ENEMY

Marriott walked along the stone slipway and stared up at his command. It was so strange to see her out of the water after so long, her spartan hull scraped and dented and still dripping with weed.

Just a few days, Meikle had said. Somehow or other the naval party with the squads of Royal Engineers had managed to clear several of the slipways, a godsend to the many smaller vessels which were working all hours to open up the harbour.

In the meantime 801's company had been put aboard one of the newly arrived accommodation ships, a huge former steam-yacht which even dull pusser's paint could not disfigure. There had been more than a few moans from the messdeck. Most of the hands had hoped that the boat would be sent back to Felixstowe for a well-deserved overhaul. At least aboard the accommodation vessel they would be able to enjoy baths and showers, catch up with their dhobying and *jewing*, as the sailors called repair work on their uniforms.

163

Marriott saw the Chief talking with a plump official in a boiler suit, his instructions being translated by another former German petty officer. It was odd when you thought about it. None of the naval personnel who was working under the British was allowed to wear either his former rank markings or rates, and yet the divisions between them were as rigid as ever. Even the few German officers who were employed here seemed little different, despite bare patches where their stripes and Nazi eagles had once been worn.

It was easy to feel more like an intruder than the occupying power, he thought.

Adair saw him and saluted. 'Take a look at this, sir.' He pointed up with an oily finger at the port outer screw. It was badly scarred and buckled.

He added, 'I think it was when we were at Neustadt, sir. Must have hit some underwater wreckage.' He gestured to the plump man in the boiler suit. 'Klaus here thinks he can get it fixed. He's got a good machine-shop in the yard despite all the bomb damage.'

'I'll be guided by you, Chief.' Marriott glanced along the gunboat's boxlike hull. So it was *Klaus* already. So much for non-fraternisation. It was to be allowed only within the needs of duty, Meikle's little book had instructed. So in this case . . . He saw Adair hand a cigarette to the German, who bobbed his head and grinned before placing it carefully in a little tin and stowing it in his boiler suit.

The new currency, Marriott thought.

He heard Fairfax coming down the slipway and wondered how he saw his skipper now.

He thought of Neustadt. It had all been a waste

164

of time anyway. The sappers there had blown up the offending wreck without waiting for the navy's explosives. Somehow the wires had got crossed. Another cockup, as Cuff had put it.

Marriott had stayed there for two days awaiting orders, before returning to Kiel and this unexpected slipway. Neustadt had been unsettling. Groups of soldiers standing on the shoreline watching the sea, trying to identify the drifting wreckage and lolling corpses that were still coming ashore from the final days of the Russian offensive. As if it was some kind of gruesome contest. The town was ravaged, and he had noticed that, unlike Kiel, the British heavy artillery had not been stood down or reduced. Quite the reverse. He had seen the gunners busily throwing up new emplacements while German labourers carried out other defence work with concrete and steel supports.

The thing was that all the guns were pointing not inland but towards the Russian sector and the Baltic. A measure of trust—or the lack of it?

Passing a bombed church where only the tall pillared windows had remained, he had heard first classical overtures then strident jazz from the organ, and had discovered a rather scruffy gunner sitting amidst the fallen roof, oblivious to all but his music. They had shaken hands. The gunner had gone to school with Marriott. What a winding mixture of trails had brought them both together to these bizarre surroundings.

Fairfax said, 'I've got the lads all settled in, sir.' He stared at Adair, who was gesticulating, then laughing with his two Germans.

Marriott said quietly, 'I know. It takes some getting used to.'

He thought of the ML's final seconds, and then pictured some postman, probably like Ted at home, delivering the telegram to Duncan's family. A letter would follow from some senior officer who had probably never known the Devonian lieutenant, nor understood what had happened. Beri-Beri had been blaming himself, but evidence netted by the minesweepers had proved that the disaster had started as a fire in the engineroom, and not because of the explosives' instability.

He looked hard at the boat's four screws. So many miles, fast and slow, or momentarily stilled while they had drifted and listened for the approach of the enemy. The ML had been like this boat. Clapped-out.

On their return to Kiel Marriott had reported to Meikle, only to find him in the turmoil of changing his headquarters again, this time to the ex-luxury yacht.

He had spared him enough time to say, 'Nobody's fault, Marriott. You were lucky you didn't get alongside. I'd have had to replace *you* then!'

Leading Writer Lavender, more rabbit-like than ever, had looked up from the one remaining desk and had said, 'According to A.F.O.s, provided that any personnel killed on operations are lost *before* the end of hostilities with Japan, they will still be entitled to have their names listed on the relevant memorials.'

Meikle had snapped, 'I'm sure that will be a great relief to all concerned!' But his sarcasm had been totally lost on Lavender.

Fairfax was watching him. 'Ginger Jackson has shifted your gear to the accommodation vessel too, sir. It'll make a change to stretch our legs.' He stared past him and up at the slipway wall. 'What in heaven's name is *that*?'

That turned out to be a long-bonneted Mercedes-Benz open car. As Marriott's head rose above the slipway he wondered if there could be a larger car anywhere in the world. It had huge silver headlamps and sported a metal flag on either wing, on which the new paint only partly covered the SS emblem and swastika of its former owner.

A sad little man in field-grey sat behind the wheel and Beri-Beri lounged in the passenger seat beside him, making no effort to conceal his pleasure at their surprise.

They walked right round the car as Beri-Beri explained, 'The maintenance commander insisted I select a car from the pool. So . . .'

'*Maintenance commander? Pool?*' Marriott shook his head. 'One hell of a lot seems to have happened round here since we went away!'

Beri-Beri opened a door. 'Come for a drive, eh? First time you've been out of this place, apart from—' He dropped his eyes. 'But we don't talk about that, do we?'

'We don't.' Marriott looked at his watch. 'You can take me down to the new HQ if you like. After that—'

Beri-Beri tapped his nose and yawned. '*Temporary* HQ. Our boss has something rather grander in view, I'm told.'

Marriott looked at Fairfax and the handful of Germans who had arrived to begin work on the hull.

'Take over, Number One.'

Fairfax seemed to relax slightly. 'I've got the

167

weight, sir.'

He watched the huge car glide on to the dock road, the one which had been under thirty feet of fallen masonry and twisted girders when 801 had first tied up.

Beri-Beri said, 'Always wanted a bus like this. God, they certainly knew how to live!' He gestured to the driver. 'I'm not allowed to handle the thing. Some regulation they've dreamed up. So that if we run over some poor bastard the German driver will get the blame!' He nudged the man. 'That's right, eh, Fritz?'

The German with the melancholy face grinned and nodded. '*Ja*, Herr Leutnant! Pretty damn good!'

Beri-Beri smiled contentedly. 'It's about all he says.'

They halted at the foot of the accommodation ship's brow.

Marriott gazed at it as Beri-Beri murmured softly, 'There is some part of a foreign field etc., etc.'

The canvas sides of the brow had been painted white, as had a lifebuoy surmounted by a naval crown and the number of the Naval Party here. A proper sentry stood on the jetty, his chinstay down, his belt and gaiters as white as the lifebuoy, a bayonetted rifle in the at-ease position.

Marriott said, 'God, it's like Whale Island!'

As they approached, the sentry's eyes measured the distance, then he brought his heels together and raised his rifle to the slope. He slapped it in salute as they climbed the brow, the fresh blanco floating around him like smoke.

A writer, not Lavender, guided them to a newly

168

painted space between decks where telephones and clattering typewriters were already in full swing.

Beri-Beri said quickly, 'I'll wait on deck. Old Cuff's coming across shortly. Thought we'd take a spin, eh?' He winced when a tall figure in naval uniform, except that like the others it was bereft of rank markings, jumped to his feet and brought all the other occupants to instant attention.

As Beri-Beri closed the door thankfully behind him, Marriott faced the room's occupants with something like embarrassment.

'My name is Verner, Herr Leutnant. Herr Meikle will be here present shortly.' He waved one hand around his small domain. 'These are my staff.'

It was like hearing a British actor trying to play a Nazi officer in the ever-popular wartime films. Mr Verner was obviously very pleased with his job and himself. New masters maybe, but the same service security.

He realised with a start that there were several young women sitting at the rear of the room with files and piles of yellow cards. He tried not to let his gaze linger on one in particular. She was small and had hair like black silk piled at the nape of her neck, so that her ears were visible. Her uniform jacket, now with plain, civilian buttons, was like that of a British Wren.

She looked up and they stared at one another.

Verner caught the exchange and snapped, 'My clerks, Herr Leutnant, they are sorting out the, er, *Soldbuch*. Er—' He snapped his fingers, suddenly embarrassed because the translation had escaped him.

The girl said quietly, 'Paybook distribution, sir. For the workers here.'

She seemed to exclude the pompous Verner, and her voice, like her gaze, was directed only at Marriott. She continued in the same low tones, 'They receive pay according to their work, and the higher their level of employment so is the higher ration allowance.'

Marriott smiled. Her eyes were dark brown.

Verner nodded, both angry and relieved at the interruption.

'Thank you, Geghin—'

Marriott said, 'Yes, it's a help to know—' He felt clumsy and very stupid. Her English was excellent, with a slight accent he did not recognise. Perhaps it was local? The others were staring at him, and he thought he saw one of the girls nudge her companion.

The door opened and Meikle strode in. He nodded curtly, then rapped, 'I want a full report on that theft from Naval Stores, Verner. I don't have time to waste, unlike some!'

He glared around the room and Marriott expected to see resentment, even fear; he could guess what a loss of employment would mean in this crushed port.

But they continued with their work as before. It must be what they were used to, he thought.

Meikle seemed to see him for the first time. 'Boat slipped? Good. Make it as fast as you can. I may want you to visit the Russian sector. If somebody senior goes it will become *an event*. That I do not need!'

Verner bustled towards him with an open file. 'Tinned food, Herr Meikle. In the night. It is perhaps easy to enter and leave the docks in their present condition?'

Marriott thought of the boy the others had told him about. There were usually ways.

Meikle regarded the tall German coldly. 'For your information, the Military Government ordered the execution by firing-squad of two looters yesterday!'

Verner took a pace back. 'My Gott.'

Meikle added, 'They were Poles, displaced persons, and may have had cause for grudges against Germany. Well, you put it about, *Herr* Verner. It's the firing-squad, not a game of cricket. We can be tough too!'

He led Marriott from the room and said, 'Useful man, that Verner. If I want something to go round this command like the wind, I tell him to keep it secret. Never fails.' He turned, his head cocked as yet another telephone rang from one of the offices which had once been luxury cabins.

'Still fretting about that ML?' He studied him keenly. 'You're an odd fellow in some ways.'

'Is that all, sir?'

Meikle's guard fell across his eyes. 'For now. If you're going out with that lunatic Kidd, don't get yourself killed, OK? Not until I've found a replacement.' He shouted. 'I'm *coming*! can't be everywhere at once!'

Beri-Beri was waiting for him in the car, but with Cuff already seated beside the driver where his bulk was less noticeable.

'Hard time, Vere?'

Marriott looked at him. He could ask him anything. About the young girl he had just seen. And she *was* young, seventeen or eighteen at the most. He was being plain, damn stupid, even if fraternisation was allowed.

171

'No. Just the same as ever. I'll bet Hitler never realised there was Meikle waiting to take over from him!'

The car roared away in twin trails of hot dust and through the gates.

Cuff said cheerfully, 'I brought a couple of bottles along.'

Beri-Beri chuckled. 'Why, aren't *you* having any?'

Marriott joined in the laughter. Just the three of them.

At journey's end. Almost.

*　　*　　*

Acting-Petty Officer Townsend held his arm up to a bulkhead mirror and studied his reflection, then smiled approvingly. 'Nice job your tailor did, Ginger.' The crossed anchors and crown on his left sleeve were like keys to another world. The next real step.

Ginger Jackson grinned broadly and looked around their temporary quarters in the converted steam-yacht.

'This'll do me. Like the bleedin' *Mauritania*!'

Craven entered and waited to catch Ginger's eyes. Then together they walked out on to the perfectly scrubbed deck and leaned on the wooden guardrail. It was certainly not what they were used to.

Craven said uneasily, 'Jack Rae's ready for the shore, Ginger.' He glanced sideways at a painted rope barrier which separated the temporary accommodation from the HQ's section. There were a bored-looking sentry beyond it, and some German workers busy with pots of paint on the sleek

172

superstructure.

Ginger said, 'Makes a change not to 'ave some of us doin' that job! It's yer fruits o' victory, that is. Quite right and proper.' He watched the leading seaman and added, 'Wot's up? Cold feet, then?'

'I was just thinkin'. I don't want to end up in the brig. Not for a few bloody Kraut watches.'

'There'll be more than that, mate. You'll see.' Ginger considered the tins of coffee he had secreted in a locker, a few packets of cigarettes and some chocolate. It would do for starters, he thought.

Craven sighed. 'Well, let's get on with it.' They both stared at two young women in overalls, carrying mops and pails, and Craven added bitterly, 'No fratting either! I'll bet the officers do all right, just the same!'

Ginger chuckled. The battle was almost won. 'Sure they do. But don't give up 'ope.' He tugged down his skintight jumper and adjusted his cap. 'From what I 'ear all their young blokes are either in the bag in Russia, or still tryin' to get 'ome.' He picked a thread from his friend's sleeve. 'You didn't say nuthin' to our new PO, did you?'

'I'm not that simple, Ginger. 'E's one o' Them now.'

Ginger grinned. 'Right then. We'll meet my *whiter-than-white, never 'eard of 'itler* Nazi, and find a suitable place to barter.'

They walked along towards the ratings' gangway where an unknown sub-lieutenant was staring gloomily at the filthy water between the hull and the jetty.

In one of the offices below deck and just level with the brow, Petty Officer Evans paused and looked out of a scuttle as he heard their voices.

Craven and Jackson. Up to no good if he was any judge. He found it hard to accept that none of them was any longer his responsibility. He returned to some open files on the desk. Meikle had put him in the screening and security section. It might be a long search. But he had the rest of his life to do it if need be.

He peered at each photograph in turn, as if to stare the face into submission. It was the first file he had found which gave known details of the unsmiling photographs. Physical abnormalities, name, rank, serial number, allegiance to the party or not, where he had served, which unit; the work was painstaking and endless. Army and SS, security units and a few, a very few, known members of the Gestapo. It would be easy enough to slip into another man's identity, once you had the means to purchase it. It was said that many senior enemy officers who had not yet been captured had already fled to South America, even the United States.

His heart felt as if it had stopped. But the empty face in the photograph meant nothing to him. It was the wording of service details which stood out like letters of fire. *Served in the Channel Islands, Security division St Helier, Jersey.*

The face he longed to discover was not this one; he might not even still exist. But after leaving the Channel Islands he had been reported first in Copenhagen and then in Lübeck. Evans pounded his fist on the desk until he drew blood.

Lübeck was only about fifty miles from here. Furthermore, Kiel had been listed as a suitable place for vetting prisoners and suspects before sending them to transit camps and eventual release.

Evans felt trapped. *Release.* For what they had

174

done to his family they deserved far worse than death. But to find that one face would be a beginning.

Meanwhile, outside the main gates, Ginger Jackson and his two companions, smart and jaunty in their best uniforms and gold badges, paused to study their surroundings.

There were signposts everywhere. Some pointed to the various divisional or battalion headquarters, others directed you to individuals, like Town Major, or Provost Marshal, Hospital or NAAFI Canteen. There were boards which pointed to Lübeck and Hamburg, Eutin and Schleswig, with the distances carefully recorded. At the top of one post some wag had fixed a sign which announced sadly, *To Canada—3,000 Miles!*

A jeep containing several redcapped military policemen idled against the pavement, and a corporal called, 'Watch yer step, lads. Don't go into the Out-of-Bounds parts or you'll be in real trouble!'

Ginger had been used to dodging coppers in Kentish Town since he could walk, and asked innocently, 'Why's that, guv? Is that where the officers go?'

Surprisingly the redcaps laughed and roared away in a cloud of dust.

'Red light district, eh?' His eyes twinkled. 'That's where we make our meet with my new pal, as it 'appens!'

Craven fell into step with the others and said fiercely, 'Just my luck to get nabbed by the redcaps on my first run ashore!'

Ginger strode forward. 'Stop drippin'. 'Ere's our geezer!'

A tall, hollow-cheeked man in a shabby but well-pressed suit stepped from a doorway.

Rae and Craven hung back while Ginger conversed with him in low tones.

'This 'ere is Oskar. Used ter be with the 'amburg-Amerika Line, chief steward, so 'e speaks our lingo a treat. My tailor bloke arranged it.'

The man named Oskar gave a furtive bow. 'You bring the goods?'

Ginger held up one hand. 'Tch, tch, that don't sound like you trust us!'

Oskar tried to smile. His teeth were quite yellow. 'I am *sorry*, Herr Ginger. It is difficult.' He looked round as if expecting to see the police. 'But I trust *you* of course.'

'Good.' Ginger winked at his companions. 'Take us where we can talk, right? Maybe get a drink or two?'

The man considered it. He must have seen from the tight 'tiddley-suits' that they were certainly not carrying anything for bargaining.

'Come.' He stepped into an alley and pushed open a sagging gate. They followed him across some back-gardens, now covered with roof-slates and charred timber. Practically all the houses were completely gutted and open to the sky.

The three sailors trod carefully, almost daintily, to keep their best uniforms from scraping against the filth.

Rae muttered, 'I'd have dressed up if I'd known it was going to be this formal!'

Past another doorway where the inner rooms had been shored up with heavy timbers and corrugated iron, a few odds and ends of furniture pulled together to make a pretence of home.

176

A woman sidled into the doorway. She had bleached blonde hair, and wore so much make-up it looked as if it had been put on with a brush. She smiled at them and said, ''Ello! You want good fuck, Tommy?'

Oskar snarled something at her and she retreated into the building.

Craven exclaimed, 'Christ, I wouldn't screw her with *your* wedding-tackle, Ginger! She must be knocking sixty!'

Ginger glared. 'What'd you expect, a bleedin' nun?'

Rae pointed. *'Civilisation!'*

It was the last dwelling in the row and Oskar gave a half-bow by the door.

'My home. Please to enter.'

Craven slipped his hand inside his jumper to touch his seaman's double-bladed knife. Just in case.

But there was no need. A pleasant-faced woman in her thirties was sitting at a table, smiling gently and playing with a battered teddy-bear.

Oskar sat down and said bluntly, 'I will send word where we meet next. I take many risks. You must bring the goods next time!' He spoke openly at some length, eager to get it settled.

Ginger looked at the woman. 'Your wife?'

Oskar nodded, his eyes vacant. 'It is all correct to speak in front of her.'

Craven shifted uneasily. 'I'm not too sure about that, Ginger. If he's taking so many risks why does he let *her* stay?'

Oskar took his wife's hand and held it for a full minute.

Then he said, 'The bear belonged to our *kleine*

177

Kinder.' He watched her empty face as if he still expected to see the return of something. But nothing happened and Oskar held up a framed photograph of a small girl. The bear was in the picture too. He shrugged wearily. 'She waits for her to come home. But she died here when the bombs came down.'

Ginger stood up awkwardly and touched his shoulder. 'Never mind, Oskar old son, we'll take care of you. Just you give the word when you want the stuff.'

Oskar walked to the door and called, '*Ich komme später zurück!*' But only the bear moved.

He led the sailors back to the main road and then left them.

Craven groaned, 'Well, I guess it's the bloody NAAFI for us after all!'

Ginger said, 'Poor little bastard. Not fair when it's kids some'ow.'

Rae lit a cigarette. 'You'll have me in bloody tears, you will!'

Ginger brightened up. 'Still, when we get goin' proper we won't 'ave to see no one else but Oskar!'

But behind the good humour Ginger was feeling uneasy. Somehow dirty.

★   ★   ★

Directed by Beri-Beri's appalling German and the liberal use of a map from the Royal Marines, the great car finally nosed along a cobbled road, flanked by trees and open fields, with here and there the glitter of a peaceful lake.

It was beautiful countryside after the ravages of Kiel, and the sights they had passed along the way.

178

Ditches filled with upended vehicles of every kind. Half-tracks, their black crosses punctured by cannon fire or buckled like cardboard from attacking fighter bombers during the final rout. Cars and lorries, some equipped with their strange inflated gas-bags which had replaced petrol and diesel for all but the *Wehrmacht*.

Marriott could smell the endless litter of wrecks, left where they had been pushed by the tanks to keep the road clear. There were still probably corpses buried amongst the debris, as there were beneath the ruined houses, in the smashed submarines and the mud of the harbour.

Considering he had arrived in Germany only a matter of days ago, Beri-Beri was a mine of information. He had been driven to Kiel from Denmark right down the full length of Schleswig-Holstein. It sounded a far cry from the harbour. Hans Andersen-style farmhouses and sleepy villages, darkly beamed inns and cobbled squares.

Marriott asked, 'Where are we now?'

Beri-Beri said, 'There's apparently a big fuel dump just a mile up this road. It missed the bombing—too far out in the country, I expect. The RN's taken it over for all of our vehicles.' He patted the seat. 'Including *this* one!'

Eventually they came to a heavily sandbagged and barbed-wired enclosure. There were armed sailors on the gates, and a guardhouse with slitted windows just inside.

One sentry saluted and checked their identity cards as well as examining the blue disc on the windscreen. It all seemed casually thorough.

The car advanced through the gates where several

other khaki or camouflaged vehicles were waiting to be fuelled. German workers were employed for that, Marriott noticed, and because the petrol and diesel had to be pumped by hand it was taking a long time.

Beri-Beri said, 'Let's stretch our legs.'

'Can I help, gentlemen?'

They saw a stocky chief petty officer with the collar badges of the Supply Branch on his immaculate jacket, standing in the doorway of an office.

'Any tea going, Chief?'

'This way, sir.' The CPO added as an afterthought, 'My name's Hemmings, by the way, sir. I'm in charge here, at present anyway.'

The mention of tea made Cuff mutter, 'I'll wait by the car. I need something a bit stronger.' As he walked out he noticed a woman standing in another room across a corridor, her back towards him. She had strong hips, and her arms, which hung by her sides as if she knew he was watching her, were very tanned. Cuff liked what he saw and he stifled a chuckle as he strolled into the sunlight. Old Chief Hemmings must have his feet well under the table, unless she was one of the authorised staff here . . .

He saw their mournful little driver walking towards a large shed which had a protective canvas awning dangling over its entrance.

A man in overalls also saw the driver and waved his hands sharply.

'*Bitte gehen Sie weg! Eingang verboten!*'

The driver shrugged untidily and changed direction. Cuff smiled. Maybe the little sod was looking for a place to piss. Then he hoisted his belt over his belly and strode towards the canvas awning.

The same man tried to block his way but Cuff grinned and said dangerously, 'Fuck off, or I'll put you through that wall!'

In the office Marriott and Beri-Beri finished their tea.

'Thanks, Chief,' said Beri-Beri. 'See you around.'

'*Any* time, sir!'

Marriott glanced at him. It was quite cool in the roomy office but Hemmings was sweating badly. It was pretty obvious he was glad to see them leave.

Cuff was leaning against the car. 'All topped up. Ready when you are!'

They drove to the gates and then Cuff slapped his pockets and barked, 'Stop the car! I've left my cigarette case in the guard-hut!' They watched him stride back into the compound, his neck bulging over his collar as usual.

Cuff slammed heavily into the office and realised that the woman he had seen across the passage was here too. She faced him, her buttocks against a table, her hands resting on its edge as if waiting to spring at someone. She wore a white blouse tucked into a skirt tightly tied with a leather belt. She faced him with a mixture of curiosity and defiance.

'You're back, sir?' Hemmings was on his feet, several printed forms slipping from his fingers and on to the wooden floor.

Cuff said sharply, 'Yes, I'm back right enough. What did you expect?'

Hemmings blurted, 'I must protest, sir!'

'Do so, and it'll be your lot!' Cuff reached into the passageway and dragged a long sounding-rod into full view. He saw Hemmings go pale and knew he had hit the mark.

181

'There's over an inch sawn off this rod, Hemmings.' He did not wait for further protests. 'So, with all this fuel in your charge, every time a loaded tanker pulls in you sound each well with *this*, right? That'll give you one-and-a-half inches of diesel or petrol, all to yourself! And since every tank is about the size of a small bungalow I reckon you've got a nice little black-market business going here.'

'I have every right to a proper chance—'

'*Balls*! This is it! Your *only* bloody chance! If I choose, I can take you in right now.' Then he looked at the woman, at the way her full breasts were rising and falling under the blouse. 'As for you, madam, I'm afraid it will be even less pleasant, but a lot quicker, I'm told.'

He heard the Mercedes-Benz horn blare like a trumpet and scowled.

'I found some engines in that shed too. Look like army spares to me.' It was so easy he almost laughed. 'I'm not some half-hard little ponce from university—I'm one of the blokes who *won* this bloody war!' The horn sounded again and he said, 'I'll come back shortly. We can do business, *if* you behave yourself.'

He crossed the room and put his fingers under her chin.

'There's no time right now, but—' He let his hand fall until his fingers were between two of the buttons of her blouse. He could feel her skin pressing against them.

And the whole time she stared right back at him; she did not even flinch as he touched her.

'After all, Chief Hemmings, you know what they say? *Honi Soit Qui Mal Y Frat!*' He tugged the blouse very lightly then swung away, his blood pounding so loudly he barely heard what Hemmings was babbling about.

Beri-Beri greeted him indignantly. 'You took your bloody time, Cuff!'

Cuff climbed aboard, careful to avoid Marriott's searching glance.

'Doing my best to set an example. Just what Meikle told me to do.'

In the doorway, the CPO watched the car roll on to the cobbled road. Over his shoulder he said brokenly, '*You bitch!* I'll fix you!'

She released her grip on the table very slowly, her palms wet with sweat. A close thing.

She replied in careful English. 'I think not. Not any more, *ja?*'

Then she walked into the other room and stared at herself in a mirror. The British officer was big, ugly and probably violent. She touched her lips with her tongue. *But a man.*

CHAPTER NINE

OLD SCARS

This time the dream would not release him, nor would the stark pictures fade or lose their horror. *Nearer . . . Nearer . . .* Marriott fought free of the sheets and tried to struggle upright in the bunk, his mind cringing from the sights and the soundless screams.

He stared for several seconds at the unknown face which was peering down at him. Round and

183

youthful, with staring, frightened eyes.

The face exclaimed anxiously, 'Herr Leutnant! *Was ist los?*'

Marriott felt his heart losing its rapid beat as his reeling mind tried to return to normal.

The unknown face was that of a German steward, one of the many carried aboard the accommodation ship. He saw his white jacket, splashed now with coffee which he must have dropped to the deck outside when he had heard Marriott's voice as he had relived the nightmare.

Marriott reached out and tried to reassure him, and himself.

'It's all right.' He saw no understanding. '*Ich brauche*—' But nothing would come. He darted a quick glance at the other bunk and let out a gasp of relief. He was sharing the cabin with a lieutenant commander who was doing something or other on the N.O.I.C.'s staff. Marriott had gathered that the man, old for his temporary rank, had been a stockbroker before the war. Not that he had really needed to be told. In the cabin he spent most of his time studying the stock-market share reports in whatever newspaper he had managed to get from one of the RAF's flights from the UK.

The steward seemed to have accepted that he was not dangerous or mad and offered politely, 'I bring *Kaffee*, Herr Leutnant!'

Marriott groaned and rolled over on the bunk. His pyjamas and sheets were clinging to him like a shroud.

He struggled out and crossed to a scuttle, then dragged it open. Sunshine without warmth. He peered at his watch. It was only five in the morning. He ran his fingers through his hair and after a

184

momentary hesitation put his raincoat around his shoulders like a dressing-gown and stepped out on to the beautifully laid side-deck.

He leaned on the rail and stared across the devastated harbour. The only movement was a far-off police-launch, while the partly submerged wrecks, and those already dragged to the 'Hindenburg Graveyard' in the shallows, shimmered in the frail light as if they were no longer dead and useless.

Marriott rubbed his forehead. It was chilled with sweat. *How much longer?* He tried to jerk his mind from it, to think of all those lost times when rich, leisure-seeking Germans had stood at his rail. Probably at this hour of the day after a night of dancing and drinking. The women with their fine gowns and tanned shoulders, the music, and lights on the harbour.

A world which had gone for ever. And not just in Germany, he thought. He turned as the steward returned with the coffee-pot and cup, trying to conceal his surprise at Marriott's appearance. It seemed that German officers had been more conscious of their appearance before their subordinates.

'Thank you.' He saw the man watching the cup in his hand. It was just the usual coffee, which he had consumed in a thousand different situations, before and after an engagement, or in the club-like atmosphere of a shore-based wardroom. But to the Germans he had already realised it was something of a miracle. For years they had been forced to exist on *ersatz* substitute coffee which was allegedly made out of acorns. No wonder there were all the stories going around about a flourishing black market.

185

Marriott had heard that the stewards employed by the navy even saved the leavings in cups and pots to be hoarded and used again like some precious discovery.

Even the sailors' clothing aroused surprised glances, and one lieutenant had told Marriott that the Germans had at first suspected that 'my lads had been decked out specially in real woollen gear just to impress them'!

So how had the German war machine lasted this long? Fighting the Russians on one never-ending front, the Allies in France, or smashing through Italy, without proper oil supplies; no wonder everything was *ersatz*. Their old allies, the Italians, had soon changed sides once Sicily had been invaded, and the Japanese had never really been regarded as true comrades in arms.

And yet it could have so easily gone the other way. Marriott sipped the hot coffee and allowed his gaze to wander around the harbour. Even here it was evident. The Battle of the Atlantic had turned in the navy's favour after years of hitting back and losing thousands of tons of shipping every week. But despite the devastation to German dockyards as in Kiel, the U-Boats had kept on appearing in the Atlantic. They had achieved this by spreading all their ship construction and using prefabricated parts which had been made in remotely situated factories and then transported and assembled far away from the danger zones. There was a large team of submarine experts here right now, they said, and discoveries of an even newer class of U-Boat had caused a few awed glances.

Somewhere a bugle blared, and from a nearby minesweeper Marriott heard the trill of a boatswain's call over the tannoy.

Then the quartermaster's voice, pitiless and uncaring for those he was rousing from bunk and hammock.

'Wakey, wakey, rise an' shine! All hands, all hands, rise an' shine! Hands off cocks an' on socks!'

He smiled despite his tense nerves. What did the Germans make of that, he wondered?

He yawned and decided to have a bath before the watch-keeping officers formed a queue.

Inside the cabin again he stripped off his night clothes and stared at himself in a mirror. Then he saw a newspaper lying on the other officer's neatly made-up bunk and glanced at it casually.

He felt the hard pressure of a chair under his naked buttocks and found that his hands were shaking. It was yesterday's paper. That meant that today's date . . .

The cabin seemed to swim round in a wild dance, objects merging together, so that when the steward clattered the coffee-pot and tray together beyond the door he felt like calling out, even as a last spark of sanity told him it was useless.

Today was the day. Exactly one year ago.

In his mind's eye he could see it all so clearly. A dawn like this one, the sunlight misty with smoke, not from underground fires and the sappers' clearance of rubble, but from guns. Guns from the sea, from over the horizon and beyond it. Barges spitting out thousands of rockets, hurling tons of high-explosives on to the Normandy coastline. The houses nearest to the coast were all ablaze, the shallows full of beached landing-craft, or those wrecked in the first attack. The troops were somewhere inland, the tanks swallowed up beyond

187

the fires, leaving only the knocked-out ones as evidence of their contested advance. Others lay half-submerged where they had fallen from shelled landing-craft, their crews trapped inside.

And yet despite the din and the casualties, the sight of ships being straddled and apparently destroyed, then emerging through the spray and smoke, their guns high-angled and shooting inland to cover the advancing armies, there was an unspoken feeling that given time and luck they would eventually win a total victory.

The waiting and the foul-ups were behind them. The impossible reality that they had succeeded in taking all their beach-heads at the first attempt had got home to them. Thousands of vessels great and tiny, millions of men with all the weapons and transport to support them had been got ashore. The rest was up to the generals and the air marshals. Marriott's boat had been working offshore near Arromanches, liaising between the British on Gold Beach and the Canadian Third Division at Juno.

To this day Marriott was unsure what exactly had happened after the collision. The tide had been on the ebb, and the first bombardment of the day had made all thought almost impossible. *Or perhaps I won't let myself think about it.* The bridge of the MGB had been packed, for apart from the usual team they had been carrying five Canadian officers, who had been planning where they would build fresh supports for the tank reinforcements which were expected the next day. A very early breakfast before things *hotted up*, as the coxswain had put it. The usual passing round of cigarettes and tobacco pouches, nervous grins, waves to some of their consorts as they rode above their sleek silhouettes

188

on the oily water, thoroughbreds amongst the flotsam of war.

Beri-Beri's had been the nearest boat when Tim had yelled that there was an obstruction in the water. A huge anti-tank device, missed or ignored by the frogmen who had worked even before the landings to destroy them.

'Wouldn't get me doing that job!' someone had said. 'Posthumous VC if all goes well—Jerry firing-squad if it doesn't!'

Marriott had felt it immediately and had used the contesting power of his screws to fight clear of the hidden iron girders.

He was on his feet now, oblivious to his shivering nakedness. '*We must get her off*!' He spoke aloud, as he had on that day a year ago. 'Number One, prepare an anchor and the boat lowering-party. We'll kedge her free before it's too late!'

But it was too late already.

An abbreviated whistle, then a violent bang, salt water cascading all around, soaking, ice-cold, tasting of cordite.

Beri-Beri's boat had come about and was standing bows-on, increasing speed, while an armed trawler was also steering towards them.

Tim had called, 'She's hard and fast, sir!'

Marriott remembered running along the after deck so that he could see the jagged tank-trap shimmering just below the surface, like a creature from a horror film.

In no time at all it would be impossible to free her. The sea was dropping lower every minute.

In his mind he could still hear a loud-hailer across the water. '*Bale out!* The bastard's got you zeroed-in!'

189

One more try. Spoken or thought, he did not know. There was just a chance at full power to rip her free. It would mean a dockyard job but—

It had all stopped right there.

He had jammed one foot on the bridge ladder when a shell had hit it on the opposite side. Shaking like a drunk he had dragged himself up the rest of the way and had felt his stomach collapse at the sight. The bridge was already ablaze, signal flares and belts of machine-gun ammunition joining in a shattering chorus over and amongst the corpses. *Corpses?* They had not been even that. Bloodied rags and gruel, burning clothing, blue and khaki, and something which still clung to life, which was screaming, and continued to scream for an eternity after the flames had engulfed him. No arms, his face gone, it could have been any one of them.

The next shell had hit the hull directly abeam. Even now Marriott still believed he had seen it ripping across the water towards him. Witnesses had agreed it was a flat-trajectory shell, the sort mounted on or used against heavily armoured tanks.

Marriott could not recall hearing anything. Or perhaps there had been no more to hear. The fire had burst up from the engineroom and he had seen vague figures running about the deck or vanishing over the side, burning like human torches.

She had gone down quickly, her bows dipping and spurting out compressed steam from the fires between decks even as Marriott had found his first lieutenant pinned under the derrick used for hoisting ammunition and loading stores. The steel had been raw in the sunny haze, cut clean in two by the shell as it had exploded.

190

They had lain with their faces pressed together while the flames had spurted along the deck towards them.

Tim Elliott, his first lieutenant and friend since they had commissioned the boat together.

Marriott had been unable to believe it. How could it be? He must have pleaded, shouted his name a hundred times, unable to accept that the eyes were without understanding. That there was barely anything left of him below the waist.

Two seamen had dragged him to the side and together they had fallen into the sea. The rest were blurred incidents. A last, dull explosion, then groping hands, dragging at his burned skin and torn clothing, the feel of a boat backing and thrashing away from flaming fragments.

Then Beri-Beri's face as close as his had been to Tim's.

'*Let it go! Don't fight it!*' He had tried to cover him with somebody's duffel coat, as he had when the ML had brewed up just nights ago.

Marriott gripped the side of the bunk and tried to control his shivering limbs.

The door opened and the elderly two-and-a-half ringer stepped quietly over the coaming.

He saw Marriott and gave a startled gasp. 'Sorry, chum, did I disturb you? I was at an all-night poker party in the Guards' mess.'

Marriott stared at him. Ashamed and yet grateful to the ex-stockbroker who had saved his reason just as surely as Beri-Beri had once done.

'It's all right, sir. Couldn't sleep.'

The other man sat down. He did not seem to notice Marriott's nakedness. But he had already seen the livid scars of the phosphorus burns on his wrists and legs and shoulder. The rest he could guess.

'It'll take time.'

Marriott stared at the deck. 'I expect so.' He gripped his hands together as tightly as he could. *Otherwise I shall break down.* Like that time in Iceland when he was 'getting over it', as the MO had called it. He had burst into tears and hadn't stopped crying for a week. Just like that. Bomb-happy, round the bend, over the hill. The things he had often said about others.

'Care for a quick snort?' The officer pulled a silver flask from his coat. 'Vodka, I'm afraid. Got it off the Russian liaison chap.'

Marriott took it and let the raw spirit flow over his tongue. *Getting like Cuff.* 'Thanks, sir.' He could feel his stomach protesting and his eyes watering. 'Just the job!'

They smiled at one another like conspirators, then the lieutenant commander handed him his old dressing-gown.

'Have a bath. You'll feel more like it, eh?'

The ex-stockbroker waited for the door to close. He had had one shore job after another. Too old for sea duty, they had insisted. But he had met others like this young lieutenant. Gone to the limit and past it just once too often. *It takes time.* He opened a drawer and took out the framed photograph of his wife. She had been killed in an air-raid four years ago.

He thought of Marriott's sensitive, strained features.

'And *I'm* not over it yet, my dear,' he whispered.

★   ★   ★

Marriott's old seaboots scraped across rusty sheets of steel left by the sappers, and then thudded on some of the original cobbles. A bright and surprisingly cold morning. He glanced up at the now-familiar silhouettes of hanging girders and gutted buildings and wondered if it was just his imagination, or if it was really getting cleared away.

Overalled figures moved amongst the dust, while across the water from the most obstructive wrecks he could see the diamond-bright gleam of acetylene cutters as the work continued without a break. They had been at it all night, every night and round the clock.

He saw the delicate mastheads of the HQ ship above some temporary huts and quickened his pace.

MGB 801 was in the water again, her small company, for better or worse, back in their proper surroundings.

In so short a reprieve they had not been able to manage very much, and even the usually optimistic Adair had shaken his head a few times.

'Too much underwater damage, sir. These damned diagonal-built hulls are no match for the work they're supposed to do.'

Marriott shivered again. It was six in the morning. Why did the navy always begin things so early?

He thought of his orders. Two oil-tankers were to be handed over to the Russians. The MGB would act as their escorts and then take off the German crews after the Russians had 'signed for them' as Meikle had dryly put it.

He had already spoken with Fairfax. It would be his job to deal with the extra passengers. Back in

193

the gunboat once again, and yet the sudden contact seemed to have made him withdraw into himself. He knew he was feeling the effects of drinking too much, brooding, waiting for the night to come with its fears and its brutal pictures. Perhaps once he was back at sea again . . . ?

He returned the gangway sentry's salute and strode up the brow. Two seamen in white gaiters were gathering the mail into their bags. *Letters home*. The same everywhere, Marriott thought, now that the fighting was over. Maybe you got a wrong impression from the newspapers after the wild excitement of victory. The headlines blared the pros and cons of the fast-approaching general election, and much of the other news was preoccupied with the latest round of industrial strikes. It was amazing and sickening.

The war in the Far East only found a place on page two usually. Bombardments of Japanese islands, air strikes on the mainland, but all so vague it was hard to tell how much longer it might take. The Japanese had resisted every seaborne attack on the Pacific Islands and the battles to retake them had been savage and relentless. The Japanese had never found any honour in surrender and would likely fight all the harder when their homeland was under attack. It might still be a long campaign.

One of the 'postmen' looked up and saluted casually. 'Anythin' still to go, sir?'

Marriott smiled. He had stil not written to Penny. 'No. Not this time.'

Inside the makeshift operations room it was unusually deserted. A young sub-lieutenant scrambled from his desk and said breathlessly, 'I'm Gilmour, sir.'

194

Marriott shook his hand. God, he looked younger even than Lowes. Straight out of *King Alfred*, if he was any judge.

Gilmour added, 'Lucky to be here, sir. Got in from Cuxhaven yesterday. They only let me come because I speak German.' He blushed and looked about fifteen. '*Some* German.'

Marriott smiled. 'That's the idea. Don't tell *anyone* in this regiment the whole truth!'

He walked to the table and leafed through the Met reports. He had not been mistaken. It *was* cold for this time of the year. He smiled to himself. Not gin, the Wardroom Devil, after all.

He glanced at the other long table where the girls had been sitting. They probably came aboard later on.

The young subbie was watching him all the time. He could feel it with his back turned.

'Where's Lieutenant Glazebrook, Sub? He's in charge of this escort.'

'Oh—' Gilmour flushed again. 'I—I'm sorry, sir. I was to tell you. Lieutenant Glazebrook's boat has had some engine trouble.' He groped around for an envelope. 'You are to take over, sir.'

Marriott frowned and slit open the envelope. Brief, curt, no more than the bones of an explanation. The navy's way. So Cuff was staying in Kiel. One of the MLs was being sent instead as back-up.

'Very well. He'll be sorry to miss it.' But in his mind he believed otherwise. You never really knew with Cuff.

Gilmour said, 'I—I wish I was coming with you, sir.'

Marriott looked at him. *You're upset because*

you've missed the war.

'Perhaps another time. I'll see if I can fix it.' He thought, *sooner than you think if Lowes goes mooning around like a dying duck as he is at present.*

'Where is everyone?'

The subbie brightened up. 'Commander Meikle has gone to Plön, sir. He'll be moving there once the Royal Marine Engineers have finished clearing up.'

Somewhere a telephone rang, while on the nearby jetty a giant saw split the air apart as it began to bite through useless lengths of charred timber.

The subbie said, 'I'll fetch the duty operations officer, sir. He said to call him before—'

He broke off as three girls filed through the other door and seated themselves by their files and telephones.

Marriott barely heard what Gilmour had said. The girl looked exactly as he had remembered her. But in the hard sunlight through the scuttle above the table he could see the shadows under her eyes, the tired way her hands moved to unfasten the waiting piles of files.

'Do you always start as early as this?'

She looked up at him as if she had not seen him before.

'Yes, Herr Leutnant. There is much to do.' She watched him steadily. 'You are leaving today, sir?'

He felt the others watching him even though their fingers were sorting through their work.

'Yes.' It was like trying to speak in a crowded restaurant. He could hear more voices and somebody sneezing. The Ops officer and the childlike Gilmour would be here soon, and no doubt the imposing Verner too.

196

He said, 'It will take a few days.' He glanced at the clock and imagined he could hear the muffled roar of 801's engines. The ML would come in handy. Without her, there would not be much room for the German crews. When he looked at her again she was busy with a file, while with her free hand she picked up a telephone and spoke quickly into it, first in German then in English.

The Ops officer strode in, a pipe jutting from his jaw.

'Morning, Marriott. Nice day for a cruise, what?'

He gestured to the nearest girl. 'Get my tobacco pouch, will you?'

As she hurried away he added, 'The whole pouch would go walkabout if I left it for long!'

Gilmour picked up another telephone before it had rung twice.

'For you, sir.'

The Ops officer snatched it. 'Yes? *Golf?* Where did you find the place?'

Marriott turned back to the table.

'Do you live around here?'

She glanced up at him, her face suddenly close.

She said in a whisper, '*Please*, Herr Leutnant. Do not ask these things!' She darted a glance over his shoulder. 'It is not *good* for me.'

Marriott wanted suddenly to grip her hand, to explain that it was not like that.

And then he thought suddenly of Penny. How he would have felt if things had gone against them. What he might have thought if he had seen her being chatted up by a German officer.

It was like a blow in the face, and he felt ashamed.

'I am *sorry*, Fräulein. I did not mean to—' He

197

swung away to hide his confusion.

The Ops officer was puffing smoke and discussing a newly discovered location where he could play golf.

'I'm off then.' Marriott picked up his folder of instructions, the one which should have been Cuff's, and walked to the door.

Gilmour called, 'You won't forget about the—' But the door slid shut.

The Ops officer put down the telephone, then tapped his pipe into a brass shell-case by the desk. It was all there. Poor little bugger.

Gilmour said, 'Do you know him, sir?'

His superior thought about it as he refilled his pipe with great care.

'Vere Marriott. Yes, I sort of know him. *Of* him anyway.' His voice was faraway, the pipe momentarily forgotten.

'A very gallant young bloke. Lost his command shortly after the landings in Normandy. Just three survivors. I think he blames himself for being one of them.' He jabbed the pipestem at the young subbie. 'He's what they call a hero. But take a good look, sonny, and you'll see past the gongs to what it's cost *him!*'

Neither of them saw the girl by the scuttle until the pencil she had been holding snapped apart in her hands.

★　　★　　★

The fuel dump looked innocent enough in the fading light as Lieutenant Cuff Glazebrook steered his borrowed jeep noisily through the gates in the barbed-wire barrier. Apart from a sentry there

198

seemed to be nobody about, so without more ado Cuff walked heavily into the office. Like the pumps and tanks in the yard the office was brightly lit.

A Leading Supply Assistant, always known as *Jack Dusty* in the navy, got hurriedly to his feet, a tattered magazine with a nude on its cover falling behind him.

Cuff grunted. 'On your own?'

The youth nodded. 'I'm afraid I can't issue petrol or diesel, sir. It's the rule. After sunset we—'

Cuff interrrupted. 'It's Chief Petty Officer Hemmings I want.'

The leading hand relaxed. 'He's not here, sir. Gone to Hamburg for something.'

Cuff nodded. He already knew about Hamburg, but it seemed prudent to check.

He gestured through the door towards the other buildings. 'When I was here a few days back I met the woman—'

'Yessir. That's Frau Ritter. She still lives in part of the building. The rest was commandeered for the staff.'

Cuff waited, frowning, knowing he would get more out of this dimwit.

'She and her husband used to have a garage and farm supply business here, sir. That's why the German army built their dump on the same site.'

'What happened to *Mister* Ritter, eh?'

The Jack Dusty shrugged. 'Not sure, sir.'

Cuff wandered from the office and adjusted his eyes to the enclosing shadows. *A nice little set-up.*

He saw the sudden gleam of light from an upstairs room, then her silhouette as she peered down at him.

'What do you want?' Somewhere a dozing sentry

199

coughed in the shadows and she added quickly, 'You had better come in.'

She spoke good English. *Just as well.*

He closed the door behind him and waited for her to come downstairs. For a long while they faced each other across the room. It was an untidy place, Cuff thought, with most of the personal furniture and ornaments all crammed into this one room.

She said, 'He's not here.'

He watched her, made himself stay calm, outwardly at least as he took her in. Her full breasts were barely restrained by her shirt, but she met his stare without flinching.

Cuff said, 'I know. Hamburg. That's why I came. But you already know that, Frau Ritter.' He saw her hand move to the front of her shirt and asked, 'Where's the nice blouse?'

She looked surprised, suddenly off-balance because he had remembered.

'It is the only one I have.'

Cuff could feel the blood pounding through his skull, his collar half-choking him.

Then he strode across the carpet and gripped her wrist. 'I've thought a lot about you.' He seized the shirt and dragged at it.

With surprising strength she pulled herself away. 'Not here. Someone might come—'

Cuff said thickly, '*I* will in a minute!'

He followed her up some stairs and found himself in her room. A sloping ceiling, chintz curtains, pine furniture, and a large bed. Cuff took off his jacket and tossed it on a chair. He pulled her against him, expecting her to threaten, even to call out. Then he began to unbutton her shirt and when one button caught he tore it open, and all the time he pinioned

200

her with his other arm, pressing her into his body so that she should feel him and his need of her.

She did not move as he struggled with her belt, then laid her shoulders bare in the lamplight, murmuring into her neck while he continued to strip her.

He pushed her on to the bed and stood away while he feasted his eyes on her naked body, her firm thighs, exactly as he had known they would be.

He managed to gasp, 'Don't fight me—' He hesitated. 'What's your name?'

She lay back and watched him tearing at his clothes. 'Hertha.'

Just the one word and then he was on her.

There was no resistance, quite the opposite; and Cuff was dazed, stunned by the animal frenzy they seemed to release in one another.

She felt his big hands thrusting beneath her, lifting her still further until he gave a groan and fell astride her like a cut-down tree.

Cuff had never experienced anyone like her. No matter what he did, she could find something else to inflame him to a kind of madness. If he lay helpless on his back she could still find the skill to rouse him yet again and he pleaded, *'For Christ's sake! I'm shagged out! Just give me time—'* But she did not.

When at last he lay in an exhausted sleep she leaned over him and ran her fingers over his great belly.

She had seen the look on his face when he had come to take her. He had wanted her so badly; and afterwards he would have left.

All that had changed. She continued to stroke him so that he groaned in his sleep. Now he *needed* her, and she knew he would not be able to stay away.

She raised herself on one elbow and stared at her reflection in the mirror. She could see the reddened marks, probably bruises on her fine breasts where he had held her and fought with her.

Perhaps tomorrow might be different. But in Germany now, you lived one day at a time.

CHAPTER TEN

VODKA DIPLOMACY

Marriott slid from his chair as Lowes's shadowy figure appeared on the bridge, and other shapes groped their way to their stations for the Middle Watch.

'She's all yours, Sub. Cape Arcona is about three miles to starboard, course due East and revs for ten knots.' He tried to keep his voice matter-of-fact, informal, but even in the darkness he could sense Lowes's pouting resentment.

The reports came in as usual.

'Lookouts closed up, sir!'

'Leading Seaman Rae relieving the wheel, sir!'

But no guns, not this time.

He added, 'Call me in an hour when it's time to alter course. I'm going to have some coffee and a smoke.'

He glanced at the green glow of their starboard light and following astern he saw the pattern of navigation and masthead lights which revealed the two oil-tankers, while in the far distance he could just make out those of their attendant ML.

It had been a better day than he had expected, after the first delays while the two tankers had been marshalled into formation for their passage to Swinemünde in the Russian sector. After being 'tidied-up' in Flensburg for their transfer to Russian control they had finally made the rendezvous off Kiel Bay. More delays while an armed escort had been taken off by tug, and naval boarding-parties put aboard to replace them. Fairfax was back there now in the leading tanker with a handful of armed ratings. Any form of trouble was unlikely, but no German wanted to go inside the Russian sector even under the White Ensign.

The ML's first lieutenant had a similar task on the sternmost ship. In the unlikely event of an attempt to sabotage the ships, the bridge and engineroom of each had to be watched at all times. Fairfax would be remembering the ill-fated *Ronsis*, and would need little prompting.

The incident with Lowes had happened on the bridge in the final moments of the last dog-watch. Up until then the visibility had been fairly clear, but as dusk had closed in there had been typical Baltic mist. Marriott had been down in the chart-room making additional calculations with the aid of some pilotage information the Russians had sent to Kiel to further the interests of safe navigation and the movement of coastal shipping, escorted or otherwise.

He had been thinking of the girl in the operations room. If she had struck him he could not have felt worse. He should have known. Vaguely above the thuds and groans of shipboard sounds he had heard muffled voices on the bridge, hushed and yet urgent.

Marriott had climbed up the ladder to see a powerful-looking freighter crossing the bows from starboard to port, her bridge well lit-up with cargo lamps, and her side clearly revealing a bright Swedish flag painted on the hull.

There had been no immediate danger, but a few more minutes might have made all the difference. Marriott had taken over the con and had altered course even as Silver had clattered off a signal to the ships astern to follow their example.

All the while Lowes had stood staring at him, his fists clenched, his face screwed up as if he was about to burst into tears.

Once on course again with the Swedish ship well clear after giving an admonishing screech on her siren, Marriott had taken Lowes down to the chart-room. Craven had been on the wheel and he suspected he had been the one to urge Lowes to take some sort of action.

He could hear his own anger now as he had exclaimed, 'What the *hell* is the matter with you? Didn't they teach you even the basic rules at *King Alfred*, or were you too busy worrying about getting into the *fun* before it all ended?' He had seen Lowes wilt and had known it had not been all his fault. He had been thinking of the girl with the brown eyes, her rebuff—or was it disgust?

'There *is* the old simple rule, y'know! If to starboard red appear, it is your duty to keep clear—remember that?'

Lowes had nodded, too wretched even to reply.

'If you still want to be a good officer it means more than a pretty uniform and being addressed as *sir, right?*'

Marriott looked at the sky. Very small stars beyond some mist and low cloud.

He said quietly, 'If you are in some kind of trouble, John, tell me about it, eh? I may be able to help. It goes with the job, you know.'

He saw Lowes staring at him through the darkness, either surprised at the use of his first name after he had given him such a bottling, or perhaps imagining he knew already what the real trouble was.

Lowes mumbled, 'It's nothing, sir. I—I can manage.'

'I'm glad to know that.'

Marriott lowered himself to the wardroom and saw his passenger sitting comfortably in one corner, a glass at his elbow while he read another copy of *The Times* which he had found at Flensburg.

So that was why his cabin companion in the HQ ship had been absent since that morning when Marriott had awakened in a rash of terror. Lieutenant Commander Arthur Durham, who did 'something-or-other' on the N.O.I.C.'s staff, was in fact attached to the ships disposal section, and had chosen to travel in the MGB rather than the arguably more comfortable quarters in one of the tankers.

Or was it really that Meikle had warned him that he might create another *incident* with the Russians, which his presence aboard would prevent? They had not had much chance to speak. Durham had been studying his documents, which he would have to give to the Russians, and Marriott had been too busy working watch-and-watch with Lowes.

'All quiet up there?'

'For the moment, sir.' He tossed his cap and

205

duffel coat into a chair. Durham had probably heard about the trouble with Lowes. There were few secrets and no privacy in an MGB.

Ginger Jackson peered in. 'Coffee, sir?'

'Please.' He asked, 'Why haven't you turned in, Ginger?'

The messman grinned. 'Doin' me accounts, sir. 'Sides, 'oo else would look arter you?'

He hurried out, whistling softly to himself, and Durham said, 'Bloody priceless, that one. I reckon he *could* look after you too!'

Marriott glanced away as a cloud crossed the man's face. He had heard about Durham losing his wife. There did not seem to be anyone who had not lost somebody like a relative or close friend.

'What is expected of us in Swinemünde, sir?'

Durham removed his horn-rimmed reading glasses and snapped them shut. 'This whole business is like a giant jumble-sale. The Russians agree on which vessels they want through the dispersal agreement, then after they get them they start to complain that we're trying to cheat them. It's been like that all the way from Cuxhaven. They may be brave chaps and strong allies but they give me a pain somewhere!' He grinned. 'Their diplomacy is vodka, so watch yourself.'

'Well, we're just passing Cape Arcona, sir. In a while I shall alter course to the south, a straight passage all the way to Swinemünde. Should anchor around 0900 with any luck. You ought to turn in while you can.' He had made Durham as comfortable as he could in his own tiny cabin. But, like himself, he seemed unable to sleep.

Durham watched as Ginger reappeared with some fresh coffee and two mugs.

206

'It will be strange to get back to my old job.' His eyes were distant. 'Upon the eight-ten every morning, back on the six-twenty-five. The City with a capital C, the old chop-house or the *Wig and Pen* for a deep discussion and too many gins while we rebuild the stock markets!' He looked at Marriott. 'What about you? You're too young to have done much before the balloon went up.'

And probably too old to settle to anything afterwards. Marriott said, 'Be like my pal Beri-Beri. Take off to some quiet place away from the sea and go fishing!'

Durham smiled, but he did not press further. 'He sounds an interesting chap.'

'My Number One wants to stay in.'

Durham nodded. 'Could do worse. There'll be too many chaps looking for too few jobs when they finally get demobbed, I'm afraid.' He tapped the newspaper. 'The election, for instance. My guess is that the service vote will change things completely. If I was a betting man, and I know people insist that you must be one to play the stock market, then I'd say Labour will oust this government. A Socialist Shangri-La with equal shares for everyone!'

Marriott had not thought very deeply about it. But now the idea that anyone would vote Churchill out of office seemed incredible.

Durham had read his thoughts. 'Churchill won this war, even the Americans realise that. But run the country, now that it's all but over? I'm not so sure. Remember, it's a government they will be voting for, not a single personality. I've been looking at your young sailors. I can't see them lining up for the dole and selling their medals like their fathers had to do after the Great War. It's not in their nature. And why should it be, after what they've had to do?'

Marriott smiled. 'Anyway, I think they might have waited until we've seen off the Japs!'

Durham sipped his drink and said, 'That's what troubles me. It doesn't fit the pattern. It's as if somebody *knows* something. Like one company buying shares in another without letting it out to the public.'

Marriott glanced at the bulkhead clock. Almost time to go up and change course. It had gone quickly and he had not noticed it. That was rare these days.

Durham asked, 'Have you got anyone special waiting for you?'

Mariott stood up and thrust his hands into his pockets. Unlike Durham, he did not even have anyone to miss.

'Not really, sir.'

'I knew about your brother. Bad show all round.'

'Yes. I always looked up to him.'

Durham watched his changing emotions and wished they had had a son like him.

'You'll find somebody. Then she'll be able to look up to you.'

Marriott pulled on his stained duffel coat and wondered what Durham, nice as he was, would say if he told him about the German girl at HQ.

It is not good for me. Her words would not fade. What did she mean? That she would lose her job if they found out about her breaking the non-frat regulations? Or was it simply that beneath it all she nursed a deep hatred for the victors? Another thought probed through his mind. Maybe she had

208

somebody else, right there at HQ, another British sailor?

'I'm off then, sir. Breakfast will be early. I want the hands in the rig of the day when we meet the Russians.' He forced a grin. 'Especially now that I know England's about to go over to Karl Marx!'

Durham lay back against the battered cushions and refilled his glass from his own private bottle. It had started off as a Horse's Neck but was now almost neat brandy.

He wondered about the girl Marriott had carefully not mentioned. Just what he needed. To look forward to. To share. He glanced at his watch and swore quietly. It had stopped.

Ginger Jackson cleared away the coffee mugs and asked casually, 'Broken, 'as it, sir?'

'No, it's getting a bit rusty. Like its owner.'

Ginger thought of the little pile of loot which was gathering through their contact with the sad-faced Oskar. Ten fine watches and two Leica cameras, and some jewellery which might be welcome in any pawnbroker's or, equally, bloody useless.

He said, 'I think I knows where I could lay 'ands on a good 'un, sir.'

'Really?' Their eyes met and understood one another. 'I'll think about it.'

'I'd make sure you wasn't done, sir.'

Durham smiled. 'You'd better make certain *you* don't get done, my lad!'

Ginger sauntered away. Tomorrow or the next day and they would do business. After all, the two-and-a-half would be used to dealing on the side in his old job.

On the bridge Marriott consulted the charts once more, then said, 'Stand by to alter course, Sub. We shall steer South-Twenty-East.'

'Aye, aye, sir.' The response was as before. *Still sulking*.

'You ready, Bunts?'

He could hear the smile in Silver's reply. 'Ready-aye-ready, sir!'

'Make to convoy and escort. *Alter course in succession!*'

He leaned against the compass and saw the six-pounder shining in the reflected glare of the lights. It was still uncanny to see the gun unmanned, and covered with its canvas hood.

'All acknowledged, sir!'

Marriott straightened his back. *Forget it. It's over, finished*.

'Starboard fifteen—steady—Steer South-Twenty-East.'

'Steady on South-Twenty-East, sir.'

Marriott crossed the bridge to watch the navigation lights astern. Little triangles of white, green and red. Follow my leader.

'Got her, Sub?'

'Yes, sir.'

'Call if you need—' He did not finish it but lowered himself into the oily warmth of the companion ladder.

The wardroom was empty. Marriott saw Durham's empty glass sliding and rattling this way and that inside the fiddles to the boat's slow roll.

Just one Horse's Neck. Or a strong brandy with a cup of black coffee. He thought of his mother as he threw himself down and covered his face with the duffel coat.

That would be all she needed. A court martial in the family.

What would the neighbours say?

When Jackson entered to switch off the deckhead lights he paused and looked at Marriott's sprawled figure.

It would be strange if he ever went back to general service in some battlewagon or cruiser where the officers were always at a distance. Here you could see them as people, human beings.

He grinned as he turned off the lights and thought about the watch he would offer to Durham. Well, *almost* human.

★　　　★　　　★

Marriott paused on the big floating pontoon and watched as his men made final adjustments to the mooring lines. It was a strange feeling. Still part of Germany, the Third Reich as it had been for so long, and yet because of the Russian presence it seemed so completely different. *Foreign*. He smiled at his choice of description.

It was surprisingly warm, even humid, with a noon sun high overhead in a sky empty of cloud.

He saw Lowes salute as Lieutenant Commander Durham and the Russian officer who had boarded the MGB from a fast launch stepped down on to the pontoon. Far beyond them the two oil-tankers lay at anchor, high in the water with only ballast aboard for the journey. The ML was tied alongside one of them and all were hemmed in by busy launches as the passage crews were taken aboard for transfer to the naval vessels, and Russian sailors sent out to replace them.

He had told Lowes to keep an eye on everything, had rammed each point home until he had seen his

211

youthful face stiffen still further like a fractious child's. He knew he was being unfair but he had given the same instructions to Townsend and Adair. This was not Chatham or Felixstowe; to all intents it was Russia.

Durham was in deep conversation with the Russian, a scholarly-looking lieutenant named Butuzov. Marriott had heard Ginger Jackson already refer to him as *Boots-off*.

They had been at it all morning, visiting the two tankers, making notes, while the obliging Butuzov had translated all the demands and complaints. It was much as Durham had predicted.

Durham said, 'We're going to meet the top man.' He gave a brief wink. 'All downhill from now on.' But his eyes suggested differently.

The Russian attack on the port area had been overwhelming. It had taken place within sight of the war's end, and with the German divisions in full retreat or surrounded with no ammunition or tanks left to fight with. It must have been like hell, he thought. Great areas of houses and shops scorched away by rocket-fire, *Stalin-organs* and then flamethrowers as the last fanatical defenders had been harried and defeated in a street-to-street, room-to-room carnage.

Lying alongside a crumbling jetty was a Russian destroyer. She was one of the old *Woikow* class, which like the British V & Ws had been launched in the closing months of the Great War. She was heavily armed, and seamen with machine-pistols guarded each brow and both ends of the jetty. Her three funnels gave her a quaint old-world look, but there was nothing ancient about her guns and torpedo tubes.

212

'What now, sir?'

They walked up the first brow and saluted the limp white ensign with its blue stripe and prominent star, hammer and sickle emblems.

Durham said in a stage-whisper, 'We talk. But first, we drink.'

Marriott could only stare at the destroyer's quarterdeck. It was almost covered with bicycles, with several baby-prams lashed beside them under a canvas canopy.

Through a door and down a ladder to the wardroom. There was barely a space here either. Wireless-sets and gramophones, clocks of every kind from ornate pendulum ones to humble alarm versions. Boxes, crates, suitcases, some bursting open to reveal women's clothing and a few fur coats.

'What's going on, sir?'

Durham watched as the interpreter opened a door and ushered them forward. He replied shortly, 'It's how they do their shopping. At gunpoint!'

The destroyer's captain was introduced, and then the senior officer with four gold rings on his sleeves stepped forward and gave Durham a hug. He was a heavily built figure with tousled black hair, and very shaggy eyebrows.

Marriott noticed that he was careless in his dress, and his jacket was open from the throat down, revealing a none-too-clean shirt.

The lieutenant, whom Marriott could now only think of as *Boots-off*, introduced him as Senior Captain Sakulkin.

They all sat down around a beautiful mahogany table. It had certainly not come from any dockyard, Marriott thought.

They waited while a Russian seaman poured vodka into small glasses, then left the bottle beside its twin in a big bucket of ice.

Then came the toasts, each one carefully translated by the unflappable Boots-off.

To Stalin, and Churchill, to victory, and to the total destruction of Fascist Germany.

Despite his caution Marriott could feel the vodka making his head swim. Once he glanced at Durham, but apart from his reading glasses steaming over he showed very little change.

Marriott turned as the senior captain used his name.

The lieutenant looked at him impassively. 'Captain Sakulkin bids you welcome.'

The captain grinned and raised his glass.

Boots-off added, 'And says it is good that you want to share in our great Russian victory.'

Marriott smiled and lifted his own glass. 'Tell Captain Sakulkin that we were quite busy too.'

They all roared with laughter.

Then the lieutenant said wearily, 'Now we return to Article Three of the Allied Ships Dispersal plan.'

Marriott felt a drop of sweat fall on his hand. It was like an oven, and he noticed that all the scuttles were screwed shut. Perhaps this was how the Russians broke down resistance to their arguments.

A hand reached over his shoulder as the sailor refilled his glass. As it withdrew Marriott saw that the man was wearing at least three watches on his wrist before his sleeve slipped down again. He thought of the rules and regulations in Kiel, the eagle-eyed redcaps and naval patrolmen. Some rules would always be broken, but not to these extremes. What did they do? Rob the civilians and loot their homes, or did they do that as a matter of course?

Durham pushed his glasses on to his forehead so that he looked like a benevolent owl.

'I would refer the captain to the report given at Flensburg three days ago by your naval surveyor. He was most satisfied with these vessels, and said as much of two further tankers which are now being refitted.'

More translations.

The lieutenant said, 'Captain Sakulkin says that this interpretation displays a lack of trust between allies.'

There was a discreet tap at the door and an armed seaman stood stiffly in the doorway.

There was a brief exchange and then Sakulkin gave a curt nod.

Boots-off explained, 'It is one of your officers, Lieutenant Marriott. The captain has excused you.'

'Thank you.' Marriott walked carefully through the door and climbed thankfully towards the sunlight. After the sealed cabin it felt like the Solent.

He had been half-expecting Lowes, worried about some unexpected setback, but it was Fairfax.

'Hello, Number One. All finished out there?' He hoped his voice did not sound slurred.

Fairfax tore his eyes from the great heap of bicycles.

'The Russians have taken one of our passage-crew, sir.'

'What?' He took his arm and led him away from the watching gangway-staff. 'Tell me!'

'We were transferring the German passage-crew to our boat and the ML when suddenly they pulled out one of the young sailors. It seems he had no proper authority, sir. Everyone else did.'

'Bloody hell! Somebody has made a damned mess of this. There's not much we can do. The rules come from the top—' He stared at him and added, 'That's not all, is it?'

'It was one of *my* passage-crew, sir, in the *Augsburg*. After all this happened the German skipper told me that the youth is the son of the senior German officer at Kiel. Von Tripz, I think he said his name is. The skipper assumed it was okay and didn't want any trouble.'

'Well, he's got it all the same, the bloody idiot.'

It was all coming back through his foggy brain. Von Tripz had been the captain of the dockyard when the port had fallen to the British. He had stayed on under RN control as his knowledge and experience would prove invaluable. He had been cleared by the officers investigating war crimes and Nazi connections. A man of honour, they had said. And now his son was in Russian hands.

Fairfax was watching him anxiously. 'We *could* make a signal—'

'It would be too late. There's more to this than meets the eye. Quite a coincidence, wouldn't you say?'

He felt the anger running through him with unexpected force. Another *incident*—well, so be it. The Russian's *share in our victory* had been almost the last straw. Pictures flashed through his mind. The final drink with Stephen, and then the newsreel shots of the *Repulse*, all those other faces, from Alexandria to Malta, North Africa, Sicily and on to Salerno. And that was just the part he had shared. *And then Normandy*.

He exclaimed, 'Well, this time they can bloody
216

well get stuffed!'

A seaman made to bar his way but relented as he re-entered the furnace heat between decks.

They were still around the table, the documents exactly as they had been.

Captain Sakulkin barked something at his subordinate and the interpreter asked, 'What is the meaning of this intrusion?'

But Marriott ignored him. To Durham he said, 'They've snatched one of the passage-crew, sir.' He was amazed that his voice sounded so calm. Like listening to a total stranger. 'They claim he had no documents. I say that's a lie. The sailor's name is Tripz.'

For an instant he thought that Durham either did not understand or even care, or that he was too drunk to realise the implications. But suddenly he removed his owl-like glasses and thrust them untidily into his breast pocket.

He said gravely, 'In view of this, Lieutenant Butuzov, after you have explained the facts to your superior officer, perhaps you would tell him that we are leaving forthwith.' He gathered up the documents with great dignity. 'It is not open for discussion, either.'

The lieutenant plucked at his collar. 'He says to tell you that it is nothing to do with you.'

Durham repeated flatly, 'Not open for discussion.'

'He says your admiralty will hear of this!'

Marriott watched. It was like a ball being played back and forth by experts, without waste, without pity.

'And so will Moscow, be sure of that!'

'He says you are threatening him!'

217

Durham eyed them each in turn. 'No, it is a *promise* I will keep.'

Captain Sakulkin suddenly threw back his head and roared with laughter.

Boots-off said, 'He says it was a misunderstanding.' He sounded very grateful. 'If you will sign for the transfer of these, er, *fine* ships, your lieutenant can recover the foolish young seaman and take him on board.'

Marriott faced him quietly. 'I never said a word about his age.'

But the interpreter did not translate it, and Durham's eyes said, *leave it there*.

It was a silent procession back to the pontoon. The MGB's engines bellowed into life as if Adair had his own peep-hole to watch their approach. The deck was crammed with anxious-looking Germans, and from one corner of his mouth Durham said, 'A small victory, Marriott, but a victory nonetheless.'

Marriott did not speak until he saw Fairfax at the guardrails.

'Got him, Number One?'

Fairfax nodded. 'In the wardroom, sir.'

Durham turned and solemnly saluted the Russian officers who had come to see him off.

Then he murmured, 'Now let's get the *hell* out of here, eh?'

'Single up all lines! Stand by to let go springs!'

'Take over, Number One.' Marriott ran down the ladder to the wardroom and saw Ginger Jackson at the table, a basin and swab in his hands as he bent over a half-naked youth in soiled white duck trousers. The youth turned and looked at Marriott. He tried to speak but his fear would not let him, and there were tears running down his cheeks and

218

across a livid bruise where someone had hit him in the face. He was at a guess about sixteen.

'Can you manage, Ginger?'

Ginger glanced at him, his eyes blazing. 'Look what them bastards did!'

Marriott rested his hand on the boy's bare shoulder. It was like ice. On the opposite side was a swastika which somebody had cut with a knife.

'Give him a tot, Ginger.' He forced a smile to contain his anger. 'One for yourself, too.'

Ginger wrung out his swab in the pink water and said, 'Ta, sir.' With great care he laid a dressing over the bleeding furrows and added, 'Must 'ave bin quite a party, sir.' He gestured with his head towards the door to Marriott's cabin. They could hear Durham throwing up as if he might never stop.

Marriott swung round as Fairfax yelled, 'Ready on deck, sir!' He paused and saw the boy staring after him, trying to convey his thanks, when everything must have seemed like a nightmare.

Marriott smiled at him. 'I'm taking you home. I don't know if you can understand what I'm saying, but it's where you belong.'

Fifteen minutes later the MGB, followed by her consort, thrashed away from the land and headed for the sparkling horizon.

Marriott half-listened to the mounting growl of the engines, something he had grown used to, always dreading a flaw, some new sound heralding another much-needed repair.

Fairfax had the watch once they were clear of the land. Marriott removed his cap and jacket and carefully lit his pipe beneath the shelter of the screen.

It was an odd discovery. For the first time since he had stepped ashore in Kiel he felt as if he had achieved something worthwhile.

CHAPTER ELEVEN

OUT OF LUCK

Beri-Beri watched enviously as his German driver brought the great car to rest on a grassy verge which lined the cobbled road, and gestured towards a distant town. 'That's Preetz, according to my map, Vere. There are supposed to be some really beautiful lakes beyond it, where the new naval HQ is going to be.'

Marriott stared at the rather forbidding-looking house on the opposite side of the road. Why had he come? What was the real purpose? The big house had all but escaped any damage. Some tiny figures were working on one of the rooftops replacing tiles and removing tarpaulins.

An official residence, once that of the dockyard's captain but now partly occupied by the British Army. A small tank was parked by the gateway beside a lawnmower.

Beri-Beri yawned. 'I'll wait out here. I've had a gutful of senior officers of late, *theirs* or *ours*, it doesn't seem to matter!'

Beri-Beri had told him that while they had been in the Russian sector he had been back north again in Flensburg. 'They're gathering a new convoy. Nobody seems to know what for, but I think *I'm* involved. It's all so secret that you'd think war had broken out again!'

Marriott climbed from the car and saw an armed sentry draw his feet together at the gates.

'Won't be long, Beri-Beri.' He smiled and crossed the ruler-straight road. It was completely empty of traffic. Once he glanced back and knew that his friend had fallen asleep in his seat.

He thought of the return to Kiel, the anxious relatives of the passage-crew, peering for familiar faces, as if they had all expected the worst. And the German boy Willi Tripz, dressed completely in naval clothing which had been freely offered by some of 801's company, trying to grin as he had left the boat. He had shaken hands with some of them, his scarred shoulders held stiffly, a cruel reminder of the nightmare which Marriott had interrupted.

A naval car had been sent to collect him with an RNVR doctor and one other officer inside it.

Marriott returned the sentry's salute and stared up at the grim-looking building. The ex-German captain still carried a lot of weight, it seemed. He thought of the way the watching Germans had saluted and nodded to him when he had left the boat. Did they see him as different from all the others because he had saved one terrified youth? Or was it that their respect for his father was as entrenched as ever?

The boy had hesitated by the guardrails and then offered his hand. It had seemed determined as well as shy, and Marriott thought he knew the reason. Some of his seamen had looked on coldly and had avoided his offers of thanks for his rescue and return home.

It had been important that the man who had

rescued him should not be one of them.

He had stammered haltingly, 'I never forget, Herr Leutnant! *Never!*'

And now, for better or worse, here I am.

The house was dark inside, gloomy and unwelcoming.

A plump servant in a white jacket led the way along a high-ceilinged hall, past pale rectangles where great pictures or portraits must have hung, and where common-or-garden noticeboards had taken their place.

All military personnel report to orderly office. And more important ones like *To the Canteen* and a door which read *Officers Only.*

But once through a pair of tall double-doors Marriott found himself in Germany again.

There was a certain grandeur about the huge room which even the dusty curtains could not diminish.

On one wall there was a large picture of Hipper's cruisers steaming into the attack at Jutland. Marriott had seen several reproductions of that famous sea-battle to end all sea-battles in the Great War, but this he knew was the original.

It was a twist of fate that the ship named after one of Germany's finest commanders should be lying wrecked and partly submerged in the harbour.

The man had been sitting in a high-backed chair by an empty marble fireplace so that at first Marriott did not see him.

Manfred von Tripz, until just two months ago a senior Kapitän-zur-See in Hitler's navy, was slight in build, and yet even as he moved displayed great presence and dignity.

He faced Marriott and looked him slowly up and down as he would one of his own lieutenants. If he displayed any surprise it was at seeing Marriott standing at attention.

He said quietly, 'Please be at your ease, Herr Marriott.' A brief smile. 'You are the victor, not I.' He gestured to a chair. 'I am afraid I can offer little refreshment as yet, but I am glad—' He shook his head as if he had heard a silent voice. 'No, I am *grateful* that you came to see me.'

Marriott tried to see the fair-haired boy with the crude swastika carved on his shoulder in the little captain. Perhaps he had also been fair? Now he was grey, with a neatly clipped beard which seemed to put him straight back in that other war, the one depicted by the gallant picture of Jutland.

Marriott sat down in a chair which had never meant to be comfortable. It probably went with the official residence, he thought.

Von Tripz asked, 'May I ask how old you are?'

'Twenty-six, sir.' It was all madness. It had to be. Sitting here with a man who had probably controlled the supply and repair work to half the U-Boats which came from and went to the Atlantic. And calling him *sir*. And yet it seemed to fit. He added haltingly, 'I feel much older.'

The other man smiled properly for the first time. 'I know how that can weigh on a naval officer!'

Marriott watched him as he moved to a tall cabinet. His father must have been very like him, he thought. He had seen pictures of him too, in his boyhood magazines, where he had read about that other war.

It was hardly surprising that the Germans looked up to Von Tripz; his father had commanded one of

223

the most famous commerce-raiders, the *Cobra*, in that so-different war when men had still clung to their beliefs of honour and example.

Von Tripz came back with a framed picture and said absently, 'I do not display this, because of his uniform.' It was said without rancour or contempt.

The young officer smiling at the camera was about Marriott's age. Again that same uncertain feeling. All the years, fighting an elusive enemy. The uniform with its Iron Cross and Nazi eagle on the right breast. It was an abhorrence he might never lose.

'My son Walther.' He replaced the picture in a drawer. 'His first cruise in command of his own *Unterseeboot*, lost to the Atlantic.' He swung round and looked at Marriott as if he wanted to memorise every detail. 'My remaining son Willi is very dear to us. The Russians would know it. They would have tried to use him to influence me.'

Marriott recalled Meikle's insistence that the Germans would do anything to sow ill will between the Allies, especially where it involved the Russians.

He realised he had discovered the one similarity between father and son. The eyes were unusual, tawny, which appeared to change colour in the sunlight.

What had they nicknamed the *Cobra*'s elusive commander in 1917? *The Tiger of the Seas*.

Marriott said, 'Your family has a great naval tradition.'

'True. Like many in England also.' He smiled sadly. 'Even Willi was a cadet in the barque *Gorch Fock* until the—' He hesitated, then added bluntly, 'Until we surrendered.'

He took out a pocket-watch and studied it. 'I have an appointment with your Commodore Paget-Orme. I must not be late.'

Marriott stood up. It was over.

Von Tripz said, 'If ever I can do anything for you, Lieutenant.' Once more the brief smile. 'Although you are maybe thinking it would be the other way round?'

'I understand, sir. I'm glad I was able to get your boy out of that place.' He found that he meant it. 'He has his whole life ahead of him.'

'Thanks to you.' Von Tripz held out his hand. 'Do not forget what I said, Lieutenant. My father once told me, in war you have enemies, afterwards you have only survivors!'

Marriott left the house and felt the sunshine close around him. He realised how cool it had been inside. *Cold with memories.*

Beri-Beri stretched and yawned. 'All done then? What's he like?'

The car throbbed out on to the cobbles and Marriott replied, 'I liked him.' He felt suddenly embarrassed. 'For a German, that is!'

Beri-Beri studied his profile affectionately. 'You really are a funny old bugger, y'know!'

On the drive back to Kiel, Marriott thought a lot about Von Tripz and other Germans like him. So-called men of honour who had been cleared of any implication with the kind of war crimes which were daily making the world's press.

And yet how could they have survived under the same regime which had perpetrated such horrific deeds?

He was still thinking about it as the car slowed down at the dockyard gates.

225

He said, 'Maybe we can meet up later for a noggin?'

But Beri-Beri was staring at the unusual activity at the gates. More redcaps than usual, some women in battledress, plus the white belts and gaiters of naval patrolmen.

'What the hell is all this flap about?'

A Royal Marines sergeant saluted and grinned at them. 'Security check, sir!' He was a Londoner and sounded like Ginger Jackson's brother. 'I wouldn't mind searchin' 'er, an' no mistake!'

Marriott noticed that the door of an army hut had been left open because of the heat.

A young German girl had been ordered into the hut, picked out at random, he supposed, from the many workers who were finishing their shifts in the dockyard.

Two of the women in battledress had opened her coat and were running their fingers expertly through the pockets, feeling the lining. Another worker, this time a man in a boiler-suit, was called off the road and ordered into another hut where some redcaps were waiting to search him.

When he turned back Marriott saw that the girl's shirt had been deliberately opened and one of the tough-looking women was pulling some sort of bag from her waistband.

He looked at Beri-Beri as the girl, humiliated and distressed, burst into tears.

The marine said, 'Coffee, most likely. That's 'er for th' 'igh jump!'

'Drive on, for Christ's sake.' Marriott stared at the twin masts of the HQ ship, his mind still lingering on what he had just witnessed.

Beri-Beri looked at him as he climbed from the

226

car.

'Take it off your back, old son. You know it happens.' He sighed as Marriott strode towards the brow. 'We'll talk about it later!'

Marriott entered the operations room and looked around, taken aback by its abandoned emptiness. He could hear a few telephones from other parts of the ex-steam yacht, but the filing cabinets and desks had vanished.

The door of a cupboard was slightly ajar, and as a passing vessel pushed the bow-wave against the hull the door swung open. A blue shoulder-bag fell on to the deck.

At that moment she entered the room, her eyes moving from him to the bag and back again. She was carrying a towel and a toothbrush. She exclaimed, 'It is *mine*, Herr Leutnant!' She seemed oblivious to everything but her bag, and as he stepped away Marriott noticed some bars of chocolate inside, and one of the little toy animals which had started to appear in the flourishing NAAFI canteen.

'Where is Commander Meikle?' He had not mean to sound curt, but the question came out that way.

She looked at him. 'I—I am sorry, Herr Leutnant. You should have been told. He has gone to inspect the new offices at Plön.'

Marriott nodded, remembering what Beri-Beri had said about it.

She had recovered his composure. 'May I say, Herr Leutnant, it was a fine thing you did for Kapitän von Tripz's son.' She flushed and added, 'I am leaving now.'

Marriott walked to an open scuttle and tried to see 801's moorings. *Home, escape.* It hit him like a

227

punch in the stomach. The chocolate and the toy. It explained everything. She had a child. Who had given it to her did not matter. No wonder she was afraid of him, what he might . . . He stared at his reflection in the scuttle's polished glass.

'*Why, you bloody idiot!*' He had a sudden picture of the girl with her shirt open for anyone to see, her despair as they had searched her.

That's her for the high jump, the Royal Marine had said.

Marriott wrenched open the door and ran down the brow past a gaping sentry.

It was too late already. He ran through the slow-moving throng of dockyard workers as if they were not there.

Too much time at sea or in hospital. The vague thought penetrated his mind. He was out of condition and the main gates were still fifty yards away. If Beri-Beri had been there with his car . . .

Then he saw her, walking in the centre of the road, her shoulder bag hanging against her hip, her little blue forage cap tilted forward from the coil of hair on her neck.

She was the only girl there now and he saw the same two women in battledress look straight at her, one give the other a quick nudge.

Marriott fell in beside her and said, 'Stay with me. Don't look surprised and *don't argue!*'

He saw a portly Master-at-Arms standing by the side-gate used by officers and touched her elbow. She felt stiff, probably with fear, as she realised for the first time what was happening.

'Fräulein Geghin is with me, Master!' Thank God he had heard that idiot Verner call her by name.

He thought he saw someone moving out towards them but the portly Master-at-Arms shook his head and grunted, 'Very good, sir.' Their eyes met, just for a few seconds. Then he added, 'I'll drop her card in the box for you.'

Outside the gates they stood together, and yet far apart.

Then she said in a whisper, 'You did this for *me*?' She would not look at him but clutched the bag against her body as the true implication hit her. 'I would have lost my work here! I—I did not intend—'

He said, 'Don't think about it. It was just something I saw earlier. I did not want—' But she had not heard a word.

'I had offered payment for them but—'

'I know. *But.* Such a powerful word in regulations.'

A grey-painted bus, one of the many used by personnel employed by the Royal Navy, rolled on to the concourse and stood vibrating noisily, waiting for the passengers to hurry along.

'Just be careful in future, eh?' He tried to make light of it, when all he wanted was to take her arm and walk with her somewhere. *Anywhere*. He tried to shut out the picture of her arriving home. Sharing out the spoils for the child. Laughing perhaps at her escape, at the lieutenant's weakness or stupidity.

'This is my bus, Herr Leutnant.'

She turned and faced him, her chin lifting with a kind of defiance. For just those few moments they were quite alone, oblivious to the curious glances from the passing workers and the patrolmen at the gates.

Then she said again, 'You came just to save me from trouble?'

He nodded. 'Yes. No strings.'

'*No strings?*' She bit her lip. 'I do not know this phrase.'

She walked to the bus and looked at the sign above its cab. It read *Eutin*.

She said, 'It is where we live.'

The bus shook itself into motion and then rumbled out on to the road again.

Eutin. Where *we* live.

Marriott turned and walked thoughtfully back into the dockyard. He touched his cap to the gangway staff and quickened his pace. It was little enough. And it was sheer madness, which could offer nothing but harm. In the same breath he knew there was no turning back.

In the shade of the gateway the Master-at-Arms watched him and gave a great sigh.

He had seen more courts martial than most people had had hot dinners. He hoped he had not just been a party to yet one more.

★　　　★　　　★

The sergeant with the Military Police armband opened a door and indicated a bare table with two facing chairs.

'Not much of a place yet, chum, but if you wait here I'll see if I can rustle up some char.'

Petty Officer Robert Evans removed his cap with his usual care and walked restlessly around the spartan office.

So different from the life he had become accustomed to, which he had *made* himself become

230

used to. Outside on a dusty square which had once been a school playground he could hear the regular stamp of boots, the slap of weapons and the hoarse cries of NCOs. The British army. Drilling to maintain their standard or to impress the inhabitants, it did not seem to matter which.

He stopped by a long noticeboard. No children's paintings here but portraits, ranks and numbers. War criminals, Nazi supporters, others merely wanted for interrogation, for a thousand different reasons.

A plain, dreary room, one of the many set up by the Military Government all over occupied Germany. Several of the photographs Evans had already seen in the files and ledgers at Meikle's HQ. Some had been caught in the net, others had been found dead, or been reported missing. It might take years and years.

The door opened but it was not the MP with his 'char'. It was another sergeant in a plain unmarked battledress. A lean, tired-looking man of about Evans's age.

He thrust out his hand and said, 'I'm Thornhill, S.I.B.—well, sort of.' He sat down opposite Evans and looked at him calmly over his pressed fingertips.

'I've read what your CO thinks about you.' He smiled. 'Commander Meikle doesn't strike me as a man who dishes out compliments very often.'

Evans relaxed slightly. He could not get used to thinking of Meikle as his commanding officer. Not after the boat, and Marriott.

The sergeant continued, 'But it's your record which interests me more, otherwise, Meikle or not, you wouldn't be sitting there. My boss thinks you

231

could be extremely useful with our work of vetting prisoners and suspects who come through here. My men are very experienced, but théy haven't been in the middle of it like you. You were in the Maquis before you joined up with the navy?' It was a statement.

Evans nodded. 'We had boats. So even when the Germans invaded France and overran the Channel Islands we were able to keep contact with our various *Maquisards*.'

'I see.' He looked down at his hands. 'I know about your family, what was done to them at the hands of Major Helmut Maybach of the SS, and what became of your young sister afterwards. In our work it's a common story but no less pitiful because of that.' He looked up, his eyes hard. 'And for *you*, there can be no words.'

The MP came in with two mugs of tea. He smiled at Evans but avoided the S.I.B. man as if he was something dangerous.

Thornhill stirred his tea with a pencil. 'Your experiences speak for themselves. The Maquis, then the Special Boat Squadron and work with agents in enemy territory, always with the additional risk, the *knowledge* of what they would do to you if you were captured.' His glance moved to Evans's left breast. 'Croix de Guerre, the DSM, a bar too. Not a quiet war for *you*, it seems.'

'Major Maybach was reported to be in Lübeck just before the surrender.' It was strange to speak his name, more so to hear another mention it so casually.

Thornhill took out some papers from his battledress blouse and flattened them on the table, cursing softly as some spilled tea soaked through

232

one corner.

'I will lay your hopes—would you describe them as such? To ashes, right away. Major Helmut Maybach is dead, *known* to be dead. So there will be no trial, no penalty to make him pay for the misery he caused.'

Evans swallowed hard. It could not be. All the years and the months. The face always in his mind and waking thoughts. A narrow, pointed face, with a long upper lip and receding chin. An animal who had tortured his victims even when he had believed them innocent of any unlawful act. Women especially; even children had not been spared. He could not just be dead like any ordinary man. It was impossible.

The S.I.B. sergeant continued quietly, 'It happened in Flensburg or very near to it. His car hit a landmine and was blown to bits. Nobody is quite sure how it happened. Maybe Danish resistance from across the border, or perhaps our own agents who preferred to lie low until hostilities ceased.' He leaned on his elbows and read down the top page. 'Staff Mercedes car, with ordinary *Wehrmacht* markings.' He sped through the various items of damage to nearby houses caused by the explosion, then said, 'Major Maybach's corpse was badly burned and mutilated, of course—some of it was on a roof across the road.' He smiled grimly. 'I saw the pics. Not pretty.' He looked up sharply as if to confront Evans's shattered hopes and disappointment.

'So try to put it behind you. The bastard's dead. Maybe for a second or two he felt some of the torment he gave to so many—who knows?'

'But can you be *certain*?'

'Quite. He wore a very special watch.'

Evans nodded, remembering. 'I know.'

'His name and serial number were on the back of it. The pieces of his uniform were correct, and some partly burned letters were found in one pocket.'

Somewhere a telephone began ringing insanely and the sergeant explained apologetically, 'I'm sorry I can't tell you more. But it's over as far as we're concerned. Come and see us again and I'll fix you up with a job where you can do some real good here. Right?'

Evans shrugged. *Right.* The way Marriott always said it.

He walked to the door. 'There were no witnesses at all?'

The sergeant shook his head. 'None.' He wanted to end it.

'What about the driver?'

The sergeant listened to the telephone. 'No driver.'

He accompanied him from the bare room. 'Don't take it too hard.'

Surprisingly Evans smiled. 'I will not. And thank you.' He replaced his cap and walked out into the dusty sunlight.

For several minutes he stared unseeingly at the bored-looking soldiers as they went through the intricacies of arms-drill and marching.

It had not been a waste of time after all.

For it was not only Major Maybach's watch he remembered. It was also the known fact that he could not and would not drive.

★   ★   ★

234

As the month of July drew to a close, Britain and her forces throughout Germany were informed of the news that Labour had won the general election. It was not just a victory for Clement Attlee's party but something of a landslide, as Lieutenant Commander Arthur Durham had predicted on 801's passage to Swinemünde. Many had been expecting it, but the enormity of the winning vote surprised everyone, not least the new government.

MGB 801 had just returned from another bread-and-butter trip, this time to Flensburg with some divers and their equipment where their additional experience was required to shift two difficult wrecks. Before leaving the bay for the return passage to Kiel Marriott had seen the small convoy of merchantmen which Beri-Beri had mentioned, and was struck by the air of dejection. Someone had told him the ships were to be taken out and sunk, but it seemed unlikely as they all looked in fair condition, although even with binoculars he had been unable to see anyone aboard them apart from some armed sailors.

The news of the election had been passed over the radio even as Fairfax had picked up the last fix for altering course towards the now-familiar naval memorial on Laboe.

Marriott heard some of the men cheering on the messdeck and wondered if they really knew what changes it might bring. They were mostly too young to have known unemployment or anything else before they had volunteered for the navy. One thing was certain, life would never be the same again. It was difficult to imagine Britain without Churchill, Old Winnie, at the helm. He had been the rock on which the country and their allies had depended and relied upon for strength when their own had faltered, for nearly six years of war.

Fairfax, tanned and looking fit as he conned the boat towards the dockyard approaches, refused to be pessimistic. Perhaps his second stripe, albeit temporary, had given him more confidence.

'They'll soon get sick of this lot, sir! Churchill'll be back, you'll see.'

Silver came up from the W/T office. 'We're to go to the main basin, sir.'

'Very well. Acknowledge it.' He saw the leading signalman bustle away. Did he care about the election, he wondered? And what about Adair, the Chief; would it bring his dreamed-of garage and tea shop for holiday-makers any closer?

Fairfax said, 'Commander Meikle will be in his new HQ by now, sir.'

Marriott glanced at him, but there was no particular significance in his remark. Fairfax would be unable to tell a lie or hide one no matter how hard he tried. But deep down Marriott often wondered if anyone had seen him with the girl, and had drawn the wrong conclusions.

Maybe she would be at Plön too? Although it had been rumoured that Wrens were coming out to take over some of the operational work. That would be strange, he thought. English voices, some of the girls who had shared their war, and not always at a distance. Signals and armaments artificers, boats' crews, and cooks, they had never been far away.

'I'll take over.' Their eyes met. How many times had they shared this?

'Hands fall in for entering harbour.' He no longer had to look at the gaff to make sure Fairfax had hoisted their best ensign for the purpose. Lowes

236

came to the bridge. He had not changed much and was still withdrawn, even more so since Fairfax had put up his extra stripe.

Marriott nodded to him. 'I'll see about shore leave when we get alongside, Pilot.'

He glanced over the screen where the hands were swaying in line, their proper caps on their heads, chinstays down. They had done well, he thought. Better than he had expected. A lot better than he deserved after driving them so hard when he had assumed command.

All in all as good a company as you could wish for.

Long John Silver lowered his glasses and frowned. 'No sign of Lieutenant Glazebrook's boat, sir. We was supposed to pass 'er on the way out.'

Marriott looked away. Cuff was probably putting it on again. He had something going ashore. If Meikle found out, he'd really be in the rattle this time. But he had known Cuff a long time, and he had never been able to keep away from women, any sort of women.

As dear old Spruce Macnair had once said of him, 'Cuff only uses his head as a periscope for his cock!' God help the Wrens when they arrived here.

As they wended their way through moving or anchored vessels, past the many remaining wrecks and salvage craft, Marriott thought of how much had been achieved in less than three months. The Hindenburg Graveyard was now a veritable forest of funnels, masts and shattered upperworks, evidence of the hard efforts of divers and salvage men alike.

He raised his hand to the peak of his cap as the calls trilled out and were answered by the blare of a marine's bugle. A newly moored ship, once another Hamburg-Amerika Line vessel, made a fine show against the casualties of war. A White Ensign flew from aft, and she was, Marriott guessed, the new HQ ship for Kiel dockyard and the naval party which had weekly been reinforced from England.

Silver murmured, 'All right for some, eh?'

Townsend, who was at the wheel, said from one corner of his mouth, 'I'll bet they get hard-living money even if they doesn't go to sea!'

Marriott smiled. The usual contempt of small-ship people for their larger consorts.

He shaded his eyes to watch a line-handling party of Germans preparing to receive them alongside. Just a few months ago and they might have been taking the wires of a returning U-Boat, fresh from the killing ground, the Atlantic.

Marriott raised his glasses. Cuff's MGB was here too, and there were several figures in boiler-suits walking along her deck, an officer he did not recognise speaking with Cuff's Number One.

He saw a heaving line snake over the jetty to be seized by one of the waiting Germans.

'Stop engines. Slow astern port outer!'

Fenders squeaked between wood and stone and more lines were passed rapidly ashore.

'Finished with engines.' In the sudden silence Marriott looked around, seeing the familiar haze of smoke from the big Packards, the sound of a generator quite different as the echo was cast back from solid concrete.

Fairfax clattered into the bridge. 'All secure, sir.' He hesitated. 'Anything wrong, sir?'

'No.' He looked at the idling seamen by the guardrails, Silver right in the bows just to make

238

certain that the Jack had been properly secured as they had made fast. 'That is—' He could not explain it. 'Somebody walked on my grave, I think.' But it would not go away. 'I'm getting past it, Number One.'

Fairfax smiled but his eyes remained anxious. He had heard about Marriott's nightmares. The lingering memories which would not leave him alone.

A seaman called, 'Messenger, sir!'

A youthful sailor in belt and gaiters clambered aboard, and would have fallen between the fenders had not Leading Seaman Rae grabbed his arm.

'What's your name? *Death?*'

Fairfax sighed. 'Look at this one, sir. Green as grass!'

Marriott touched his arm. 'So speaks a real old sweat!'

But it was true. The young rating in his issue clothing and heavy boots looked more like a sea-scout than a sailor.

He appeared in the bridge and was confronted by another problem. Two lieutenants. Which one was the captain?

Marriott solved it for him. 'I command here. Do you want me?'

The youth stared at him with awe. 'Y-Yes, sir. Commander Meikle is in the Base . . . Engineer's . . . office—' He broke up the sentence so that he would not miss out any detail. 'He sends his compliments and—'

'And he wants me there, right?'

The youth nodded, relieved. 'Yessir.'

'Very well.' Marriott looked at Fairfax. 'Come and talk with me while I put on some regulation

239

shoes, eh?'

He paused by the ladder as they both heard Lowes say loftily, 'How long in the Andrew, did you say? Six months? God, you should have been with *us*!'

Marriott chuckled. 'There's still hope for him after all!'

The Base Engineer's office adjoined one of the many great workshops which had been brought back into service by the combined efforts of their original crews and their new owners.

The first workshop was typical of any naval dockyard, Marriott thought. It stank of oil, dirt and cold metal, and one false step could send you sprawling down a slipway, or knocked senseless by one of the great steel tackles which dangled from the roof.

Welding torches threw harsh light over the crouching figures in their protective masks, and the noise made ordinary speech impossible. A naval rating opened a door for Marriott and he was surprised how the din seemed to fade as it was closed again behind him.

The Base Engineer Officer, a round, comfortable-looking commander with purple cloth between his tarnished gold stripes, was puffing at his pipe behind his deck. Commander Meikle seemed to shine amongst the untidiness, the hanging plans and blueprints, his beautiful cap jammed beneath one arm, the other holding some kind of document. Leading Writer Lavender was sitting on a camp stool scribbling in his note pad and did not look up as Marriott was announced.

Meikle asked shortly, 'Good run?'

'Yes, sir.' Marriott looked at the fourth figure by

240

the wall. He was a tall officer in smudged white overalls who when he stepped out of them was revealed as an RNR Lieutenant Commander.

Meikle said in the same clipped tone, 'This is 'tenant Commander Dobell.'

The newcomer said heavily, 'Sorry it has to be like this, Marriott.'

Marriott stared from one to the other. 'Like what?'

Meikle put down his cap on the deck and folded his arms.

'Your boat is to return to England. Lieutenant Glazebrook's also.'

'I see, sir.' So that was it. Something was in the air. A refit? More work perhaps?

'When do I leave, sir?'

The one called Dobell made to speak but Meikle said, 'You don't, I'm afraid. A small passage-crew will be arriving for each boat. Lieutenant Commander Dobell will be taking them to the UK.'

Marriott felt the room closing in on him. He had misunderstood; he had to be wrong.

Dobell said bluntly, 'Your boat's in no shape for further service. I've read all the reports on both machinery and hull. The hull is as ripe as a pear, but you must know that?'

Meikle glared at him. 'I'm sorry, Marriott, but there it is. The boats are to be paid-off, here in Kiel.' He looked away and added, 'So if you'd like to complete the arrangements.'

Marriott nodded, unable to find any words.

They were taking the boat away. It was all he could remember.

Meikle said, 'Make a signal when you're ready. A week should do it, eh?'

241

Outside Marriott stood with his back pressed against the wall, letting the din of machinery shock his mind back into the present. He realised that Fairfax was waiting for him.

Fairfax exclaimed, 'I'm glad your meeting's over, sir! There's some lunatic from the base staff on board asking to see our repairs log. I told him—'

Marriott looked past him. He could just see the masthead pendant of his boat showing above the dock wall.

'It's over, Number One. They're taking her away.'

Fairfax stared at him with stunned disbelief. 'I don't understand.'

He thought of Beri-Beri. 'She's run out of luck.'

CHAPTER TWELVE

THE LAST WATCH

Lieutenant 'Cuff' Glazebrook tossed his cigarette on to the road and ground it in with his heel.

His German driver picked up the jack and gently kicked the wheel he had just changed.

'All fix, Herr Leutnant!' His glance lingered on the crushed cigarette.

'About bloody time too!' Cuff heaved himself into the jeep and waited impatiently for the driver to start up.

It was not yet dusk and yet it was much darker than usual after a brief drizzle which made the road and hedgerows shimmer in the grey light.

Cuff glanced at his driver. Perhaps it was just as

well he was here. At first, when he had been unable to 'borrow' a jeep from the pound, Cuff had lost his temper. Now, having the time to think about it made him feel differently.

He had been having a drink in the new HQ at Plön, and had intended it to be the first of many. It had been a busy day, supervising the transfer of men and stores from his MGB, being driven to Plön where he had been allotted a cabin in the fine-looking barracks which had until recently been occupied by the *Kriegsmarine*.

He had been so busy that he had had barely time to think about what was happening. His boat being taken away like so much salvage. Cuff was not a sentimentalist on any level, and he had viewed the whole operation more with seething resentment than a sense of loss. But he was not so blind that he did not see a change in the future. He and his command had gone through a lot together, more than most.

He sighed as the jeep swayed around a tight bend. Perhaps it was his old luck again which had found him sober when the telephone call had come. Cuff had imagined it to be a mistake but the German steward had insisted. The mention of a fuel depot was enough to convince him. It had been Frau Ritter, her voice strangely hushed and unsteady. 'I would not call you, but—'

'What is it?' Anyone might be listening to the call, a bored operator tapping the line.

'Hemmings is here. I think he drinks—he is very *wild*!'

Cuff had tensed instantly. He had only seen Hemmings once since their brief discussion. He had not even been able to see her again. As he clung to

243

the windscreen in the swaying jeep he tried to recall exactly what she had whispered. He had noticed how strong her German accent had become on the line.

One thing was certain. Hemmings had lost his bottle over something he had heard. A possible inspection of the depot by the security boys. Properly handled, Hemmings could have coped. Now, Cuff was not so sure.

He saw the wire fence of the fuel depot in the far distance and growled, 'Slow down! *Langsam*, for Christ's sake!'

Everything looked as usual. The sentry at the gate stepped out of his box and shouldered his rifle, his gaze on the approaching jeep. The gate, Cuff noticed, was shut, and there were no German workers about. The depot had obviously kept to union rules again.

The sentry slapped his rifle. 'All correct, sir!'

Cuff looked past him. 'Where's CPO Hemmings?'

'I dunno, sir. But the place is secured.'

'Well, *unsecure* it. I want to see him.' He looked at the sailor and added gently, 'So bloody well *chop, chop*!'

The sentry sighed and slung his rifle over his shoulder. He made a big job of unlocking the gate, dragged his feet as much as he dared.

Even from here Cuff could see that the office was shut and in darkness. In the poor light anyone in there would need something to read by.

The driver revved the engine, his face unconcerned and empty, the expression of one who is not involved.

The sound of the shot followed by a scream froze

244

the sentry in his tracks, while the driver stared at the open gate as if he expected to see an attack.

There was a second shot and then silence.

Cuff unclipped his webbing holster and dragged out his heavy Smith and Wesson revolver.

The sentry gasped, 'What, what—'

'Call the guard, then get round the rear of the house.'

In his mind he knew it was her house. It had to be.

He broke into a shambling run, only half-aware of the sentry yelling for his off-watch companions.

The door was just ajar and Cuff smashed it inwards with his foot and almost fell into the room.

She was crouching at the foot of the stairs which led up to her room. She stared at him wildly, her hair falling over her face, her breasts thrusting against her blouse as she tried to regain her self-control. Chief Petty Officer Hemmings was propped against the opposite wall, a pistol in one hand and half of his head blown away. There were blood and fragments of bone on the wallpaper and yet all Cuff saw was a sealed letter.

She called across the room, 'It is written to his wife in England. He tried to burst into my room. I think he heard me telephoning you. He was mad! He was shouting that he had written to his wife to ask for her forgiveness, but all the time he kept saying his other letter to your Kapitän Meikle would destroy you!'

'What did you do with that one?'

There were things he had to know, and know immediately. At any second the others would arrive. By then it might be too late.

'I destroyed it.'

Cuff had seen too many dead men to worry about the one whose solitary eye gleamed up at him from the horror of his face.

'There were two shots.'

She nodded. 'He fired at me first.' She gestured shakily to a ragged hole beside the stairs. 'After that—'

Cuff strode over to her. It was all suddenly crystal clear. He even found time to notice that she had put on her best blouse, the one she had been wearing when he had first laid eyes on her.

He said harshly, 'The security men will be here at any moment.' He saw her eyes widen with a new fear as he reached over and tore the blouse wide open from her shoulder to her breast. As she tried to step away he struck her bare shoulder with the palm of his hand, and before she could evade him swung his hand back again and lashed her across the mouth.

Something seemed to explode inside her and he seized her wrists as she tried to struggle, to claw at his face even as blood ran from her lip and on to the torn blouse.

He waited for her to hang helplessly in his considerable grip and said harshly, 'There was blood on your sleeve. You couldn't have got that from across the room. *You* killed him, didn't you?'

She lowered her face as he released his hold on her.

'I had to. For you. For us.'

Cuff stooped down and recovered his revolver.

She was staring at his every move, waiting for him to attack her, denounce her to the sentries who were running around the back of the house.

He said, 'Remember, you called for my help

246

because you had discovered what Hemmings was doing. I was the only British officer that you knew. The rest will be *exactly* as you told me, see?'

He looked at his thick wrists and big hands. He felt that he wanted to laugh his head off. His hands were as steady as rocks.

'You stick with me, Hertha, and you'll be all right.'

They faced the door as an army sergeant and two redcaps clattered into the room.

The sergeant's dark eyes flashed in an upended table light as he took in everything at a searching glance.

'I'm Glazebrook, Sergeant. Frau Ritter called me on the phone.'

The sergeant nodded and lowered his face to within inches of the dead man's smashed skull.

'Walther P38, nine-millimetre job. Point-blank.'

Cuff realised that one of the redcaps had taken out his notebook and was writing busily.

He could feel the laugh welling up again like something solid. Just like a Manchester bobby, he thought.

The sergeant said off-handedly. 'My name's Thornhill, sir. S.I.B.'

He looked at the woman and asked, 'Did he try to rape you?'

She dropped her eyes. 'No. He, he—'

'I see.' He took the letter from the other redcap and opened it with his finger.

Cuff saw his eyes moving along the pages. Suppose she had been mistaken and Hemmings had put something about him as well?

But the sergeant seemed satisfied. 'He must have been a neat sort of cove, sir. Asks her forgiveness and so forth—' He glanced up sharply, 'And Frau Ritter phoned to tell you that Hemmings was going to kill himself, was that it, sir?'

'No. She wanted help. I'm the only officer she's met. She said that Hemmings had heard that the depot was to be investigated.' He forced a smile. 'By your lot, I suppose!'

The sergeant shrugged. 'Probably.' He seemed to come to a decision. 'I'll have my men here all night, Lieutenant—er, Glazebrook.' He looked at one of his men. 'Get this corpse taken away and have someone clear up the mess.' He looked at the woman, the reddening mark on her shoulder, her bruised and cut mouth. His glance shifted to the bullet hole in the wall. 'You were lucky, Frau Ritter.' He added, 'Go and change into something more suitable, will you?'

Cuff saw her sudden alarm but she went up the stairs without looking back. Thornhill dragged open a drawer and shut it again. 'We'll search the place properly tomorrow. Pity he had to take this as a way out though. Might have put us on to the next link in the chain.'

'What will happen to her?'

Thornhill turned his back as some RAMC orderlies entered with a stretcher and a couple of rubber sheets.

'This is her house, Lieutenant. She is well respected, some might say feared, around these parts, but by showing her readiness to co-operate with the authorities she can still be very useful.'

Cuff felt parched. He watched the corpse, hidden at last, being carried from the room. He had not even heard the ambulance arrive.

'What happened to her husband? Prisoner-of-war?'

Thornhill picked up the Walther pistol and dropped it into an envelope before handing it to his corporal.

'Nothing like that, sir. He was mixed up with the local black market, as I understand it. About eighteen months ago, I think.' He lit a cigarette and blew out a stream of smoke. 'The Gestapo came for him one night. End of story.'

Cuff thought about it. 'Are you saying that she shopped him?'

'I'm not saying anything at all, *sir*. But she stayed on here afterwards, and the men in black never bothered *her*!'

She came down the stairs again but kept her eyes away from the dark smears on the wallpaper.

She wore a clean shirt, and the same leather belt pulled tight about her skirt.

Thornhill said, 'I've just got a few questions, Frau Ritter.' He looked meaningly at the lieutenant. 'I'll not require anything further from you, sir. Many thanks for preventing another murder. He might well have killed her if he hadn't realised you were at the gates, so to speak?'

Cuff grimaced. 'You make it sound quite romantic.' He walked to the door but she followed him out into the cool, damp evening.

From one corner of his mouth he murmured, 'Sorry I was rough with you.'

She did not seem to hear. 'You will come to see me? Soon?'

Cuff looked down at her. 'Soon as I can.' He made certain that the door was hiding them from the redcaps and their introspective sergeant. 'Just be very careful. Don't change your story, no matter

249

what, and I'll back you up.' He reached out and touched her breast. Despite everything that had happened it immediately roused him and he added, 'I want you *right now*!'

She watched him until he had walked past the ambulance and some military policemen and then turned back towards the room.

Hemmings's letter to his wife had been the perfect ending. His other letter to the Royal Navy about the lieutenant's involvement, the one she had *not* destroyed as she had lied to him, would if need be save her again in the future.

Thornhill stood up for her and pulled out a chair.

'I've sent for some coffee and later I can arrange a meal, if you wish.' He leaned over to study her cut mouth. 'I can have that treated by our medical officer.'

She shook her head. 'I will be all right. But thank you.'

Thornhill had already seen a report about the misuse of fuel at this and certain other dumps. But for that, and despite the pleading letter written by the dead man to his wife, he might have suspected that the attempted murder and then suicide was because of something very different. He could imagine how the big, dangerous-looking lieutenant with all the gongs on his tunic would appeal to an attractive woman who was probably as starved of sex as he was.

He sighed as the coffee and some sandwiches were brought in by the corporal.

'My men will be on call if you need them, Frau Ritter.' He put on his beret and recalled for no obvious reason the dark-faced petty officer who had come to see him about the dead SS officer.

As the door closed and she turned her back on the drying bloodstains, her limbs began to shake uncontrollably for the first time. Then she touched her breast as he had done and would do again.

Another day. And she had won through.

*　　*　　*

Commander Meikle glanced up from his large desk and asked irritably, 'What *is* it, Lavender? I'm too busy just now!

Lavender eyed him reproachfully then glanced at his watch, the White Rabbit once again.

'It's Lieutenant Glazebrook, sir.'

Meikle looked around his spacious office. Somewhere he could work, away from makeshift surroundings and unstable communications. Most of the equipment had been installed after being changed several times until he had been satisfied. Through one of the windows he had a good view of some well-tended grass where a party of Germans were busily working on flowerbeds, with the glittering expanse of the Plöner See making a perfect backdrop. A far cry from Kiel and its shattered dockyard.

'Very well.' He added for his own benefit, 'Better get it over with.'

Glazebrook strode into the room, his head seeming to brush against the top of the doorway. He looked hot and angry. But that did not appear to be unusual, Meikle decided.

'I asked you to come—'

Cuff interrupted rudely, 'I just heard about my promotion, sir!'

'Yes.' Meikle leaned back in his new chair, one

originally used by Grand-Admiral Dönitz's chief-of-staff. 'You could appeal against the decision, of course.'

'But you think I'd be wasting my bloody time, is that it?'

Meikle eyed him coldly. 'If you continue to take that attitude here, I shall have you escorted to your quarters.' He pulled a sheaf of papers across and looked through them. He knew exactly what each one represented, how many minutes or hours he would allot to their various contents, but it would give the massive lieutenant time to cool down, to save himself from a court martial.

Meikle said eventually, 'Your advanced promotion to lieutenant commander has been curtailed. It has happened to many. If the war has not completely ceased in every theatre it has done so sufficiently to slow down, and in some cases stop, further temporary promotions.'

Cuff glared at him. He knew he was beaten, had known it when he had received the formal announcement from the Admiralty.

He blurted out, 'Well, another command then! Surely after what I've done for them they can manage that?'

Meikle thought suddenly of Marriott. How could two men who had done so much in the same demanding warfare be so different? Marriott had been to see him three times, had even sent his own request to the Admiralty—he had been prepared to plead to anyone who might listen. But not for himself. Just for his boat. Meikle had scanned the official reports for himself. He was not much of a sailor, but even he had marvelled that MGB 801 had stayed afloat this long.

252

By contrast Glazebrook had not even touched on his own boat but was thinking only of his own advancement.

Meikle said, 'The work of this naval party is vital. Everything seems fine and well organised now. But look beyond the sunshine, Glazebrook, and you'll see the winter coming. The railways and harbours are in a mess and all the goodwill in the world won't save the civilian population if we can't get the flow of food and supplies moving again.' He held up one hand as Glazebrook made to interrupt. 'You have fought a hard war, and have survived it. But all that is behind you. We have to think of survival for others now, no matter what our personal views might be.'

Leading Writer Lavender peered through the door. 'Almost time, sir.'

Meikle hid his relief. Right on cue as usual.

'I'm afraid I cannot do anything further, Glazebrook. I had hoped you would settle down and use your skills under my direction.' He watched calmly, as he would the face of a prisoner in his summing-up at a trial. 'Especially after your excellent piece of work at the fuel depot when you saved that woman from being murdered, and helped the military police in their investigations. Very commendable.' He dropped his gaze to his diary. 'If you remain here, assisting my staff, I see no reason why the subject of promotion should not be raised again.'

'By you, sir?'

Meikle nodded gently. 'Of course.'

'Well, in that case, sir.' Cuff was feeling confused by the new tactics. 'I'd like to give it a go.'

Meikle replied, 'Fine.' He stood up and patted

253

his uniform into shape. 'If that's all?'

Glazebrook swallowed his anger. 'For the present, sir.' He marched past the leading writer and slammed out of the building.

Half to himself Meikle said, 'I cannot imagine what sort of officer he really was. My only surprise is that he was commissioned at all!'

Leading Writer Lavender asked timidly, 'Can I reach you anywhere, sir?'

Meikle paused by a mirror and straightened his tie. 'The duty operations officer can deal with anything urgent.' He added distantly, 'I have to see someone who is about to do what I imagine to be the most difficult thing in the world.' He thought suddenly of Glazebrook's belligerent intolerance. 'For *him* anyway.'

★   ★   ★

'Ship's company, *'shun!*'

Fairfax wheeled round and saluted smartly.

'Ready for inspection, *sir!*'

Marriott looked him straight in the eyes, then replied, 'Thank you, Number One. Stand them at ease.'

He watched as Fairfax shouted the order and looked along the lines of uniformed men he had come to know so well. Each one in his best blues, the red and gold badges, the very few good-conduct stripes which would show if a man had behaved himself for three years on the trot. Three years' undiscovered crime, as the old skates would have it.

Lowes in front of the main division of seamen, Adair, the Chief, at the head of his stokers and motor-mechanics. From commanding officer to the greenest recruit, twenty-nine souls in all, now that Evans had left them.

In harbour, rare enough before VE-Day, this kind of routine within the family had kept them going. A moment when they were all together, not divided by watches or at nerve-searing action stations off some enemy coast in pitch darkness.

A moment for them to moan about, to be nagged by their officers, petty officers and leading rates, but one which was secretly cherished because no outsider could share it, still less understand it.

But this time it was not like that at all. Marriott clenched his fists and pressed them against his trousers to steel himself. Each day he had tried to keep it at the back of his mind, to lose himself in the endless chit-signing and stocktaking which were part and parcel of handing over even the smallest warship.

A week of seeing the gunboat through different eyes, like trying to pack a lifetime into seven days. Now it was all behind him. Not next week, or even tomorrow. It was now.

He had hunted down Commander Meikle and had tried to get him to fix a postponement but to no avail. Marriott had even produced a whole batch of requests he had made over the months for spare parts and the chance of a longer refit for a hull which had been worn out by relentless and unending service.

To the people watching from the dockside the motor gunboat probably looked no different from usual except for the extra smartness of her company. Cuff's boat had gone to the outer yard yesterday, which only seemed to add to the finality of the occasion.

Marriott saw there were a lot of onlookers standing in the bright noon sunshine. Some were from ships in the harbour as well as several of Cuff's disbanded crew. Once he caught sight of Meikle's oak-leaved cap at the rear of the crowd, here for reasons of his own, as a spectator like the rest.

With a start he realised that Fairfax was waiting for him. He wanted it to end and at the same time he did not want to begin it.

Some faces he had seen at their best and worst in battle, eyes staring into the flashes, voices shouting unheard words of encouragement or hatred into the clattering din which had been their world. Some he had seen rather too often across the defaulters' table. Hurt, innocent, reproachful, they were usually the most guilty, like Scouse Arkright, now standing with his cap in his hand, its huge tiddley bow hidden against his flapping trouser-leg.

'Sorry it's over, Arkright?'

The eyes shifted from a point beyond Marriott's shoulder.

'Not arf, sir. Back to th' Pool soon, eh?' But his eyes did not respond.

Telegraphist Knocker White, the one man who had kept them all in touch with hope and support, who had brought news of victory together with that of loved ones lost in air-raids at home. Paler than most of the hands because he saw little of the sunshine, cooped up in his W/T office. He was to be transferred to the big Signals Section at Plön. But as he had said when he had been told, 'I'll miss this old bucket, sir!'

Stoker Gilhooly, who had seen so many fights and brawls each time he had stepped ashore that his

256

nose and eyelids were bruised and scarred beyond recovery, answered Marriott in much the same fashion.

'I wanted to finish in 'er, sir. Not ponce about in some flamin' barracks!'

So it would be the defaulters' table again for him, Marriott thought. A lump of a man, but one who had saved several of his mates from blazing fuel when his previous boat had brewed up.

Acting-Petty Officer Arthur Townsend gave a brief grin. 'I'll go for my full rate, I suppose, sir.' He shrugged, summing it up. 'An' what for? All dressed up an' nowhere to go!'

Leading Seaman Rae, their crackshot machine-gunner, said much the same. Perhaps one of the best seamen Marriott had met. Just a hostilities-only recruit like the vast majority of the wartime navy, and he was one to be proud of.

Rae had been an errand-boy for a local grocer's shop before joining up. Riding a bicycle with a basket of groceries on the front for fifteen shillings a week. It seemed unlikely he would be content to go back to that.

And at the end of the line, strangely subdued, Ginger Jackson, who apart from the bridge-team Marriott probably knew better than any of them.

'I've arranged for you to be with us, Jackson.' Marriott studied his homely features, the bright ginger hair flapping in the harbour breeze. 'After that, well, it will be up to you.'

A quick grin, but sad all the same. 'Not Kentish Town, sir, never in a thousand years, not after 801!'

As Marriott moved along the second rank he saw the figures staring down from the dockside. Petty Officer Evans was there, as he had known he would

257

be. Harder for him perhaps? He had been so much a part of her. The hinge on which all else had depended.

Usually calm, always dependable no matter how bad the circumstances. Marriott had once believed Evans to have no feelings at all under the occasion when tracer shells had ripped just feet above the bridge to sever Silver's halliards like cotton threads. It was the only time he had heard the impassive Evans drop his guard and let loose a stream of curses in voluble French.

Marriott paused and faced Leading Signalman Silver. Like most of his breed he had shared just about everything with those who stood their watches on the bridge. In battle, he was as exposed and as vital as anyone in the tiny nerve-centre where the protective plating was not thick enough to withstand a heavy bullet's direct hit, let alone a cannon shell.

'What about you, Bunts? Will you go back to the dogtracks when you finally get demobbed?'

'Shouldn't wonder, sir. It's as good a bit 'er graftin' as any, an' I reckon they'll all need somethin' to take their minds orf fings.' He gave a sad grin. 'Still, I'll miss the tots an' the 'ot kye an' runs ashore in Alex.'

Fairfax followed closely on his heels, missing nothing, sharing each contact, and just as quickly feeling it slip away.

He had been right through the boat followed by one of the B.E.Q.'s officers. The latter had done everything but cluck with impatience, as if it was just another job number, an irritating formality.

But to Fairfax it was stark and moving, like these last farewells. For even if they worked together

258

again while they remained in Germany it could never be the same. No longer of one company.

The messdeck, the largest space in the hull apart from the engineroom. Stripped bare; they had even taken their beloved pin-ups with them. And yet still filled with the sounds and faces, movement, and the comings and goings of shadows.

Empty tables where they had written their letters, done their 'jewing', and sometimes slept when the whole deck was awash in heavy weather. The W/T office, the only place with a lingering air of life, but with an unknown telegraphist from the passage-crew sitting in White's metal chair.

Lastly the wardroom. Again so empty, without glasses in 'the bar', no pistols in the rack by the King's portrait, or where the picture had been.

Did boats really have their own personalities? Did they care or sustain hurt? After this, Fairfax knew they did.

He thought of his interview with Commander Meikle. He had gone to his new offices, all smelling of fresh paint and raw timber, hopes high after his application for transfer to the regular navy.

Meikle's attitude had been a disappointment; worse still, he had made Fairfax think of his father, blunt and uncompromising.

'You know what I think, Fairfax? I believe it would be a waste of your time and experience. Even if a transfer is effected, it may not be for very long, or until the navy settles down again to its peacetime torpor.' Fairfax had been astonished by his scornful tone. 'Then where will you be? Out in the cold, no job, and few prospects, unless you are well connected with the Old Boy network.' He had added sharply, *'Are you?'* Without waiting for a reply Meikle had finished by saying, 'Think about following your father's advice. Medicine. We will always need good doctors.'

Fairfax saw Marriott's expression as he walked towards him. As if he was reliving what he had just lost.

'Ready, sir?'

Marriott glanced past him at the silent watchers. 'Yes.' Just one word.

Fairfax looked at Lowes. 'Carry on!'

The hands arranged themselves into a new formation and faced aft.

Silver stood by the empty depth-charge racks, his cap at his feet as he loosened the White Ensign's halliards. In the bows the telegraphist was doing the same with the Jack.

Marriott climbed on to a ready-use locker and stared across their heads, his back towards the people on the dockside, excluding them.

'No speeches.' It was surprising how his voice carried. It was as if the dockyard din of cranes and pumps had been hushed for this final moment. 'We did a lot together. Few will ever know how much.' For the first time he dared to look at their faces, now blurred and indistinct so that others seemed to replace them. 'I shall miss you all, and I shall miss the boat, more than I could have believed. Later on, perhaps *much* later on, she will stand us in good stead when things go against us, no matter how or where we all end up. *We shall remember*, each and every one of us, and we will gain strength from it.'

He turned quickly to Fairfax. For just a few seconds he felt himself freeze, as if he could not move or speak again.

It was not Fairfax who stood there watching him,

his eyes in shadow from his cap. It was Tim Elliott. He was back. To share it.

Fairfax saw some of the men moving uneasily and called, 'Ready aft, sir!'

Marriott nodded. 'Yes. Thanks, Number One. Carry on.'

The calls shrilled the *still* and then very slowly the ensign and the Jack crept down their staffs, each keeping perfect time with the other.

'Sound off!'

The two boatswains' calls shrilled the *carry on* and the small masthead pendant vanished from the truck.

Marriott heard a launch start up its engines and knew the passage-crew had been hanging about nearby, waiting for this last, sad ritual. Like undertaker's men they would come and make it respectable and final.

Leading Signalman Silver strode up and saluted. ''Ere it is, sir.' He handed the tattered little pendant to Marriott and added, 'It's not much to show what you done, sir.'

Marriott took it and returned his salute. Then he stepped down from the locker and walked to the brow.

Only once did he look back. There were boiler-suited figures already on her deck, eager to go, unaware perhaps of what they had done.

Then he walked past the faceless figures on the dock wall and saw no one until Beri-Beri blocked his way and said, 'I've got the car. We'll go somewhere and get an enormous drink.'

'Thanks for coming.'

They walked together to the road, the various groups of figures parting to let them through. It was

261

all there, curiosity, indifference, sympathy. Beri-Beri had been watching with all the others, knowing what it was costing his friend, as it had once cost him.

He glanced at the young girl he had seen working at HQ, so pretty with her coiled black hair and brown eyes.

He had not noticed her on the dock until he had heard her sobbing quietly as she had watched the MGB's last rites. When some Germans had asked her to translate what Marriott had been saying she had not appeared to hear, but had kept watching him. In retrospect, it had seemed as if she had been willing him the strength to get through it.

She saw his glance now and lifted her chin as if to show she was all right. But her eyes returned to Marriott and told a very different story.

CHAPTER THIRTEEN

WITHOUT FEAR OR FAVOUR

Marriott rested his elbow on the table and looked out of a nearby window. It was a small office, as yet unallocated for any particular purpose, and like most of Meikle's headquarters smelled of paint and floor-polish.

He said wearily, 'I don't see why I need to have a German driver. What's the point of it now?'

Beri-Beri lowered a newspaper and eyed him gravely. 'Orders. It's the same for everyone.' Two days since MGB 801 had left Kiel on probably her

262

last passage anywhere, and Marriott was still feeling it badly.

Perhaps that was why Meikle had given him barely time to settle in to his new quarters at Plön. Nobody could argue with him on that score, he thought. Meikle himself seemed to work right around the clock.

Marriott watched a man watering some flowers and saw him glance up as if he could feel the scrutiny. Was he thinking perhaps of the officers who had worked here just three months ago?

A tall white mast and gaff had replaced the one smashed down in a final attack by RAF fighter-bombers. A large White Ensign curled lazily in the hot breeze while, from the masthead, Commodore Paget-Orme's broad pendant would act as another reminder that these premises were under new management.

Marriott turned back to the six folders of ex-German sailors who were available for use as drivers. All the rest, he assumed, had been selected by senior officers and military government officials. They had to be whiter-than-white, able to speak good English, and be capable of driving all the usual types of military or commandeered vehicles. One of Meikle's staff had explained tersely, 'The choice must finally be yours, old chap.'

Marriott had been in the navy long enough to know that, translated, that meant, *so too was the final responsibility*.

'They've been checked right through, of course, no dyed-in-the wool Nazis or that kind of fellow. Still, you can't be sure.' He had finished brightly by adding, 'After all, you're the one who'll be stuck with him!'

263

Beri-Beri said suddenly, 'You'll be with me for some of the time. So you'll need a driver who knows the whole of Schleswig-Holstein, not just round here.'

That was another mystery, Marriott thought. His new job required an officer with a watchkeeping certificate and some experience of command. A small-ship man.

He tried not to think of that last farewell. The way the once-familiar faces looked so out of place now whenever he passed one in the barracks. It was a demand on his own nerves too. To awake each morning without the usual standing orders, requestmen and defaulters, the routine of running a compact fighting unit with each man's problems your own. He had never believed he could have missed it so much.

Beri-Beri crossed the room and looked at the six folders. Marriott had seen three of them already. Impassive, well trained, withdrawn. He knew that Marriott would never get along with any of them.

'Try the next one. He seems to be, or *have* been, a regular.'

Marriott pressed a buzzer and a tall, broad-shouldered man in the now-familiar 'civilianised' uniform reefer jacket entered and waited across the table from him.

From his folder Marriott knew that his name was Heinz Knecht, and he was twenty-nine years old. Like Townsend he had been an acting-petty officer when the surrender had been announced. He had been doing an advancement course in Kiel where he lived with his young wife and daughter.

Meikle's aide had confided briefly that this man Knecht was a doubtful choice, in his opinion. The

264

folder explained that he had been a member of the Party, although like most servicemen he had had little to do with outside functions. Knecht had spent all his war in U-Boats, mostly in the Atlantic, and had been a survivor from one of them; his submarine had been depth-charged by an unseen Sunderland flying-boat when they were all but in sight of home. With casualties so high in the U-Boat arm of the *Kriegsmarine* he was lucky to be here at all.

'How long have you been in this command, Knecht?' The man looked like many people's idea of the typical German sailor. Light brown hair, neatly cut, blue eyes which although troubled by this interview showed a hint of humour.

'I was six months in Kiel before the end, Herr Leutnant.'

His voice was as Marriott had expected. Low and rounded, what he had already come to recognise as local.

'You have answered all the questions in the folder.' Marriott made no attempt to speak slowly or carefully, and the man named Knecht had no difficulty in following every word.

'You speak good English.'

'I wanted to do well in the navy, Herr Leutnant.' He gave a small shrug. 'We were expecting to win, you see. English would have been a great aid for promotion.'

Marriott stared at him. But there was neither insolence nor resentment in the blue eyes.

Knecht added, 'I have driven several cars here. I am good mechanic also.'

Marriott glanced at Beri-Beri who was looking at a newspaper at the other table, his head propped in his hands. He doubted if anyone else would realise that he had fallen fast asleep.

'It says here, Knecht, that you were a member of the Nazi party.'

A cloud seemed to pass across his features. 'That is so, Herr Leutnant.'

None of the others had been classified as ex-Nazis. They had professed to know little about anything which had happened in Germany before the surrender.

Marriott said quietly, 'Tell me about it.'

Again the shrug. 'There is nothing to tell. I entered the navy as my career, a life's work. I wanted to,' for the first time he groped for the right phrase, '—wanted to *get on*. So I joined the party. Those who say differently—' he looked at the floor. 'May I go, Herr Leutnant?'

'Do you have a family?'

Knecht looked up at him, surprised by his prolonging the interview.

'We have a little girl, Herr Marriott. Her name is Friedl. She is three years.'

Marriott frowned. 'How did you know my name?'

Knecht smiled, but it made him look vaguely sad.

'I was there when you came into the dockyard. That first day. I was near the one with the white flag. I saw and heard everything. When I heard about Kapitän von Tripz's son I was curious. I was there also when you—' He hesitated, 'Pay off your ship.'

Beri-Beri's elbow slipped off the table and he exclaimed, 'What? What was that?'

Marriott stood up and held out his hand. 'I've

just got myself a driver.'

The German stared at the out-thrust hand and then his face slowly split into a huge grin.

'*Danke sehr*, Leutnant Marriott!' Surprisingly, he wiped his face with the back of his hand. '*Danke!*'

Marriott said quietly, 'Report to me tomorrow, and I'll see what sort of Rolls-Royce they're going to give me.'

The door closed silently and Beri-Beri said, 'Good. He'll give you something else to worry about!' But inwardly he was glad. Companionship, anyone's, was what his friend needed above all else. He thought of the black-haired girl and wondered if he should mention that she had been on the dockside too. But he decided against it.

They left the bleak office together and walked across a patch of grass in the shadow of Paget-Orme's broad pendant. There was a small board which proclaimed that this place was called the *Quarter-Deck* henceforth, so they both saluted.

Beri-Beri chuckled. 'You always know when the Royal Navy is around. If it moves, salute it, if it doesn't, paint it white!'

They mounted the steps of the new wardroom and paused to hang up their caps with all the rest.

It was then that Marriott looked at the open doors where the other officers were sitting or standing at the bar, but nobody was speaking. It was like going stone deaf.

Then as the hubbub of voices boomed out again, Meikle left the big room and picked up his cap before saying, 'I'm afraid you missed my announcement.' His eyes moved from Beri-Beri to Marriott and stayed on him.

'It has just been cleared by Operations. Today,

267

the American air force dropped an atomic bomb on the Japanese city of Hiroshima.'

Marriott grappled with it. He was not even certain what the news implied. 'What happened, sir?'

Meikle dusted the peak of his cap with his sleeve before replying. 'The city was completely wiped out. Not a brick left standing, not a soul expected to be alive.'

He walked to the other door and took a deep breath as if to rid himself of the knowledge.

'It *means*, gentlemen, that to all intents and purposes, the war is over.'

Neither Marriott nor his friend moved or spoke for several seconds after Meikle had disappeared.

Then Marriott said, 'It's hard to take in, bloody nearly impossible.'

There was a burst of cheering from the wardroom and Beri-Beri said, 'That'll be the new subbies who arrived from England yesterday. Never heard a shot fired and now they're *all for it*!'

Marriott looked at his clean-cut features, the sun-bleached hair which usually poked from either side of his cap like wings. The sort of face you noticed, young but no longer young.

Beri-Beri said, 'They never stop to think, do they? Suppose it was London, or my old stamping-ground, Winchester?' He spoke with such anger and bitterness Marriott hardly recognised his voice. 'And it had to be our side to use a weapon like that, didn't it?' He snatched his cap from the rack and said, 'Let's just walk, shall we? If I go in there right now, I think I'll kill someone!'

Marriott fell into step beside him as they crunched along a broad gravel driveway.

Some would hail the news as brutal justice, punishing the enemy which had shown little respect for the rules of war. The Americans might claim that it was worth it if only to prevent more of their sailors and marines dying in the Pacific as they winkled out each Jap-held island with bayonet and flame-thrower.

Marriott might have expected Beri-Beri to be one of the former; he had been in the Far East and Burma, had lost his own command in the fighting. But his clear-sighted comparison between his home town and a hitherto unknown place called Hiroshima moved him more than he could say.

They reached the side of the great lake and Beri-Beri dragged out his worn and blackened pipe and waited for Marriott to produce his pouch. 'We'll be doing this when we're old men.' Beri-Beri shaded his pipe with his hands and held a flame above the tobacco like a true sailor. Then he said abruptly, as if he was giving himself no time to change his mind, 'You've done a lot for me, Vere, over the years, I mean.'

Marriott gripped his unlit pipe and watched the change of mood. 'For each other.'

'Maybe. But the war's finally over. Something which we knew must happen, and yet probably we still can't accept it. We were lucky.' His eyes moved to Marriott's decorations. 'And I don't mean the Glory Boys.'

'I know that.' Marriott looked at the shimmering water which stretched endlessly past the tall trees. 'All the blokes who bought it. Others back in hospital right now who most likely wish they had. It's that kind of luck.'

Beri-Beri nodded. 'I feel it's been given to us for

269

a reason. Not because we *won The War*, not as a reward. But as some kind of second chance.' He smiled suddenly. 'That's why I'm going fishing when I get demobbed. A labrador, maybe two, that's all I'll need.'

'No girl?'

'Well, maybe later.' He said quietly, 'That girl at HQ was on the dockside when you paid-off.' He felt as if he had betrayed some kind of trust, but knew instantly he had done the right thing.

Marriott stared at him. 'I've hardly spoken to her. But she's German, and—'

Beri-Beri raised an eyebrow. 'You surprise me. Does that matter?'

'I didn't mean it like that. Anyway, why the hell should she care?'

'You wouldn't ask if you'd seen her. She was with *you* and nobody else that day. I wouldn't lie about it, but then you know that too.' He clapped him on the shoulder. 'Come on, we'll go over to the Guards' Mess and cadge a drink, or two.' He watched his friend and added gently, 'Her name's Ursula, by the way.'

*   *   *

As Marriott had expected, the mood in the wardroom was more mixed that usual. The aftermath of the Bomb, and how it was all kept secret until it had become a terrible reality, raged and died like a forest fire.

Lieutenant Commander Arthur Durham sat in a corner engrossed in a copy of *The Times* which he had obtained from one of his private sources. He half-listened to the young officers arguing for and against the merits of the US attack on a Japanese city, but many, he thought, were more concerned about the war ending and leaving them high-and-dry, than with how it was achieved. However, his main attention was as usual on the closing prices at the stock exchange.

Cuff was lounging in a deep chair, halfway through his eighth gin and feeling more at ease than he had for several days. The S.I.B. had completed their investigations and the fuel depot had been handed over to a lieutenant from the supply branch. A worried young man who, Cuff had made it his business to discover, was deeply in debt. A *very* suitable contact, he had decided.

Then there was Hertha Ritter. He had seen her again, and was hoping to visit her tomorrow after the depot was shut. Cuff had experienced all kinds of women in his tempestuous service life, and even before that. But Hertha was head and shoulders above all of them. Whatever he did, no matter how hard he tried to overwhelm her, she could give him back such sexual passion that he was more often than not left exhausted. Then in minutes she would begin on him again until he would plead for mercy.

She had some friends in the nearby town who might help with their proposed deals. They would have to be doubly careful now, and it would be madness to allow too many strangers to become involved.

He twisted his head as Lieutenant Commander Durham said above the noise, 'Have you read this?'

Cuff frowned, but he saw no harm in the elderly, owlish staff officer.

Cuff was sick and tired of hearing these twits all arguing about the Japs and the atomic bomb. Who

271

cared? He had other things to dwell on. The end of the war meant no half stripe, no new command. He would be out in civvy street like all the rest. Anyway, the Japs had it coming, so what?

Durham said, 'Right here in *The Times*?'

Cuff grinned and swallowed the rest of the gin. 'Not my sort of rag, old son!'

Durham glanced at him over his horn-rimmed glasses. Pissed again, he thought sadly.

He said, 'You come from York, don't you? You must know this fellow. Charles Glazebrook of Glazebrook Engineering—'

Cuff almost choked. '*Know* him? It's my bloody father! What's he done now, gone in the nick?'

Durham laughed. 'Hardly. The new Labour Government has seen its way clear to give him a knighthood!'

Cuff took the proffered newspaper and waited for his blurred vision to clear.

'I don't bloody well believe it!' He pictured his father. He was only half his size, everyone's idea of the pig-headed Northerner. All beer and whippets. He exclaimed, 'Christ, he's ignorant as shit! He must have done a few favours for someone, eh?'

Another lieutenant commander, this time a regular officer, snapped severely, 'Watch your language in the mess!'

Cuff was still floundering at the news. '*You* can kiss my arse!'

The other officer jumped to his feet and strode across to the sprawled lieutenant.

'*What* did you say?'

Cuff focussed his eyes on him. 'Now that I've seen you close to, I withdraw the offer!'

'Why, you foul-mouthed—'

272

Durham rose and stood between them. 'Remember this.' His voice was mild, but his words had bite to them. 'This is my home too, until I can get out of uniform for good. So behave yourselves. There are German stewards here. Don't take away *all* their illusions.'

Someone laughed, and the noise of voices washed around the little group like waves on a rock.

Cuff nodded as the other lieutenant commander stalked away.

He said, 'Gone to whine to Meikle, I s'pose.' He chuckled. 'Fair enough, sir, I take your point. No hard feelings. And thanks for telling me about my father.' He shook his head. 'He'll never change though.' He could almost hear him, 'good old Charlie Glazebrook', down at the Royal York with his cronies, doing another deal and promising full support for the returning servicemen. *Aye, nowt's too good for our lads*, especially if it helped him to line his pockets in the same way the war had done.

Another thought struck him. His father might sell all his business, or do something daft with the cash.

He needed to talk about it. There was only one he could trust. He looked at the clock. She might even be expecting him.

He lurched to his feet and walked unsteadily to the door.

One of the newly arrived subbies said, 'God, what an awful type!'

Sub-Lieutenant Gilmour, who had met Marriott and most of the others who came and went from headquarters, said, 'I'd keep your voice down, chum.'

The youth turned on him and asked hotly, 'Why

273

should I?'

'Because he's killed more people than you probably know by their first name!'

The new subbie glowered. 'But that was the *war!*'

'No, my little friend, *that* was Cuff Glazebrook. Even his own men say that of him. He actually enjoys it. So watch it!'

Sub-Lieutenant Lowes walked through the doors and found a chair in one corner, hidden from most of the others by a giant potted palm. He wanted a drink badly. *Needed it.* He had been walking up to the wardroom still thinking of the letter which had come from his mother. *Dearest Johnnie*—that beginning had always warmed his heart. Now the words stuck in his throat so that when a German messman hovered over his chair he could barely order a drink.

She was going to marry that brute he had come face to face with on that awful night. Marry him. Lie with him. Allow him *to do things* to her. *'Oh God!'* He flushed and stared at his lap as some of the officers at a nearby table turned to look at him.

She treated him like a child. She always had. Now he was unable to see his way to do anything without her. If only . . . He pictured himself running into the old house and pitching the man down the stairs and throwing his uniform after him. He almost cried out aloud again. The brute of a man could have thrashed him with one hand!

The messman brought him a Horse's Neck, like he had seen Marriott drink. 'Another, please!' It had meant to sound defiant, *a man of the world*, but it came out like a whimper of despair.

He thought suddenly of Ginger Jackson who had accidentally bumped into him that morning. Like

274

some of the other junior officers in Meikle's command Lowes was employed in assisting the Officer-of-the-Day, either at the main gates, or doing the rounds of the foreshore and sentry posts. Jackson had asked him if he had any spare cigarettes for barter. Lowes had considered telling him it was off when he had thought of his mother again. He would give her no more duty-frees. If she really was going to marry that oaf, *he* could take care of everything for her!

Ginger Jackson had seemed surprised at his eagerness to provide more cigarettes, and had then touched on what his 'accidental' meeting with Lowes had really been all about.

'The bloke 'oo's 'elpin' with me business arrangements, sir, 'as asked us to meet someone really special-like.' He had waited, watching Lowes's troubled eyes. 'A lady, she is, a countess no less. Lots of good contacts, jewellery, no rubbish, just the job.'

Lowes had waited. 'How does that affect me?'

Ginger Jackson had almost laughed aloud. 'Well, *you*, sir! That's the difference! An officer an' a real gent, the sort of toff she'd be used to, with 'er sort of class!'

Lowes had decided to ignore the idea. Now, sitting with his second Horse's Neck inside him and a third on the way, he was changing his mind. *I'll show them. All of them. Fairfax with his second ring, Marriott who treats me as much like a child as my mother does, and that brute who's taking her away . . .* He stopped his reeling thoughts. What did he mean by that? He felt suddenly embarrassed and ashamed, and lurched up without waiting for the next drink.

Yes, he would show all of them.

In the large canteen which was used by other ranks below the rank of petty officer, Ginger Jackson sauntered towards a beer-covered table and grinned reassuringly at Rae and Craven, who looked as if they were going to make a night of it.

Craven looked at him warily, his eyes red-rimmed. 'Well, wot did he say?'

Rae glanced at his new watch, a real beauty, with tiny diamonds set around the face. 'Yes, Ginger, how did Snow White take it?'

Ginger clapped his hands together and his grin widened. 'All fixed. The bite 'as bin took, my friends! I don't know what they put in them wardroom drinks, but our gallant Mr Lowes is ready to do 'is bit!'

Craven nodded gloomily. 'So God bless all of us!'

Ginger glared at him. 'Don't be so bloody sarky about it, Bill. Oskar's not let us down now, 'as 'e? If 'e says this bint is on th' level, countess or no bleedin' countess, then that'll do me, see?'

Rae grinned lazily. 'Might be enough of her for all of us!'

*   *   *

Meikle's operational section was in darkness but for a solitary desk light when Fairfax arrived from the wardroom. A messenger looked up from some signal flimsies and said, 'Commander Meikle is expecting you, sir.' He gestured to the big office with a strip of light showing under the door.

Fairfax had been getting ready to turn in after a noisy dinner where the arguments had carried on, back and forth, discussing the merits or the horrors

276

of the Bomb and all its implications. Some of the mess bills would be extra large, he thought, and might soon arouse the first lieutenant's attention, if not that of Meikle himself.

He straightened his jacket and hoped his collar still looked fresh. To call for him so late at night was unheard of. Bad news could always wait. So it had to be something about his application.

He tapped on the door and heard Meikle say, '*Come!*'

He was at his huge desk, his hair unusually dishevelled. And when he glanced up he looked tired.

'Ah yes, Fairfax. Sit, will you.'

That too was unusual.

Meikle said, 'I've sent a report to the commodore about you for his approval. You'll have to be patient. Especially now that the war is almost certainly finished. I believe that the Japanese have made approaches on surrender terms. But everything is so vague.'

Fairfax tried to dispel the disappointment Meikle had aroused. He was, after all, offering to help; at least he seemed to be. So why had he sent for him?

Meikle looked at him searchingly. 'A lieutenant, even an *acting-temporary* lieutenant, must expect all kinds of duties to come his way, especially in territory newly taken from the enemy.'

'Yes, sir.'

'Some of the tasks are hard, some more difficult than others. But they have to be fairly and equally shared by the occupying forces, and *seen* to be shared without fear or favour.'

'I see, sir.' How inadequate it sounded.

'Two displaced persons, Poles to be exact, were

arrested and charged with looting and attempted murder.'

Fairfax watched as one of Meikle's hands moved away to flip over some loose papers, as if it was acting apart from its owner. Where was this all leading?

'They were found guilty by a military court at Lübeck and sentenced to death.' His eyes never wavered. 'The executions will be by firing-squad next week. You will be in charge of one of them.'

Fairfax found that he was on his feet, his skin suddenly chilled despite the warm night.

'Is that an order, sir?'

'You may request to be excused. That is all I can tell you. Your name was selected in secret. But I fear your refusal to carry out this unpleasant duty would *not* remain secret for long.'

'I understand, sir.' He felt sick, and wanted to leave the room.

'I doubt that, Fairfax. But nothing can be achieved here without maintaining law and order. The fact that the victim was a German, and her attackers people from an oppressed country, must matter not one jot if we are to succeed.'

'A *woman*, sir?'

Meikle gave a cold smile. 'It touches your sense of honour, does it?'

He rang a bell and the same messenger appeared as if on a wire.

'Off you go, Fairfax. Just be ready.'

Outside the room Fairfax walked slowly into the deep shadows. What difference should it make? He had seen men die in battle, bravely, or screaming with terror until death offered its release. Thousands they said had died in Hiroshima, with many more to follow if all the rest of it was true.

So why should one man count? He was guilty.

He tried to think of Marriott's summing-up when he had spoken about a regular commission. *All for it.*

It was what he wanted more than anything. Was it enough?

*   *   *

The Staff Operations Officer stood with his arms folded and stared up at his huge wall chart, which showed in detail the Schleswig-Holstein Command. Wrecks considered safe enough for general navigation, wrecks awaiting salvage or destruction, a few remaining minefields; the endless litter of war.

Marriott had not been in the main operations room before and was struck by its quiet efficiency. He sensed that Meikle's hand was behind it although it gave the impression it had been here for years.

The commander said, 'You'll go up to Flensburg by road; there you can contact the local operations section who will take care of you. There's a ship to be towed into the Baltic for scuttling. Probably the first of many, but because it's a towing job we can't wait for the weather to change against us.' He glanced at the sunlight streaming through the windows. 'You know the Baltic—nice as pie one minute, but as the summer passes on it can get really ugly.' He eyed him keenly. 'You're a good navigator, I hear. Small-ship chaps usually are.'

Marriott smiled. 'Have to be, sir.' He added, 'Can I ask why it has to be scuttled so far out, sir?'

'You can now, but it's still officially secret. The army have discovered several great storage dumps of poison gas, a last resort probably, but never used, thank God. My father was a soldier in the last lot. He was gassed in Flanders. Never got over it. Coughed out his life while I was still at school.'

Marriott pictured the silent and deserted ships he had seen at Flensburg. He had thought they had looked sinister then; now that he knew their contents it did not surprise him.

The commander said, 'It's properly stowed. Nothing for you to worry about. Lieutenant Kidd is up there now, supervising the job. A friend of yours, I gather?'

Marriott did not get a chance to answer as a signalman sitting at one of the telephones covered the mouthpiece and called, 'For you, sir!'

The commander frowned. 'I said not to be disturbed until—'

'It's the N.O.I.C., sir.'

He shot Marriott a quick grin. 'In that case.' He took the phone, but apart from announcing himself he did not appear to say anything further. He replaced the telephone and said to the signalman, 'Send a messenger around Ops. I want everyone here. Right now.'

He moved out of earshot and looked at Marriott, his face suddenly very tired.

'What is it, sir? Bad news?'

He did not answer directly but walked over to fling open a window. Later, Marriott was to remember it very clearly. Like Meikle when he had drawn those deep breaths outside the wardroom.

'Apparently they decided that one was not enough. They dropped the second atom bomb on

280

the town of Nagasaki. Exactly the same result. Everything and everyone wiped out by a single blast.' He clenched his fists. 'It's obscene! Are we no better than the ones who have been guilty before us?' He seemed to recover his self-control and added, 'You can shove off, Marriott.' He tried to smile. 'The job goes on. Like the Windmill, we never close.'

Marriott walked along one of the freshly painted corridors, so bright it was like a hall of mirrors.

A few Germans, still wearing their naval uniforms, were working on some wiring, but their hands were barely moving, and they watched him pass as if they were afraid.

They knew. How could anyone expect to keep something like Hiroshima and a place called Nagasaki a secret for long?

He could feel it as he passed open office doors. Inside he saw a Petty Officer Yeoman of Signals sitting with his hands folded and staring at a flowering plant which somebody had put on his desk. He might have been praying for all the notice he was taking of those around him. Past another door marked S.D.O. where as if to a silent signal all the typewriters and teleprinters stopped as one. *Now they all knew.*

A door at the far end near Meikle's office opened and she stepped outside, frowning as a file slid from the pile she was carrying. Marriott reached down and scooped it up, seeing her sudden surprise and recognition.

'I—I am sorry, Herr Leutnant.'

At the end of the corridor was a division like a large letter T. He would take the left passage, she the right one to her new office.

281

He tucked the file under his arm and said, 'I'll carry it for you.' They walked together and he realised how clumsy she made him feel. They would part. It was, after all, only a dream.

But she said quietly, 'I was sorry to hear about your ship. I am beginning to understand such things. Before—' She shrugged. 'It is different, you see?'

He did not understand what she meant. 'You were there?'

She met his gaze, her eyes very bright. 'I was. It was sad, I think.'

'I am going up to Flensburg.'

She looked away, suddenly embarrassed. 'I know, Herr Leutnant. I had to translate some of the details.'

They both stopped and she watched him over the pile of cardboard files.

He asked, 'Did the child enjoy the chocolate?'

She nodded. 'She did.' Again that shrug which seemed to tug at Marriott's heart. 'She has not known such luxuries.'

'I'm glad.' He had to say something. 'I wondered if we could talk sometimes. I know I upset you before. I didn't think—'

She did not reply directly. 'You will be going home soon, to England, yes?'

'Perhaps. Nothing is tied up yet.'

She smiled, her teeth very white in her tanned face. 'You use expressions I do not understand!'

'You speak perfect English.'

'Thank you. I try. I need the work now.'

'The family, you mean?'

She looked past him, her brown eyes in shadow. 'My father is missing, somewhere in Russia they

282

say. Also my brother. There has been no news. He has never seen his little girl. Never.'

Marriott wanted to touch her arm, to try and help.

It was not her child after all. Even if it had been . . . His mind was in a spin.

He said, 'When I return, perhaps we could meet?'

She faced him again. 'I am not sure, Herr Leutnant.'

Lieutenant Commander Durham, his glasses perched on the top of his bald head, walked past them. He was about to speak, but decided against it. They had not even seen him. Maybe she was the girl Marriott had not told him about on passage to Swinemünde?

She said softly, 'When you are gone from here they would say things, think things—'

'It mustn't be like that.' So close he could feel her warmth, taste the scent of her coiled hair. And all the while she was slipping away from him.

A door opened and Meikle's voice cut across them. 'Some of us have work to do, Marriott, even if you do not! I thought you were supposed to be on your way to Flensburg.' His glance flickered just briefly between them. 'I suppose you heard the news?'

Marriott placed the extra file on the others and watched as she walked down the opposite corridor.

'Yes, I heard, sir.'

'Well I just hope they know what they're doing by unleashing all this on the world!'

He looked round as a door slammed shut.

'Very useful girl, that one. English student before she was called up. The best interpreter I've got at

283

the moment.'

'She was telling me about her family, sir.'

'I suppose that loosely ranks with *in the line of duty*, eh?'

He watched Marriott's eyes and added, 'Her people run some sort of inn, a *Gasthaus* over in Eutin. Pretty little town from what I've seen of it.'

He consulted his watch. 'Conference time.' He looked at Marriott and said, 'Cut along to Flensburg. Put everything else on the shelf and forget it.' As he walked away he called, 'I see that you chose Knecht as your driver. Knew you would. Just your style.'

Marriott walked down the steps and looked at the sky. Perhaps Meikle was right. *Just forget it.*

He found Heinz Knecht waiting for him beside their authorised vehicle. It had begun life as a *Wehrmacht* scout car, neat enough from the outside with its spare wheel on the bonnet, and enjoying a coat of blue pusser's paint with *ROYAL NAVY* in white letters on either side. But the interior was sparse and unwelcoming, with plain slatted seats. It definitely did not compare with Beri-Beri's Mercedes.

Knecht beamed at him. 'Maybe we get better one next time, Herr Leutnant!' He looked very fresh and neat, his skin glowing as if he had just had a shower.

He thought of Meikle. *Just your style.* He certainly knew how to needle and irritate people.

Knecht had seen to everything. Marriott's small case was on the back seat and a sealed tin which the wardroom chef had sent over with some sandwiches, plus a bottle of wine in a rubber bag filled with ice. He heard Knecht humming to himself as he prepared to start the car. At least he was happy. Getting the job, or being back in a world he understood, it was hard to tell which.

Marriott tried to make himself comfortable. Flensburg was about eighty miles from here. On these seats they would feel every one of them.

As the car bumped towards the main gates Marriott asked, 'How long would it take to drive to Eutin?'

Knecht tore his eyes from the gates. 'But Herr Leutnant, that is in the other direction!' But he saw Marriott's expression and added, 'Fifteen minutes, no more.'

They passed through the gates and Marriott returned the sentry's smart salute. Then he said, 'I don't want to *visit* anybody there, you understand?'

'Yes, Herr Leutnant.' Knecht's blue eyes gleamed in the driving mirror. 'You give the orders, I obey.'

He thinks me mad. He is probably right. Marriott watched the green countryside flashing past. *I only want to see where she lives, that's all.*

Knecht relaxed slightly. It was a strange experience to be driving one of the old enemy. Stranger still that he was able to enjoy it. What was in Eutin that meant so much? He glanced at the lieutenant's profile. How different from some of the officers he had served in his time. When they returned from Flensburg he would tell his wife all about it, and make her laugh. That would be the best part.

Marriott winced as the wheels bounced over a loosely filled bomb-crater.

Dreaming of a girl he could never hope to know, being driven by an Ex-U-Boat sailor who had spent

285

his war trying to blow the backsides off British warships and merchantmen alike. And soon to put to sea again with a cargo of deadly poison gas. The schoolfriend who had been playing jazz on the organ in a bombed church, and rescuing von Tripz's son from one of their own allies.

By comparison his war seemed almost sane and commonplace.

CHAPTER FOURTEEN

THE SAME MEN?

Marriott moved the overhead light very slightly and concentrated on the Baltic chart, all its latest references and bearings marked with surprising neatness. By glancing to starboard he could see the vessel's master, a solid, rugged-faced professional sailor, peering beneath the peak of his battered cap, his hands thrust into his bridge-coat pockets. It was hard to imagine those same hands making such delicate calculations.

He straightened his back and looked at his friend, who was leaning on the chartroom voicepipes, an unlit pipe clenched between his jaws. Such a different feeling from the motor gunboat, he thought. Strange and alien. Not the thrusting, uneven rolls when throttled right down to minimum revolutions, or planing across the crests when at full throttle; the big German salvage tug *Herkules* felt as if nothing could resist her. Also, unlike the base or Kiel harbour, everyone around him was speaking German, and only when directly

286

addressed would one of the new petty officers translate his wishes into direct action.

He said, 'About twenty minutes.' He walked to the rear of the wheelhouse and studied the long towing hawser, the obedient merchant ship which had dragged astern at a mere five knots, all the way from Flensburg Fjord. To navigate the narrows and busier parts of the journey they had had the assistance of a second tug, *Tail-end-Charlie*, which had controlled the towed ship's progress with a long stern-wire. They had passed Bornholm in the night, and had altered course to the north-east when the other tug had left them to it. Marriot was glad they had made contact with that island under cover of darkness. In his mind it would always represent something bad, where men and women had died to no sane purpose.

Together Marriott and Kidd walked out on to the open bridge wing on the opposite side, leaving the German master to his privacy. He doubtless knew these waters and this kind of work better than anyone; certainly a lot better than two ex-Coastal Forces officers. But he seemed content to accept their instructions. Maybe only because he had no choice.

Beri-Beri said, 'We'll board her and then I'll take you below. It's dead simple really, but you'll be doing it on your own next time. Don't want to lose my *old mate* now that I've only just found him!'

Marriott raised his binoculars and levelled them on the vessel under tow. She had been in service until the last year of the war, when she had sustained a near-miss from a heavy bomb which had put her engines and shafts out of alignment. Too costly to repair, she had been patched up and used for various other tasks, from accommodation vessel to prison hulk for Russians captured on the Eastern Front. Now, loaded with tons of poison gas, in shells and bombs, cylinders and all the deadly equipment required to release it on the enemy, she was on her final voyage. There was something sad and yet menacing about her spartan outline. Stripped of everything except some emergency rafts, she must offer little comfort to her small passage-crew of German sailors. They would give a sigh of relief when the powerful *Herkules* went alongside for the last time and took them off.

Beri-Beri pointed over the rail to the after deck which, with all the weight of the two pulling against her, was almost awash.

'Look at him. Happy as a sand-boy!'

Marriott nodded and smiled. The young German Willi Tripz was squatting on a hatch-cover, his legs crossed and arms wrapped around his knees as he stared at the activity around him. His feet were bare, and his fair hair was blowing unchecked in the wind, as if he felt no discomfort from the spray which pattered over the hull like tropical rain.

He was here at his father's request. It had come through Meikle's office, so he had obviously approved it for unknown reasons of his own.

Beri-Beri grinned. Real bit of hero-worship, that one!'

Marriott looked at him. 'Don't be so bloody daft! I think you were out in Burma a bit too long!'

Beri-Beri was unmoved. 'He follows you everywhere. All kids need a hero—you happen to be it. At the moment anyway.'

Marriott shrugged. 'I'd have thought he'd seen enough of the Baltic after the last run.' He thought

288

of the swastika carved on the boy's shoulder, and wondered if he would always carry it.

He swung away and shouted across the chartroom, 'Stand by, Kapitän!'

The tug's master, whose name was Horst Krieger, raised one massive fist, then strode unhurriedly to a voice pipe.

Beri-Beri murmered, 'I can just see him at Jutland, eh?'

The tug's small crew turned-to and bustled aft to prepare for casting off. A signal lamp clattered from the upper bridge and a diamond-bright acknowledgement came instantly from the vessel astern.

Marriott turned his eyes from the bridge. He had almost expected to see Long John Silver there.

Beri-Beri was watching him. 'More memories, Vere?'

'A few.' He heard the winches whine into action, felt the tug's tightly packed hull lift its thousand tons of iron and steel, her screws thrashing astern to take off the way.

Marriott wrapped one arm around a compass-repeater and felt the hull swaying over into a deep trough. *A cross on a chart.* Who would ever question the sense of what they were doing, or even remember it? Fifty fathoms down, three hundred feet, where all that cargo of poison and mustard gas would lie harmless in the depths.

Beri-Beri jammed his cap more tightly over his unruly hair and watched as the tow was cast off, and the big winches brought it whining through the water and up to the stern swivel before it could snare a shaft or some hidden, unmarked wreck.

Marriott saw how well the crew worked together.

Few orders, hands and arms moving like machines. One man dropped a spanner and the boy Willi Tripz snatched it up and handed it to him, then turned and looked up to the bridge, as if to seek him out.

Beri-Beri smiled gently. '*Told you.*'

Even now *Herkules* was swinging round, butting into the choppy crests with disdain as she altered course towards the drifting hulk. They had lowered fenders and two ladders; were wasting no time, Marriott thought.

Then he and Beri-Beri hurried down to the raised forecastle and waited while the gap narrowed between the two hulls, and the other ship seemed to tower over them like a flaking cliff.

'*Up we go!*' Beri-Beri judged the moment then swung on to the ladder, climbing fast while Marriott waited for the two hulls to fall apart, spray spurting up between them, before he could follow his example and swing himself across. It was a matter of timing. Too soon and you might fall. Too late and you could be crushed between the hulls as they surged together again.

Up and over the bulwark where they stood, regaining breath, staring around at the deserted and abandoned decks. The eyeless bridge where anxious lookouts had watched for aircraft and the tell-tale periscope. Storms and frozen nights in the Baltic, hopes, fears, all the things which every ship must know.

Beri-Beri led the way. Down one ladder, through a watertight door, where battery-driven lamps lit the handrails and catwalks, and then down the next.

The deeper they went the more distant and

290

muffled the sea sounds became. It was eerie, creepy, as they groped along the shining catwalks where countless men had gone before them. On and off watch, to enter or leave harbour. As the ship had carried many wounded back from the Russian Front, it was more than likely there had been many sea-burials too.

Beri-Beri levered open a door and flashed his huge light inside. It was one of the ship's four holds. 'See, they've made a good job of it.' The massive piles of gas shells and bombs in this hold were covered in cement. No wonder she felt so heavy in the water despite being stripped of her fittings.

Marriott said, 'I'm glad you've done this before. I'm bloody well lost!'

Beri-Beri's teeth gleamed in the lights. 'I studied the plan until I knew it backwards.' He dragged up another hatch and said, 'Last hit, old son.'

Here, at the very bottom of the hull, it felt even more oppressive. The sea was just a far-off booming sound, while the gurgling slap of trapped bilge-water seemed to be all around them.

Beri-Beri clung to a vertical steel ladder and studied the long array of explosives. Again, more concrete so that the full blast would go straight down, blast a hole in her bottom without breaking her back to strew the deadly cargo across the sea-bed. 'Like a bloody great Bangalore torpedo!'

Marriott stooped over the nearest pile. It had to be done this way. To scuttle the ship might take too long, so that she would drift for many miles, her final resting place unknown or wrongly marked on the charts. To blow her up by gunfire would be even more dangerous. Insanity.

They checked their watches. Up in the damp air of his bridge, Kapitän Kreiger would be doing the same. He had his orders too. Marriott thought he was not the kind of man to act without or against them.

Beri-Beri remarked suddenly, 'We do meet in the oddest places.'

Then he stooped over and unlocked a well-greased metal plate. 'It's very simple really. There's a line just here which is connected to a friction-type igniter set. You pull it, and the thing fires. After that—' he grinned up at him. 'You've got fifteen minutes. Piece of cake!'

'Suppose it misfires?'

'There's a second one next to it. But I've never known one to fizzle out.' He chuckled. 'Not yet, that is.'

The hull rolled suddenly and Marriott heard a chorus of metallic groans and shudders. Like a protest. Like something alive.

He said, 'Let's get it over with.'

Beri-Beri nodded, suddenly serious. 'Let's.' He dragged at the line and there was a tiny spurt of sparks and smoke.

He stood up and licked his lips. 'Time to go. You first.' He gripped the ladder and waited for Marriott to clamber up towards the oval hatch while he stood and watched the inert mass of concrete.

Marriott gripped the rim of the hatch. He might get used to it. He had been in dying ships before, and in the Med had even helped to fit charges to vessels they had found working for the enemy amongst the Greek Islands. But this was different, although he could not explain why.

There was a sharp click beneath his feet and he

heard Beri-Beri exclaim, '*Hold on!*' Then the lower half of the ladder veered round, swinging on a single bolt, before that too parted and Beri-Beri fell straight down on to the concrete.

He struggled to get to his feet and fell on his side. '*Oh, shit!* My bloody leg!'

Marriott clung to the remains of the ladder and peered down at him. 'I'm coming! *Don't move!*'

Beri-Beri almost screamed. 'You can't do anything! You'll never be able to lift me up there!' He was sobbing, pleading. '*For Christ's sake get out while you can!* This lot'll go up—'

Marriott hung by his fingers for a few seconds then dropped lightly to the bottom.

He bent over his friend, felt him tense as he tried to move the leg folded under him at an unnatural angle.

Go! In the name of God!' He was gasping with pain and despair.

Marriott cradled his shoulders in his arms and crouched down beside him. All at once, after the stark spasm of fear, he felt completely calm.

'I'm not leaving you, you silly old bugger.' He pulled him closer, and tried not to listen to the lapping bilge-water, while the smell of the acrid fuse seemed to be everywhere like an invisible threat. Once he thought he heard a loud thud, the vague vibration of engines, and could picture the tug standing away. They had already overstayed their time. And why should Kreiger risk his ship and his men? Just months back they had been fighting each other. Killing and dying. Kreiger had no cause for regrets, even if he could do something.

He thought suddenly of his driver, Heinz Knecht, when he had ordered him to remain at

Flensburg with the car until they returned.

He had protested. 'You might need me, Herr Leutnant! You are my officer now! It is my *place* also!'

How right he had been, he thought. Something slid from a catwalk and seemed to fall for a long while before it clattered down below.

Beri-Beri groaned, 'You've still got time . . . if you jump for it, you could make it to the top—'

'I thought you'd dropped off again.' He hugged him tightly. 'Forget it.'

Beri-Beri seemed to relax. Then he said hoarsely, 'That girl.'

'What girl?' He felt it probing through him, already missing what he had never shared. 'It was hopeless.'

Beri-Beri gritted his teeth. 'How long have we got?'

But Marriott would not remove his arm to look. It would be quick anyway. If it was enough to take out a ship's keel . . .

He stared with disbelief at a rope bowline as it dropped down by his legs. He stared up and saw the boy's face peering at them, another shadowy figure beyond, the sound of feet on metal.

Marriott struggled to his knees and dragged the bowline around Beri-Beri's shoulders. He did not know what he was saying to him; the words just seemed to flood out as he tried to secure the line. All he could think was that they had not left them to die. *They had come back*. It might be too late already but . . . He gasped, '*Haul away!*'

Beri-Beri cried out just once, and then mercifully fainted as they dragged him up and over the rim of the hatch. Marriott took a deep breath and then jumped for the upper part of the ladder. Hands reached down to guide him through, and then they were all lurching along those same eerie catwalks, pausing only to haul and thrust Beri-Beri's limp figure through one hatch after another until Marriott saw daylight, tasted salt spray, and felt almost sick with gratitude and disbelief.

He saw the tug's tall funnel rising and dipping close alongside, the master peering up at the ship's bulwark, his real feelings hidden by a mask of watchfulness.

Orders were barked, lines cast off, and then with powerful dignity the tug *Herkules* thrashed stern-first clear of the side.

Marriott saw his friend being wrapped in a blanket, while someone placed a lifejacket under his head like a pillow.

The explosion when it came was surprisingly subdued, but the tell-tale bubbles and spreading pattern of floating rust told him that the explosive charges had done their work.

Marriott walked into the spacious chartroom and leaned over the same calculations, before marking the position and initialling the deck-log.

He was vaguely aware that the tug had gathered way and was forging ahead once more. The master's shadow fell across the chart and for a long moment their eyes met and held.

Marriott had faced death many times. He had persuaded himself he had been able to accept it, if not the actual dying.

Today he had surprised himself. He had accepted both without hesitation.

The master nodded very slowly.

'I send radio signal, Herr Leutnant. They will

295

have doctor waiting.' He gave a rare smile so that his weatherbeaten face seemed to be all wrinkles.

'Now I know the war is *kaputt!*'

Marriott saw the bare-footed boy staring at them through the door and replied, 'You took a great risk, Kapitän Krieger.'

The older man shook his head. 'To go to sea is a risk, Herr Leutnant.' He held out his hand. 'I have some schnapps. It is a good moment.'

'None better.' He saw them carrying Beri-Beri to the shelter of the bridge. *Leave him to die? Not in a thousand bloody years!*

He did not see the expression on the German's craggy face, nor did he realise he had spoken so fervently, and aloud.

★   ★   ★

Captain Eric Whitcombe of the Army's Special Investigation Branch was sipping his first mug of scalding tea of the day while he read slowly through a copy of the *Daily Mail*.

He was a big man, with a sun-reddened face and a dashing ginger moustache. His battledress was neatly pressed, and he was still unused to the comfortable quarters and German servants which had been available to him since his arrival in Kiel.

Through the door he could hear his department coming to life, somebody whistling, while out in the yard one of his MPs was unsuccessfully trying to start a motor-cycle.

The headlines on the front page were huge. Larger, if anything, than those on VE-Day. It was all over. Officially. August 15th would henceforth be   remembered—'celebrated'   hardly   seemed

296

suitable—as VJ-Day. The Japs had finally thrown in the towel. But for the bombs' horrific casualites, Whitcombe doubted if the war would have ended even next year. He straightened his back and walked to the window. He walked and stood like a policeman, which indeed he had been before joining up for the duration. His last nick had been a busy one in North London, Jews, the rag-trade, and clashes with Mosley's blackshirts every Sunday. A kind of local entertainment, and always busy for a newly made-up inspector.

It would be strange to begin all over again, he thought. School-crossings, pickpockets, Saturday night punch-ups, drunks, and vagrants. A copper's lot. In many ways he would be sorry to go back. This was a different world which even some of the occupying forces did not know existed. The black market, troops flogging stores and petrol, officers who were not slow to make a dishonest quid when the choice offered itself. But deeper still there was depravity and squalor which made a London knocking-shop seem like a kindergarten.

He was proud of his team. Most of them were ex-coppers, and the majority were from the Met like himself.

The door swung open after a brief tap and Sergeant Jim Thornhill walked in and saluted.

'Morning, Jim.'

Thornhill slumped down in a chair and gratefully took a mug of tea.

'Thanks, Guv.'

To the army they were captain and sergeant. To one another they were the Guv'nor and his Skipper. It was their own defence against the rest, their world within a world.

Thornhill was unshaven, and there was dirt on his battledress elbows and knees.

'How'd the obbo go, Jim?'

The sergeant suppressed a yawn. 'Caught a couple of the buggers out by the Ravensberger Wasserurm. Pair of displaced persons, Poles again. Had a load of gear on them. Ration cards *and* faked petrol permits.'

'Hmm—bad business. The Poles seem to be trying to get their own back. They won't though. A couple of them are being topped today. That might help to cool them down.'

The sergeant was looking at the newspaper's front page. *'They'll* not be around to celebrate VJ-Day, that's for sure!'

Thornhill frowned and said, 'I've been thinking about that navy bloke, Petty Officer Evans—'

'Ah!' The captain tugged a file from his briefcase. 'I've been looking into it while you've been away on the job.'

Thornhill raised his dark eyebrows. 'I thought we'd done with that case. Major Helmut Maybach of the SS is just a bit of dirty linen now, surely?'

Captain Whitcombe put on his glasses, something he hated to do in company. 'I had the forensic boys go over it all again. They even exhumed the corpse, or the bits which were available.' He grinned, knowing it was pointless to try and shock his sergeant. He had been a CID officer in Bethnal Green and had seen just about everything. What he had missed there he had certainly made up for in Germany. He continued, 'Managed to get one good fingerprint. A bit messy for our lads, but they got a really clear dab.' He looked at him impassively. 'That man Evans was right. It wasn't Maybach after all. We already had his prints with his other details. The SS were very methodical, even—or should I say especially—with their own lot.'

Thornhill put down his mug, the tea, the long nights of observation, even bed, forgotten.

'That means he may still be here? Christ, I'd like to feel *that* bastard's collar!'

Whitcombe took out another sheet of neatly typed information. 'You know about Evans's background, but you may not have seen this.' He held the paper to the light. 'Evans's father had been using his fishing-boat to pass messages to the Maquis on the French mainland—he was good at it apparently. Then one day he had to bring half-a-dozen members of the Maquis to Jersey, to hide them before using his fishing permit to smuggle them to England. Can you imagine that? In a twenty-five-foot boat? It must be all of a hundred miles, and with their patrols everywhere.' He gave a deep sigh, picturing it in his mind. 'He took them to Guernsey first. He had friends there.'

Thornhill nodded slowly. 'But somebody shopped him?'

'Yes. The Channel Islanders had their collaborators too. Maybach did the interrogation himself. He knew Evans's father wouldn't crack so he tortured his wife right before his eyes, didn't even stop when he spilled everything. She died under the torture, and then Maybach took his men over to Guernsey and captured the others. He did the same to them, and from their agony was able to send information to the Gestapo on the mainland, then even more members of the underground and their families were arrested. Most of them ended up in the gas chambers.'

Thornhill asked quietly, 'And his young sister?'

'She was just sixteen then. Maybach had her stripped and raped in front of her father before they took him out and shot him. Hung him from a tree in his garden so that everyone would know the penalty of non-co-operation. Then she was taken away to some French brothel used by German troops on leave from the front. Reports say she lost her mind there, so she followed the others to the death-camp.'

Thornhill pictured Evan's intent features, his carefully worded questions and explanations. He must have always been preparing himself in case he was captured and his true identity revealed.

'You think Evans knows?'

Whitcombe removed his glasses. 'I'm bloody sure he does. Something you must have said to him triggered it off in his mind.'

'Well, I'd better have a word with him, Guv. Together we might—'

'No. I think I've a better idea, Jim. Pick a good man to tail him, two if you think it best. The best you've got. If we show our hand to Evans he might blow the gaff, and Maybach will go to ground. My guess is that the bastard's trying to fix a passage out of here, maybe to join some of his mates in South America. Remember, Jim, plenty of ships run from Hamburg to the South Atlantic, or they did, and they will again if Mil. Gov. is going to get things moving.'

'I'd like to be on this detail. I'll take Taffy Hughes along with me.'

'Fine. But just catch him, eh? A nice feather in our caps. Won't do any harm when we get back to the Job, will it?'

They both laughed. In their work they had to, to keep sane.

* * *

Not very far from the S.I.B.'s local headquarters stood an old artillery barracks, or the half of it which had not been bombed flat. It was walled off from prying eyes, and any gaps left by the many air-raids were filled with sandbags and barbed wire. Off-limits to civilians and servicemen not actually on duty, it was a dismal place which smelled of charred wood, damp and decay. Even its former owners had not used the place since the heaviest raid had made it uninhabitable.

In a small army hut another of MGB 801's small company was waiting, standing quite still, like an actor about to move on stage and still uncertain of his lines.

Acting-Lieutenant Mike Fairfax RNVR, Mentioned-in-Dispatches for bravery under fire and still only twenty-one, was facing the worst morning he could remember.

He felt lost and trapped at the same time. There was nobody to share his thoughts with. Marriott for instance might have helped him to cope, to understand. There was nothing. He saw his reflection in the dull glass of the window. In his best uniform, as if he was going on parade. Every sudden sound made his heart leap and he found himself wondering what sort of man was going to be shot. He felt his throat contract. If he was sick he knew he would never be able to do anything.

The door swung inwards and a massive chief petty officer with freshly blancoed belt and gaiters stamped to attention.

''Awkins, sir. Chief Gunner's Mate.' As his mouth snapped open and shut with the precision of a breech-block, his eyes flitted critically over Fairfax's general appearance. He seemed satisfied enough and added, 'Firin' party is fell in outside. All gunnery ratin's, sir.'

Fairfax swallowed hard. The chief gunner's mate was one of a mould. In every barracks and establishment as well as many of the larger ships, you would always find a Hawkins. They could bawl and bellow until even the thickest sailor could work a gun or handle a rifle and bayonet. He could arrange a guard-of-honour for a visiting dignitary, a burial-party or, like now, a firing-squad.

As a breed Fairfax disliked them *all mouth and trousers*, and could recall how one of them had taken such pleasure in tormenting the young would-be officers at the *King Alfred* training establishment.

Now, on this unusually dull morning, he knew he was never so glad to see anyone in his life.

'Will it take long, Chief?'

'*Long*, sir?' He pondered on the word while all the time he took in Fairfax's demeanour, his ability, and whether or not he might screw it up. 'Nuthin' to it, sir. It's all in the book. I've spoken to the 'ands—they know what to do.' He repeated, 'Nuthin' to it.'

Fairfax persisted, 'Have you had to do this sort of thing before?'

'Well, only once, sir. Anyway, that was a wog.' He made it sound as if it barely counted. 'Caught nickin' the stores.'

He added, 'Word of advice, sir.'

'*Anything*, Chief.'

302

'The Provost gentleman who is in charge 'ere . . . is a bit *odd*, if you'll pardon the term, sir.'

It was getting more unreal by the second. 'In what way, Chief?'

Hawkins kept his face quite stiff. 'A bit of a poof, sir.'

He faced the door. 'That'll be 'im now, sir.' His thumbs were exactly in line with his trouser seams as he glared at the entrance. 'Don't take no stick from 'im, sir. We're not in the bleedin' army!' He was in charge again.

The door opened and a languid-looking captain wearing a Military Police armlet entered and smiled. He had a leather swagger-stick beneath one arm and wore a heavy revolver in a webbing holster.

He nodded, *bobbed* would be a better description, and said, 'You're Fairfax, I expect?'

Fairfax could almost feel the chief gunner's mate steaming.

'Yes. The firing-party is outside, I understand?'

The man pouted. 'I *had* been expecting marines, but still—' He examined his watch. It looked expensive. *Loot*.

'Time to get started. This way, er—Fairfax.'

They left the hut and walked through a sagging gate and into a bare courtyard.

There was a long plank supported at regular intervals by posts. About shoulder-high, so that a firing-party could rest their rifles on it to take aim. No chance of a stray shot or a miss.

Hawkins marched across the yard, his boot heels cutting little horseshoes in the dirt. He touched the plank and sniffed. 'A coat of paint wouldn't come amiss, sir!'

For the first time Fairfax made himself look at

303

the opposite wall. There was a post some eight feet in front of it, behind which was stacked a neat barrier of new sandbags.

Fairfax stared at the post. It was exactly what he had been expecting. Like a film. Not real at all. *That was the worst part.*

The Provost captain gestured casually with his swagger-stick. 'I've had the rifles covered with some newspapers. We're not expecting the weather to change just yet, otherwise—'

He sounded petulant, and reminded Fairfax of Lowes. He saw the shining butt-plates of the twelve rifles just protruding from the untidy line of newspapers.

The captain added, 'All loaded.'

Fairfax tasted the bile in his throat again. The captain even had a lisp.

'I see.'

The chief gunner's mate growled, 'I'll march 'em in, sir. Gettin' close to the time.' He saluted smartly and managed to exclude the Provost captain completely.

Eventually the firing-party, smart and businesslike in their belts and gaiters, marched to the plank in single-file, halted, and turned right towards the wall.

The big chief petty officer strode up and down the line and said, 'In a moment you will make one pace forward an' take up arms. Each weapon 'as its safety catch on, an' don't you bloody well forget it, *see*?' He stood in front of them, one hand resting on the plank. 'On the order *take aim*, you will do so in the prescribed manner. There will be an aimin' mark, so nobody will 'ave an excuse for missin'. You are gunnery ratin's, not a bunch of tiffies,

304

right?'

Fairfax watched as one of the seamen hurried along the line and gathered up the newspapers before stuffing them around the gate. As he ran back to his place Hawkins thundered, 'Now stand *easy!'*

He marched back to Fairfax and saluted. 'All ready, sir. One of the squad was askin' if there is a blank cartridge amongst the rifles?'

The Provost captain touched his chin with his little stick and tittered. 'He's been reading *Boy's Own Paper*, I expect!' But he did not answer the question.

Fairfax knew that the sailors had been picked from various sections and ships in harbour. Only one he recognised. It was Leading Seaman Rae. Neat and alert in his uniform, his cap tilted just an inch above his eyebrows. He saw Fairfax and gave a slight blink of recognition.

The captain walked away, saying, 'I'll tell them you're ready.'

You're ready. The casual remark brought Fairfax out in a cold sweat. He looked desperately at Hawkins. 'Carry on, Chief!'

Hawkins barked, 'Squad, *'shun!* Take up, *arms!'*

Fairfax walked along behind the single rank as Hawkins stood them at ease again.

They were murmuring quietly to one another. To show they did not care? Or was it an outward bravado to cover their true feelings.

Fairfax heard one man whisper excitedly. 'Yeh, they got *Frenchman's Creek* on at the E.N.S.A. Cinema next week! Must see it. Missed it when it was on in Chatham!'

Another was saying, 'Did you see the match

305

between the Guards an' the Pioneers at the Kilia Ground on Thursday? Gawd, they was useless! Couldn't 'it a ball wiv a bloody elephant!'

Only Rae who stood at the end of the line, the Lee-Enfield gripped loosely in his right hand, remained aloof. He heard Fairfax pass behind him and could guess what he was going through. Good enough as Jimmy the One, soft as shit for this kind of caper. He felt his new watch heavy on his wrist. There was a girl too. He would give Ginger and Bill Craven the slip soon and see what she was like. A tin of coffee should be enough.

He heard the chief gunner's mate hiss, 'Comin', sir!' Then Fairfax cleared his throat before calling them to attention.

Fairfax watched as the silent procession entered the yard via another gate. A squad of redcaps, two officers of the Military Government, a massive sergeant-major, and then the prisoner. He was a pale-faced young man held on either side by two more MPs.

Then last of all came a priest, his robe very clean against the dull brickwork.

The Provost captain stood near Fairfax and murmured, 'Not long now.' He could have been discussing the weather again.

It was when the prisoner was led to the post and his arms suddenly pinioned behind him that he seemed to understand what was happening. It was all done so swiftly and efficiently that it was almost too quick to follow.

One of the Mil. Gov. officers was reading from a buff sheet of paper. Then he stood aside and waited while the priest started to murmur a prayer from his book.

306

The prisoner stared straight ahead, directly at the line of sailors without seeming to see them.

The sergeant-major hung a bright red disc around the Pole's neck and arranged it carefully on his chest, before fastening a blindfold with the same practised skill. It was then that the spell broke, and the prisoner lunged against his bonds and began to weep. He was peering towards the prayers, obviously pleading even as the officers, redcaps, and the sergeant-major withdrew, leaving him and the man of God isolated.

In the sudden stillness the man's anguished sobs seemed very loud.

Leading Seaman Rae licked his lips and muttered, 'Here we bloody well go!'

Another near him said, 'Even the God Bosun can't 'elp 'im now!' But his face was as pale as the prisoner's.

Fairfax realised that the officers were all looking at him, that the priest was walking very slowly towards the gate, his closed book held to his lips.

Fairfax could feel Hawkins willing him to act.

He said, 'Firing-party, *ready*! *Present*!' From a corner of his eye he saw the twelve rifles rise and settle on the long plank. 'Catches *off*!' He wanted to turn away as the prisoner began to shriek with terror. Pictures flashed through his mind. 'Take *aim*!' His father going on about the profession, Meikle's suggestion that his time might be better used in medicine. His brother, always playing golf with other doctors. He felt his muscles go wire-taut. '*Fire*!'

So loud and instant was the fusillade that it sounded like a single explosion, the echoes hanging in the yard, making the pale smoke writhe up towards the dull-coloured sky.

Leading Seaman Rae had always been an excellent shot, and had even been in a naval team when still under training.

He watched the bright red disc move slightly as the prisoner wrenched helplessly at his lashings, his head thrown back as if to peer under the blindfold.

Rae had taken the first pressure before Fairfax had managed to get out his orders, and then at the last second had eased the foresight up very slightly until the man's blindfold was dead in the centre. That way he had known his shot had found its mark. The others had smashed through the man's body with such force it had the same effect as a cannon shell.

It seemed an age until the chief gunner's mate shouted, 'Ground *arms*!'

Rae glanced at the figures already moving towards the lolling corpse. Poor old Jimmy the One had not been able to get the command out this time.

Hawkins yelled, 'Right *turn*! Quick *march*! 'Eads up there! Swing them arms!'

Hawkins came back after seeing the sailors into a waiting lorry. He asked, 'All right, sir?'

Fairfax stared past him. Even in the dull light he could still see the great splash of scarlet. The thing which they had killed.

'Thank you, Chief, *yes*.'

'I've got a tot in the truck, sir. Drop o' Nelson's blood!'

Fairfax retched. 'Thanks.'

The two Military Government officers walked past, and one, a lieutenant colonel, asked irritably, 'Don't they teach you to salute superior officers in the navy, Lieutenant?'

Fairfax stared blindly after them, unable to speak, knowing at the same time that had he been able, he would be under arrest himself.

When he looked again, the post was empty, and some Germans were raking sand around it like gardeners.

Inside the little hut Fairfax waited as the chief gunner's mate produced a flat bottle and two chipped cups.

Did it really happen? Or might he awake suddenly from a nightmare, the sort which kept Marriott company on so many nights?

Have we changed that much, or are we really the same?

''Ere, sir.' He watched him over the cup. 'Down the 'atch!'

Fairfax left the hut a few minutes later and was confronted by some men pushing a plain coffin on a hand-cart.

He watched until it had vanished around the corner, and then he leaned against the hut and threw up.

★ ★ ★

Leading Writer Lavender pattered towards the big desk and announced, 'Lieutenant Marriott has just driven through the gates, sir.'

Meikle was standing by a half-open window looking out across the freshly cut grass. Such a timeless, satisfying smell, he thought. Cut grass. The sound of a cricket bat on a lazy summer's afternoon.

He sighed. 'I know. Bring him in as soon as he arrives.' He had seen the stubby little scout-car in

309

its new blue paint almost as quickly as they had telephoned from the main gates.

He turned and looked at his desk and all the neat piles of papers which awaited his attention. *Urgent. Immediate. Never.*

He glanced up at the wall clock and checked it against his watch. Over. A few minutes ago. How had Fairfax taken it? Lavender would probably tell him that too. He would have made an efficient spy, he thought. The door opened and Marriott stood there watching him. He looked very good, Meikle thought. Better than he had for some time. A lot better than he had expected.

'Sit down.'

Marriott lowered himself into a chair. His legs were stiff. Partly from Knecht's fast drive down from Flensburg, which had mostly been in silence. Marriott felt it had been a kind of protest, a rebuke, after what had happened.

'How is Lieutenant Kidd?'

Marriott wanted to yawn. Instead he smiled. *Too much like Beri-Beri.* They kept him in the army hospital in Flensburg, sir. A fracture, but not too bad, according to the "experts".'

'You took your time.'

Marriott met his gaze. How typical of Meikle, he thought. No wastage. Straight to the point without any trimmings.

'I stayed over for two days until he was settled in, sir.' He waited for some sharp retort, felt himself rising to meet it.

'Yes. Probably the right thing to do.' He turned away. 'You had a close shave by all accounts.'

'But for the German tug crew I'm not certain—'

'Spare me. They probably hope to gain a few

310

favours from you after this.' He faced him again and gave a dry smile. 'Anyway, you completed the job.'

Marriott thought of Beri-Beri's face when he had last seen him in the army hospital. The nurses were all British, probably the first over here. He might make a good impression on one of them. It had been a sad parting all the same. Too much to say, too much unsaid. As soon as he was well enough they would shift him down here again. What a party they would have that day.

'Any feelings about VJ-Day?'

Marriott shrugged. 'Too soon. Out here, we don't seem to belong. It'll take time.'

Meikle nodded. Apparently satisfied. 'Any comments about the ship you disposed of?'

Marriott leaned forward. 'Well, yes, sir. I've thought about it on the passage back.' Again the secret smile. He had nearly said *home*. 'I think the charges should be separated, halved.' He pulled a pad across the desk and scribbled a rough plan on it in pencil. 'It would lessen the chance of breaking a ship's keel before she can settle on the bottom.'

Meikle watched the experienced hand on the pad. 'I forgot. You used to prepare plans for building, not "destroying"?'

Marriott grinned. 'That's right.'

Meikle folded his arms. Marriott was thinking about this new job. The first promising sign.

He said, 'I'll be getting you some home leave quite soon. But the commodore hopes to cram in a few more sinkings in the Baltic before the weather closes in.'

'Thanks, sir.'

Meikle returned to his desk. His bastion. 'You

311

might look up your old first lieutenant when you get a moment. He was in charge of a firing-squad today.' Another glance at the clock, his driving force. 'About fifteen minutes ago to be precise.'

Marriott stared. 'Firing-squad? Who the hell thought up that idea? He's not a—'

'Not a *what*, Marriott? A *soldier*, were you going to say? We share all of it, or we lose the peace just as efficiently as we won the war!'

He did not look up until Marriott had left his office.

Marriott strode along the corridor, angry with himself and Meikle. It was not his problem, and yet—he looked round and saw the girl staring at him as if she had seen a ghost.

He asked, 'What is it? Tell me. Has something happened?'

But she stood quite still, searching his face as if she was mistaken. '*No!* It is not that! I thought, we heard—' She lowered her head very suddenly and he saw droplets of tears fall on her jacket.

He took her shoulders in his hands, expecting her to pull away, and asked, 'What did you hear?'

'That a lieutenant had been hurt aboard that ship! I did not know another officer was to be there! I thought—I thought—' More tears ran down her chin.

'You thought it was me. I didn't think it would matter to you.'

Then she did tear herself away. '*Matter? Care? But of course I do!* What sort of woman do you think I am?' Then she turned and went into her office and slammed the door.

Meikle heard the slam and looked up from his work.

312

Perhaps the sooner he sent Marriott on leave the better it would be for him. He closed the folder and ran his fingers through his hair.

For them.

CHAPTER FIFTEEN

INNOCENCE

The little scout-car completed its turn around the wide, shrub-lined driveway and halted outside a magnificent entrance. While his driver, Heinz Knecht, had woven along the quiet roads with regular bars of shadows made by the tall trees, Marriott had watched the proud-looking castle rise higher and higher, like something from a fairy-tale.

It was by no means the largest *Schloss* in the area, but the commodore had certainly picked himself a splendid one. Two turrets and a high, sloping roof, again with a Hans Andersen flavour, with the ever-present Plöner See making a perfect backdrop.

'I won't be long, Heinz.' It was surprising how easy it was to call him by his first name. Perhaps because of their run to Flensburg and back, a trip they had now done twice together. This last time had been to supervise the tow of another hulk, a ship crammed with weapons, machine-parts which were of no further use, and several tons of defused bombs. The timed explosion had worked perfectly, and when he had visited the hospital before returning to Plön, Beri-Beri had said, 'Told you, old lad. You were taught by the master!'

He had told Beri-Beri about Fairfax and the

313

firing-squad.

Beri-Beri had shaken his head and suppressed a yawn. 'It will likely get worse. If there's a bad winter—well, you know how it is.' He had suddenly brightened up. 'There was a bloke here today explaining about demob. It's to be a system of numbers. The longer you've been in, the faster you're getting out!'

It had sounded like being released from jail.

Marriott had seen very little of the girl, and when they had come face-to-face she had been polite, but nothing more; and he had respected the invisible barrier which seemed to rear between them.

Knecht watched him from beneath his cap. 'Fine place, Herr Leutnant. Very senior officer of *Luftwaffe* was here before—'

Marriott looked up at the impressive frontage. Almost baroque from this angle.

A Royal Marine sentry saluted and opened one of the tall doors for him and he entered, feeling the coolness of marble enfold him. A wide spiral staircase, the entrance hall dominated by the largest chandelier he had ever seen.

He smiled. Just the place for Errol Flynn and Basil Rathbone to fight that last duel in *Robin Hood*.

'This way, sir.' The steward's Scottish voice seemed totally out of place here.

They entered a long room, well furnished and hung with deer-heads and other trophies.

Sitting near some glass doors which overlooked the gardens was the commodore.

'Take a pew, Marriott.' He was smoking a big cigar, his pink, crab-like hands resting for the while in his lap.

314

Marriott sat.

Commodore Lionel Paget-Orme watched him with amusement. 'What d'you think of my new HQ, eh?'

Marriott shrugged. 'It's magnificent, sir.' He did not know what else to say.

The commodore eyed him bleakly, disappointed perhaps.

He stood up and walked to the glass doors. 'I find luxury adequate.'

Marriott wondered if he had tossed off that comment before. He followed the plump commodore down some steps and on to a lawn. Here the unreality continued.

Seated around a painted, wrought-iron table were Kapitän von Tripz and Meikle, and two other officers Marriott did not know, obviously from Paget-Orme's staff.

A German servant in a white jacket was pouring wine into crystal hock glasses and approached instantly as the commodore snapped his fingers.

Paget-Orme said, 'We are having a meeting. Routine amidst fine surroundings.'

Marriott glanced at the ex-Kapitän-zur-See. How did he feel? He must have visited this great house many times before the White Ensign replaced the swastika.

But the bearded German met his glance with only a faint smile. As if he was reading his mind, and was able to find amusement there.

Two more men strode on to the lawn, both Germans, each an ex-naval officer. Marriott could even see the darker patch on one of the jackets where he had once worn the infamous eagle.

Paget-Orme remained standing, his eyes

315

watching the smoke drifting from his cigar while he sipped a fresh glass of hock.

It was a beautiful wine, Marriott thought. Like nothing he had ever tasted. As in England, not everyone had had to tighten their belts here.

Meikle said, 'You're to go on one more job, Marriott. My writer can let you have the details. You'll be alone again, but I think that suits you well enough?' As usual he did not expect an answer. 'The bigger gas convoys will be on the move soon. They are to be code-named *Scran*.' He did not explain why.

Paget-Orme signalled the servant and said, '*Very* pleased with your work, Marriott. I've told the admiral as much. Pity you're not a regular, all this would be invaluable; could still be if you want to stay on after your release date.' He gave a baby-like smile. 'Civilian life under a bunch of Reds won't be too exciting, I'd have thought?'

Meikle waited for his superior to pause and said, 'After this one I shall send you on home leave. I understand that your sister is about to get married.'

'Yes, sir.' How did he know that? 'I didn't realise it was already fixed.'

He held his breath, his sister and the marriage thrust aside as he heard footsteps on the stone steps. He knew it was her without even turning.

When he did look she was walking to the table, her arms full of paper files. She wore her white shirt and blue uniform skirt. Even so plainly dressed she brought every eye from the table. Except Meikle's. He was watching Marriott.

'Well, if you're all ready, gentleman?' Paget-Orme turned to Marriott and said, 'Just wanted you to know I think highly of your work in

316

this command.' He was smiling but it was a dismissal all the same.

The Scottish petty officer steward coughed politely.

'What *is* it, Dundas?' The commodore obviously hated interruptions.

But the steward was looking at the girl. 'There's a call for *her*, sir.'

Meikle snapped, 'A telephone call, *here*?' Then he said, 'Go and take it, Fräulein Geghin. We have all we need here, by the look of it.'

She hurried away and Meikle said, 'We're still waiting for the captain of the *Sea Harvester*, sir.'

They all looked at their watches and then began to shuffle their papers. Marriott walked into the cool room again, his eyes almost blind after the sunshine.

Through a window he saw his driver gossiping with one of the gardeners. You could be forgiven for thinking there had been no war here at all.

He heard her voice and then saw her by an ornate, gilt table where she was speaking quickly into a telephone. Close by, as if he expected her to steal something, was Dundas, the commodore's personal steward.

'I didn't expect—' Marriott's voice hung in the still air as he saw her face. She looked quite pale, like the time she had broken down in Meikle's HQ. *Desperate.*

'What is it? Tell me!'

She looked at him but seemed to stare through him into the distance. 'Bernadette has been hit by a car! I—I don't know what—'

Marriott did not have to be told. It was the child, the one he had thought was hers.

317

'Where is she?'

She seemed to have difficulty in answering, as if her ability to translate and to understand had been shocked out of her.

'Hospital. In Eutin.' She dabbed her eyes with a handkerchief. 'Oh, my God, she is only three!'

Marriott saw her make a move towards the glass doors. 'No. Come with me. I'll explain to them later. I'm taking you there, right now!'

She stared at him as he took her arm and guided her through the great doorway.

Knecht nodded approvingly but said nothing, as he realised something was wrong.

Marriott waited for her to slide into the back of the little car and snapped, 'Just drive, Heinz!' He had seen the steward hurrying to the gardens. At any second someone might try to stop him from taking her.

Heinz gunned the engine and roared around the curving driveway.

'Eutin, Heinz—the hospital.'

They were out on the road now. It was all as before except the angle of the shadows had changed.

Marriott could hear her quick breathing behind him. *No, nothing was the same.*

She said huskily, 'The children's hospital, please.'

Heinz relaxed, his strong hands guiding the little car with ease around two gaping women with bundles on their heads.

This was a new drama. Someone was ill? Why should his officer be concerned? He had seen over twenty other cars in the driveway. He glanced quickly at Marriott's expression. It must be

318

important to him. She was certainly a most attractive girl. Who would blame her? But perhaps he did not see her in that way?

Marriott said, 'Watch your driving, man! Or we'll *all* end up in hospital!'

Heinz concealed a smile. There was an unusual edge to the lieutenant's voice. Oh yes, he *did* see her that way!

★   ★   ★

The children's hospital turned out to be part of a small convent. Black-habited nuns glided down spotless corridors, or could be seen bending over beds, doing the work of nurses.

Although close to the main road it was quiet, isolated even, and sad.

Marriott said, 'Wait for us here, Heinz.' He saw his quick nod of understanding. *In case we have to leave immediately because the child is dead.*

The girl said, 'I will ask . . .'

A young British soldier left the hospital and threw Marriott a quick salute. Following behind him was a local policeman wearing the same uniform as before the occupation, with the old-world style shako. Only the Nazi eagle had been removed.

He saw them standing beside the scout-car and ambled across. He began to explain something in German and Heinz interrupted with a jerk of the head.

'He thinks you are here about the accident, Herr Leutnant.' He kept his voice steady but it was an effort. 'He says there is nothing to worry about. It was British army truck!'

Marriott thought of the young soldier who had just passed them. *No further explanations needed.* He was one of the occupation forces.

Marriott asked coldly, 'What about the child?'

The policeman smiled, relieved perhaps that this officer was not going to make his life difficult.

Marriott felt her fingers tighten suddenly on his arm as she whispered, 'She will live.'

A sister met them in the entrance and led them through the building. Marriott's first impressions changed immediately. Clean and peaceful it certainly was, but so overcrowded that each ward was crammed with beds or, in the smaller cases, cage-like cots. They were wedged end-to-end, with just space enough between them for the nuns and visitors to squeeze through. There were others in corridors, and in one ward Marriott saw the more badly injured ones. Small, pale, and pathetic, some without limbs, others with bandages over their eyes.

Heinz was still smouldering over the policeman's sickening indifference. There was not that much difference in the child's age and that of his own little Friedl. It might easily have been her.

Marriott asked, 'Those children in there, Sister? Who are they?'

Either she spoke no English or preferred not to. The girl translated for him. 'They are from the last air-raids. They are—' She frowned, trying to re-discover the word. 'Orphans now.'

The sister led the way into a small ward, her habit swishing on the polished floor.

Beside one cot was a young, fair-haired woman sitting on a stool, staring into the face of the little girl named Bernadette.

'This is my brother's wife, Leisl.'

The other woman had obviously not heard their approach and stood up quickly, staring first at the girl, then at Marriott and his uniform. She clenched her fists and could barely control her despair and what Marriott recognised as anger. The woman called Leisl obviously thought that he was the one who had knocked down her daughter.

But she listened to her sister-in-law's quiet voice, then together they looked into the cot.

The child was very pale and breathing jerkily, her head and shoulder heavily bandaged, one eye almost hidden by a bloodstained dressing.

The girl said softly, 'She will be well again.' She bit her lip. 'She has to be. She ran out of the door before Leisl could stop her. The soldiers brought her straight here, otherwise—'

Otherwise. Marriott thought of the soldier who had saluted him without seeing him. Nineteen at the most, like 801's company, probably at the wheel of one of those countless Bedford trucks the army seemed to favour. Going home, being one of the victors—nothing would have meant much to him if he had killed the child. Or would it? Did war slip even through the guards of humanity? Did it harden you so much that you could think only of your own survival?

He heard the girl murmuring to the child's mother and caught the mention of Willi Tripz. Leisl studied him openly for the first time, as if to see something for herself. She looked tired and drawn and Marriott recalled what he had been told about her missing husband and that he had never seen his child. Did he resemble Ursula, he wondered? Was it possible that he was still alive or,

321

like their father, lost in the wilderness of snow and ice around Stalingrad?

She spoke with great care. 'I thank you, Herr Leutnant, for bringing Ursula to me so quick. We are much help to each.' She swung round, everything forgotten as the child gave a tiny whimper. The nun was there in a flash, her shadow swooping down over the cot like an avenging angel.

The girl said, 'We go now, I think.' She reached out and stroked the young woman's hair. 'She will wish to stay.'

'My driver can wait and take her home.'

She looked at him curiously. 'We *are* home. It is only a short walk.' She faltered, emotions making her fumble for words again. 'If you wish, Herr Leutnant, my *oma* will make some chocolate for you—'

He stared at her so that she dropped her eyes. 'If you are sure?'

She nodded, some loose strands of hair falling across her forehead like black silk.

'Twice you help me. Would I not repay that?'

They walked out into the sunshine. It seemed wrong that the sky was so bright and clear when there was so much suffering, all that innocence. She climbed into the car without protest. Marriott knew it might offend if she was seen walking with an English officer. Those who criticised rarely took time to find out the truth of the matter.

'Here it is.' Heinz bobbed his head and swung the car into a cobbled yard. Marriott climbed out and offered his hand. He wondered briefly if Heinz had realised why he had asked him to make that detour through Eutin on their first trip to Flensburg? Funnily enough, this was not the

Gasthaus he had picked out for himself as her home. It was smaller and probably much older, leaning over the cobbled yard as if drowsing in the sunshine. He thought of Fairfax and decided he would bring him here to cheer him up. In the same breath he knew he would not.

She stepped down and looked at him. 'You are welcome here.'

He squeezed her hand. 'I am very happy to be here.' She did not return the pressure, but she did not take her hand away for several seconds.

'I will remain with the car, Herr Leutnant.' Heinz watched them. Again that clear-eyed understanding. So that it would look *official*. An officer from the base perhaps, where she worked to help support the family. A family of women. How did they manage?

'How old is your brother's wife?' It was something to say while he followed her towards the stout, studded door with an old double-headed eagle painted above it.

'Twenty-five. She is still young.'

Marriott looked away. He had thought her ten years older than that.

Inside the door everything was dark, polished wood, and half-litre tankards hanging in line from one of the beams. There was a huge fireplace with logs beside it and a hand-carved box full of pine cones. It would be a cosy place when the winter came, he thought.

The girl's mother came to meet them and Marriott could see where Ursula had inherited her fine features. She was not much taller than her daughter, with the same dark hair, although hers was streaked with grey like frost. She was

323

courteous, and smiled as her daughter explained how Marriott had helped her. She spoke no English at all. Eventually she left to fetch something to drink.

In an adjoining parlour Marriott had seen two British Tommies sitting with a seedy-looking civilian. They all got up and left with unseemly haste.

The black market in action?

She made him sit on one of the long polished benches at an equally shining trestle table. She took his cap and looked at the badge as she said, 'My mother is Lithuanian. I was born there also.'

'Where?'

For the first time she laughed, her teeth very white in her tanned face. 'You would be no wiser, Herr Leutnant! It is called Palanga! My father was a salesman of schnapps and beer—he was from Schleswig. So when he came to Lithuania to do business he met and fell in love with my mother.' She waved his cap around the old, black beams. 'So they came here.'

She tried to laugh again but it eluded her. 'I think we shall not see him again. He was not strong, but they put him in the infantry all the same, my brother also.'

That explained her appearance, Marriott thought, so different from the fair-haired Leisl who was worn down by her despair for her missing husband. And now the Russians were in Lithuania. Marriott thought of the Russians he had met across the unmarked frontier. It seemed unlikely they would ever leave, any more than they would let go of Poland.

'Who is your *oma*?'

324

'What you call a grandmother!' She walked round the table and touched it with her fingers. 'She is of great age and very fierce. You must show her great respect or she will call down the wrath of God!'

'You speak English so well.'

She gave the little shrug he had come to look for. 'I expected to teach, you see?'

Her mother brought some hock, not the chocolate he had been expecting.

'She says you are to drink.' She shot her mother a searching glance. 'And that you are always welcome here.'

Marriott waited until her mother had left the room and then asked, '*May* I come again? I will not, if it should cause you embarrassment.'

She did not answer directly. 'Soon you will go home. Then you will forget. I heard Herr Meikle saying that your sister is getting married, yes? Then you too will find a nice English girl, I think, and marry also.' Only then did she look at him, her eyes filling her face as she added quietly, 'It is hopeless, you see. We are lost before we begin.'

Marriott could feel the contact slipping away even as he clasped the wine in his hand. He was *speaking* to her, to nobody else, not surrounded by telephones and naval routine. It had been only a dream before.

He asked, 'What did you say to Leisl about Willi Tripz?'

She stared at him, surprised at the question. 'I told her how you brought the boy out of Ivan's hands.' Her dark lashes hid her expression again. 'That you are a good man, a brave one also.'

He said, 'It must not end. We cannot turn our

325

backs, Ursula.' He saw her catch her breath at the use of her name. 'I would not harm you, or use you wrongly—'

She shook her head, 'Please stop! You are harming me by speaking like this! When you smile or touch my hand it is like pain to me! How much worse would it be after you leave?'

Marriott stood up. 'I am going now. I shall explain to Meikle about the accident.' He barely knew what he was saying. 'He told me you are his best interpreter.'

She stood facing him and handed him his cap. Then very softly she said, 'Perhaps it were better if I spoke no English at all. Or is silence no protection either?'

He took her hand and kissed it very quickly. Afterwards he thought how strange it must have seemed, and yet in those old surroundings with all their own private memories, how right.

He heard himself say, 'I shall never forget, Ursula. Never.'

He did not remember returning to the car or even leaving the room. Only once did he look back, like the moment when he had handed over 801. He thought he saw a curtain move in the room they had just shared for so short, but so precious, a time. Or was that just one more delusion?

But she had watched the car until it was out of sight around the corner. She reached for an apron and glanced at the tall clock without understanding. *Oma* would be rising from her afternoon rest very soon, and Leisl might be hungry when she returned from the hospital. But still she remained there by the little window, looking at her hand, remembering the touch of his lips on her fingers.

Then she slipped her fingers through the front of her shirt and laid them on her skin. Her body, like her face, was suddenly flushed, as if shocked and ashamed by the thought in her mind.

Then she sat down on the same bench and began to cry silently into the apron.

She was still crying when she felt her mother's arm encircle her shoulders.

So it was no longer a secret.

*　　*　　*

The town of Neumünster lay some twenty miles to the south of Kiel. The British army and their signboards seemed to be everywhere, and even the soldiers' recreation clubs bore regimental and divisional crests.

The three sailors in their blue raincoats and bell-bottom trousers stood out here, and brought several rude whistles from passing khaki vehicles.

Leading Seaman Bill Craven leaned in a doorway and muttered, 'Goin' to piss down with rain too. How the hell do we get back to barracks anyway?'

Ginger Jackson sighed. Always moaning. He should never have got involved with him in the first place. You could never trust a bloke from Brum.

He said wearily, 'I got you 'ere, didn't I? Just stop drippin' an' trust me, see?'

Leading Seaman Rae lit a cigarette and smiled to himself. All for a bit of loot. But it was worth it if only to hear these lunatics going on at each other.

Craven persisted, 'But he's a bloody officer!'

'*So?*' Ginger was losing his patience completely. 'Then 'e's got more to lose, ain't 'e?'

Rae said, 'Here comes Oskar anyway.'

327

The Hamburg-Amerika Line chief steward stepped from an overloaded bus and hurried across the road which led all the way south to Hamburg.

'Not here yet?' He wore a hat, pulled down over his eyes so that he looked furtive, guilty even.

Ginger said airily, ''E'll be 'ere. After that it's up to you, Oskar, me old china.'

'I do what I can.' Oskar watched the road. It was shining with a light drizzle. Unusual for the time of year. He added, 'She is what *you* call a countess. Of old family, von Lorenz, from East Prussia.'

None of it meant a thing to Ginger and his friends. She was a German, and needed them more than they did her. That's how they had to think of it anyway. A few deals with some one who knew the market, then pull out of it and roll on demob.

'Christ, here he is too!' Rae sounded surprised for once.

'*See?*' Ginger felt his muscles relax slightly. There had been a few moments when he thought he had made a bad blunder. Once, when a jeep full of nosy redcaps had cruised towards them, he had even thought that Lowes had panicked and then gone squealing to Meikle and shopped them.

The car stopped and Lowes got out, pausing to say something to the driver. Then he laughed and waved elaborately as the car drove away. When he turned towards them they saluted as if the meeting was a pure accident.

Craven whispered, 'Jesus, look at 'im! Pissed as a fart!'

Ginger bit his lip. 'Easy lads. Let me 'andle this.'

Craven glowered. 'Bloody welcome, mate!'

Lowes adjusted his cap and surveyed them cheerfully. 'And who is *this*?'

328

'This is Oskar, sir. Good bloke, 'ated the *Nasties*, an' respects all British officers!'

Ginger breathed out slowly. He really was pissed, otherwise even Snow White would have seen they were having a go at him.

Lowes eyed the ex-steward severely. 'Good man. Now about this countess—'

Ginger did not have time to withdraw the offer, to make some excuse to keep Lowes out of it until he was sober. He had never seen him like this before.

But Oskar said quickly, 'The house around the corner, sir. I take you.' He shot an anxious glance at the others. 'Okay?'

Ginger asked carefully, 'Bin celebratin', sir?'

Lowes turned his gaze on him with some difficulty. 'My mother got married today.'

So that was it. Ginger saw Rae about to make some suitable remark and shook his head. It was not the time.

Lowes nodded several times. 'I hope they—' He did not finish it.

'Lead on.' He glanced at the three sailors. How simple it was to take charge. Always complaining, but when it came right down to it, they had to come crying to an officer.

He thought of the army club he had visited after leaving the wardroom. He could not remember clearly how many drinks he had consumed; he did not much care any more.

He had seen Fairfax in the mess but had avoided him. Ever since the firing-squad he had been like a duck in a thunderstorm. The comparison made him giggle. *I'd have shot the bastard single-handed if I'd been there*. At this moment, he even believed that.

329

He realised that Oskar had led him up the steps of a once-imposing residence. Half of the building had been boarded up after being bombed, but the door opened smartly enough at Oskar's knock, and a burly servant regarded them both with suspicion.

Lowes thought he looked more like a boxer than a butler.

The big man shut the door and ushered them into a room which despite the daylight outside was all in shadow.

It had a faintly musty smell, and Lowes noticed that the chairs and sofas were of dark red velvet; well, pre-war, he thought vaguely.

He was feeling very dry, and his head was throbbing painfully. If only there was more light. He sat down gingerly on the nearest sofa while Oskar prowled around the room like a caged cat.

Lowes could hear the throb of music and decided the house was larger than he had imagined.

Oskar said, 'She is coming, sir.'

Sir, The right sort of respect. Lowes got to his feet and almost fell over. But as the door opened and the woman came into the room he managed to recover his wits enough to say, 'Countess von Lorenz, I believe!'

The countess was tall and slim and dressed all in black. She even wore a wide-brimmed black hat, so that in the shadows it was impossible to determine either her features or her age. Her hair, what Lowes could see of it, was blonde, almost silver in the dull light. She was smoking a cigarette and even managed to make that look elegant and relaxed.

She remarked, 'You are very young.' Her accent was strong but her English easy for Lowes to follow. 'What may I call you? Your first name?'

Lowes was taken aback. He had expected formality, with him controlling the conversation. The British officer and the impoverished aristocrat. He stammered, 'My name is John, but—'

'Sit down, John.' She sat on the sofa and crossed her legs.

Lowes knew his mother's expensive tastes and recognised the stockings as pure silk, war or no war. In England they were just a memory. He seated himself beside her, suddenly very aware of her perfume, the nearness of her body.

She said, 'You have had some bad times in the war, *ja*?' She laid one hand on his knee.

Lowes stared at her hand, unable to move and barely able to answer. 'Well, yes, as a matter of fact. But you learn to master fear—' It was surprising how easily the lie came out, to be followed by others. 'I've seen some horrible things, Countess.'

Her hand moved along his thigh. '*Nein!* Call me Elisabeth!'

Lowes gasped, 'I want—I thought—' What was happening? He could do nothing. The pressure of her hand seemed to burn through his uniform, while with the other she continued to smoke her cigarette, her eyes hidden by the brim of her hat.

She stood up quite suddenly. 'You will have a drink perhaps?'

Lowes nodded dumbly. At least it would give him time to think. He watched her as she moved with effortless ease to a cabinet and produced a decanter and glasses.

When she sat down again he fumbled with her arm but with the same easy grace she removed his hand while she poured the drinks.

She said softly, 'No, John. I am not for you. Partners maybe when we know each other, *ja*? Just a little better.' She offered the glass, her eyes watching and judging his disappointment as his blurred mind grappled with the new developments.

'I have someone for you in my house.' As Lowes made to lower the glass she took his wrist and lifted it again while she waited for him to drink.

'Have no fear, John. *Trust* me. It is *safe*, you understand?'

Lowes felt the drink running through him. Like nothing he had ever tasted, sweet and yet fiery. He was sure it was clearing his head and not adding to his earlier discomfort.

He thought suddenly of his mother and that brute. *Married*. What did marriage count? He must have had her whenever he wanted to, long before this.

The countess was on her feet again. She spoke quietly, but the door opened immediately. Lowes half-expected to see Oskar, but he had gone somewhere. Instead it was the burly manservant.

She touched Lowes's lips with her fingers. 'Karl will take care of you.'

Lowes swayed and might have fallen but for the man's iron grip on his arm.

He felt cheated, out of his depth. On top of the wedding . . . Then as the man led him from the room he saw several officers' caps lying on a table. All army, but it made him feel safer.

She called after him, 'My home is yours, John. We will talk later.'

Up some stairs and along a passageway. The music was more muffled now, and the drink made him feel light on his feet.

A door opened and closed behind him and he saw the girl standing by a window.

She was very young with short blonde hair. Her eyes were heavily made-up, so that she looked gentle, like a fawn. She wore a plain, silk gown with a gold chain around her waist. Her feet were bare.

Lowes had never touched a girl in his life, and after joining the navy had always been terrified by the stories of catching some terrible disease from a contact. The sailors joked about it. *Getting a dose. Catching the boat up. Having a full house.* They took great pleasure from it if he was within earshot. Even some officers who spoke of *Rose Cottage*, a nickname for the officers' VD hospital, as if it was all a huge joke. He swallowed hard, his pulses racing. 'What is your name?'

She did not answer but crossed the room and took his hand, like a child leading another child.

They sat side by side on the bed and then she put her arms around his neck and kissed him on the mouth. It did not stop and he found he was clutching her shoulders through the thin robe, returning her kiss even harder, his mind reeling as her tongue darted between his teeth.

She was kneeling on the floor, although he did not see her move. She took off his shoes and socks and kissed his feet. She began to undress him, touching him confidently while she worked, so that he could feel his body rising to her. There was another blank, and he was on his back, quite naked while he tried to see what she was doing. She came to bed very slowly, her eyes on him the whole time. Then she stooped over him and kissed him once again.

Lowes thought his mind would burst. He tugged

333

the gold chain away and reached up through the thin robe to discover an erection to match his own.

He knew he should have been shocked, disgusted, but he was far beyond that now. The boy slipped out of the robe and lay down beside him while they explored each other like lovers.

Around the corner in the adjoining street the three sailors waited for Oskar to report on progress.

Ginger asked, 'Where is 'e?'

Oskar turned up the collar of his threadbare coat and looked at the steady drizzle. He was thankful to be out here, even in the rain.

'He is staying there. With the countess.'

Craven growled, 'Hold on, chummy, that's not what we planned!'

Ginger eyed the German shrewdly. 'Bent, is she?'

'Bent?'

Ginger exclaimed, 'Fer Gawd's sake don't keep repeatin' everythin' I say! I *mean*, was it all a bloody lie?'

'No.' Oskar looked at him unhappily. 'She has much influence. But the officer is maybe *too young, ja*?'

'Then wot's 'e doin' right now?'

Rae tossed down a cigarette and stepped into the road as he saw an army lorry splashing through the drizzle.

'It's goin' our way. Let's cadge a lift.' He sighed as the lorry began to pull over. 'Oskar means that your trusted officer-pal is having it off with some tart while we stand here like whores at a christening!'

Oskar looked for his bus. It did not harm at all to let them believe the officer was with a woman.

He said, 'There will be other times.'

The soldier driving the Bedford lorry yelled, 'Wot's up, lads, lost yer boat?' He banged the side. ''Op in, I'm goin' all the way to Kiel!'

Ginger sat with his back to the vibrating side and tried to think. He saw Craven watching him, the faintest hint of a smirk on his face. Ginger said, 'Just *one word* from you, Bill, an' that will be your soddin' lot!'

Rae was thinking about Lowes. 'Didn't know he had it in him. Always thought that with him it might be the other way round.'

Ginger held out his hand as Rae pulled out his tin of duty-frees. 'Give us a fag, Jack.'

He said it only to cover his excitement. Without knowing it Rae had hit the bloody nail right on the napper.

Everything was not lost after all.

CHAPTER SIXTEEN

UNTIL WE MEET AGAIN

I pronounce that they be Man and Wife together.

Marriott considered the words yet again as with the other guests he made his way into the little church hall for the reception. The day had started with clouds and a hint of rain but by mid-morning the sun had broken through, and now the sky was clear and blue.

The church by the duckpond had been almost full, for although the numbers of guests were limited, most of the locals had known Penny since she had been a small child. Marriott had wondered

335

if they had seen and felt the difference too as she had walked up the aisle on her father's arm. All in white, her cheeky smile absent for the moment, like the uniform everyone had got used to on her leaves from the fighter-station. And with those words she had seemed to change once more while she had faced her man—*My Jack* as she always called him, revealing a happiness she had rarely shown, and a new maturity whch Marriott had found both moving and disturbing.

He had taken Jack out for a last stag drink the previous night at the old Harrow. He was a friendly man whom Marriott had liked instantly despite his own inexplicable protective feelings about the man who was to marry his young sister. For one thing, he was not at all what Marriott had been expecting. He was older, maybe in his thirties, with the wartime rank of squadron-leader, one of Penny's 'Wingless wonders', the senior Met officer on the base.

After talking to him over pints of mild-and-bitter he began to understand what she saw in him; what she needed after her own war at the fighter-station, in the front line as much as anyone. A comfortable, intelligent man who would take good care of her. Their love for one another had been quite obvious there at the altar.

And she was here now, with her bouquet of tea roses and a ready smile for the arriving guests, while her Jack stood beside her beaming and shaking every hand.

As one of the airmen in the church had been heard to say, 'Jack looks like the cat who's swallowed the cream!'

Most of the visitors in air-force blue had been

336

fairly senior, or of Jack's own rank. What of the others now that they were no longer needed? Sitting in the deck-chairs, thinking and dreaming, staring at the sky, waiting for the shrill order to *Scramble!*

And there must have been many, many more who Penny might have remembered on this day. The lighthearted affairs she had touched upon, youngsters like herself who had flown one sortie too many and had ended up ditched in the Channel or in the burned-out carcass of a Spitfire.

Marriott knew that feeling and could share it without effort.

Most of the airmen were Canadians like Jack; they would soon be gone. Marriott remembered his sense of astonishment at the way his home, his roads, where he had cycled as a boy, had all changed even since that last, brief leave. No barrage balloons any more, floating above the Hawker aircraft factory at Kingston, no anti-aircraft batteries, their muzzles pointing into the far skies over London. The air-raid shelters too, were just long humps of grass in the fields and on the village green. It had been a wet spring, and the grass had done its best to cover the dismal shelters even if it could not wipe out their memories. Crouching against damp or dripping concrete, feeling the ground shake, wondering if the house would still be there at first light . . .

But there was something even more disturbing. The wild rejoicing, the crazy dancing in the streets after VE-Day, had been replaced by apathy. As if these same civilians, who had faced the blitz and everything the enemy could hurl at them, had used up all their energy, were no longer interested in the next step forward. There were still shortages of everything, rationing and austerity, as if peace was still a mirage, that it could not be taken for granted.

He saw his mother with some of her friends. A few were in their wartime Women's Voluntary Services uniforms, others had dug out flowered hats for the occasion, doing their best for Penny.

Marriott saw *the man from the ministry*, or the creepy lodger Chris, as Penny referred to him, watching from a corner, a faintly superior smile playing on his lips.

Marriott looked at his mother again and tried to guess her feelings. He hoped he was mistaken, but he had thought her to be more excited about the lodger's own engagement announcement than her daughter's wedding.

Chris had joined them at the pub, pointedly ordering a glass of tonic water, and had immediately launched into his involvement with the girl he would marry, 'once we have both completed out studies for advancement'.

Jack had grinned. 'What are you studying exactly?'

Chris had given a deep sigh. 'Too complicated to go into just now, I'm afraid.'

He had told them that he had met this girl at a Fabian Society Summer School in Devon.

Commodore Paget-Orme's voice had intruded into the conversation. *Civilian life under a bunch of Reds* . . .

But it had not lasted long, and when he had left the Harrow Jack had remarked, 'What a jerk.'

Marriott had tugged out his wallet to pay for another round and a card with a rose pressed flat inside it had dropped to the floor.

Jack, big though he was, scooped it up and

338

handed it over. Then he had said quietly, 'So there *is* a girl? I'm bloody glad.'

Marriott had tried to cover it. 'You're even beginning to talk like a Limey!' But it had not worked.

He slipped his arm around Penny's waist and kissed her. 'You were great. Just marvellous. An old married woman now, not my kid sister any more!'

He held her hand and studied her. Her Jack would not have had time to tell her about the rose. But he would, no matter what he had promised. They were not the sort to keep secrets from each other.

He asked, 'How did Mum take it about you-know-what?'

She looked up at her tall husband. 'Jack may never get another chance like it, Vere. They've offered him a good job in Toronto—Met consultant for the airlines. They're all getting back on the job again—it's just too good to miss. Of course Mum took it badly. But there it is. We've got our lives, we've found each other. I'm on extended leave, which means that I'm out of the WAAF for good.' She waved her bouquet around the room. 'Special licence, a honeymoon in some crabby cottage his lordship's got lined up in Dorset, and off we go!'

More guests were arriving now and Marriott said, 'We'll talk later.' He held her very tightly so that when he stood back he saw the pain in her eyes. His leave was over in five days. The last time he would see her for—

She said quietly, 'Steady the Buffs, Vere! Jack's getting a super job—I'll not have to scrub floors for the pennies after all. No more passion-killers

339

either—the first thing I'll buy is some really daring underwear!' They laughed but her eyes were anxious as she watched. 'Don't *worry*. We'll meet.'

Marriott drifted to a table and picked up a glass of wine. His father joined him and murmured, 'Went off well, I thought. So glad you could come over beforehand. It was a big help all round.'

Marriott saw his mother watching them from across the room. *I'll bet*, he thought.

His father was talking to one of his friends from the disbanded Home Guard. It was good to see the Old Man so cheerful. Life had not been all that easy for him. He heard some of the RCAF guests making jokes and thought of all the many hundreds of Canadian soldiers who had been camped around here. Who had become a part of the place and the people. When the local population had awakened on the morning of the Normandy invasion they had all disappeared. *Vanished*. Their accents, their funny games in the pubs, their adopted families, it had all stopped right there. His mother probably saw Jack like that. As if Penny was deserting, or that he was stealing her from their own home.

There were no naval uniforms here. How good it would have been if Beri-Beri had been able to make it. He would be up and about by now. He felt a sudden urge to see him. It was as if he did not belong here any more. Like the air-raid shelters, his old life was overgrown. Lost.

He had thought about it a lot since his return home. Of the way he was treated by the crew of the tug *Herkules* and her skipper, the 'ancient mariner' who would now share a joke and a pipe of tobacco on their runs into the Baltic. It was ridiculous, but equally so to try and explain it. The youth, Willi

340

Tripz, who was always around looking for odd jobs and his companionship, the people who worked at the docks; they had come to mean more than just names and faces. They no longer seemed to resent his authority; perhaps he had proved that he could take as much care of them as he had of his own command in 801.

He had thought about that too. How the tight community of a small warship had been broken up and scattered. No longer of one company, but individuals again, the good and the bad, the keen and the lazy, without the drive or danger to hold them together.

Was that what was happening here in England? The war was over, but where was the peace?

His father was introducing him to another of his friends. 'This is my boy, Ted. How does he look, d'you think?'

The man called Ted shook his hand warmly. 'Like a hero. We're all proud of you, Vere. I'll bet you'll be really glad to get home for good!'

Marriott smiled. 'Yes, of course.' Whatever he might think, he would have not said otherwise. He knew this man had lost both of his sons, one at sea, the other flying over France.

He saw the women preparing the buffet and glasses, dominated by a huge wedding-cake.

The cake, like a lot of the food, had caused another rift. With the rationing and shortages, it would have been impossible to lay on such a spread. Jack and some of his Canadian friends had had it sent to the reception in good time.

His mother had snapped, 'We've put up with the rationing! We don't need charity!'

Marriott wondered how his father had got round

that one. He heard Jack give a loud laugh and imagined them when it was all over, at the *crabby little cottage* in Dorset. In bed together.

He thought too of the *Herkules* tying up in Flensburg, the last, strangely solemn handshake he shared wth Kapitän Kreiger when he had given him a tin of pusser's pipe tobacco.

He had been expecting to see the girl named Ursula. Had bought her a present in Flensburg. Had thought of little else even when the tow had snapped and they had faced a bad night fighting the sea until they had secured it again.

At the wardroom there had been a little parcel waiting for him, the rose pressed inside. He had read her note several times until he knew the round handwriting like his own. Meikle had gone to Minden for a court martial, some stupid subbie who had been caught flogging stores, and had taken her with him. Was that his way of hinting how he felt, and that he really knew what Marriott was doing? Had he made sure she would be away when Marriott had returned in the *Herkules* and then gone straight on leave?

He took out his wallet again and opened it carefully.

She had ended with, *Take care of yourself. Auf wiedersehen.* Until we meet again.

Someone confronted him with a tray of white wine.

He took a glass and saw Penny staring at him through the laughter and the babble of voices. For her it should have been champagne.

Then as his father called out a toast to the Happy Couple, Penny looked up at her tall husband and smiled.

Marriott swallowed his wine and gave a rueful grin. They could see nobody but each other.

He saw Chris, the creepy lodger, bending to whisper something in their mother's ear, his father's brief frown of annoyance.

The speeches followed next, and the telegrams; all were fairly predictable, and those from Jack's old squadron pretty close to the bone.

Then it was just as suddenly over, the crowd spilling out on to the road, more confetti and cheers, old boots and cans tied to the back of the hired car before they roared away to change their clothes at a local pub. But for just a few seconds more Penny and Vere looked at each other alone. Then she tossed him the bouquet and laughed, as if she were symbolically casting off her past life.

She cried out above the din, *'Take her the rose, Vere! Do it if—'* The rest was lost as the car vanished in a clattering chorus of tin cans. Marriott stared at the empty road for a full minute.

So he had told her. He touched his uniform and felt the wallet there. He was suddenly glad. Sharing it. For the first time in his life.

He went back into the room and knew he wanted to get away to think.

He heard his mother say, 'And this is our Chris—always so busy, and yet never slow to help me when I need him!'

Marriott moved away and was confonted by a wing-commander with a chest full of decorations and a moustache as wide as his jaw.

'I'm Peter Winters.' His Canadian accent and his medals marked him out as one of Penny's fliers.

He added, 'So you're Penny's brother, eh? Heard a lot about you.' He seemed nervous, on edge; then he blurted out, 'Did you ever meet a Canuck serving with you guys—a Bob Winters? Lieutenant Bob Winters? He was my brother. So I guess we've got something in common.'

Marriott stared past him as the vision flashed through his mind. A motor-gunboat rolling over at full speed, having just taken a direct hit from an armed trawler off the Belgian coast. The scream of machinery as it tore apart, spurting flames, then oblivion. He remembered this man's brother very well. He always wore a big red maple leaf painted on the back of his leather jacket. Now nothing; like Stephen, like Tim Elliott.

The wing-commander asked gruffly, 'Had enough?' He looked at the door. 'I've got a bottle of good old Canadian Club down the road. Like to share it?' As they strolled through the dying sunlight he went on, 'Jack's a lucky guy. Got a wizard girl like Penny, and now a good job waiting for him.' He touched his pilot's wings and medal ribbons with quiet affection. 'Me? I've got fuck-all, but what the hell!'

Marriott grinned. 'You shouldn't have joined!'

They laughed together. 'If you can't take a joke!'

*   *   *

Lieutenant Mike Fairfax stood near a busy derrick and watched the last net of stores being hoisted from a tank landing-craft and lowered expertly on to the dockside. It had been a scene of constant activity since first light when three such vessels had entered Kiel, each fully loaded with stores. They were mostly cans and tins of food, not for the forces here but for the German population.

Fairfax had tried to keep up to date with affairs, just in case he was summoned unexpectedly to face a board who would consider his appointment to the regular navy. He often thought about the firing-squad, of the man's terrible screams which had continued in his brain long after the hail of bullets had smashed him down, and the sailors had been marched away by the formidable CGM named Hawkins.

But in the passing weeks he had made himself accept it. Nobody discussed it with him, and there had been several more summary executions throughout the command to make it somehow acceptable. Or so he told himself.

Of one thing he was certain; his longing to remain in the navy had strengthened, as if he had passed some harsher form of test. He looked at the teeming figures who were hauling the stores on to trestles before being loaded into army lorries. It took good teamwork, with German interpreters ready to iron out mistakes made by impatient and frustrated NCOs.

With the Kiel Canal cleared of hazards, wrecks and abandoned mines, smaller vessels were running a regular shuttle service back and forth to Dover. Food, blankets, building materials—somebody in Whitehall was obviously planning well ahead for a hard winter.

Fairfax wondered how Marriott was getting on in England. He should be back soon. Perhaps he might be able to arrange a similar duty for him? It would enable him to keep his hand in, to improve his ship-handling, something else to stand him in good stead when so required.

Meikle had mentioned leave for him too in the

near future. He had said nothing when Fairfax had offered the opportunity to another lieutenant. Suppose his one and only chance of an interview arrived when he was on leave in England? Besides which, he quite enjoyed his work here: the mess life at the barracks, the evenings at a local theatre of café. He had made several new friends, mostly about his own age, but so far had avoided mentioning his desire to 'stay on'.

What he would really like was an appointment to a warship, large enough to gain more experience. He could still smile at the thought. Small enough *to be noticed*. Several destroyers had visited Kiel. One of them would be just fine.

He realised that a chief petty officer from the Supply Branch was looking up at him from the landing-craft's side deck.

'What is it, Chief?'

'I've been over this vessel *six* times, sir. My Jack Dusty has checked every item with me. It doesn't tally.' He eyed him challengingly. 'Take my word for it, sir!'

Fairfax replied, 'I will, if you explain, Chief.'

The chief petty officer frowned. He was not dealing with some green amateur after all.

He said in a more patient tone, 'Two nets are missing. That's about sixty tins of meat.'

The implication filtered through Fairfax's mind. 'Are you sure?'

'I'm sure. According to this pad, it all left Dover, and everything's been unloaded, so it's gone.' He pushed his cap to the back of his head. '*Walked*.'

Fairfax stared at the nearest lorries. Sixty of those big tins. Enough to feed a platoon. He saw the CPO's expression. Or to make a small fortune on the black market.

'I'd better warn the main gate.'

The other man regarded him with a pitying stare. 'Too late for that, sir. It should have been checked *twice*.'

There was a heavy tread on the deck and Fairfax saw Lieutenant Cuff Glazebrook striding along the bridge, pulling off some oil-stained gloves.

'What's th' bother?'

Fairfax said, 'I didn't know you were in command of this thing.'

Cuff grimaced. 'Thing is right. I'm just standing in. Had a good run-ashore in Dover.' He made a vulgar gesture. 'Fixed up a nice bit of crumpet in the Stag—d'you know it?'

The chief petty officer coughed. 'About these missing stores, sir. They should have been checked twice, like I said.'

Cuff turned towards him as if noticing him for the first time.

'They *were* checked. By me, as it happens.' He stuck out his jaw. 'I signalled Dover and the stores are still in the shed there. They'll be across in a day or two.' He stared at him belligerently. 'So what are you bellyaching about? Haven't you got something useful to do?'

The man flushed. 'I was only doing—'

Cuff snorted scornfully. 'Your duty? Not another arselicker, surely? A *regular*, too!'

The chief petty officer stammered something and then hurried away.

Fairfax said, 'That was a bit hard. The Chief was trying to sort it out.' He was relieved all the same. He had seen himself held responsible for the misplaced tins of meat.

347

'Trying to pass the buck, more like.' Cuff's Yorkshire accent intruded suddenly. 'His sort make me want to spew!'

Fairfax smiled awkwardly. There was something unreal and fearsome about the burly lieutenant. 'Thanks, anyway. I'm glad about the blessed stores.'

Cuff grinned hugely. 'That was a load of old flannel I gave him. Of *course* the stores have walked—someone's nicked them, that's what!' He laughed at Fairfax's astonishment. 'This is Germany, remember? Either they're on the road to some secret dump by now, or they never left Dover in the first place!' He fixed Fairfax with a cold stare. 'Forget it. They're all at it.' He considered telling Fairfax about his passage to Dover. Amongst a mixed cargo of secret U-Boat parts collected by submarine experts from the dockyard, he had also carried a lovely fifteen-ton yacht. There had been no papers, no explanations, other than it would be collected by a long-loading truck, and there his responsibility would end.

Cuff had been amazed that it had been so easy. No customs officers, no officials, no query about the yacht, which was to be delivered to a Hampshire address without delay. The rest had been simple. The information had come from the commodore's secretary, and the address for final delivery was Paget-Orme's.

It could prove useful if things got a bit dicey, he thought. Before, he had proclaimed it was not what you knew but *who* you knew that mattered in the navy. But in this instance, it was *what* you knew which might come in very handy.

So instead he said, 'Just stay out of it. Especially

if you intend to soldier on in this regiment. I reckon you need your head testing.'

A car lurched over some train tracks and ground to a halt, and a woman's voice called, 'I say, do you know where Operations are?'

Fairfax swung round and stared at the girl who was leaning out of the window. She was fair, with candid blue eyes, and very pretty. She had her jacket and tricorn hat on her lap and he realised she was a third officer in the WRNS. He had heard they were sending some to the Schleswig-Holstein command, but he was bowled over all the same.

Cuff was not so bashful. 'Now here's a fine little piece! Just get out and walk towards me slowly, my love!'

Fairfax exclaimed, 'For God's sake, man, what's got into you?'

Cuff held up a big hand to his face and made a mock aside. 'I'd be more interested in getting into *her*!.

She was still smiling from the car. 'Who's your fat friend?' Then she laughed. 'With a bay-window like that I don't think he could get near enough to do much damage!'

To Fairfax's surprise Cuff turned and stormed back on board the L.C.T.

'I don't think he's ever been spoken to like that.' He looked at her again, still embarrassed by what Cuff had said. 'I'm Mike Fairfax. I'm going to Ops myself. I can direct your driver.' He hesitated. 'We're not all like that, you know.'

She watched him climb into the car and smiled. 'Jill Wheatley. You can point out the landmarks as we go.' She smiled again. 'I *can* tell the difference, you know.'

The German driver headed for the gates, where Fairfax noticed some military policemen searching one of the dockyard workers.

Then he watched the way the sunlight shone in her hair, the damp patches on her shirt. She must have been on the road for some while.

He said, 'Welcome to Germany, um . . . Jill.'

The sixty tins of meat were already forgotten.

★   ★   ★

The khaki and camouflaged Bedford lorry with its divisional markings on front and back was parked close to the street-junction. It was an open lorry and the back was crammed with sports equipment. Marker flags, machines for making white lines, bench-seats and several crates of loose gear, all of which was covered by a tightly secured net. There were only two occupants in the cab. One wore a bright football jersey, the other was in army battledress. They were both smoking and drinking tea from a thermos.

Vehicles like this one were common enough on the road to Hamburg. A big match was to be held there very shortly, the first time a top-notch team would have come out from England to play against the services. To bored and lonely servicemen it would be the event of the year.

The one in the football jersey was Sergeant Thornhill, the other, his chosen assistant, Sergeant Hughes.

Thornhill said, 'Can't stay here much longer, Taff. Someone might twig us. I've laid on a baker's van for tomorrow.'

The other man yawned and stretched. 'I think we

350

may have struck oil this time. It's more than a bloody knocking-shop, that's for certain, see?'

'I still don't understand how chummy got wind of it. Luck, d'you reckon?'

Hughes thought of Evans's set features, the latent dedication of the man. 'No. Not the type to rely on luck. Any more than he's a bloody Welshman!'

Thornhill stiffened. 'Look, another one!'

An army officer had just left the building, and, after a quick scrutiny up and down the road, hurried away, his cap tugged over his eyes.

'It's that major. RAMC.'

Hughes chuckled. 'Rob-all-my-comrades, eh?' He became serious again. 'I think the *countess* is into the drugs business too.'

Thornhill nodded. 'That's when it sticks, Taff. Where's the connection? Petty Officer Evans has been watching the place, we know that. Is he after information about Major Maybach? If so, why doesn't he just walk in and threaten the old bag?'

In the driving mirror Thornhill saw some small children hanging about the back of the truck. '*Was wollen Sie?*' When it had no effect he shouted, '*Sod off!*' That worked.

He said eventually, 'He could blow the whole thing, that's what bothers me. the Guv'nor says he can't wait much longer.'

His friend tapped his knee. '*Who's that?*'

Thornhill sank down in his seat. 'Quite a reunion, it seems.' He watched Sub-Lieutenant Lowes walk past, look both ways, then hurry up the steps. The door opened and shut, as if the house had swallowed him up.

'I know him. Served in Marriott's boat, along with the one who took charge of that firing-squad,

351

remember?'

Hughes looked at him. 'Are you going to tell me, or do I just have to guess?'

Thornhill's eyes gleamed. 'I reckon the countess has got that subbie hooked. He probably went there to use her—'

Hughes exclaimed, 'Christ, she'd have that little baby for breakfast!'

Thornhill touched his arm. 'Drive on. I think it's time we had a little chat with chummy. Otherwise Evans will be into something he can't handle.' The Bedford growled into life, but Thornhill's mind was still working. 'It'll mean a whole squad, some from Hamburg as back-up.' He glanced at the house as they rattled past. 'I'll tell the Guv'nor.'

Hughes smiled. Just like old times. Major Maybach would have to wait. This job would mean breaking up a whole black-market gang and nailing their contacts. The pale-faced subbie who had walked past the truck without even a glance was probably about to be blackmailed, if he was not in the countess's trap already. Just how did we manage to win the war, he asked himself, and not for the first time.

A white-overalled bill-sticker who was putting up posters about the forthcoming football match watched the lorry from beneath the long peak of his cap.

Evans smiled. Thornhill was good. But not that good. After all, he had never had to contend with the Gestapo or the SS.

He realised with a start that he had pasted the bill upside down. It was not all that surprising, he thought. *Maybach was there*. Less than fifty yards away, in that house. His mission was nearing its

352

close. With a slight frown he daubed the poster with a large V made of paste. As some had done on the walls and houses in the Channel Islands, and who, in Maybach's hands, had paid dearly for it.

*　　*　　*

The children's hospital at Eutin was exactly as Marriott remembered it. He left Heinz with the car and walked past the wards, his mouth quite dry at the prospect of seeing her again.

He was reminded of his thoughts at Penny's wedding, his sense of not belonging there any more. Here it felt vaguely like home, familiar, so that when he had arrived at the barracks he had found himself seeking out faces, waving and greeting those who were still awaiting leave, and did not know what to expect when they got there.

There were several visitors crammed amongst the lines of cots, and then he saw her standing beside the one where he had seen the child, Bernadette. Her sister-in-law was speaking to one of the nuns, her gestures animated, her face quite flushed.

The girl looked up and saw him, her hand going briefly to her throat as if she had caught her breath.

Marriott squeezed himself past two women who were staring down at a sleeping child and reached across the cot to take her hand.

'I heard you were here. I couldn't wait, so I came right over.'

She searched his face with dark steady eyes. 'But you are only back an hour or so since?' She smiled suddenly. Like sunlight breaking through a hill-mist. 'It is *good* to see you.'

Around them other people jostled and apologised

353

to one another as they found their way to the various cots, some clutching small gifts, toys and picture-books. Marriott wondered who visited those other children in the silent wards, with their pain and their fears.

'I got you a present when I was in Flensburg.' He gripped her hand and held it on the side of the cot. 'I'll get it later.' He looked at the empty cot. 'Where's Bernadette?'

She watched him, her eyes troubled. 'We are taking her home today.'

'She's quite recovered?' It was so hard to speak, impossible to avoid the press of visitors, the occasional cries and laughter from the sick and injured children.

'Almost.' She gave the little shrug. 'They need the cot, so—'

She did not take her hand away and Marriott somehow knew she did not care what people thought, even if they had noticed.

There was something wrong. He could sense it between them. And yet it felt at a distance, like a threat.

He asked, 'How is Leisl? She looks excited.'

He felt the hand tighten under his grip. 'What is it, Ursula? Has something happened?'

Once more, the use of her name made her stare at him. She seemed unable to make up her mind. As if she was withholding something.

'I thought of you very much.'

He replied, 'I've still got the rose. It was a lovely thing to do.'

She reached up and held his hand between hers and said huskily, 'There was a man, who came to Eutin on his way home.' Now that she had begun she could not stop. 'A soldier—Ivan had held him prisoner for a year.' She shook her head despairingly. 'Like a skeleton. I did not recognise him and yet he used to be a carpenter here. Poor man. What a welcome. His wife went off with another when she thought he had been killed at the front.'

Marriott waited. It was all too common in war. A girl he had grown up with at home had gone off with a Yank when they had reported her young husband missing in Singapore. That too had been a mistake, and he would likely be on his way back to England right now. Except that in his case the other man had gone, and there was a baby instead.

But there was more to come, and he asked gently, 'Will you tell me, Ursula? Maybe I can help.'

She lifted her chin and tried to compose herself. 'This soldier told us that he saw Lothar, my brother, in the prison camp. He is alive. Sick but *alive*!' She could not keep it up and whispered, 'He is being sent to a work-camp on the Baltic. But he is sick. It might kill him.'

Marriott forced his way around the cot and put his arms around her. For a few more moments they were both oblivious of the curious stares, a few children standing in the cots to watch. Even the nuns who had been chattering excitedly while they examined the parcel of coffee, soap and chocolate which Marriott had brought for them gathered together like crows to peer at them.

Marriott felt her sobbing quietly against his jacket, her tears soaking through his shirt. He held her tightly, protectively, not wanting to release her. *Ever.*

You've just about had enough, haven't you? Aloud

355

he said, 'When you're ready, Heinz will drive you all home.'

She prised herself away and took his handkerchief without answering.

He said, 'Even the Russians can't hold everyone prisoner.'

She looked up at him. '*Ja. Ja.* I know. But a winter would kill him. The soldier said—'

He took her arm as two nuns carried the child from another room. A third nun began to strip the cot without even glancing at them.

At the door she exclaimed, 'I'm so selfish! The news of my brother is good, yes? Yet here I am spoiling your return! Come, you can tell me all about the wedding—I think it was a very grand affair!'

She was acting, and Marriott had the feeling it was not for the first time.

Grand affair? He thought of the little church hall, Chris the lodger, and the wing-commander who had lost his brother in the North Sea. Penny would soon be in Canada with her Jack. She was doing the right thing. There were too many who were preparing to pick up where they had left off before they had joined up. They ought to be thinking of a future, not the past.

While they waited by the car Marriott handed her the little parcel. 'It's perfume.' He hesitated. 'If it's not right for you—'

She opened it, slowly, prolonging it, and held the little cut-glass bottle to the light. 'It is so *beautiful*!'

Marriott watched her, drinking in every moment, each reaction. Like a child again.

She said, 'I will wear it for you.' She spoke so firmly that Marriott impetuously gripped her arm.

Heinz, who lounged against the car, his arms folded, missed none of it. On that last drive down from Flensburg Marriott had told him to stop at a big NAAFI shop in Schleswig. He had come out eventually with that same parcel and a huge bag.

When Heinz had dropped the lieutenant at the barracks he had been astonished when he had handed him the large bag and had said awkwardly, 'For the family.' Then he had walked away, embarrassed perhaps by his own kindness. The bag had been filled with cream cakes and custard tarts of the sort apparently very popular with the Tommies.

A toy for little Friedl, chocolate too. It had been like Christmas three months early. Like one his daughter had never seen in her life. Now as he watched the dark-eyed girl and the grave young lieutenant he thought he knew why, even with all against them, fate had guided them together.

And later that evening, when Heinz returned to the ancient *Gasthaus*, he knew he was not mistaken.

Marriott stood by the door and looked at the sky. It was already much cooler. She was probably thinking about her brother. Found alive, and yet still beyond reach.

He said, 'I have to go to Hamburg tomorrow, to the harbour.' He took her very gently and pulled her against him. He could feel the tension in her body, like fear.

Into her hair he said, 'I will never harm you, Ursula. I promise.'

She raised her face slightly and he caught the scent of the new perfume on her skin.

'I know. Do not be angry. It is only that I do not understand—'

He kissed her very carefully on the cheek and held his mouth there. Then very slowly she moved her head until their lips touched. He felt her trembling. Afraid of love? Or fearful of what it would do? Then he walked to the courtyard and called, 'I shall see you soon!'

She raised her hand and watched him as he climbed into the little car. *He wants me and I know that I want him. It has never happened; it must never happen.*

But her thoughts mocked her and she was ashamed at the way she felt. At the same time she knew she could not wait until she saw him again.

CHAPTER SEVENTEEN

VICTIMS

Marriott clung to the bridge wing and squinted through icy sleet which within an hour had reduced visibility to a few yards. Beside him, the *Herkules's* skipper, Kapitän Horst Krieger, peered up with alarm as the shadow of the *New York's* listing hulk crept out of the gloom like a reef.

For once Marriott felt that his knowledge of Kiel was a match for the German's, especially in its present state. It was strange not to have Heinz with him, but he had left Flensburg with the car after *Herkules* had received orders to make for Kiel.

Another ship to be towed out and dumped perhaps? Marriott shivered. He could scarcely believe that any sea could change so quickly. There was a bite in the air which took his breath away, and with the blinding sleet all around them it seemed like evening instead of noon.

Krieger remarked, 'Plenty of wrecks, eh, Herr Leutnant?'

Not as many as there were when 801 arrived, Marriott thought. He said, 'We should be up to the jetty soon.' A green wreck-buoy winked out of the downpour, its bell clanging mournfully, as if for the dead.

Maybe they would stay here for a while? He would see Ursula as soon as he could get free from his duties. *Duties?* He grimaced into the stinging sleet. He felt more like a scavenger and scrap-dealer rolled into one.

He thought of the walk they had shared before *Herkules* had carried him out into the Baltic again. Along the beach of the Plöner See, through the dark green woods where they had found an old track and bridle-path, a reminder of better times when there had been horses here.

Once, when they had crossed a small stream, he had held her hand in case she slipped. He had not released it, even when two forestry workers had gone past.

She had not mentioned her brother again, even when he had pressed her. At first he had thought she was too worried to talk about him, but later had the feeling she knew more than she had told him.

A lamp blinked through the sleet and Marriott saw the end of the pier taking shape off the starboard bow. It probably seemed like matchless navigation to the crew who huddled in the bows with lines and fenders. Marriott was just thankful they had reached the bay before the skies had fallen on them, or they had been forced to make the final

359

approach in the dead of night.

He knew the skipper was watching him as he moved to the wheelhouse voicepipe. *'Volle Kraft zurück! Ruder mitschiffs!'* He sensed the grizzled skipper nod, with relief or approval he did not know.

Marriot felt the power rising to take the way off the tug's forward thrust and saw vague figures moving along the jetty towards them.

'Maschine stopp! Langsam fahrt voraus!'

He wondered how his stilted German sounded now to the tug's crew. He had learned the basic commands by listening and watching. At first, the seamen had stared at the bridge with astonishment, but now they seemed to accept it, as they did the only British officer on board.

'Maschine stopp! Klar zum Ankern!'

At the jangle of the telegraph again the powerful engine gave a shudder and fell silent even as the lines snaked ashore, and the bulky tug nudged purposefully against her big rope fenders. He turned and faced the other man. Krieger nodded and said. *'Good*, Herr Leutnant! I prefer you to me that time!'

They both laughed and Marriott felt his voice shake as he gave the last order to ring off the main engine.

'Maschinen abstellen!'

He saw the bridge light up to some frail, watery sunshine, as, like a solid fence, the sleet moved away across the wrecks and the swirling grey water. Krieger's lined features lost their smile as he stared hard at the pier.

He exclaimed, *'Herr Meikle!'*

Marriott saw the long bonnet of a staff car parked
360

near one of the new cranes, then Commander
Meikle as he stepped on to the wet stones. He
turned up the collar of his raincoat before walking
to the edge to watch the sailors passing up the
heavier mooring ropes.

Meikle seemed to come to a decision, and as the
brow was hauled across and secured, he walked
very carefully on the wet treads towards the
Herkules's bulwark.

The tug's boatswain bellowed, *'Besatzung
stillgestanden!'* then saluted smartly as Meikle
stepped down from the brow.

He returned Marriott's salute and commented,
'They don't forget, do they? To us she is a useful
tug. To them, still a unit of the *Kriegsmarine!'*

Marriott guided him into the small cabin abaft
the wheelhouse and watched as the commander
removed his cap and patted his iron-grey hair.

'I had to be in the yard anyway. Heard you were
arriving, so I thought I might offer you a lift,' He
eyed him shrewdly. 'From the weather reports it
seems unlikely we shall have many more operations
in the Baltic this year.'

A larger vessel surged abeam and the tug rocked
heavily in her wash. Meikle swallowed. 'I cannot
imagine what anyone finds enjoyable about serving
in small ships!' He retrieved his cap. 'If you're
ready, Marriott?'

Marriott followed him on deck again. Meikle had
been as near to being sick as any one he had seen. It
was almost unnerving to discover he had human
weaknesses like everybody else.

Meikle watched as Marriott and the skipper
solemnly shook hands before they parted.

He remarked, 'You do form the *oddest*

relationships, Marriott.' The bite was back again.

They got into a smart staff Humber, while a Royal Marine driver bustled around with Marriott's small bag, opened and shut doors with the zeal of a Mayfair chauffeur.

Meikle sat back and stared out of the window as they picked their way along the dockyard road.

'Thought it would save time to have this talk.' He turned suddenly and said, 'You have been seeing quite a lot of Fräulein Geghin of late?'

Marriot said nothing. He knew by now there was no point. So that was what it was about. A reprimand, or a warning.

Meikle said calmly, 'She asked to have a meeting with me, as a matter of fact. About her brother—the one in Russian hands.' This time he did pause.

Marriott replied, 'Yes, she told me about him, sir. It's still not known where he is.'

Meikle tapped the marine sharply on the shoulder. '*Stop the car!*' He wound down the window and beckoned to a petty officer who was walking with some seamen along the road. Several of them were smoking.

'*You!* You know the regulations, PO!' He did not raise his voice, but the petty officer was gaping as if he had just hurled a string of obscenities at him. '*March* those men! You're not a sloppy civilian just yet!'

The car lurched forward and Meikle said in an almost matter-of-fact tone, 'Fräulein Geghin's brother is in Swinemünde. She came to tell me that she had received some definite news from another former POW.'

Marriott looked at him questioningly. 'She asked

your help to get him out, sir?'

'No.' He saw his surprise. 'She pleaded with me to make certain you were *not* sent to Swinemünde. She was afraid you would do something impetuous to release him.' He gave a thin smile. 'She obviously understands you pretty well.'

Marriott glanced away. 'Protecting me?'

'Yes.' His tone sharpened. '*Would* you have done something?'

Marriott faced him. 'I might have acted personally, sir. I can't say. But I would have had the *Herkules's* crew as my responsibility too. I couldn't risk having them seized, and the whole thing blown up into a confrontation betwen the two governments.'

Meikle regarded him impassively. 'What I hoped you'd say. I'm glad those pieces of lace on your sleeve mean more than *rank*, to you anyway.'

'So what can we do, sir?' He thought of her face when he had last seen her. She might even have known something when he had been at the hospital.

She loved her brother, and yet she was prepared to stand back for his sake. It must have been a terrible responsibility, a secret which meant far more than a gesture of friendship. At a guess, Ursula's mother, and her sister-in-law, the strained-looking Leisl, might already have put pressure on her to persuade her *British lieutenant*.

Meikle was watching the emotions on his sensitive features.

'So it is true. You're not just using the girl?'

'No, sir!'

'Don't jump down my throat, Marriott. I have to know.' He stared moodily at the glittering waters of the Plöner See as they turned on to the last lap for

363

Plön. 'I might be able to help.' Again the brief smile. 'Not *officially*, of course.'

Marriott said, 'I suppose you think I'm making a fool of myself?'

'Not at the moment.' He nodded approvingly as a squad of Germans, still in their old uniforms, leaped to attention as the car roared past.

Marriott said, 'I think they're all scared of you, sir.'

'That *was* my intention.' It was so casually said that Marriott stared at him, remembering the tug's crew when Meikle had stepped on board. He added, 'But they also respect you, there's no doubt about that, sir.'

Meikle shifted in his seat as the barracks appeared at the end of the road.

'That too was the intended outcome. Remember how I came down on your ships' companies like a ton of bricks when you arrived here? Strolling about in your combat gear, like a bunch of heroes on show, eh?'

Marriott made to answer as he continued ruthlessly, 'Heroes are well enough in war. In the aftermath they can only create resentment, non-co-operation. How would you have felt if you'd seen Germans swaggering about in Piccadilly, clanking their Iron Crosses all over the place? You might have been wary of them. But respect? I think not. That has to be earned, and only by example!'

Marriott saw the sentry at the gate and the O.O.D. salute as the car swept through.

The word was out. *Commander Meikle is back.*

'Word of advice, Marriott. Don't raise her hopes too much. She's a good girl. Let her down and you'll hurt her irreparably.' He waited for the

364

marine to open his door. 'And you will have *me* to reckon with.'

They strode into Meikle's HQ section where several people were busy on teleprinters or peering at their desks.

Meikle snapped, 'I'll bet it's the first work they've done today!'

He thrust open his office door, just in time to see the rabbit-like Lavender on one of the telephones. 'For you, sir.'

Marriott noticed that the leading rate had vanished from his sleeve. He was a petty officer now.

Meikle muttered, 'I should hope so!' He snatched the telephone and snapped, 'Meikle?'

Then he looked at his writer while he replaced the telephone and said, 'Get my car back, at the double.' As Lavender spoke urgently into another phone Meikle said, 'You come with me, Marriott. In a way you are concerned.'

He picked up his cap and looked at it as his car squealed to a halt outside the building.

Then he added quietly, 'There's been a shooting in Neumünster.'

Marriott almost had to run to keep up with him.

A shooting. But from the bleakness in Meikle's voice, it sounded very much like murder.

*   *   *

Captain Eric Whitcombe glanced first at his watch and then at the sky. It was clouding over again and would make the dusk come early. After that it would be too late, too much of a risk that the whole operation would blow up in his face.

365

He shifted his balance to the other knee and cursed softly as the wet charred woodwork ground through his battledress. Like several of the houses on this side of the street, this one had been bombed into an eyeless shell, the whole place littered with rubbish, all soaking wet from the last downpour.

The young lieutenant of the Military Police watched him dubiously.

'Should all be in position by now, sir.'

Whitcombe pressed his binoculars against a hole in the hoarding which ran along the front of the bombed buildings. Why did people make such pointless comments, he wondered.

The street was as before, empty but for two overalled figures with sledgehammers who had been breaking up old paving stones to clear more space for the salvage squads.

Whitcombe ignored them. They were two of his own men. He moved his glasses slowly to the tall house at the end. Four storeys, if you included the basement and some cellars. A barn of a place but Whitcombe, like his officers and NCOs, had been studying the plans of the building since daybreak. They had obtained them from the local *Rathaus*, on the pretext that more bombed buildings around it had to be made safe. You never knew who you could trust. Who might sell his own sister on the black market.

He wanted a smoke but dared not. Around and behind him about fifty redcaps and some of his own S.I.B. squads waited and fretted. The whole place stank. There were probably still some rotting corpses buried in the debris, although the town hall had assured him the street had been evacuated during one of the last devastating air attacks.

366

Someone wriggled up between him and the lieutenant. It was Sergeant Thornhill.

Whitcombe asked tersely, 'Find chummy?'

Thornhill shook his head and tried not to let the captain see that he was peering at his watch.

'I reckon Evans slipped past us, Guv. He was last seen in uniform. Then our chaps lost him.' He nodded firmly. 'But he's there. I'm sure of it.'

'If he screws this up, I'll, I'll—' Whitcome sounded fed up.

Thornhill loosened the revolver in its webbing holster. 'Taff Hughes is around in the back garden, sir.' The *sir* was for the lieutenant's benefit. 'You know what they say, every rat has two holes.'

Whitcombe looked at the sky again. People would be coming home from work soon, or to queue for rationed bread at one of the army's cookhouses. It would be too damn dangerous then. He tried to picture the other squads of police, military and civil, who were hidden further back in the adjoining streets. It had to go like a clock, or fail completely.

Thornhill said, 'I'll slip back, Guv. Taff might need a hand.'

Whitcombe nodded. 'Ten minutes then. All I can spare.' But Thornhill had already gone.

He whispered, 'Pass the word. Ten minutes.' He saw his communications orderly with the radio on his shoulders edging towards him, the shoulders bowed to conceal the wagging aerial.

In burned-out rooms his men were getting ready. Guns drawn, safety catches checked, jaws tight with expectancy.

'I don't want anyone allowed near, all right? All vehicles to be stopped, searched too if need be.' He

367

swung round as a shot echoed through the buildings, followed shortly by another.

Whitcombe exclaimed, 'Christ!' Then he snatched the walkie-talkie from his orderly and shouted, 'This is Hotspur! *Go! Go!*'

*   *   *

The garden was full of muddy puddles and scattered slates from a roof, but the trees, still heavy with rain, afforded good cover as Evans felt his way towards the tiny door beside a collapsed glasshouse.

There were old cellars here, probably used as air-raid shelters—he had seen them on the plans. The clerk at the town hall had told him that others had already been looking at them. Evans might have smiled if he was not so tense. Every muscle was bar-taut, his mind clear and cold as if he was on the gunboat's open bridge instead of in this stinking garden.

He eased the heavy pistol from inside his jacket and found time to glance at his Croix de Guerre. How apt, how perfect for this final moment.

Two more steps and he was at the small door; there were some stone stairs down, each treacherous and slippery from the sleet. There was some kind of light in the cellar, while from overhead in the main building he heard a woman give a shrill laugh.

They were all in for a shock, Evans thought. *The last laugh.*

He held his breath and very gently pulled back a thick, damp curtain, apparently made of sacking. He could scarcely believe it as his eyes took in the scene with the instant understanding of a camera.

A German uniform hanging on a chair. A small
368

suitcase. A table lamp which allowed a trail of black smoke to rise straight up towards the stained ceiling. His eyes registered everything and then settled on the sleeping figure, covered by a blanket.

So this was what they used to call a safe house in the Maquis. Perhaps Maybach had intended to make this a final stopping-point before being aided by his friends upstairs to board a ship, or to make his way to France and across to Spain where he would have a better chance of completing his arrangements. And all the while Maybach would be thinking that the security forces thought him dead. Evans felt the bile rise in his throat as he reached for the blanket, the pistol levelled. But first of all he would make sure this bloody murderer knew who his executioner really was.

With a jerk Evans dragged the blanket away and then stared at the purple, contorted features of a British army sergeant. His eyes had bulged almost out of their sockets and his tongue was poking through his bared teeth in one last terrible attempt to live. He had been garotted, the wire pulled so savagely that it had vanished into the flesh.

Evans heard just the slightest sound from a corner of the cellar. He swung round, but all that his mind had time to record was the face, the cold eyes he had recalled in every waking moment.

The sound of Sergeant Hughes's revolver was like a thunderclap in the confined space.

Evans tried to raise his pistol but could feel himself falling. There was no pain, but when he tried to shout it was like being filled up with scalding fluid. Then as understanding faded from his eyes, and his blood gushed from his silent scream, the other man, once Major Helmut

369

Maybach of the SS, shot him again in the nape of the neck.

Something flew through the air and hit Maybach on the jaw. Before he could recover the gun which he had taken from the murdered Hughes, Thornhill bounded across the cellar and hit him with all his strength across the face with his pistol-barrel, slashing the skin so that the jawbone looked white in the flickering lamplight.

'*You bastard! You bloody bastard!*' He hit him again, his ears deaf to the sudden pandemonium in that other world outside. Sledgehammers smashing down the front door, yells and screams, the sounds of vehicles roaring into position, boots clattering on stairways.

With his chest heaving, Thornhill bent over the unconscious Maybach and tugged his hands behind his back to snap on some handcuffs. Then he stood leaning against the wall, gasping for air, knowing how close he had been to murder himself.

He stared, sickened, at Evans's blood-soaked corpse. Even at the end Maybach had cheated him. Then he looked at his dead friend and retched. A good cop. An even better mate.

Savagely he kicked the unconscious Maybach in the stomach, then turned as Whitcombe burst in with three redcaps close on his heels.

'All right, Jim?' His eyes moved from the drawn revolver to the two corpses. Then he crossed to the handcuffed Maybach.

'That's him, then?' He was watching his sergeant anxiously, moved by what he saw. 'That took guts, Jim. Me, I'd probably have blown the fucker's brains out!'

Overhead whistles shrilled, and then there was

370

complete silence. Whitcombe nodded to the redcaps. 'Take over here.' He put his arm around Thornhill's shoulders and led him from the cellar and its smell of death.

In the garden Whitcombe took out his hip flask and said, 'Here, Jim, have a good swig.'

Thornhill thrust his revolver back into its holster.

'What, Guv, *on duty?*' He laughed but almost broke down until the whisky had done its work.

Together they walked out on to the road. How different it looked now. Cars and vans, ambulances, and dispatch-riders on motor-cycles. Soldiers everywhere, some grinning, as if relieved they had succeeded, none knowing that two men had died in the process. At either end of the street was a human field-grey barrier of civil police, the *Polizei* in their old-fashioned shakos. More like spectators than participants, Whitcombe thought. But he had noticed that with the Germans. They rarely got too curious or interfered where police were concerned. The old order may have gone, but the shadow of Hitler, dead or not, was always present.

The MP lieutenant came up smartly and saluted. 'All taken, sir!' He looked very pleased with himself. 'Enough loot to fill a convoy, *and* some useful prisoners.' He saw his expression and waited, his smile fading.

Whitcombe said, 'Taff Hughes has bought it. There's an RN petty officer back there too.' Afterwards he wondered why he had not mentioned the capture of a most-wanted war criminal. While there was life there was hope. And Maybach was still alive.

Someone called, 'Here comes the navy, sir!'

Meikle's staff car swept through the police
371

barrier, making two of the *Polizei* jump aside for their own safety.

It pulled up with a screech and Meikle with a young lieutenant stepped on to the wet cobbles.

Meikle listened without a word of interruption as Whitcombe gave him his report. It sounded as if the raid had been a huge success. It could also be of some embarrassment when the officers found in the building were put in front of a court martial, although it would deter others. For a while.

Thornhill looked at Marriott. 'It was Evans, sir. Tried to do it single-handed. A brave lad. That bastard Maybach killed a mucker of mine too.'

'I'm so sorry.'

Meikle shot him a glance. Marriott's face told him a lot. He was blaming himself for Evans's death. Without reason.

A corporal shouted, 'Stretcher party, round the back, chop-chop!'

Marriott said tightly, 'I'll take care of him, sir. He was one of mine. The best coxswain I've ever had.' He could not go on.

'No! Wait.' Meikle turned as the first of the prisoners were pushed and bundled down the steps and into the waiting vans.

Youths wearing make-up, some almost naked, staring around in terror as the redcaps hurried them along. Prostitutes too, trying to swagger, their eyes bold until they were loaded into the vans like so much rubbish. Then came the countess. All in black as usual.

She saw Whitcombe and said, 'There were British officers also. I am not the only guilty one.'

Close to in the grey light she looked much older. Haggard.

372

Whitcombe said softly, 'You will be charged.'

'Please address me properly!'

Whitcombe knew that he wanted to hit her but replied evenly, 'You're as much a countess as my arse! I repeat, you will be charged under the articles of the Military Government, with unlawfully keeping stolen or bartered property.' He watched her lip curl in a contemptuous sneer as he had known it would. He added harshly, 'But *also* you will be charged with harbouring war criminals and being an accomplice to the murder of two British NCOs.' He rocked back on his heels. 'No smile now, Countess? But me, I'll be happy to drive you to the gallows myself!' He gestured angrily. 'Cuff her, and take her in.'

Thornhill nodded as she was hurried away. The Guv'nor was a shrewd old copper. The countess would do anything to stay alive. She would sing like a bird.

He lit a cigarette and saw his hand shaking.

None of it would bring Taff back.

Meikle said, 'And don't take this on your back either, Marriott!'

Sub-Lieutenant Lowes was being escorted down the steps; he was hatless, his eyes wild and desperate as he tugged feebly at the grip of a massive MP.

He saw Meikle and Marriott and shouted, 'It's not my fault! Tell them it wasn't like that!' His voice broke into a shrill scream. 'It was *her*! It was all *her* doing!'

The van door slammed shut but they could still hear his cries as it moved towards the junction where an escort of outriders had lined the road.

'*Her* doing?' Meikle said mildly. 'I wonder which

one of them he meant?'

He saw Marriott's expression. 'It's nobody's fault. That young man may have missed the war, but he was one of its victims nonetheless.'

He watched Helmut Maybach being carried, still dazed and bleeding, to one of the cars. Slight and harmless enough, until he stared round and you saw his eyes, as so many of his victims had done.

Meikle touched Marriott's arm. 'Quite a day. I suggest you get cleaned up. Then tell your *Nazi* driver to take you out to Eutin.' He beckoned to his own car and it started up. 'If you like, Marriott, you may tell Fräulein Geghin that her brother will be safe.' He nodded to Marriott's strained features. 'I shall see the commodore. I may have to remind him of a few points of law, but I'm certain he'll see it my way in the end.'

Marriott stared from the window as the car glided away. Soldiers smoking and chatting, clearing up. Others carrying boxes and books from the house while a few were to be seen at the upper windows, investigating further corruption.

He watched the ambulance take station behind Meikle's Humber.

Petty Officer Evans would be going home. Even if he had not taken Maybach himself, it had been his finger which had pointed the way. Others would hear what he had done. That revenge if not justice had been carried out.

*   *   *

Lieutenant Mike Fairfax walked slowly through another barbed-wire barrier inside Kiel dockyard and continued towards the slipways.

It was cold, and, but for a swaying line of little electric lamps which were suspended from a single overhead wire, it would have been pitch-dark.

He should have had the duty petty officer with him, but he had sent the man around the other side of the old U-Boat pens to seek out the sentries there and save time.

Doing Rounds in Kiel dockyard was never welcome duty at night. The place was sinister with memories and tall stories which could make a new recruit throw a fit. There was the story of the U-Boat, now crushed beneath its fallen concrete pen, which had had an extra officer when it had sailed for the Atlantic. The officer was said to be one who had been lost at sea, washed overboard while watchkeeping on the conning-tower. Newly joining officers always swore they had been greeted by his ghost. Now the boat was wrecked down there, but it was bandied about the messes that the same ghost had been seen on the slipways. Watching the harbour, waiting perhaps for the returning U-Boat which would never come.

Fairfax paused by a telephone box and dialled for the correct time. The recorded female voice announced that it was two in the morning. He replaced it. *Had it come to this?* So hungry for a woman's voice that he was dialling the talking clock!

He watched the line of swaying lights. Each one made a small disc of white on the stones, while the darkness isolated one from the next. It would be impossible to walk here without them, he thought.

Fairfax had heard about the big raid in Neumünster, and how Evans had been killed there. All their little company was being scattered, and he

375

knew Marriott felt like that too. Evans dead, their 'hinge' when he had been 801's coxswain. Even his memory would blur in time. Others too would be leaving the navy in the next few months.

He thought suddenly of Third Officer Jill Wheatley. His ideal girl. She was always pleasant to him, and had soon settled down with the others. But whenever he had tried to get closer neither of them seemed to have anything in common. Even she intended to get out of the WRNS at the first opportunity.

If he only knew if or when a Board might summon him to make the only decision he cared about. One more week and he would see Commander Meikle again.

He stiffened as he heard footsteps on the wet stones and stood quite still in the shelter of the telephone box.

He watched the feet move from one circle of light towards the next. When the figure was directly beneath one of the lights he saw it was Cuff Glazebrook, his gait slightly unsteady, but that was nothing unusual. He was heading towards the LCT moorings and Fairfax toyed with the idea of speaking to him, but rejected it immediately. He was probably too drunk to talk reasonably, or was in one of his foul moods. All you could say for him was that *he* certainly did not lack confidence.

Fairfax stared as another pair of feet appeared in the swaying light beam. Khaki trousers. A soldier. He was speaking with Cuff, the two pairs of feet isolated in the solitary disc of light, like shoes on a hotel landing.

Fairfax could hear their voices and thought that Cuff was getting angry; the other man's tone

376

seemed equally sharp.

The voices stopped and Fairfax heard footsteps again.

He felt a chill run down his spine. There was only one pair of feet now. He removed his cap and wiped his forehead. Despite the bitter air he felt the sweat on his fingers. He was going round the bend! He tried to recall how many drinks he had had at dinner and afterwards. Very little. When he was O.O.D. he was very conscientious for all sorts of reasons. Then how—

The petty officer stepped from the gloom and flashed his light. 'All correct at the pens, sir. Both sentries alive an' well! Nippy though, ain't it, sir?'

'Er—yes.' Fairfax fell into step beside him. The PO would probably laugh his head off if he told him. After what he had heard about poor Lowes it would bring further discredit on the lot of them, amd Mciklc's spies would soon get to hear about it.

'Let's get it over with, PO.' He quickened his pace. *Just forget it.*

But the next morning at breakfast the news broke over the table as a new topic of disaster.

A lieutenant exclaimed, 'Did you hear about last night? Some army officer fell into a basin in the dockyard!'

Fairfax kept his voice level only with difficulty. 'Oh really? What happened?'

The others looked up from their newspapers, each one propped on a little stand so that an officer could read without being disturbed while he ate his breakfast.

The lieutenant spread his hands. 'Well, for God's sake, Mike, it smashed his skull in! It must be all of a sixty-foot drop there!'

Fairfax turned sharply as Cuff looked over the top of his *Daily Mirror*. 'Surprised I didn't hear something. I was aboard one of the LCTs last night.' His eyes moved and then rested coldly on Fairfax. 'Said all along it's a dangerous place if you don't know your way about.'

Fairfax wanted to look away, to break the contact, but it was like being mesmerised. *He knows. He must have seen me.*

Cuff folded his paper and stood up. 'A brown job, you say?' He grinned. 'Well, you know what they say about soldiers!'

He walked heavily to the door and tossed his newspaper to one of the German messmen.

Fairfax stared at his plate and the congealing sausages. What should he do? Meikle was bound to question him. After all, he had patrolled the dockyard as O.O.D. And what might the petty officer say?

He thought of Cuff's bleak stare. *They might not even believe me!*

As he stood up to leave he knew he would tell nobody. Not yet anyway.

The petty officer of the guard was waiting in the lobby.

'Mornin', Mister Fairfax, sir. Commander's compliments an' he'd like to see you.' He grinned. 'A bit sharpish.'

Fairfax groped for his cap. He could feel his world falling apart.

'Hello, old son!'

Fairfax stared as Marriott's friend Beri-Beri, propped on two sticks and assisted by a messenger from the main gate, lurched through the doors.

'Welcome back!' Fairfax could barely get it out.

378

Beri-Beri regarded him cheerfully. 'Thought you'd be at *least* an admiral by now!' He ignored Fairfax's anxiety and added, 'I heard Meikle is leaving too. Up the ladder of plenty, it seems!' He balanced himself on his plastered leg and winked at the petty officer. 'This comes off very soon!'

Fairfax slipped away, his mind already busy with Beri-Beri's information. Probably just a rumour, another 'buzz'. But if it were true, there would be nobody to speak up for him at the Board.

So later, when Meikle watched Lavender's busy pen darting across his pad, it was easy to deny that he had seen anything untoward.

Meikle nodded and replied, 'The soldier was apparently an S.I.B. officer. Lavender, get Captain Whitcombe for me, will you? After that, I'd like an appointment with the commodore.' He raised his eyebrows. 'So you're still here, Fairfax?'

There was a huge pile of letters and signals to be dealt with. One letter which he had to send himself was to Lowes's mother and stepfather. Lowes was being sent to a special wing of a naval hospital. With luck he might escape with a mental discharge. Without it, he would face a court martial. Not an easy letter to write.

He faced Fairfax and said severely, 'There are one hundred and twenty junior officers in this command who are seeking the same transfer as yourself. Just do your work and stay out of trouble. The rest is up to their lordships.'

Fairfax left the office. There was still hope after all.

As soon as the door was closed Petty Officer Writer Lavender said, 'Do you expect the commodore to agree, if I might ask, sir?'

379

Meikle smiled. Outwardly timid, but there was quite a lot to Lavender. He had already asked him to stay with him, and later to join him in chambers in London.

'Oh, about Fräulein Geghin's brother? I think so. Just dig out that confidential file about the commodore's new yacht. This might be an excellent time to remind him.'

He did not speak with Captain Whitcombe very long. Like himself he was always in demand, especially with the enormous task of sorting out the evidence his men had gathered in the raid.

Whitcombe sounded abrupt, tired. 'Yes, sir. One of my team. A Lieutenant Sanders. I had my people there when the body was discovered. All the usual checks.' Meikle heard him sigh. 'But it was a long drop into an empty drydock. Not a lot to go on.'

Meikle stared at the opposite wall. One of the maps was slightly crooked and he gestured at Lavender to straighten it.

'May I ask what your officer was doing there? It is in confidence, but I need not tell you that.'

Whitcombe answered, 'He went to speak with Lieutenant Glazebrook, sir. He had apparently been up late at some party or other.'

'Trouble?'

'Well, no, sir. I just thought he might have some information about a German woman, the one who's employed at the fuel dump. I know he once tried to help her, so I thought he might have heard something.'

'Thank you.' Meikle's eyes gleamed. 'I was sorry about your sergeant.'

He put down the phone and rested his chin on his interlaced fingers. But Glazebrook had not seen the officer. Neither had the O.O.D. He glanced at Lavender on the other telephone and smiled to himself. *Curiouser and curiouser.*

'The commodore, sir!'

Meikle lifted the other telephone connection. 'I wonder if we could meet, sir—about the transfer of a German prisoner?' He frowned until Lavender had the wall-map exactly right. 'Well, *I* am busy too, sir. I also wanted to discuss the standing regulations and A.I.s on the Customs and Excise requirements at Dover.'

He put down the telephone and said aloud, 'Yes, *sir*, I thought that might make a difference!'

CHAPTER EIGHTEEN

A PROMISE KEPT

When winter struck it was swift, and with such intensity that few of the civilian population in Kiel and its immediate surroundings could recall anything like it. Snow, freezing rain and strong winds off the Baltic rendered their existence another battle, a fight for survival itself.

Broken sewers were soon blocked with ice, and the problem of trying to heat an individual house or even a room presented enormous difficulties. The British armed forces worked around the clock, for although they were provided with ample rations and heated quarters, they were very aware of the desperate civilians who had come to rely on them. The battered streets were always filled with the mouth-watering smell of baking bread—both the army and the navy provided bread as fast as they could, but it was still far from enough.

With the food shortages came crime. Many of these were committed by displaced persons, the Military Government's polite term for refugees. Like the one who had faced Fairfax's forgotten firing-squad, a lot of them were Poles. Invaded first by the Germans and then by the Russians, they had been made to fall on the mercies of their old enemy.

The first to suffer were children. Two small boys sent by their mother with ration cards to collect their bread from the army. It was common enough with so many of the men killed or missing, and the women often doing manual work to provide for their families. Both children were stabbed to death, their bread stolen.

A witness saw the incident, however, and justice was short and sharp. But the executions did not stop it. Surprisingly, it seemed to draw the British and the Germans closer to one another. Or as Lieutenant Commander Arthur Durham had described it, 'The cowboys and the Indians working together until the cavalry arrive!'

Marriott had seen very little of Ursula, although he had called on her at the inn as often as he could. Her brother's whereabouts were carefully avoided in the conversation, and they always seemed genuinely glad to see him.

Even Ursula's fierce, white-haired *oma* had softened slightly when he had presented her with some cocoa, freshly ground coffee, and more chocolate for the little girl.

As Christmas drew near Marriott was deeply aware of the passing of time. Like his companions he worked day and night and in all weathers.

Clearing roads and unloading ships and barges, the cargoes usually food, flour and medicine.

Every shipment of cargo had to be guarded until is was safely delivered to the various distribution points in the Schleswig-Holstein command, while hoarding at the expense of others was regarded almost in the same vein as armed robbery.

But despite the hardship and the cold, some attempt was made to revive the Christmas spirit. Paper flowers, hand-made greeting cards and even carols near the bombed-out churches gave an extra meaning to this, the first Christmas after the war.

The sailors were busy speculating on their demob dates. Some were already consulting their divisional officers, who had been supplied with lists of training schemes, further education, new jobs. Perhaps Christmas was more like a final truce than a religious celebration, a reminder of personal suffering and loss irrespective of flag or language.

There were all the usual mistakes, of course. Like the new naval chaplain who had been asked to choose the hymns for one Sunday divisions at Plön. He was young and he was earnest and he loved the majesty of the words when he chose his selection. Unfortunately he did not think of the music. So that when the grinning sailors roared out the old and familiar hymn while they hid their glee behind their prayer-cards, the young chaplain was scarlet with embarrassment. It was exactly the same tune as the German national anthem, 'Deutschland über Alles'! Outside the building, German workers stared at each other with surprise and wonder that their old enemy should make such a gesture.

Marriott had also hidden a smile when he had stood with Ursula outside a church while a choir

383

had rendered a Christmas hymn, 'Tannenbaum, the festive fir tree'; it had been the same tune as 'The Red Flag'.

But there was disappointment and tragedy too.

Two weeks before Christmas Fairfax was requested to go to Meikle's HQ. He arrived there with mixed feelings. Was it about the dead S.I.B. officer? Had something worse happened?

Meikle was dictating letters, to another leading writer; Lavender appeared to have his own office now.

He said. 'The day after tomorrow, Fairfax. It'll give you time to collect yourself—' He glanced at the writer. 'Where was I?'

The leading writer repeated, '*With reference to your signal* . . .'

Fairfax stammered, 'Collect myself, sir?'

Meikle regarded him with a wry smile. 'The Board meets here then. The other interviewees have no active-service experience so—' His black eyebrows rose together. 'Think about it!'

As he walked past the operations desk the duty officer called him over.

'Job for you, Mike. Ride shotgun on a ration train to Hamburg this evening.' He grinned. 'Congratulations, by the way. I'll lay odds that the Board will select you, with your record.'

Fairfax was walking on air. He did not relish the idea of a trip to Hamburg with a line of ration-trucks and no shelter or heating. He had already done one such trip and had been glad to get rid of the precious rations into the army's care.

It had to be right this time. He pictured his father's face, and those of his friends when he appeared for the first time with straight stripes on his sleeves. Meikle must have made out a first-rate report. That, with the commodore's endorsement, might just make all the difference.

But within a few minutes of reaching their destination Fairfax realised that something was wrong. His party of twelve armed seamen, the number constantly reminded him of the firing-squad, was crouching behind the tarpaulin-covered crates trying to find shelter from the icy snow. It tore down across the train like white flak; stung their eyes and faces until they felt raw.

The petty officer was Arthur Townsend, still not made up to full petty officer, still wearing his square-rig as he had in 801. He had been bemoaning the fact to Fairfax, saying he would be glad to quit the Andrew now and find a job that was useful rather than profitable.

It was good to see him again. All the others were young ordinary seamen, just out from England, excited like a bunch of kids as the train rolled slowly along the bumpy and much-repaired track.

Townsend stood up and said, 'God, look at the *crowd*!

Fairfax said, 'Don't worry, the army will be waiting. There's always a crowd watching these trains, especially the ones with rations!'

Anyway, it would soon be over. Back to Plön. A drink or two, maybe tell Jill Wheatley about the Board.

Towsend shattered his thoughts. 'The track's been taken up, sir! *We're stopping!*'

Fairfax climbed up beside him on top of the wagon. He almost fell as the train halted sharply, while the driver and his mate stuck their heads out

385

to see what was happening.

At first Fairfax thought it was an accident. Then he saw the great black mass of people begin to move towards the train, along either side of the track, soundless, as if it was one great force under a single control.

Townsend swore. 'Where's the bloody army?'

Fairfax tried to clear his mind. There was an explanation. Must be. But he was in charge. He looked at his squad of sailors. Not laughing and joking any more, but gripping their rifles, watching the approaching crowd. In a moment they might panic.

Townsend said harshly, 'Look, sir! They're cutting the lashin's of that truck! God damn them, they're goin' to pinch the lot!'

'Like *hell* they are!' Fairfax dragged out his revolver and fired it above his head. He felt the kick of it jar his wrist and forearm, the sensation helping to steady him, and control his sudden fury.

Everything stopped, and only the muted beat of the engine gave any hint of life.

It worked. Fairfax shouted, 'Get back! *Stopp! Zurück!*'

Somebody may have shouted, or it might have been several voices. Then with something like a roar the whole mob, men and women alike, was surging up to the train, tearing at the lashings, yelling at the young sailors, who without warning were suddenly cut off from one another. A man leaped on to the leading truck and Fairfax saw Townsend jab at him with his boot. But he slipped on the snow-encrusted tarpaulin and slithered down the side, only preventing himself from falling to the track by seizing one of the lashings. The mob was

386

clawing at him or trying to lever the lower crates over the side.

Fairfax suddenly noticed a man wielding a long crowbar, his eyes crazed as he lashed out at the helpless Townsend.

Townsend had lost his cap, and was staring up at him, his voice cracked and pleading.

'Help me! For Christ's sake, *help me!*'

The man with the crowbar stood slightly away, preparing to strike, then he looked up and saw the revolver.

The crowbar started to swing down and Fairfax fired.

Before the crash of the revolver shot had died the air was split apart by sirens, and the sudden clatter of boots.

A voice, clipped and tense, yelled, 'Second Platoon! *Fix—Bayonets!*'

Headlights swept through the snow and Fairfax saw a gleaming line of levelled bayonets advancing on the train, the mob falling back, and then all at once stampeding away from the helmeted soldiers.

Then he could only see the woman who lay on her back in the snow. He vaguely recalled her in the crowd, near or beside the man with the crowbar. He must have ducked while she—

He dropped to the ground and tried to raise her shoulders, but took his hand away as blood reddened the snow beneath her. The heavy bullet had hit her in the temple. Fairfax pulled her skirt down to cover her legs and stood up.

An army captain walked over and looked at the body. 'We were just in time, it seems. This must have been organised by the size of it—your chaps okay?'

Fairfax clenched his fists, the revolver hanging at his side.

'Where the *hell* were you?'

The captain eyed him curiously. 'Two trucks in collision. We had to take a different route. Still, nothing broken or lost. My colonel would have been most displeased about *that*!'

Two soldiers, their slung rifles bouncing at their hips, hurried across, and in the glare of headlamps dragged the woman's body across the snow. She lost a shoe, but they did not retrieve it. Fairfax heard a tail-board slam shut, the sudden revving of engines.

The captain said, 'We'll back the train to the last intersection. Then you can carry on and unload as planned, right?'

Fairfax was still staring at the wet patch of blood. It was pinker now as the snow got heavier and more persistent.

Townsend watched the captain marching back along the line where some railwaymen had suddenly appeared.

'Well, *I'm* not bloody sorry, sir! But for you I'd be dead, not her!'

But Fairfax knew that his luck, like 801's, had run out.

One of the three commanders put it rather differently when Fairfax re-entered the room where the Admiralty Board was meeting.

'We know that these things happen in such difficult circumstances. I am sure that we all agree that there will be nothing recorded against you, and for myself I see no reason why you should not continue with peacetime training in the voluntary reserve. And with your fine wartime record, should

388

there be another national emergency I feel certain—'

Fairfax did not hear the rest. *He was finished.*

As he walked towards the privacy of his quarters he thought of Cuff, and the man found dead in the dockyard. He had failed to report that, and now all he could think of was the woman lying in the snow, her eyes wide with disbelief and shock.

I didn't mean to kill her. The echo came back like the crash of the firing squad. *But you did!*

*   *   *

Keil's central mainline station, *Hauptbahnhof*, was not so busy as usual, and, compared with the weeks and months after VE-Day, it was barely moving. Marriott stood beneath a little stone archway and turned up the collar of his greatcoat as more snow filtered down from the dome-like shell of the station's roof, which because of other priorities was still open to the sky.

He had left Heinz in the adjoining square and found himself wondering why he had come. If Meikle's brief message was true he would feel left out, an intruder again. If it proved to be false, he would have to be witness to their despair.

For the hundredth time he glanced at his watch. He had been here for three hours. How much worse it must be for Ursula and Leisl. If he leaned forward just a bit he could see them by a barrier on the far side of the concourse, the child Bernadette shifting between them.

He looked at the tall hoardings which lined the exits; they had become as much a part of the once-thriving station as the people who ran it.

389

Hundreds and hundreds of old photographs. Faces of husbands, sons and lovers. But even they lacked the urgency they had once had. Some were curled by the weather and damp air; a few had fallen unheeded on the splinter-chipped stones, as if all hope had gone, or confirmation had been received that those countless portraits would no longer be needed.

Marriott could remember his first visit here. The way the women had pushed against the barriers and the lines of military police who met every train, especially those bringing released prisoners from Russia.

'My son! Have you seen my boy?' Or frantic eyes seeking out a familiar uniform or regiment. 'My husband was with you! Have you seen this man?'

The soldiers had for the most part shrugged them off, pushed past, eyes straight ahead as if they feared that, by stopping, their new freedom would vanish.

Today, there was just a handful of women. Watching the closed gates and the station clock which miraculously had survived the bombs. Staring at the gleaming tracks as if they could see or hear an incoming train.

He watched Ursula stamping her booted feet on the wet stones, her hands in her coat pockets. He realised that he had never seen her with her hair down before. When she turned, it swung across her shoulders, shining despite the grey light.

For her brother perhaps? He felt the same ache, the longing to cross the concourse and join her, to share either her joy or her grief. But if Lothar did come back today he would be like all those others he had seen. Startled by the sight of so many British

390

uniforms, the navy, the army provost men; even the RAF police were here. Before, the only foreign uniforms they would have seen would have been Russian. It would be like suffering defeat for a second time. The last thing Ursula's brother would want was to see a British officer in the welcome-home party.

He wandered how Meikle had done it; if indeed the Russians could be trusted. After Swinemünde, Marriott was more than doubtful. He had heard that Meikle had exchanged a wanted prisoner, and with full approval from the Military Government.

It might even have been Helmut Maybach, although he could not fathom out the connection.

He thought too of Fairfax. Always so buoyant and trusting, and never without courage when it had been needed in those terrible nights in the Channel and North Sea.

Marriott had taken Ursula to a local theatre, the small Schloss Theatre and Casino in Eutin. It had been crowded with servicemen, officers and other ranks as well. He had guessed that she had never been to the place before even though it was in her own town. He had recalled Meikle describing her as a good girl. Innocent, he had really meant.

There had been a scantily clad girl in a spangled jacket and tiny pants, wearing a stetson while she rode a white horse around the dance-floor, the gestures with a cowboy pistol leaving little to the imagination. The servicemen had cheered and waved their beer mugs, and at least one officer had slipped away soon afterwards to the dressing-rooms. There had been a singer too, a fair girl not much older than Ursula. She had wandered among the tables singing some of the old melodies which the

Germans had enjoyed before their fortunes had changed. A spotlight had followed her through the smoke-filled room, making her face shine, adding to the atmosphere of memory and loss.

It was when she had begun to sing 'Lili Marlene', the song beloved by both the Afrika Korps and Montgomery's Eighth Army in the desert, and now every one's favourite, that Marriott had seen Fairfax.

He had been sitting alone at a small table, his chin resting on one hand, a half-empty bottle of gin or schnapps by his elbow.

The girl had seemed to sense something, to pull herself from the thoughts and dreams she could share with no one. She had wanted only to sing, and was able to ignore the whistles and the cheers; but Fairfax, as completely alone as herself, had penetrated her solitude.

She had taken his hand and pressed it to her waist. Ursula had gripped Marriott's arm until he could feel her fingers biting into it.

Fairfax had looked up as if seeing her for the first time. Had held out his arm so that she could sit on his lap, her heavily powdered face just inches from his.

Marriott had expected her voice to be drowned by the noisy audience. But in the large, smoke-filled room, apart from the piano and her lilting, haunting voice, you could have heard a pin drop.

When they had left the casino and walked through the slush in the darkened streets towards the *Gasthaus*, Ursula had whispered, 'I will not forget that. It was the saddest thing—and yet so perfect!'

Marriott looked at his watch once more. He

thought he could hear bells ringing and knew it could only add to the poignancy of their vigil. Christmas Eve. A family's time to be together. He had already checked with the R.T.O. There were just two more trains. After that—

The child was playing up, bewildered by the unexplained waiting, and probably cold in spite of the coat and woolly hat which would cover the scar on her forehead. How *could* she understand?

Her mother Leisl was crouching down to placate her. How did she feel? Was she still full of hope, or would she be dreading the questions? How had she lived and behaved in his absence? It was never easy.

He felt Heinz slip into the archway beside him.

Heinz glanced over at the small, isolated group. He had witnessed it all before, and thanked God he had been in Kiel with his family when their world had collapsed.

'Not here yet, Herr Leutnant?'

'No. There's still time.'

Heinz shrugged. 'They will miss the lights.'

The lights. The F.O.I.C. had ordered all ships in Kiel to turn on their searchlights, and sound their sirens. There might be fireworks too. A night to remember, to cling to.

Marriott looked at them. Ursula had lifted the child and was speaking quietly, rocking her back and forth.

There was not much anticipation now. Despondent, resigned, and not knowing what to do about it.

Heinz said, 'I will be with the car, Herr Leutnant.' He tried to manoeuvre his words into order. 'You were—most kind to us.'

Marriott thought of his face when he had given

393

him a parcel for his own family Christmas. Mostly food, but some toys too from the White Knight shop in Flensburg.

'We remember you afterwards—' He could not go on, but thrust a small package into Marriott's gloved hands and hurried away.

Somewhere a bell jangled noisily, and around the concourse the remaining figures seemed to come alive again.

Like a scene from an opera, Marriott thought. The mourners and the ghosts. The drifting snow filtering through the overhead lights like in some ancient cathedral.

He watched Leisl straighten her coat and fluff out a bright neck-scarf to lessen the drabness of her clothing. She had been very pretty once.

Marriott had seen her go through the same motions so many times today.

Ursula had put down the little girl and was gripping her hand while she stood close to the barrier. She tossed her head, and Marriott felt his heart jump as the long hair drifted over her shoulders.

An old woman who had been here all day was gripping her two photographs. Enlargements of her husband and son, but now dog-eared and grubby with constant handling.

The MPs in their red-topped caps, some yawning, the naval patrol in white belts and gaiters, and the usual collection of officials gathered. Marriott could hear the train now, saw its light cutting over the gates, the screech of the big wheels as it slowed down for the final approach. *The end of the line*.

He saw Leisl dabbing her eyes with a

handkerchief, shaking her head hopelessly while Ursula spoke to her, as if offering some encouragement.

The inspectors manned the gates, the police moved closer, and then the train was suddenly here, the doors opening along the side like scales, pouring out men on to the platform in a living tide.

It was exactly the same train as all the others, Marriott thought. Field-grey, threadbare uniforms, some with parcels or kitbags, others walking as if on a last parade, eyes lifted, trying to escape.

Marriott saw the child holding the little teddy-bear which Ursula had been taking out of the dockyard when he had guided her past the place where they had been searching the women. The child was never without it. Even in the hospital.

The old woman was through the barrier with her pictures, holding them up, asking the hurrying spectres if they had seen them.

Marriott heard an MP say to his mate, 'She can't keep it up for ever, Tom. They're both dead and she knows it. She just keeps coming, poor old cow.'

Marriott stared, then looked away. Another side to the war which he had just discovered.

When he looked again the platform was almost empty, and Ursula was bent over the child, wrapping her up carefully for the return journey to Eutin. Then Marriott saw Leisl take a few faltering steps towards the gate, watched as she lifted both arms, unable to speak or move.

The soldier was tall and thin, and from this distance bore no resemblance to his sister. He was almost the last, and was limping badly, and one hand, probably maimed by frostbite, was poked into the front of his ragged greatcoat.

Marriott blinked, and then they were all together, hugging and kissing, the child somehow wedged amongst them. Leisl was laughing and crying all at once, and for these wonderful moments she was the same pretty girl the soldier had married, and left behind.

They turned away, but the child had dropped the teddy-bear, for once without noticing.

Ursula stooped to recover it, looked up, and saw Marriott in the archway. She ran across the snowy concourse, and pressed against him while he held her with both arms.

'You *came*! You are here all the while!'

He felt her hair against his mouth, could smell the perfume he had given her.

'Always when I need, you are here!' She leaned back in his arms, her eyes bright with tears, but laughing. She half-turned to look after the others and said, 'They do not miss me. Time to talk—to say things—to give thanks is all they want.'

With his arm round her shoulders they walked out into the snow and down the steps to the square.

The sky was criss-crossed with searchlights, and the clouds suddenly lit up with exploding fireworks and what Marriott knew to be Very lights and distress rockets. And all the while the bells were ringing. People stared up at the display, for once without fear, the dread of the first stick of bombs.

Marriott saw her turn towards him, saw her eyes dancing in the sparkling lights, felt the tension drain out of her, as if she knew, as if she had always dared to hope, as he had.

Her lips were slightly parted as he kissed her once, and then again; they were cold, but as he held her the warmth returned. With one hand he

396

brushed the snowflakes from her face and hair and said, 'I want to *marry* you, Ursula. If you'll have me, I'll make you happy.' He touched her mouth very gently. 'I don't know how, but I shall find a way. I've never loved anybody, but now I know what it's like.'

She stared at him for several seconds, the snow melting on her face like tears.

But there were no tears. 'I knew when you first spoke to me. I was afraid then.' Her chin rose slightly. 'We *shall* find a way.' She stood on tiptoe and kissed him on the mouth. 'If we have to be parted, we will still be together. *This I know.* It is all I want.'

Heinz came out of the darkness as the fireworks began to flicker and die.

'Car is here, Herr Leutnant!'

Marriott stood back from her, but his hands were still on her shoulders. To Heinz he said, 'Drive this lady home. You will find her brother on the other side. Take them all back to Eutin.'

Heinz nodded, uncertain of what to do. 'What about you, Herr Leutnant?'

Marriott helped her into the back seat, their faces touching as he withdrew. He said. 'You must go now. But you were right. We *are* together.'

'I know why you are doing this.' She held on to his hand. 'I have a gift for you. Please come soon.'

Marriott watched the car glide over the churned-up snow until it was lost amongst the other vehicles.

He began to walk along the road but a naval car stopped within ten minutes. The marine driver asked, 'Goin' to Plön, sir?'

Marriott got in and saw two naval lieutenants

slumped fast asleep in the back. The driver grinned.

'Some bloody Christmas, eh, sir?'

Marriott dug his hands deeper into his greatcoat pockets and watched the snow-covered bushes which lined the road.

'The best yet, as far as I'm concerned.'

Later he would have to start asking questions, filling in forms; there *had* to be a way.

But for the moment, as the wheels purred over the tightly packed snow, he was not going to share it with anybody.

We shall find a way. He could almost hear her saying it. *It is all I want.*

She had bought him a gift. He smiled. Her words were the greatest gift in the world.

CHAPTER NINETEEN

WHITE GUNS

The woman lounged against the pillows and tried to cover her bare shoulders with a woollen shawl. It was not out of modesty, for although the room was well heated by a wood fire, the windows were crusted with ice-rime, the field beyond white with snow.

She watched as Cuff struggled into his trousers and tugged them up under his belly.

She said, 'You were very quick that time, Cuff.'

He paused and looked at her reflection in the bedroom mirror. 'On and off like a fly, that's me!'

He stared at her full breasts and felt another thrill

398

run through him. Just to touch her had been enough, even though on this visit it had been unintentional.

He started to knot his tie, his body still heaving with exertion. He blamed a lot of his condition on the Christmas celebrations, or what he could remember of them. That was all of three weeks ago and yet his head was still muzzy, and he knew it would take a few drinks to pull him together again when he got back to the barracks.

'They took the officer away.' She was watching his face in the mirror, her legs sprawled carelessly apart. 'But they said nothing to me, Cuff.'

Cuff paused, his fingers around his tie. 'I know. I heard all about it.

He almost laughed aloud. The poor stores officer who had been so much in debt had not even realised how they had been using him. A court martial, and probably prison in England. Cuff felt neither pity nor remorse. The man had been an amateur and a fool to boot.

He said, 'You're in the clear, just as I told you. You'll remember me when I'm back in Blighty, eh, Hertha?'

She reached out and fondled some of the silk underwear Cuff had bought for her.

'You have been good to me, Cuff. I knew you would have to go one day.' She shrugged. 'We have had some exciting times, yes?'

He breathed out noisily. 'Not half!' He turned and looked at her. 'You'd better clear the little dump when I've gone. Keep that idiot's share for yourself. He'll not be needing it in prison!'

She bit her lip, and then reached into a drawer of the bedside table.

Cuff asked, 'What have you got there?'

She hesitated. 'When Herr Hemmings—died—downstairs, I told you a lie.' She handed him the envelope. 'I did not destroy this other letter, the one about you.' She watched his expression, more curious than afraid of his reaction. She added, 'I did not *know* you then, you see?'

Cuff gasped and then gave a huge grin of admiration. 'Why, you saucy bitch!' He flipped open the letter and glanced quickly through it. 'Yes, it would certainly have made things hot for me!' He pushed it into the fire. 'Just in case I get pissed and someone finds it on me!'

They both laughed but Cuff turned away in case she should see the sudden gleam in his eyes.

So many near-misses. It was a bloody good thing he was getting out tomorrow. Like that interfering S.I.B. bastard on the dockside. Cuff still could not recall exactly what had happened. The man had begun to question him about the woman who now lay naked on the disordered bed. Through his fuddled brain Cuff had misunderstood, had not realised until afterwards that the soldier had been making nothing more than a routine enquiry. They had been about to arrest the stores officer anyway, but Cuff had not waited. He had stuck out his foot and thrust the soldier backwards. There had been no sound. *Nothing.* Once or twice he had seen Fairfax looking at him. Did he know? Had he seen what happened?

He gave a slow grin. One worry at a time. Fairfax had enough on his plate by all accounts. Anyway, he had left it too late to stick his oar in now.

He reached for his heavy greatcoat and then bent over the bed. 'I'll miss you.' He kissed her roughly

400

on the mouth, his hand exploring her thighs, until he knew he must stop. He forced her back on the pillows and looked at her demanding body.

'So long, girl. May see you one of these days.'

For a long time she stared at the closed door, even after the sound of his car had melted into the snow.

Then she touched herself and grimaced. She was a real mess.

She picked up the lovely underwear and thought about her next strategy.

Two hours later Lieutenant Cuff Glazebrook strode into Meikle's office and was surprised at the unusual disorder. There were files everywhere, metal boxes, and more files in neat lines, numbered and ready for transportation.

The commander was the most unusual of all. He wore no jacket, and sat at his desk in shirt and tie, a telephone to his ear.

'Wait a moment, Glazebrook.'

Cuff shrugged and went to the window. It was a strange feeling to be leaving here. But it was time. He had seen the commodore privately; he had been unusually agitated about the mention of the yacht, but had agreed to Cuff being sent home. His service and seniority, plus the fact that his father had been taken ill, were sufficient reasons. Cuff suspected that he was relieved that he was leaving anyway. *Not as much as me.*

His father had had a slight stroke during the Christmas festivities. Now he would need Cuff on his board. If he had *his* way he would soon be running it.

Meikle put the telephone down and said, 'So you are going?'

'If *you've* no objection, sir?' It was as close to insolence as he dared go.

'Actually I'm very glad you are leaving, here, and the navy. I think you're a disgrace to both!' He waved down any interruption. 'I believe they were supposed to teach you O.L.Q.s when you were accepted for a commission? Officer-like qualities, right? They obviously failed badly!'

'Now look, sir—'

'No, Glazebrook, *you* look! One more interruption and you will be under arrest!' He made an effort to calm his voice. 'Are you still certain that you have nothing to add to your statements about the fuel depot, and the missing S.I.B. officer who was found dead in the dockyard?'

'Well, hardly, sir—'

'That woman, Frau Hertha Ritter, the one you tried to *help*—remember?'

Cuff looked solemn. 'I thought she needed a break, sir.'

Meikle stared at him coldly. 'She was arrested an hour ago, and charged with possessing stolen goods, government property, and with being one of several involved in selling fuel on the so-called black market.'

Cuff shifted his feet. It gave him time to control himself, although he was almost bursting. It had been so damned easy, and had reminded him of one of those awful films. While he had telephoned the police in a disguised voice to tell them about Hertha's private dump of loot, he had wanted to laugh. The police had been trying to stall him so stupidly, while they had frantically attempted to trace the call.

They had acted a lot faster than he had expected,

402

but she would not involve him, even if she suspected his betrayal. He had burned the evidence, and she knew he carried the secret of Hemmings's murder.

'Well, I never, sir! It just goes to show, doesn't it?'

'Be off with you. But remember, Glazebrook—one day you will make the fatal mistake. Please go now.' He looked down at his desk again.

Cuff paused by the door. 'What will happen to her?'

Meikle did not trust himself to raise his head. 'It depends which way she looks at it. If she's lucky, fifteen years in prison. If not—' He waited for the door to close, and then he did look up.

In his heart he knew Glazebrook was a part of it. But there was no proof. Captain Whitcombe had told him that CPO Hemmings's body had been taken back to England and cremated. But even if it hadn't been, there would have been no point in exhuming it. They would already have thought of that.

There was a knock at the door and Lieutenant Commander Durham, his glasses on the top of his bald pate as usual, entered with the inevitable newspaper.

'Yes—what *is* it, Arthur?'

Durham glanced at the upheaval. Many would be pleased that Meikle was being moved. Personally, he would miss him and his abrasive efficiency, which marched side-by-side with a genuine desire to sustain the people who were his responsibility.

'Thought I saw Cuff Glazebrook just now, sir.'

Meikle nodded wearily. 'Why does he always make me so *angry*, I wonder?' He rang a bell. 'Tea for two, please,' he said to a head in the doorway. 'He's being released. His father had a heart attack or something. I would have liked him to stay for a bit longer, to look into a few things, although I admit I detest him and all his sort.' He recovered his normal composure. 'Anyway, what did you want to see me about?'

Durham held out the newspaper. 'I don't suppose he's seen this, sir. I only just got it myself. But now I can understand why his old man had a stroke.'

Meikle read the headline. *Newly Knighted Business Man Charged With Bribery Of A Government Official and Tax Evasion.* He looked up and gave his first smile in a long, long day.

'I think we'll leave it as a surprise for him, eh?'

As he stirred his tea the owl-like staff officer said, 'Sorry you're going, sir.'

'You'll just have to get someone else to worry about what colour the regulating office is to be painted, or what proportion of potatoes is to be issued to German workers.' But he stared at the piles of packages and carefully wrapped presents. All were gifts from the people he had driven so hard from the beginning. Germans, or *prisoners* as he had once described them to Marriott. It seemed like years ago instead of eight months.

He said, 'I suppose I will miss it. There's such a lot to do here.'

Durham put down his cup. 'You've got them through the winter, sir.' He stood up and beamed. 'I can say what I like. I'm too old to care!'

Meikle smiled. 'We'll talk later, Arthur.' He called after him, 'And stay away from the Glazebrook Enterprises shares! They'll be as

404

worthless as his knighthood after this!'

He turned over his diary. Marriott would be coming soon. He thought about him and the girl, their hopes of marriage when everything seemed loaded against them. He thought of his words to Durham. *There's such a lot to do here.* If there was one project he would like to complete before he left it was to dispel their anxiety.

Meikle never thought like a naval officer. He thought like a lawyer. Prosecution or defence, there was always a way out. How changed she was. She was still the same in her work as interpreter, but there was a kind of magic about her, in her eyes and in her manner, which even Meikle could not explain. Marriott must have done it for her.

The object of his interest was leaving the wardroom block deep in thought, something he had just been told hanging over him like a cloud. At the end of the corridor he saw Cuff directing two messmen to his cabin to pick up his gear. So he really was leaving.

Cuff strode towards him. 'I'm just off. Not a moment too soon, everyone's thinking!' He roared with laughter, and the smell of gin was overpowering.

Marriott said quietly, 'I just heard. Spruce Macnair has died. His heart gave out. I still can't believe it.'

Cuff frowned as his mind grappled with the news. Then he said airily, 'Well, everybody dies! Who cares anyway?' He thrust out his hand and said, 'I'll be seeing you!'

Marriott ignored the hand and said, 'They were right about you. You really are a bastard.' Then he turned and walked out into the bitter air.

405

Cuff yelled after him, '*Suit yourself!*' But the laugh would not return. He stumbled out to a waiting car and muttered thickly, 'I'll bloody well show the lot of you!'

Like the missing laugh, there was no one to see him leave.

*　　*　　*

'If you can find a place to sit—' Meikle gestured at the loaded chairs. Marriott found a vacant one. He was still thinking about Spruce Macnair. Seeing him there as he had once been. As they had all been. He had been worked to death, but at least he had seen his efforts end in victory.

Beri-Beri had told him about it; he had seen it in some report or other which he was filing for the commodore's office.

Poor Beri-Beri had got into the bad books of the top brass during the Christmas dinner. Afterwards he had insisted it was purely an act of revenge for the dirty trick done to him while he had been laid up in hospital. A senior officer had commandeered his beautiful Mercedes, and left a beat-up jeep in its place.

Beri-Beri's response had been dramatic and probably dangerous.

With a small, controlled explosion he had blown off the legs of the senior officers' serving table. The table had collapsed so that the floor had been covered with a great mash of plates, glasses, and several kinds of jelly. The explosion had not been very loud, but quite enough to send some of the war veterans diving for cover.

Like the lieutenant who had been so drunk that

406

he had jumped off the wardroom roof into a tablecloth held by his cheering and equally tipsy friends, the commodore had insisted on suitable punishments.

The rooftop jumper had broken both legs. To punish Beri-Beri he had ordered him into the morasses of his internal filing section.

Even that had had compensations. He had met Third Officer Jill Wheatley there and through his usual, casual, gentle probing had discovered that her home was about a mile from his own. For the moment at least, the isolated life of a fisherman had been shelved.

It was strange how there had been so many changes since Christmas. Countless new faces, so that the old familiar ones seemed few and far between. Some of the old hands had gone home for demob already. A few had sought him out to say their goodbyes, others had cut free, and left without a word.

One of the former had been Petty Officer Motor Mechanic Adair, 801's unbeatable 'Chief'. In his absence his young wife had put down a deposit on a dilapidated garage on the Exeter road, where there was room for expansion and, perhaps, a teashop.

'Just right for the holiday trade, sir, or soon will be. I'll do most of the work myself to begin with.' Again the well-known, toothless grin. 'I reckon if a bloke can hold an MGB together as long as I have, I should be able to manage that!'

'Now, Marriott.' Meikle was watching him. 'I've made some enquiries.' His eyebrows rose. 'Is there something you were about to ask?'

Marriott smiled. It was so unusual for Meikle to offer the first opening, just as it was incredible to

407

see him so casually dressed.

'I was wondering, sir, about Fräulein Geghin's brother being exchanged—'

Meikle plucked at his tie. 'It can do no harm for you to know. It was the SS man Maybach who was sent across to the Russians. What your late coxswain, Evans, did not know was that Maybach had once been in charge of hundreds, maybe thousands of Russian prisoners, or slaves, as Hitler's Todt Organisation called them, when they put them to work in the Channel Islands. They were worked without mercy—building underground emplacements and bunkers, a complete military hospital and many anti-tank devices for their Western Wall against invasion. Most of those poor wretches never returned. They ended up in the concrete they were pouring even as they dropped dead of starvation and brutal treatment.'

'I see, sir.'

'The Russian senior officer you made such a big hit with in Swinemünde, Captain Sakulkin, has been somewhat out of favour lately with his comrades in the Kremlin. I spoke to him on the telephone. I feel certain that by the time Maybach reached Moscow, Sakulkin would have convinced himself, and everyone else, that he was solely responsible for the capture of a criminal on the top of their lists.' He raised his hands. 'Harmony all round, and now he owes *me* a favour.'

The mood passed. Meikle said, 'Now tell me again.'

It had been a letter from Penny which had begun it after he had sent her and Jack a photo he had taken of Ursula.

Marriott said, 'The Canadian Government is prepared to assist immigrants, sir. If we were married, and could get the backing of some senior officers maybe—'

He recalled her face when he had told her of his ideas. He had added, 'Neither of us would be looking back at a country left behind. We would be sharing a new one. Looking forward—together.'

Meikle took a note pad, and said, 'Fräulein Geghin did say something of the sort to me, although I don't think she realised she was undergoing a cross-examination.' He scribbled quickly. 'I made a few notes. It is true about the Canadians. It may take time, but there are some bonus points. Lithuania was an independent and self-supporting country for twenty-two years, after being a part of the Tsarist empire. When Stalin signed his notorious non-aggression pact with Hitler he also decided to take back Lithuania and make her a part of Soviet Russia. The rest we know. Ivan is back, and has no intention of leaving ever again. But *if*, and it is flimsy, the country had remained as before, Fräulein Geghin would have been classed as Lithuanian. The Canadian Government is, ah—sympathetic.'

Marriott licked his dry lips. 'My sister and her husband would sponsor us, sir, others too—'

'One step at a time. Permission to marry.' He let the word sink in. 'I can see from your face that it is what you both want.'

A messenger peered in. 'The car is here, sir.'

Meikle stood up. 'I shall be around for a few more days until my successor gets here. One of the old school, I believe, so tell your outrageous friend Kidd to watch out!' He eyed him gravely. 'I think

409

we might just manage it. But you must make her realise it could take time.'

Marriott turned as Lavender entered carrying Meikle's reefer jacket. As he slipped his arms into it Marriott saw that there was new gold lace on the sleeves, four rings instead of three. Meikle was a captain now.

The deepset eyes fixed on him again. 'It seems that in my new appointment, all the Allied advocates are quite senior—so their lordships obviously consider this promotion justified.' He smiled. 'I am a little awed myself.'

Marriott asked, 'Where will you be going, sir?'

'The Judge Advocate's Department has a new office for me. In Nuremberg.'

Marriott guessed the implication and said, 'I'm sure they'll take notice of you, sir.'

Meikle's reaction was swift. '*Why*—because I'm a Jew? Is that what you meant?'

'I'm sorry, sir. I didn't mean that. I never—'

Meikle held out his hand. 'No, Marriott. I am the one to be sorry. Forgive my hasty judgement—it's something I have had to get used to.'

Then this strange man smiled, beneficently. 'You and Fräulein Geghin deserve one another, and I mean that. You will be missed here, you know, Marriott—you've made quite a reputation for yourself during your stay. When all this is behind you, there will be days when you wonder at and question some of the risks you had to take, the sacrifices you were forced to offer in the face of death. But, believe me, the work you have done here will stay with you even longer. It is something you and your Ursula can always be proud of.'

He took down his beautiful cap and said, 'I am
410

dining with the commodore. We shall probably discuss yachting!'

He and his rabbit-like Lavender chuckled at this obviously private joke.

Marriott stood for a long time in the deserted office.

Meikle was right. He would never forget. Nor want to.

       ★   ★   ★

Marriott and Ursula stood in the shelter of a concrete wall and watched a high-sided troopship being manoeuvred away from the dockside. It was February, but the snow had refused to budge despite occasional stabs of pale, dazzling sunshine.

Ursula was wearing a naval duffel coat, the hood pulled up over her hair as though to shield her face. He could guess what she was thinking.

Faintly across the murky water as the last line was let go, they could hear the cheering, the blast of a horn from a passing patrol vessel.

Soldiers, sailors too, some of the first to be going home for demobilisation.

She said nothing, but she was thinking of that ship's passage to England, where the servicemen would be discharged to depots and barracks, to be fitted up with civilian clothing at a grateful government's expense.

When the ship turned round, she would be coming straight back to Kiel. When she cast off again, Marriott would be aboard.

He said quietly, 'Commander Meikle has made certain that your job will be safe until—'

She turned and looked up at him, their breath

411

combining like pale steam in the stinging cold air.

'He told me. I am so glad. It will keep me closer to you.' She smiled, but her eyes were wistful. 'I cannot think of him as *Kapitän* either!'

Marriott considered the passing days. He had filled in all the necessary forms, and his application to be allowed to marry here had gone through the right channels. He had heard that a major in the infantry had managed to obtain permission, but he did not know all the circumstances.

Now he was being sent home like all the others. Officially he would receive full pay until all his accumulated leave was used up. But after that he would be seen only as a civilian. The chances of getting permission to return to an occupied Germany would then be almost impossible.

They could face it while they were still together—but when that trooper sailed again?

He watched a sleek destroyer glide past the old Hamburg-Amerika liner *Milwaukee*, another HQ ship with the White Ensign rippling from her staff like all the others.

The shrill exchange of salutes, the calls cutting across the water like the cries of demented sea-birds.

She said softly, 'Look at her guns. All white . . . the snow. They do not look so dangerous any more.'

'I know.'

Marriott had only been back to the inn at Eutin once since Lothar's return. It was as he expected, neither welcoming nor hostile. Lothar was home. His hopes, and recovery from what he had suffered, were their main concern now.

Usually they met at the barracks, or here near

412

Meikle's original HQ where he had first seen her. Now the bunker was just a paint-store, a place without personality.

They often walked in the frozen woods, found small cafés, or inns like her own home. They talked and held hands. It was often difficult not to go further. He thought of the present she had given him, a photograph of herself in a leather carrying case. On the back of it in her familiar round hand she had written simply, 'For my Englishman, who is my whole life.'

If she was afraid that he would have second thoughts when he returned to England, she concealed it well. For his own part, he often tortured himself with the possibility that she would change her mind once he was beyond her reach.

She pulled off her glove and held up her hand to show him the ring he had given her after Christmas. At first she had worn it only when they were together. Now she wore it openly, with both happiness and defiance. Marriott took her fingers and kissed them. In those few seconds they had become like ice.

After he had gone there would be none of the old faces for her to recognise. Beri-Beri would be going with him, and probably Fairfax too.

Fairfax had told him about a meeting he had had with an official from the Home Office who had come out to Germany to drum up volunteers for London's Metropolitan Police. The force had had no recruiting throughout the war, and with its end they had been compelled to release as civilians all the reservists, special constables and pensioners who had comprised it for the duration only. It had left London's blue line even thinner than usual.

413

What had persuaded Fairfax that he wanted to be a policeman, Marriott wondered? One thing was certain, he would do the work well. It would keep him busy and give him time to find his feet, perhaps look for a different solution to his problems. He was not alone. Acting-Petty Officer Arthur Townsend was going with him. After the shooting incident at Hamburg it might be a help to both of them.

Marriott smiled inwardly. Fairfax's wealthy surgeon father would just love it!

He pulled out the little packet from his greatcoat, Heinz's present. It was a beautiful carved model of a fishing-boat, styled on those which had once worked out of the village at Laboe. Heinz had modestly admitted that he had carved it himself.

He handed it to Ursula. 'For our new home. Whenever it is. Wherever we end up.'

He gazed at the destroyer as she edged towards her moorings. He was leaving this life for good. He thought of Meikle's words: *There will be days when you wonder at and question some of the risks you had to take.* But for today it was still inside him. A part of himself and all the others he had known and lost.

Aloud he said softly, 'The white guns . . .'

She had summed it up perfectly.

*   *   *

It was the last day of February, when the time of departure was minutes and not days away.

Unlike the last time they had watched the battered-looking trooper cast off, when the event had been softened by distance, close to, with the din of voices and bustle magnified by the ship's tall side, it was hard to think clearly, to find a space. To

414

be alone was impossible.

The departing sailors, some of them staggering with farewell 'neaters' or 'gulpers' of pusser's rum, clattered up the several gangways, waving to their friends, too caught up with the exhilaration to recognise the sadness that might follow.

Those already aboard lined the rails, waving their caps and cheering, while the send-off parties returned the yells with equal vigour.

Marriott put his arm around her shoulders as more figures surged past. The excitement did not reach him. His heart felt like lead.

Beri-Beri hesitated, and then saluted the girl. He was still using the stick, and admitted that his many tropical illnesses would leave him with a limp.

'Rather romantic, don't you think?' he had remarked with his usual gentle, droll irony.

But now he could recognise the passing gift of time. He said, 'See you aboard, Vere, old son. We'll meet in England too.' He leaned forward impulsively and kissed Ursula on the cheek. 'I'll look after him for you!' Then he limped away, his eyes on the ship with the plume of smoke rising from her single funnel.

A voice seemed to probe Marriott's mind. *It is now, it is now!*

He said, 'The time may pass quickly.' He saw her lips quiver and added, 'You are my whole life too, Ursula. *When* I come back we shall be married.'

Across her shoulder he saw the others who had come down to see him off. Kapitän von Tripz, contained and grave until he had put his arm around his son's shoulders.

'You gave my son back to us. We will never forget.' He had given a stiff bow. 'Until better times

415

then, Herr Leutnant!'

Willi had been unable to say anything, but had wrung Marriott's hand, tears on his freckled face.

Heinz too had been there, and had carried Marriott's cases on board the ship himself.

He had been unusually quiet until they had shaken hands.

Then he had said, 'When you come back, you will need a good driver, *ja?*'

He was smiling as, with the girl, Marriott had shown his pass to the police at the barrier.

The ship's siren gave a tremendous roar, sending up gulls from the outer harbour and bringing more wild cries from the men along her rails. Marriott took her in his arms and they kissed for a long moment, oblivious of cheers and whistles from the watching sailors. It was too precious a moment to share.

As he stepped away she bared her hand and held up the ring, her eyes shining brightly, too brightly.

'Until the next time, *my darling!*'

Marriott turned towards the gangway, the only one still rigged. At the entry port he turned and saw her, tiny in the crowd, waving up to him. Heinz was near her. Ready to perform his last duty and take her home.

'This way, sir.' The steward was watching him with interest. 'You'll be sharin' with a Mister Kidd, sir.'

'Thank you.' He pressed to the rail as the ship began to move slowly astern, a tug belching smoke as she pushed fussily with her bow fenders.

When he tried to see her again, the pier had blocked her from his view.

The deck began to shake as the ship gathered

way, her bow-wave surging untidily over one of the wrecks still awaiting removal.

Marriott followed the steward down to the cabin where Beri-Beri was sitting on one of the bunks.

'Still awake?' he said.

Beri-Beri watched him with affection and said, 'Don't feel so down, old son. I reckon you're just about the luckiest bloke I know!'

Marriott nodded and took out her picture.

For my Englishman, who is my whole life.

He touched his friend on the shoulder.

'*I know.*' Through a scuttle he saw the tall, grim pinnacle of the naval memorial gliding abeam, remembering that first time when life had seemed so empty.

He felt the keel lift slowly to the first inshore swell.

'I shall be back.'

Only Beri-Beri knew he had spoken the words aloud.

EPILOGUE

Once the troopship had tied up at Southampton, disembarkation was carried out with remarkable speed.

Most of the servicemen would be going straight home on leave. The next time they reported to their base or barracks would be their final kitting-out for Civvy Street.

Some had a long way to go; others, perhaps a mere handful, were home already. For them it would be distressing to see the devastation left by the bombing of this busy port, a city, like

417

Portsmouth, which would have to be almost entirely rebuilt.

But for the many it was a time of hazy rejoicing.

Most of them would never meet again. The war had been their one shared experience. Perhaps, years ahead, when time had blurred the bitter memories and the horrors of battle, they would, like countless old campaigners before them from Waterloo to the Somme, gather together for their brief twilight.

From the boat-deck Ginger Jackson watched the dockside and the barriers through which they would all have to pass. By arrangement they had agreed to separate for the final departure.

With a fine pair of Zeiss binoculars Ginger watched Leading Seaman Bill Craven as he pushed his way towards the line of tables, naval police and customs officers.

He did not need to be there to know what happened next. The sudden movement of two customs men, and then Craven's suitcase open on a table. Ginger sighed. He had warned him; so had Jack Rae who was some twenty places behind him in the same queue.

He knew that Craven's case was packed with loot, jewellery and watches for the most part. Even the most hard-hearted customs man would turn a blind eye to a few bits and pieces, *but this lot—*

Ginger looked away when he saw Craven being escorted back into the dockyard. Officially he was still in the navy, so it would be the glasshouse, the hateful detention quarters, for him.

Ginger picked up his own little canvas bag and, after a slight hesitation, dropped it over the side into the oily water. It was simply not worth the risk. After all, he had entered the navy flat broke, but would be leaving with a nice fat post office account. The loot would have to go.

Down at the table Leading Seaman Rae, very smart in his Number Ones, paused as a customs man called, 'Over here, son!'

Then he seemed to notice the ribbon of the DSM on Rae's jumper and relented.

'Got anything to declare?'

Rae looked round for Craven but he had already been swallowed up, lost to the machinery of naval justice.

'Not really,' he replied.

'Off you go then.'

Rae picked up his bag and whistled softly to himself as he walked with the crowd towards the docks railway terminus.

Stitched into the bottom of his bag was a brand-new Luger pistol. There was not a country on earth which could make guns like the Krauts.

After this lot nobody would have any work for an ex-machine gunner, he thought. But a beautiful pistol like that would make sure he never went without again.

Another customs officer stopped Marriott, who opened his case on the table.

The customs officer saw Ursula's picture looking up at him and smiled. 'I can see you've got the best reason in the world for coming home, sir!' He marked the case with his chalk. 'All the best!'

Marriot waited for Beri-Beri to join him. *If only he really knew.*

Beri-Beri reached him, and said, 'Call me, um, when—'

They shook hands. Each felt keenly the

419

significance of the moment. Neither knew how to express it.

'Yes.' Then Marriott asked, 'Will you come and see me through it?'

Beri-Beri gave his lazy grin. 'Best man? You bet, old son!'

The rest was lost in the bustle of more returning servicemen.

Ginger Jackson strolled by and threw up a casual salute.

'So long, gents! See you in Moscow!'

It was over.

*   *   *

The weeks which followed were the longest Marriott could remember. Without Stephen or Penny, the house was less than a home; it was like being in lodgings.

He had tried to explain, and had hated himself for sounding so defensive. His mother had exclaimed, 'Oh, how could you, Vere! A *German* girl! I suppose you'll expect to bring her here if the authorities are foolish enough to let it go through?'

Marriott had seen the anxiety on his father's face as he had said, 'Easy now—don't harass the boy after all he's been through . . .'

He may as well have remained silent. She had continued, 'What about our friends? The neighbours? She's probably doing it to get away from there! Using you!'

Marriott had answered flatly, 'No, Mother—nor is she pregnant, as you once suggested Penny was.'

He had decided to walk down to the Harrow. But something had made him stay, and see it through.

420

For his father? Or for Stephen, who would never come back?

'We love each other.' The defiance had gone, the pleading too. 'There was a war, and, because of it, we met. If anything, I'm grateful.' He recalled Beri-Beri's words about being a survivor for a purpose. 'If they do reject my request I shall find another way.'

He had heard Chris the lodger moving about upstairs. He had two rooms now. *Young men today can't find homes for love nor money*, his mother had said.

So what chance for returning servicemen, he thought.

When he was not out walking, endless walks over commons and along the lanes he had known since his schooldays, he had thought of Ursula. She seemed further away than ever, the waiting dragging them down.

At night he would lie on his bed, staring at his uniform, which hung on the back of the door. It was his link, his key to Germany, and then only with the proper authority.

He had considered telephoning Beri-Beri at Winchester several times, but knew he would only be sharing his mounting despair.

Once, his father had walked down to the Harrow with him.

He had said, 'You mustn't mind your mother, Vere. She doesn't understand. Life's not been easy. The war and everything.'

Marriott had looked at him, moved by the quiet gentleness of a man who had nevertheless taken up arms in the Home Guard, when his country was in such grave danger.

421

'It hasn't been that smooth for you either, Dad.'

'She needs someone.' He had filled his pipe with some of his son's naval tobacco. 'I know you don't like Chris, but he lets her run things for him. That's right up her street, you see?'

Marriott didn't, but said, 'If it does come off we hope to be going to Canada, Dad.'

Surprisingly, his father had laughed.

'But for my arthritis, and if I were twenty years younger, I'd be right with you, believe me!' Then he had continued in a serious tone, the one Marriott remembered from over the years. When an exam had gone wrong, or he had fallen off his bicycle.

'Look, Vere, I'm proud of you . . . more than I can say. I'm sure she's a lovely girl. Just promise me something, eh?' He had looked across the bar, his eyes far away. 'You will bring her home sometime, *before*—'

They had walked back together, an even stronger bond between them.

Marriott got up late one morning, mainly to avoid sharing the breakfast table with the all-knowing Chris.

His mother had come in from the garden, her breath smoking from the cold outside.

'Letter for you.' She had watched him impassively. 'Your final demobilisation, I suppose?'

Marriott slit open the brown envelope, hardly daring to anticipate its contents.

Then he turned over the pages, his eyes almost too blurred to read the neatly typed instructions.

His father had appeared from somewhere, a basket of firewood in his hand.

'What is it, son?'

Marriott looked up without seeing them.

'They've granted permission.' He had to listen to his own words before it finally sank in. 'I—I didn't really know—' He could not go on.

Then he saw a smaller envelope pinned to all the official papers. Printed on it was *From the Office of Captain Joseph Meikle, RNVR, KC*. The letter was short, typed Marriott suspected by the loyal Lavender.

It had obviously been Meikle's own pressure which had finally brought the action to reality.

I wish you both every happiness. Something forged out of war will be stronger than steel. He had finished his brief letter with, *In my present work I am often reminded that what you and your Ursula have found in one another is almost the only decent thing I have yet seen to come out of this war.*

Beneath his familiar spiky signature he had written a Priority telephone number in his own hand.

Marriott walked along the road and back again, to give his mind time to settle down.

With the house silent around him he called the telephone operator, and after what seemed like an age of clicks and suspicious questions and demands for official confirmation, he heard a voice say, 'HMS *Royal Alfred*.'

More squeaks and clicks and then she was here, right beside him at the foot of the stairs. *'Ja . . . this is Fräulein Geghin speaking . . .'*

'It's me!' He heard a quick intake of breath. *'Everything's all right!'*

He waited, suddenly dreading that she had changed her mind; that she had not understood.

When she spoke again her voice was shaking, but clear enough to catch the emotion of that single word.

'Together!'

It was all they both needed. The rest, was history.

Photoset, printed and bound in Great Britain by
REDWOOD BURN LIMITED, Trowbridge, Wiltshire